SAVAGE LIES

THE TRUTH IS MORE BRUTAL
THAN YOU CAN IMAGINE.

PETER BOLAND

Savage Lies
Published by Adrenalin Books
Copyright © 2018 Peter Boland
First Edition: 2018

ISBN 978-0-9935695-1-7

CHAPTER 1

T HE BAG OF BODY PARTS slid across the back of the stolen van, making a wince-inducing scrape as it travelled from one side to the other. Minchie's piggy little eyes darted anxiously towards the rear-view mirror, continually checking the status of his fragile and illegal cargo. Every time he swerved left, the bag skidded across to the right, colliding with the interior wall of the panel van, and when he turned right, it slid over to the opposite side. When he braked hard, it would catapult forward, concertinaing against the back of the van's front seats. The bag must have wobbled across every inch of the dirty payload floor.

Minchie knew he should have secured the thing before setting off or at least wrapped it in blankets, as removal men do with furniture, but in his haste to get the job done quickly, he'd cut corners.

The van he'd stolen wasn't ideal, either. He'd taken the first one he'd seen—a builder's van or maybe a plasterer's—a battered Ford Transit, its once-white bodywork suffocated with London grime turning it a mucky grey. Old yellowing copies of *The Sun* newspaper were stuffed between the windscreen and the dashboard. Empty coffee cups rolled around in the footwell. The back had been empty apart from a scattering of sand and grit and an old glove missing its other half. Minchie had tossed the medical-waste sack in, eager to get going, but he grimaced every time the plastic bag rode over the shallow sea of sharp, abrasive material. If one fragment managed to slice it open, blood would spill out, which would eventually leak out the back doors, which didn't shut properly, one of the reasons it had been so easy to steal. Nothing drew attention to you in London traffic like a van dripping blood.

Minchie didn't know the exact contents of the bag. The gang wouldn't tell him, and he knew not to ask. All they had said was to get rid of it, not by throwing it in the river or by burying it. It had to be with fire. All he had to do was point the van in the direction of an abandoned building site he knew, set fire to it, and destroy the evidence. They'd told him some other important things too, but Minchie's small brain and even smaller attention span had prevented the information from being stored in his short-term memory.

He wasn't getting paid. It was a trial, an initiation to see if he could make it to the next level, he remembered them saying. If he did well, he would be in the gang. They were a serious outfit—secretive, tooled up, and big... very big. They had the means to get things done, to change things, that was for sure, and he wanted to be part of it. If he pulled off the little task they had set without any hitches, he could forget the seedy, backstreet debt-collecting job he had with Venables. It depressed and bored him, not like this. This was exciting. This was some serious James Bond shit. In fact, Minchie pictured himself in a movie, on a secret mission for a big organisation. It made him important, glamourous even. Maybe that was going a bit far. At six feet three inches and wide as a door, with a shaved head and a heavy forehead hanging over those shifty small eyes, like a steep cliff face, Minchie looked as if he'd narrowly escaped extinction at the last ice age.

He knew he could succeed as long as that damn bag didn't split.

A tiny voice inside his head told him to pull over and at least try to stop the package from moving around, but he'd long since learned to ignore that voice. The voice also told him to call in on his old mum once in a while or check his bank statement so he didn't go overdrawn. He hated that voice. It got in the way of him doing things, so he usually ignored it. Besides, if he stopped the van and opened the back doors, someone might see inside and start asking questions. Then he'd have to put them in the back of the van and make them disappear along with the bag. He simply didn't have time to do both. No, he would keep going. Nothing would stop him.

Just then, something happened, something far worse than the bag splitting. A police car pulled out of a side road and slotted itself right behind Minchie's van. The silver-and-Day-Glo-yellow Metropolitan Police Vauxhall cruised along behind him, two coppers in the front seats. Tensing up, Minchie gripped the steering wheel more tightly and began a mantra in his head: *Just a random police car... Just a random police car...* Over and over again, he said it in an attempt to calm his nerves. But police cars had a habit of pulling over white vans, especially ones with no markings on the outside. Paranoia gripped him like the coils of a snake. *They're going to pull me over. The owner of the van has obviously reported it stolen. Right now, the coppers are punching the number plate into their onboard computer, then it will flash up "stolen."* He could imagine what would happen next. It played in his mind like a scene in a TV cop show. Blue lights would flash, Minchie would pull over, they'd ask him what was in the back of the van, his mind would go blank, and he'd say something stupid like "organic wine." They'd ask him to open the back doors. *Then what?* The scene in Minchie's head hit pause. He couldn't see beyond that part. *What about doing a runner?* Yes, he could make a run for it on foot. *But where?* Minchie took in his surroundings, a busy, slow-moving main road in South London. Tightly huddled terraced houses lined each side of the street, and no turnoffs or side streets were nearby. He wouldn't get far. That was certain.

His rear-view mirror suddenly lit up with pulsating blue lights. The police were onto him. Minchie banged his hands on the steering wheel and cursed. Instinctively, he thought about hitting the accelerator, taking the police by surprise, and escaping through the traffic in a Hollywood-style getaway, but he had nowhere to go. Both lanes were an endless stream of slow-moving bumper-to-bumper traffic, so he simply didn't have the space for a high-speed escape. Plus, the crappy diesel van he drove had been designed for shifting bags of cement, not car chases. That wouldn't have happened if he had stolen a nice fuel-injected Volvo Estate. He would have had a chance of outrunning them, but then, the police wouldn't have pulled him over in the first place if he'd been in a Volvo Estate. They would've assumed he was somebody respectable, like an accountant who shopped at Waitrose and had National Trust membership. Right then, Minchie wished more than anything that he could be an accountant who shopped at Waitrose and had National Trust membership.

For a guy as big as Minchie, his body felt weak and useless as he pulled the van up onto the pavement. His hands shook as he killed the engine, accepting his fate. He had no way of talking his way out. He wasn't clever enough. Minchie let his head slump forward on the steering wheel as he waited for the inevitable tap on the window.

Any moment now.

CHAPTER 2

THE TAP ON THE WINDOW never came, though. Slowly, he raised his head like a scared child looking out from under a duvet. Through the windscreen, he could see the two lines of traffic had parted, as if powerful magnets lined the pavement and had dragged the cars over to the side. A blast of sirens made him jump. The police car that had been behind him rocketed past, hurtling down the middle of the street. Minchie watched open-mouthed as the police car accelerated away, its lights and sirens gradually fading into the distance. All the cars around him slowly resumed their original positions, forming a slow, plodding procession along the road.

Adrenalin fizzed through his body, mixed with the elation of relief, making him slightly hysterical. He'd got away with it. One manic laugh escaped his mouth and then another. He ran his fingers over his scalp and swore rapidly, like a machine gun that fired swear words.

He couldn't drive in that state, not when he was that wired. He had to calm down, or he'd end up having an accident. Part of him—actually, most of him—wanted to celebrate his miraculous escape from the cops. Something like that didn't happen every day, not to him, at any rate. For that, he deserved to treat himself to a little sip of something to calm his nerves.

Farther down the street, boxes of produce were stacked up on the pavement with various exotic fruits and vegetables poking out of the top, protected by an overhanging canopy, the tell-tale signs of a typical London corner shop. Minchie left the van at the side of the road and headed towards it. He hated those places, normally. They were always open, for a start, even on Christmas Day, and that just wasn't right. *This is because they're run by people who shouldn't be in this country, the kind who have no respect for our traditions or way of life, like knowing when to stop working.* They were always bloody working, seven days a week, nonstop. It made decent white folk look bad, as though they were lazy.

As Minchie got closer, he felt uncomfortable. Going into one of those places went against all his principles. They were usually run by Pakis, Ragheads, Wops, and more recently, Poles or Portuguese. No matter who they were, Minchie hated all of them. Actually, he didn't mind Poles so much. They liked drinking, and some of the women were hot. With his current desire for whisky, though, he overlooked his other prejudices. Besides, the guys who'd set him on his little task would soon make places like that history. They'd send them all back to where they came from.

Minchie's hulk-like frame barely made it through the narrow shop doorway. Inside, his nostrils were assaulted by a whiff of Far Eastern spices. *Ugh, the worst kind of place—a stinking Paki store.* Sure enough, there behind the counter sat a smiley Asian man chatting away with a tiny Asian woman clutching bags of groceries. They spoke to each other in a language that, to Minchie's ears, sounded as if it had been sped up. Minchie grunted in disapproval and moved down an aisle packed floor to ceiling with all sorts of exotic foods, which Minchie would never dare touch—none of that foreign muck for him. He'd take a plate of egg and chips over all that spicy rubbish any day of the week.

Minchie passed packets bulging with dried delicacies with unpronounceable names, covered in strange writing and weird graphics that gave him the creeps. At last, he came to shelves full of beer and cider. The whisky wouldn't be far away, but he could see no sign of it. Surely, they would keep all the booze in the same place. He did another circuit of the store and still saw no sign of it. *But this place is owned by a Paki. Their brains aren't right, so he's probably put the whisky in some completely random place, like next to the beans or with the fish fingers.*

After a while, when Minchie gave up looking and grumbled his way to the door, the owner politely asked, "May I help you with something, sir?" The guy's politeness contrasted sharply to the animosity bubbling inside Minchie.

"Er, whisky," Minchie muttered.

"Yes, it's right here, sir," replied the shopkeeper, pointing to a shelf behind the counter, stocked with various sizes and brands of whisky. Minchie's eyes ran along the price tags until they landed on the cheapest one.

"I'll have that small one for five quid."

"Just one moment, sir. Let me finish with this customer, and I'll be right with you."

The shopkeeper continued his conversation with the small woman in front of the counter. They chatted and laughed and chatted some more. Minchie's temper rose. *Is this guy having a laugh?* He wasn't exactly serving the customer but probably just talking a load of boring shit about their families. That was what those people did. They had massive families, then all they did was talk about them all the time, like "My daughter's going to be a lawyer" or "My son's going to be a doctor." Minchie couldn't stand them. *Who do they think they are?*

Minchie swore under his breath. Then he spoke at full volume. "Mate, can I just get my whisky?"

"Yes, yes. Very sorry," said the shopkeeper as he turned to get Minchie's bottle. "I'm afraid this lady is an old friend, and we often get carried away. Terribly sorry."

The woman turned and smiled at Minchie. Minchie stared back with an expression he used just before a fight. The woman quickly turned away. Minchie handed a fiver to the shopkeeper and left.

"Goodbye, sir," he heard as he slammed the door behind him. Minchie wasted no time cracking open the metal seal on the bottle and taking a large slug of the strong liquor. As he lowered the bottle, the sight that greeted him made the burning whisky turn icy cold.

Hanging in the air, swaying gently from side to side, was the van he'd been driving not five minutes before. A powerful lifting arm attached to the back of a London Traffic Enforcement flatbed truck hoisted the helpless van higher and higher off the ground. They were impounding the vehicle, not because it was stolen but because Minchie had left it parked illegally in a bus lane. In London, blocking a bus lane was worse than punching the Queen.

Minchie spat out a stream of rapid-fire swear words again, in sheer disbelief at the scene unfolding in front of him, watching helplessly as the stolen van dangled above the back of the flatbed. The whine of the hydraulics sounded like tinnitus. He pictured the bag sliding everywhere, giving him a sick stab of pain in his gut, not helped by the whisky swilling around. Finally, the scruffy vehicle came to rest on the truck, its wheels swiftly secured by two men in hi-viz jackets. They took their time, checking and double-checking their cargo.

An idea popped into his head. Maybe he could reason with them and offer them a few quid to release the van, but Minchie had just spent the only money he'd had on a bottle of whisky. Perhaps he could do a trade: one slightly used bottle of whisky in exchange for the stolen van. Even to a dimwit like Minchie, it sounded like a crap deal. Besides, he knew what those people were like: they'd clamp a homeless person if they happened to be sitting on double yellow lines. They couldn't be reasoned with. He could punch their lights out. That was Minchie's solution to most problems he encountered. However, once he'd knocked them out, how would he get the van off the lorry? It looked too complicated to do by himself—lots of levers and buttons. With Minchie's track record with anything technical, he'd probably end up lowering the van onto himself. Instead, he just stood there, slowly sipping his booze.

The diesel engine of the flatbed lorry rattled to life, and Minchie watched it disappear into the busy London traffic, the van wobbling on the back of it.

That's that. It's over. He'd had one job to do and had royally screwed it up, just for a quick drink. His plan to work with a big-time criminal outfit had fallen apart like the time he tried to build flat-pack furniture. He'd been lucky with the police car, but then he was slack and paid the price.

"Oh, Minchie," he muttered under his breath. "You stupid prick."

He didn't know what he was going to say to the gang. He'd have to tell them the evidence they'd told him to destroy was now in the hands of London Traffic Enforcement and would very soon, no doubt, be in the hands of the police. They would kill him. No, he'd do what he'd always done—run away and hope for the best. Anyway, nothing was there to link him or the gang to the van and its contents. He took another slug of whisky, stuffed the bottle in his pocket, and shuffled away. He'd have to go back to Venables and his crappy debt-collecting job as long as the gang didn't kill him first.

CHAPTER 3

JOHN SAVAGE KNEW EXACTLY HOW he was going to kill himself.

In the middle of the lounge floor, he placed a table, the one he used to play poker on with friends, back when he had friends. It had once been a small dining table, but he'd covered it in green felt to make it look more professional. No cards were in sight that day, and his friends had all gone, disappeared off the radar or dead.

In the centre of the table, in stark contrast to all the fuzzy green material, rested the brutal form of a powerful handgun—a stainless-steel SIG Sauer P226 with a rosewood grip—handsome, efficient, well made and reliable. It had once belonged to an Iraqi officer during the first Gulf War until Savage had relieved him of it. Stealing that weapon had saved his life all those years ago. Ironically, the same weapon was about to end it.

Next to the handgun he placed a single bullet, standing on its end. The last remaining bullet from the original magazine, it pointed up at the ceiling like a miniature version of the Gherkin building in Central London. The rest he had used to shoot his way out of an Iraqi military facility.

On the far left-hand side of the table, Savage placed his smartphone.

One gun, one bullet, one phone.

A contest with only one outcome. Either the gun or the phone would win. Considering Savage's current state of mind, the gun had a ninety percent chance of winning, but he hadn't made a firm decision yet. Deciding to take one's life wasn't something done in a hurry.

In the meantime, Savage made sure the SIG was in perfect working order. He literally had one shot at killing himself, and he didn't want anything to go wrong. The thought of the gun misfiring and leaving him brain damaged and a burdensome vegetable terrified him more than the thought of ending his life, so while he mulled it over, he stripped down the pistol, cleaning and oiling it. That wasn't really necessary. Like any disciplined soldier, he'd maintained the weapon correctly ever since he'd acquired it. Savage was stalling, and he knew it.

After reassembling the gun, he placed it next to the phone, glancing from one to the other. *Which one is going to win today?* He still had no idea.

He had many reasons for wanting to take his life. He'd been thinking about doing it for quite some time, until it had grown to a groundswell over the years, an irresistible force made from his memories of all the people he'd killed during his career. He'd shot, stabbed, strangled and blown up hundreds of them, all for queen and country. The sheer weight of victims pressed on his conscience like the worst case of the bends. The guilt had grown into a spiked wheel that spun inside him, and as it spun, its spikes extended, reaching out farther to inflict more and more pain, so that he could barely contain it. Every day, the agony grew exponentially, compounded by the fact that he couldn't actually remember any of the people he'd killed. They had become a faceless mass, anonymous and angry, surrounding him on all sides, calling for his death.

What had really driven him over the edge, though, smiled back at him from the mantelpiece across the room: a picture of his wife Dawn and his daughter, Kelly, taken on the day she graduated.

Kelly had wanted to become a soldier like her dad. Savage didn't want that life for her, so they'd struck a deal. If she got a degree under her belt, then she could join the army. Savage had figured that the fun and carefree life of university would distract her from following in his footsteps, or she'd fall in love and want to move into a flat with a boy and get a job in the city. Neither happened. Just like her old man, she was stubborn and determined. A few years after joining the Royal Engineers, she was posted to Afghanistan, where a roadside bomb ended her life.

Nothing could've prepared him for the agony of losing his little girl. He blamed himself, of course. Savage had been trained to endure pain and torture, but the waves of guilt and grief that battered him day and night left him helpless. He'd always been the strong one, mentally tough and single-minded, but he simply wasn't equipped to deal with the crushing emotion of loss. His job had been to end people's lives, but when the life of someone he cared about ended, his brain just couldn't handle it.

Back then, his wife had to be the strong one. Not only did she cope with losing her only daughter, she also had to support her husband, whose heart and mind were breaking. She got them both through it and managed to rebuild a new life for them even though Kelly was no longer part of it.

Then, just last year, cancer took his wife. It started in her bowel, and at first, her hopes looked good. The treatment was working, and they'd cut out the infected section of her intestine. The "all clear" seemed to be just around the corner, but the cancer, vanquished from one part of her body, popped up somewhere else, then it appeared in another place and another until her body became riddled with it.

Two painful months later, she died. Savage stayed with her every day, gripping her hand and stroking her brow, watching while that horrible disease slowly ate her alive. His utter helplessness in the face of it all was the start of Savage's mind collapsing in on itself. He had always been the smart, resourceful, and determined one. He knew how to get out of impossible situations with the odds grossly stacked against him. He could keep calm when all around him wanted to kill him. Against that vile disease, though, he had nothing—no strategy, no plan, no defence. All he could do was sit and watch her fade away.

The only two people he cared about were gone. Life had no meaning.

Snatching up the SIG, Savage locked the slide back and pushed the single bullet into the chamber. He dropped the slide, which gave a deep, satisfying click, and put the gun to the side of his head. The muzzle felt cold against his skin. By contrast, once he fired the gun, a ring of skin would blister with heat as the red-hot bullet made the briefest of contact. Then it would continue on its high-velocity journey, and John Savage would be no more.

The SIG was powerful enough, and the bullet, with its full metal jacket, would easily do the job, but the powder in the round... He had no way of telling whether it was still good or not. Doubt set in.

Savage kept the gun to his head, delaying pulling the trigger. He was annoyed at himself for being so weak. Being totally honest, the quality of the ammunition didn't really worry him. The bullet in the chamber was a well-made, high-quality 9mm Parabellum round. It would still fire perfectly in one hundred years' time.

"Just pull the trigger, and get it over with," said the voice in his head. The voice had been an unwanted companion in his life for the past year, a symptom of his declining mental health, piping up at odd moments to persuade Savage to end his life. Savage couldn't walk over a bridge or near a railway without the voice pointing out that it would be a good opportunity to kick the bucket.

"What are you waiting for?" the voice continued. *"Pull the goddamned trigger. You've done it hundreds of times before when other people have been at the other end. How come you can't do it now? Coward. Come on, you have nothing to live for. You're not exactly contributing to society, are you? You're a waste of space. Nearly sixty years old, with nothing to show for your life but a trail of dead bodies and broken hearts. Just do it. Nobody's going to miss you. I mean, people aren't exactly banging down the door to see if you're okay. Nobody cares about an ex-SAS operative with a perverse love of hurting people. At least admit it: you do like hurting people."*

"No, I don't," Savage said out loud. "I'm just good at it. There's a difference."

"Rubbish," said the voice. "How can you be good at something if you don't like it? It's impossible. You're a killer. Just because you wore a uniform doesn't change that fact. Face it. You're a mass murderer employed by the government. That's the only difference between you and people doing life in prison. Come on. Admit who you are. Then you can end this all and do society a favour. One fewer psychopath in the world has got to be a good thing, right?"

However, other voices in his head were vying for his attention—two, to be exact: his wife's and his daughter's. They were small and distant at the moment but getting louder all the time. The warm familiarity of their voices melted his resolve. They were getting clearer the more he delayed his suicide.

"John, what are you doing?" said his wife. "This is madness, and you know it. Put the gun down, and stop being the tough guy. Pick up the phone and call for help. You're a good man. You loved me, and you loved your daughter, cared for us, and provided us with everything we needed."

A tear escaped his left eye and slid down his cheek, making it all the way around to his chin, where it formed a drop and fell into his lap.

"What about all the people you've helped? If anyone needed anything, you were always the one to step in. You're a generous, caring man. It upsets me to see you like this."

His daughter was less forgiving. "Dad, you stupid prick. Are you serious? Are you really going to do this? After all the missions you survived, you're going to kill yourself? What about your mates who didn't make it? What are they going to think? They're going to be pretty pissed off, and so will I. When I died, I didn't have a choice. If I had my time all over again, do you think I'd let myself get blown up by a roadside bomb? Course not. I'd want to live. Stop being a selfish dickhead, put the gun down, and do like mum says: pick up the phone. Stop being so stubborn. You're still annoying me even when I'm dead."

A little smile tugged at the side of his mouth. That was

definitely the voice of his daughter. Never one to mince her words, she was just like her old man.

Several more tears fell.

He listened to the right voices in his head, the ones who made sense.

He put the gun down.

A few seconds later, his phone was against his ear. The help line buzzed twice then answered.

"I need help," John whispered. "I'm trying to kill myself."

CHAPTER 4

Three months later

S AVAGE STOOD LOOKING UP AT a wall of glass glimmering in the early-morning sunshine. At the very top of the building, four stories up, a giant, bright-red sign announced or rather shouted its presence to the world: Motivation Health Club. It was like no gym he'd ever seen.

He'd found it by doing a search on the internet. A little map had appeared, peppered with virtual location pins showing gyms in his local area. That one happened to be the closest. On his smartphone, he scrolled through lists of reviews from the public. Motivation Health Club had an average rating of four point seven stars out of a possible five, and all the reviews were pretty positive. He never bothered looking at their website, they were bound to say they had the most amazing gym on the planet even if it wasn't. No, always go straight to the reviews for the truth—that was Savage's philosophy. Hell hath no fury like an angry consumer.

From what he read, it was clean, modern, and well equipped, although he doubted he'd have any use for the day spa or the aromatherapy rooms, but the café seemed like a good idea. He could eat after he worked out, perhaps even make a few new friends.

However, the reviews hadn't prepared him for the monolithic structure of plate glass, which gave it the appearance of a corporate bank rather than a place of exercise. Suddenly the scruffy T-shirt and jogging shorts he'd thrown into an old kit bag looked seriously out of place. *No matter.* He wasn't here to impress anyone. He was here to sort his head out.

Savage had been attending a course of behavioural therapy to change the suicidal thoughts swimming around like sharks in his head. A regular face at group-therapy sessions, he shared his experiences with other war veterans. So far, it was working, although he'd neglected to tell the therapist about the voice he kept hearing in his head. He knew what they did to people who heard voices. They pumped them full of antipsychotic drugs—drugs that dulled the senses, slowed down the brain, and changed the personality. Therefore, he kept that side of things to himself. He'd deal with the voice on his own terms, like a soldier, confronting it when he was ready and had gathered his strength. For the time being, he tried to ignore it.

Savage's therapist had suggested he do some sort of activity, either exercise or DIY. She said having something to do every day improved mental well-being and would release endorphins to help him feel better about himself.

DIY was out of the question. Savage treated his home the same way he treated his weapons. Everything had been cleaned and maintained to within an inch of its life, and nothing escaped his meticulous eye. Cupboard doors were regularly oiled. Screws holding up pictures were examined to check their structural integrity and, if necessary, replaced. New gutters had been fitted, not because the old ones leaked but because they might leak one day, at some point in the distant future. Savage was such a stickler for maintenance that he wondered whether he should add OCD to his range of problems, but he figured his therapist had enough on her plate dealing with his suicidal tendencies. DIY was not an option, as he wouldn't have enough to do, so it had to be exercise.

He wasn't in bad shape, but since he'd left the army, a fledgling pot belly had formed where an iron-hard six pack used to be. Savage had set himself a little challenge to see if he could get it back.

The sliding doors of the health club hissed open gently, ushering Savage into a plush double-height reception space complete with exotic plants, posh water coolers and sofas. It was the polar opposite of the army gyms he was used to: bleak, utilitarian places designed to hurt soldiers and push them to their limits, not cosset people. He smelled no stench of man-sweat either, just the occasional gentle waft of potpourri, probably being pumped in through the ventilation system.

To his immediate right, a large glass partition sectioned off a modern office where rows of smart, attractive people sat busily typing away at large workstations or having important PowerPoint meetings.

Why would a gym need such a large office? What are they all doing in there?

Dominating the reception area was a vast oval-shaped desk made of solid wood. A man sat with his back to Savage, decked in tight-fitting sportswear, showing off his wide-backed bodybuilder's physique. His thick neck supported a head with a shock of blond hair, shaved up the back and sides. Beyond the reception desk, another vast glass wall revealed the gym, a cathedral to exercise on two levels. Savage marvelled at the size of it. He'd never seen a two-storey gym before and could barely see the back wall for all the high-tech machines blinking with lights and display panels. He recognised treadmills, bikes and rowing machines, but that was as far as he got. Most of the equipment looked like alien technology, offering no clue as to what it did or what part of the body it exercised.

The whole place was large enough to train an army, which puzzled Savage, as he counted only seven people working out, dressed in more of that figure-hugging black Lycra, making their limbs look like liquorice. Savage couldn't be sure, but they appeared to have had makeovers before coming.

Savage walked forward and stood by the reception desk. The blond guy sitting behind it didn't turn around or acknowledge his presence. Savage edged along the counter and noticed what was distracting him. At first, he thought he was playing on his smartphone, which most people did when they had nothing to do. Then Savage noticed him filming someone, a young woman dressed in a tight red top and leggings. As she bent over to fill up her bottle from a water cooler, her small, pert backside left nothing to the imagination. She was completely unaware that the big blond pervert was digitally capturing her perfect behind.

Savage marched around the desk and stood in front of him, blocking his shot and ruining his filming. "Morning," Savage said loudly.

The guy looked up. Shocked and slightly ashamed, he threw down his phone as if it had electrocuted him. The girl capped her bottle and made her way into the gym, blissfully unaware of what had just happened.

"What?" asked the blond guy, flustered. "Sorry. I mean, yes, how can I help?" He forced a smile of perfect teeth that looked as if they'd been whitened by God himself. Not one wrinkle marred his polished skin.

Savage didn't think anything was wrong with taking care of one's appearance, but the guy looked as if he'd been CGIed into existence.

"I want to join your gym," Savage said.

"You want to join our health club," he corrected.

"That's right. Sign me up."

"So why do you want to join *this* health club?"

Savage didn't understand the question. "Isn't it obvious? To exercise."

The blond guy leaned back in his chair and steepled his fingers. "Could you tell me why you chose this particular one?"

"It's the nearest," Savage replied.

"Okay. What other health clubs have you been a member of?"

"None."

"None?"

"That's right, none."

The simple act of joining up seemed to be turning into a job interview. *Why is everything so complicated these days? Is it like this everywhere?* Savage's fists were tightening and his heart rate increasing as anger took hold of him. *Calm down,* Savage told himself. *This guy's probably been told to ask these things for market research or something.*

The guy sighed as if he were about to impart some sagely wisdom. "First, let me tell you a little bit about what I do here. My name's Brett, and I'm the brand ambassador for Motivation Health Clubs. I'm just on reception because our normal receptionist is off sick."

In Savage's experience, the person with the least important job always got put on reception when the real receptionist was away.

"What's a brand ambassador?" asked Savage.

"Think of me as a guardian who protects our brand. Keeps it safe and relevant, maintaining our message and championing its image as the UK's premier health club."

He had clearly memorised the line from his job description.

"Actually, this is not just a health club," Brett continued. "This is the headquarters for our entire chain of over five hundred gyms throughout the UK, and we have hundreds more across Europe. That's why I work here and why we have that big team of staff you see behind the glass. It's quite an operation."

"Wonderful," said Savage, "Now, where do I sign up?"

"You know, they do a lot of good exercise classes down at the local community centre. I think that place might suit you better."

At five feet nine inches, with a receding hairline and an expanding waistline, on the wrong side of middle age, with no taste in gym attire, Savage clearly didn't fit their demographic. That made him want to join even more. "No, no. I think I like the look of this place. So get out the forms, and let's get the ball rolling."

"Ah, that maybe a problem, as we're currently full up."

"Really?" Savage looked over at the handful of people currently working out in the vast, hangar-like gym.

"It's a quiet time." Brett replied. "After six o'clock tonight, this place will be heaving."

"That's okay. I only want to exercise in the daytime."

"I'm afraid we can't go over our membership levels. It's against health and safety."

"When did you go over your membership levels?"

"Oh, months ago."

Savage swivelled around a leaflet dispenser sitting on top of the reception desk so Brett could see it. "Why's this here, then?"

The headline on the leaflet read Recommend a Friend to Join, Receive a Year's Free Membership.

Brett stared at the words on the leaflet as if, by using the power of his will alone, he could change them to something else. Eventually he said, "That's an old leaflet, out of date."

"I thought you said you were the guardian of the brand, *keeping it safe and relevant, maintaining our message.* This message is out of date, Brett." Savage grabbed the leaflets in his fist and dropped them in the nearest recycling bin. "Better get rid of them. Otherwise, the brand's going to suffer."

Savage headed toward the door to the gym. "Maybe I'll just let myself in, start having a workout while you sort the forms out for me."

He was nearly at the door when Brett rushed out from behind the desk and blocked his way. Easily half a foot taller than Savage, it was like staring up at a Viking... if Vikings had strict grooming regimes.

"I'm going to have to ask you to leave, I'm afraid," said Brett.

"That's okay. Just let me send a text first." Savage got out his smartphone and started thumbing away.

"Sorry, you have to leave."

"Are those muscles for show, or can you actually do anything with them?" Savage asked.

"Look, I really must warn you, I'm a trained martial artist."

Savage had only been in the place five minutes, and he had already provoked a fight. His therapist would not be happy.

CHAPTER 5

S MILING AT THE BLOND BRUTE staring down at him, Savage said, "Okay, take it easy. I'm leaving, but before I do, you better know I've just seen you taking suggestive footage of a young lady without her permission, and now I'm texting your managing director to tell him so."

"What?" Brett said. "That's rubbish. You don't have the MD's number."

Savage cleared his throat and spoke while he texted. "Brett, as well as being an inefficient brand ambassador, you're also a sloppy receptionist. You left the staff list of contact numbers on the desk for everyone to see. I'm guessing you took it out to call the receptionist to see if she was coming in today, or maybe you called someone else to see if they could fill in so you wouldn't have to do this job because you think it's beneath you. You should have put it away because it's a confidential document. You never know who could be watching. That's how I got your MD's number. I had to read it upside down, but while you were spouting rubbish, I managed to memorise it."

Brett ran back to the desk, grabbed his mobile phone, and frantically deleted the footage.

Savage followed him. "So what are you going to do now?" he asked.

"Nothing. You still have to leave."

"I don't think so. You have six security cameras up there in the ceiling. That's a lot for one room, even one this big. Security must be important to this organisation, but you'd probably only need four at the most for that, so I'm guessing customer service is equally as important, which is why you have six cameras, so management can keep an eye on how customers are being treated. It looks like a top-of-the-line HD system, possibly with video analytics so they can see everything that's happening in great detail, right down to someone recording a young lady's backside on their smartphone. Am I right?"

Brett nodded and swallowed hard. "It's on a network, too," he said quietly, "linked to all our clubs." Even in defeat, Brett still sounded as though he was quoting from a corporate brochure. Clearly, he took his job very seriously even if he wasn't particularly good at it.

Just at that moment, a smart-suited man with immaculately parted hair emerged from the office on the other side of the glass partition. With a brisk, determined walk, he did up the buttons on his suit jacket one-handed without missing a stride then adjusted the cuffs of his crisp white shirt, readying himself for business. He looked like the kind of guy who kept a fully charged Dust Buster in his car and a nasal-hair trimmer in his desk.

Brett went white. "Please," he said to Savage like a small child. "I'll lose my job."

"Do you have a girlfriend?" Savage quickly asked.

"Yes. Please don't tell her."

"Not going to. Does she work here?"

"She works in Camberwell Green."

The manager approached the desk, straightened his rimless glasses, cleared his throat and smiled politely. "Hello," he said with a soft Scandinavian accent. "Are you Mr. Savage, the man who just texted me?"

"Yes, I am."

"Hello, I'm Carl Hansen," he said, extending his hand in Savage's direction. Savage shook it. "Can I ask how you acquired my mobile-phone number?"

Savage quickly changed the subject. "You know, I owe you a huge apology. I thought Brett here was filming someone without their permission. Turns out it was his girlfriend. She dropped by to show off a new outfit. Brett filmed her in it. I got the wrong end of the stick. My apologies."

"Oh, okay," said the manager. "Brett, just make sure you don't do that sort of thing in here again. It's not professional."

"Yes, Mr. Hansen," Brett said. "Sorry, Mr. Hansen."

"Now, Mr. Savage, may I ask how you came by my mobile-phone number?"

"That's a Norwegian accent you have there, isn't it?"

"Yes," Hansen replied, brightening a little. "Most people mistake it for Swedish."

"Let me guess. You're from Bergen."

"Right again," he said, pleasantly surprised. "I must say you have a good ear for accents."

"Ah, no." Savage waved away the praise as if his observation was nothing remarkable. "It's a bit of a hobby of mine, spotting accents. I've worked with lots of nationalities over the years, and one of them was from Bergen. I recognise the way you pronounce your *n*'s. It's exactly the same as his." Savage left out the part about his friend being the best sniper he'd ever worked with, who could put a bullet through someone's eye socket from two thousand yards, until he decided to put a pistol under his chin and blow the top of his head off.

"So, Mr. Savage," said Hansen.

"Please, call me John."

"John, will you be working out with us today?"

"I'd love to. Brett was just about to sign me up, weren't you, Brett?"

"Er, yes. Yes, I was."

"Wonderful," said Hansen, shaking Savage's hand again. "Welcome to Motivation Health Clubs. Brett will sort you out with an induction and get someone to give you a tour. Our facilities are quite extensive, and our staff are second to none."

Perhaps with the exception of Brett.

"From day one, all our staff do a three-week induction course to ensure our exacting standards, whether they're managers or maintenance. Did Brett tell you about our free health screening?"

"I think he was just about to."

"Well, included in your membership is a full medical check-up carried out by our very own qualified doctor. Most other clubs just check your pulse and blood pressure before you join, but we're more thorough here. You get a full health assessment, checking for everything from cancer and heart disease to liver damage and bone health. The same service would cost over £200 if you had it done in a private hospital."

A full health check-up by a doctor? Those guys didn't do things by halves, and his wife would certainly approve. Before she died, she'd pestered Savage every day to get his health checked. He promised he would, but after her death, his own health was the last thing on his mind.

"Sounds good to me. Let's get those forms out, Brett," Savage said, winking at him.

Brett looked far from happy. Savage hadn't had so much fun in ages.

CHAPTER 6

AFTER THE FULL TOUR OF the club, Savage knew Hansen wasn't lying when he'd said their facilities were extensive. Six tanning rooms, five massage rooms, two aromatherapy rooms, one beauty salon, a juice and smoothie bar, a restaurant, a raw-food bar, a coffee shop, saunas, steam rooms, swimming pools, tennis courts—the list of facilities went on and on, and Savage wondered if he would ever get around to actually exercising.

Before that could happen, Savage had to have a medical in the club's clinic. He was shown to a pristine white waiting room, where a smiley receptionist groomed like a catwalk supermodel spoke to him as though reading from a script, just like Brett. She went to great lengths to explain their menu of services while offering him an espresso, freshly squeezed fruit juice or mineral water. Savage politely declined them all, figuring that the addition of a beverage might prolong his time there. Instead, he politely listened and nodded in all the right places as she spoke with great passion about treatments, therapies, osteopathy and acupuncture. Most people's brains would have shut down by then, but Savage was trained to take in details, whether he liked them or not. She'd just started on the subject of sports massage when the doctor emerged from one of the side rooms to call Savage in.

The picture of health and beauty, the doctor was ridiculously handsome, with piercing blue eyes, thick, chestnut-brown hair and clear, unblemished skin moisturised to a faint glow. Savage noticed a slight, almost imperceptible hesitation when the doctor caught sight of him, as though Savage wasn't what he was expecting.

"Pleased to meet you," he said. "I'm Dr. Stevens. Come in. Can I get you anything?"

"No, I'm fine," said Savage, taking a seat in front of the doctor's desk. On the wall behind it hung an array of certificates for awards, qualifications and memberships of professional bodies, all smartly mounted in hardwood frames.

"Would you mind filling in this form for me?" asked the doctor. "It's just some personal details of your medical history."

Savage sifted through the three pages, skimming the questions to check if there were any about the state of his mental health. There weren't. The form was all to do with physical things: Did he smoke? When was the last time he'd had an operation? Any allergies?

Suddenly, the voice in Savage's head spoke up. *"You should tell them you hear things,"* said the voice. *"They have a right to know you're a maniac."*

Shut up, Savage replied, mouthing the words but not speaking out loud.

The voice continued, *"They can probably already tell you're not right. That smug doctor knows. I bet they all know. Then you'll be in trouble. Next stop, psychiatric hospital. A white van will come and drag you out of the gym in front of everyone. The shame of it. Just think of all those beautiful, normal people watching while you get hauled away, kicking and screaming."*

Savage gripped the pen in his hand, almost crushing it.

"Everything okay?" asked the doctor.

"Fine. I'm fine," replied Savage.

The voice spoke with mock worry. *"You need to leave this place. You shouldn't be here. You're putting these people at risk. What if you lose it and start killing people? You could lose it right now and stab that smug doctor in the neck with the pen. He hates you, you know."*

I don't kill innocent people, Savage said to the voice in his head. *Now, go away and leave me alone.*

"He's not innocent. Look at him. Vain, pompous, stuck up. Thinks he's better than you. Besides, he's a fake. Trying too hard to play a part, if you ask me. The smooth, sexy doctor. Prick thinks he's George Clooney."

You can't kill every person you don't like the look of, Savage said in his head.

"Why not? It'd be easy. He wouldn't put up a fight. He's the sort that gets others to do that for him, you mark my words. Hides behind other people."

The doctor had noticed Savage had stopped writing and was staring at him coldly.

"Sorry, those forms are so long," said the doctor, smiling uncomfortably.

Savage came out of his daze. "What? Sorry?"

"I know they're a bit dull, but the more we know about you, the easier it makes my job. Is there anything you want to tell me not covered on the form?"

"Tell him you're a murdering, suicidal freak," said the voice.

"No!" Savage replied out loud.

The doctor looked shocked at Savage's outburst. "Okay, that's fine. Just thought I'd ask."

"Sorry, Doctor. That came out wrong." Savage nervously ran his fingers through what little hair he had. "I'm just not used to filling out forms. Been a while."

"Quite all right," replied the doctor.

"Finally, you've said something truthful. When was the last time you filled a form in? Ah yes, when little wifey died. Ah, boo-hoo."

Polka dots of sweat appeared on Savage's forehead. He wanted to throttle that voice, silence it for good. It always chose the most inappropriate times to mock and belittle him. Savage could feel his grip on reality falling through his fingers like water. Rational thought had been put on hold, and he could sense darkness sweeping over him, eclipsing his mind. He was losing control. The doctor appeared to be miles away, as though seeing him at the end of a long tunnel.

"Are you okay, Mr. Savage?" The doctor's words were weak and echoey.

Savage started to speak, but his mouth wouldn't move. He gripped the pen in his hand like a dagger.

"That doctor knows you're not right. He'll blow your cover, soldier. Better stick that pen in his neck. Silence him."

Against his will, Savage felt himself rise from the chair. The voice was taking control, forcing Savage to do something he knew he would regret, but he didn't know how to stop it.

CHAPTER 7

SAVAGE CLUNG LIKE A DROWNING man to the last bit of rational thought he could muster. He had to fight. The voice was the enemy, and he had to take it on, otherwise it would completely destroy him and anyone around him, including the pretty-boy doctor. Savage would become that guy on the news who went on a killing spree then ended his own life. He wasn't about to let that happen.

Why had the voice chosen now to go on the offensive? Pulling out all the stops to make him lose it? Perhaps it felt threatened. Maybe it didn't want him joining the gym because it knew the gym would be good for him and would help his mental health, as his therapist had said. *Yes, that's it. The voice is scared.* Suddenly, he felt it lose some of its control. Savage regained some of his composure, took a deep breath, and sat back down, putting the pen on the desk in front of him. He pressed forward his advantage, addressing the doctor but really aiming at the voice.

"You know, Doctor, I'm really glad I decided to join this gym. I think it's going to be really good for me. I think I'll be a regular here. Nothing's going to stop me coming here. Exercising is also really good for your mind as well as your body, isn't that right?"

"Oh, yes. Studies have shown that the release of endorphins is very good for mental well-being. Keeps everything in balance."

Your days are numbered, Savage said to the voice.

It didn't respond.

Savage's mind cleared. The voice relinquished its grip on him completely, and Savage's mind returned to business as usual.

The doctor noticed a change in Savage's demeanour. "Are you

sure everything's okay, Mr. Savage? You seemed a little anxious back there."

Savage nodded his head. "Never better," he said. He had no intention of telling Dr. Stevens about the voice or his recent suicide attempt. He didn't want anyone to know about it, and even though he was sure the doctor would keep it confidential, he wasn't naïve. In places like that, secrets had a tendency to turn into rumours, and rumours turned into gossip. He didn't want the rest of the club to know a trained killer with suicidal tendencies had gym membership. He wanted the place to be a haven where he could leave his past and that damn voice behind.

Picking up the pen again, he swiftly scribbled the answers to the questions and handed the form back to the doctor, who scanned through it. Savage sat patiently as Dr. Stevens read, his eyes darting backwards and forwards across the page. Occasionally, he would mutter, "Uh-huh," pausing to jot something down.

Eventually the doctor said, "Very good. That all seems fine. I'll take your blood pressure, heart rate, and some measurements from you then, if it's okay, collect a few vials of your blood so we can screen it to check for anything nasty that may be lurking. You're not squeamish, are you?"

Savage had probably seen more blood and guts than the doctor. "I think I'll manage."

"Good. Now do you have any questions for me?"

"Do all Motivation Health Clubs have an on-site doctor?"

"Only this one, as it's our flagship club. All of them offer the health-screening service, but it's carried out by part-time nurses."

"Wow, that can't be cheap, what with five hundred clubs."

"True, but it's a great benefit to our members, a good USP, as our marketing department calls it."

"USP?"

"Unique selling point. Something that sets us apart from the competition. Makes us more attractive to the public. I actually came up with the idea of offering free health screening."

Savage thought for a moment. "No offence, but most people

in your gym are in their twenties. Are they really interested in that stuff?"

"You'd be surprised. Twentysomethings are a lot more health conscious these days, taking care of what they eat, how much they drink..."

Savage agreed with that. Younger people were pickier about what they ate and how they lived. But the idea that someone in their twenties would join a gym because it offered free health screening—he didn't buy it. This age group was about as interested in health checks as it was in retirement homes or bus holidays.

"Okay, would you mind rolling up your sleeve?" Stevens asked. "Let's collect some of your blood."

Savage watched as the doctor drained blood from his vein, filling up different-coloured sample bottles, one after the other. The doctor informed him that each one would cover a different set of tests, seventy-two in total. He rattled them off from memory, never pausing to take a breath or look at any notes. Savage wondered how many times Stevens had sat there and done that. Savage kept a tally of every test the doctor mentioned, counting them in his head. By the end of it, Stevens had only mentioned fifty-six tests. Savage couldn't be bothered to pick him up on it. Besides, he didn't really care. They could have been testing him for alien DNA, and he wouldn't have been interested.

Savage understood the reassurance it was supposed to bring him but couldn't help feeling the whole thing was a little over the top, which he put down to the fact that he'd tried to kill himself three months before. Health care wasn't exactly high on his agenda.

"All done," said Stevens. "In about ten days, we should have the results, so if you make an appointment with the receptionist on your way out for, say, two weeks from now, we can go through the results, okay?"

"Great," said Savage, rolling his sleeve down.

He walked straight out of the clinic without stopping to make an appointment with the receptionist.

After two hours of being at the club, Savage finally made it to the gym. One of the club's personal trainers, another leggy blond supermodel called Tyler, gave him a crash course on how to use everything.

Savage learned quickly and was champing at the bit to work up a sweat. Tyler was reluctant to let him stay on any of the machines for more than a couple of minutes, first because he hadn't exercised in ages and second because he'd just had a needle stuck in his arm. Savage mostly ignored her pleas for him to get off, especially the Nordic skier, which felt a little too enjoyable to be called exercise.

As noon approached, the club got noticeably busier with people popping in for a quick lunchtime workout. Nearly every machine was occupied. Savage felt a little twinge of guilt for Brett, who might not have been lying after all about the club reaching its full membership.

As Savage looked around, he struggled to find anyone remotely near his age, making him feel like a dad at a disco. He flipped the negative thought around, deciding to show them that old didn't mean out of date. He'd get fit, get his six-pack back, and give them all a run for their money.

After his workout, he showered, making sure he tried out all three complimentary shampoos in the cubicle, got changed, and walked home.

An odd sensation rose up from his core, reaching out across his body to his very fingertips. Like a warm glow, it lit up his mind and put a spring in his step. Savage couldn't quite grasp what it was until he dug back into his past, way back before any of the darkness had sucked the joy from his life.

He felt happy.

Maybe *happy* was too strong a word for it. Mild contentment would be more accurate. So his therapist and the doctor had been right. That brief hit of exercise had released endorphins into his bloodstream, sending a positive charge around his body and mind. He liked it. Although he knew it probably wouldn't last, he decided to come back the next day to get another hit. More importantly, it would keep that pesky voice at bay.

* * *

For the next few months, he became a regular face at Motivation Health Club, alternating between exercise and his therapy sessions until those hopeless thoughts that had once threatened to take his life dissolved into background noise. Eventually, they would disappear altogether, his therapist had said. At the time, he didn't believe her, as they'd held siege on his mind for so long that he thought the only option was to surrender to them. However, he was winning, and getting stronger every day, both mentally and physically. For the first time in a long time, life felt mildly enjoyable. The voice had also fallen silent, too. He couldn't remember the last time he'd heard it shaming him.

The pot belly had gone, and while his six-pack hadn't emerged yet, given a little more time, a rack of muscles would be popping from his midriff. He'd also treated himself to a new gym kit, but not the skin-tight Lycra stuff. He wouldn't want to inflict the sight of that on anyone—well, apart from Brett, who still averted his eyes whenever he saw Savage coming the other way.

After another successful workout, Savage walked his usual route home, zigzagging his way through the posh houses near the gym, which gave way to more affordable homes, until the final leg of his journey passed rows and rows of tightly packed, low-rent social housing. Most people would've called it a dodgy area and would have taken a long detour, but after having fought in hellish conditions in Iraq, the tatty houses with rusted satellite dishes and broken windows didn't even register with Savage. In fact, after being discharged from the army, many of his colleagues had wound up in places like that, scratching out a life on a meagre pension. They'd risked everything to protect their country and had ended up with nothing. It wasn't right.

Savage wasn't going to let anything bring him down, though, not on a beautiful September morning when the air tasted sweet and the sun warmed his face. After dumping his gym gear back at home, he thought he might jump on a train, take a trip into the centre of London, maybe wander round a park or two, then watch the multitude of foreign tourists snapping away at the famous landmarks. That was what he loved about London: one could stroll through the capital and walk past just about every nationality in the world. That gave London a colour and vibrancy unlike anywhere else in the world.

He made up his mind. He would have some lunch at home then walk to the Oval underground station and ride the Northern Line to Embankment, where he'd get off and just see where his feet would take him. Maybe he would instead forgo lunch at home so that he could go straight into the centre and treat himself to a sandwich from one of those fancy chains dotted everywhere. He relished the idea of sitting with all the city workers, eavesdropping on their hurried conversations as they wolfed down their lunches.

His mouth watered at the thought of a bacon, brie and avocado sandwich. That indulgent little thought got interrupted when he heard screaming.

CHAPTER 8

THEY WEREN'T SCREAMS OF TERROR, more screams of protest: a woman's voice, angry and loud, peppered with cursing. Savage's mind went on high alert, his eyes and ears immediately searching for the source of the trouble. It wasn't hard to find. Up ahead, a man was dragging a woman out of her front door by the arms.

"No, no!" she screamed, trying to resist, pulling back with all she had.

Even from a distance, Savage could see she was no match for the man, who towered over her. Without thinking, Savage ran towards the scuffle, shouting as he went.

"Hey! Hey! Leave her alone!" As he got closer, he realised his first assumption had been incorrect.

Abduction wasn't the man's intention. It was to snatch a laptop out of her hands, and she was currently losing. The woman refused to let go as a typical South London thug with a shaved head and leather jacket yanked her across the pavement.

The woman struggled against him, but he was an unstoppable force. She had no intention of letting go, so he punched her in the face. In an instant, she collapsed to the ground, relinquishing her claim on the computer, which Savage noticed was plastered in bright stickers.

Savage put on a spurt of speed, but he was just too far away. The thug looked at him, smiled wickedly as he got into an old Range Rover parked by the curb and sped off.

When Savage reached the woman, she was still dazed by the blow, her head wobbling around as though it might topple off.

Small built, a little too skinny, with strawberry-blond hair scraped tightly back into a ponytail, she would have been pretty had it not been for the rack of worry lines crisscrossing her forehead. Savage put her in her late thirties.

He knelt beside her, steadying her back with his arm. "Are you okay?"

"He took the laptop," she mumbled.

"Shall we try getting you up, get you inside?"

She tentatively touched the cheek where she'd been hit. It was already swelling up and glowing red. "Ow," she said in a small, woozy voice.

"Come on, let's get you up. I'll call an ambulance."

"No," she said, suddenly coming to her senses. "No ambulances."

"Okay, no ambulances. Let's get you inside and put something cold on that cheek to stop the swelling."

Savage helped her to her feet, guiding her into the narrow hallway of her home, which was darkly lit and smelled of fried food. She stumbled a little as she went but quickly regained her balance.

"Let me sit here a second," she said, dumping herself down on the step of her tatty, threadbare stairs. "I think I dropped my keys outside. Could you get them for me?"

"Of course," Savage replied. "Just don't try to move, okay?"

"Okay."

Savage went out onto the pavement to scout around for the lost house keys but could see no sign of them. Maybe she was wrong about having dropped them. As he turned to go back into the house, the door slammed in front of him, making the doorknocker flip up and down angrily.

"Miss? Is everything all right?"

"Go away," came the voice through the cheap UPVC door.

"Please let me help you. You've been attacked, had a nasty shock."

"Go away."

"You're hurt. I want to check you're okay."

"I'm fine. Just go away."

"Who was that guy? Did he break in? You need to call the police."

"They won't do anything. Now get lost and leave me alone!" Despite her angry words, her voice was tinged with fear. Savage had seen that reaction all too often. Defensive and ashamed, she was in no mood to be helped, and nothing he could say right then would change that. Pestering her to accept his help would only make things worse, but he couldn't leave her stranded without at least doing something useful.

Savage found a pen and a scrap of paper in his bag and scribbled down his mobile-phone number.

"I'm John, and this is my number. If you ever need someone to talk to, just give me a call," he said, pushing the folded piece of paper through the letter box. "I'm going to go now. I won't bother you again, but if you need me, give me a call on that number, any time. It's no trouble."

John listened for a response, but none came.

He hung around for a while, unsure what to do, pacing up and down the pavement just in case the thug came back, but the street remained quiet.

He made one more attempt to help the woman, knocking on her door again, but heard no response. Flipping open the letter box, he called out to her. "Listen, I'm going to go now, but my offer still stands, or if you see any sign of that idiot, call me, okay? And I'll come and help. Just keep hold of my number."

Savage closed the letter box and carried on home, looking back occasionally to see if the woman had emerged.

She didn't.

For all he knew, she could be tearing his number to shreds.

CHAPTER 9

FOR THE NEXT FEW WEEKS, on his way to the gym, Savage took the same route past the woman's house, where the scuffle had occurred. He didn't knock on the door or linger, but he never saw any sign of the woman or the thug who'd stolen her laptop.

Weeks went past, and he'd almost forgotten about the incident when his phone buzzed.

"Is this John?" asked a woman, quiet and unsure.

Savage didn't recognise her at first. "Yes, speaking."

"It's Theresa." She paused then added, "You probably don't remember. You helped me a while ago, and I was a bit rude to you. I slammed the door on you. I'm very sorry." Her voiced cracked on the last syllable.

"Oh, yes. Hello, Theresa. I remember. Please, don't apologise. It's not the first door I've had slammed in my face." He added a laugh to show he wasn't serious. "How are you? I was worried about you. Has that man been bothering you again?"

Desperate sobs punctuated by short gasps bubbled out of the phone.

All Savage could offer in return were soothing words. "It's okay... It's okay."

That kindness only made things worse. Theresa's sobs turned into wails of heartache.

When the tears subsided and her unnecessary apologies for crying ceased, Savage proposed they meet somewhere, perhaps a coffee shop, where they could talk properly. At first, she refused, saying she didn't want to burden him with her problems. Savage wasn't having any of it. Plucking up the courage to phone a complete stranger must have been hard for Theresa. She obviously had nowhere else to turn. He wasn't about to let her slide back into whatever oblivion she faced. He wanted to help.

They met at a café opposite Camberwell Green, which was also a cycle shop. Bikes 'n' Beans sold those strange narrow bikes with no brakes and no gears that all the trendy kids were riding. Smart pastel-coloured bicycles lined one wall while, on the other, skinny white guys with thick beards busied themselves with the grind and hiss of preparing coffee. In between was an assortment of scruffy mismatched tables and chairs.

Savage noticed Theresa immediately. Her pale, lonely face stood out as a beacon of worry among the smiling faces and happy chatter of the other customers. She sat as far away from the door as possible, her chair wedged into a corner at the back. As Savage approached, he noticed her lip had been recently split, judging by the lopsided swelling and vertical scab on her mouth. A blue-grey bruise also hung below her right eye.

Savage had planned a nice, getting-to-know-you-type conversation, but that evaporated the moment he saw her injuries.

"Who did that to you?" he asked, slotting himself into a chair opposite her.

Theresa bowed her head, staring at the crumbs on the table.

"Was it that thug I saw outside your house?"

She nodded slowly.

"Who is he?" Savage asked.

She didn't reply. He could sense fear emanating from her like radiation, choking her, silencing her. Defeat was written all over her downcast face, fixed in an expression of permanent worry, where the only news she received was bad. People phoned her with it, sent her emails full of it, or knocked on her door to deliver it. Her life resembled a conveyer belt of crap that kept dropping on her, one crisis after another. Savage could see she was on the edge with nothing left, not an iota of hope dwelling in her.

"Okay," said Savage, softening his voice. "Let me get us some drinks first. What would you like?"

"Mocha, please," Theresa replied without looking up. "Let me give you some money." She reached into her bag.

"Don't be so silly," Savage said. "These are on me."

He got up and returned a few minutes later with a steaming cup of tea for himself and a mountainous glass of coffee topped with swirls of cream and chunks of marshmallow and bright confectionery. It looked more like a dessert than a drink. He sat in silence, watching Theresa attack her beverage, barely pausing for breath. He wondered where someone as petite as Theresa would put it all, but put it away she did.

He waited until she fished out the last marshmallow and said, "I have a daughter, too."

Theresa's eyes snapped wide open. "How did you know I had a daughter?"

Savage realised he'd said the wrong thing. It made him sound as though he'd been stalking her, and he quickly attempted to salvage the conversation. "The laptop that thug took from you. I noticed it was covered in stickers. They looked like pop bands. My daughter used to put stuff like that all over her wardrobe, so I'm just guessing you have a daughter."

"I do," she said, looking down into her empty cup. "She put those stickers on it when she was younger. They came free with a magazine. She would pester me to buy it for her every week. She stuck them all over her laptop, never bothered to take them off when she got older."

"How old is she?"

"Bella's twenty-two," Theresa replied. "How old is your daughter?"

"Kelly would have been thirty-five this year. She passed away, I'm afraid."

"I'm so sorry." Theresa began to cry. "I'm so sorry."

This isn't going well. He was supposed to be helping the woman, not reducing her to tears the minute after they'd met properly. He should have opened the conversation some other way, not by talking about his dead daughter.

"It's okay. I've learned to live with it." He pushed a napkin across the table for Theresa to wipe her eyes.

"How did she die?" she asked, dabbing her eyes.

"Roadside bomb in Afghanistan. Kelly was in the Royal Engineers."

"That's terrible. I know how it feels to lose a daughter."

"What happened?"

"Bella went missing about a year ago."

"I'm sorry." Savage couldn't think of anything else to say and didn't know how to react. His daughter's death had been more agony than he could bear, but at least he could attempt to deal with it, to make some sense of it and try to get closure. Theresa, however, lived in a whole different world of pain, one where questions hadn't been answered, and indeed, she might never know the truth. In a purgatory of perpetual heartache, she would never find any closure. She wouldn't move on, her imagination conjuring up new and sinister scenarios of what terrible fate might have befallen her daughter, the worst torture possible.

"I can't imagine what that's like," he said.

"It's like a shitty version of *Groundhog Day*. You know that film? Every day, you wake up, and it's the same. No matter what I do or how upset or angry I get, nothing changes. My life's in limbo, and I miss her so much." Thick tears slid down her cheeks.

"What have the police said?" Savage asked, trying to distract her.

"Oh, they're next to useless. They're not interested in missing people. 'Not enough resources,' they say. Did you know over six hundred people a day go missing in Britain?"

"I didn't know that."

"That's their excuse every time I ask them what's happening. They say they haven't got the time to deal with individual cases."

"Is it possible she's run off somewhere?"

Theresa shook her head. "Something horrible's happened to her. They found her womb."

"Her womb?"

"Yes, her womb. Police found it in a medical sack along with loads of others."

"What the hell? Where was this?"

"They were in a stolen van dumped on Camberwell New Road. They managed to identify one of them. It belonged to Bella. She got in trouble with the police when she was seventeen, nothing serious, but her DNA was put in a database—that was how they identified it as hers."

"So she'd had her womb removed. What did the police say?"

"Police think it was dumped there by some backstreet abortionist. But that doesn't make sense. Why would a backstreet abortionist go to the trouble of removing her womb? And who goes to a backstreet abortionist anymore? Unless they're ultra-religious and frightened of being found out. We certainly aren't religious, and I wouldn't care if she was pregnant. She'd have told me if she was. She tells me everything. We'd have got it sorted on the NHS."

Savage's mind jumped to the possibility that she'd been raped and was too ashamed to tell her mum, or maybe she was the victim of some bizarre serial killer who removed women's wombs before murdering them. He kept those thoughts to himself. Adding to Theresa's misery with new, unfounded theories wasn't appropriate. She was right about one thing, though. An amateur abortionist wouldn't go to the trouble of removing the womb. They wouldn't know how to. A procedure like that required surgical skill and anaesthetic, not a coat hanger and blind luck. The police were fobbing her off.

"So the police think she's had an amateur hysterectomy and disappeared?"

"Yep. They're not interested anymore, never have been. They've got hundreds of other missing people to worry about, they said. And my daughter's out there somewhere. On her own, frightened." Theresa's eyes began tearing up again. "Or lying in a ditch. I just want her to come home. She's such a beautiful girl, too. Look at her."

Theresa took out her phone and scrolled through some

pictures. She was right. Bella was a stunner, but not the usual peroxide-blond Barbie-doll clones seen posing along the King's Road or around Mayfair. She had thick fiery-red hair that curled around her shoulders and bright hypnotic amber eyes. Unlike most redheads, though, her lashes and eyebrows were dark, in contrast to her pale, unblemished white skin and full red lips. The blend was intoxicating.

"You're right, she's beautiful."

"Thank you."

The conversation stalled, so Savage went to get more drinks, the same again. Theresa greedily spooned away at the cream and marshmallows topping her mocha, as if all the talk of her daughter's disappearance had depleted her strength, leaving her hollow and ravenous. Savage dunked his tea bag, waiting for his brew to hit maximum potency.

"So who was that guy who took her laptop and did that to you?" Savage asked.

"That's Minchie. He's a debt collector for a local loan shark called Venables. Are you sure you want to hear all this? I've got more problems than the third world. I'm bad luck to be around."

"I'm sure. Go on."

"Well, after Bella disappeared and it was clear the police weren't going to do anything, I hired a private detective to find her."

"What's his name?"

"Hackett, a sweaty, disgusting man. Anyway, he was all I could afford. I spent everything I had on him. Said it would take him about a week to track her down—that was the usual scenario for a missing person. You can't believe how happy I was. He was sure he could find Bella, so I paid him seven hundred pounds. Then he came back to me a week later, saying he was close but needed another three hundred pounds. I didn't have it, so I borrowed it off Venables. I know I shouldn't have, but I was desperate to find Bella. I gave the money to Hackett to finish the job. A week went by, and I heard nothing. So I rang him, and he told me he'd exhausted all his leads and he was sorry but there was no sign of her. I went to his office and demanded my money back. He said no. I shouted and screamed. Told the police about him. Threatened to sue him. Nothing happened. He'd just been stringing me along, conning me. I realise that now. But I'm a single parent with no money. What could I do?"

"So you borrowed three hundred pounds off Venables, and now how much do you owe him?"

"Two and a half grand."

"Two and a half grand! On a three-hundred-pound loan!"

"And it's more every week."

Savage shook his head in disbelief. He knew rates were high for loan sharks, but that was crippling for anyone. "Was that why Minchie was at your house, to collect money off you?"

"Yeah, I've got no money to pay them, and they've already taken anything valuable, so they knock me around a bit and take my daughter's things. Not because they're worth anything but because they know they've got sentimental value."

"Like the laptop."

"Yeah, it's got loads of her pictures on it, right back from her school days."

"Bastards."

"So you see, my life is crap and is getting crappier."

"Would you like me to help you?"

"You can't get involved. Besides, I've got nothing to give you."

"I don't want anything from you—let's be clear about that. No money, no favours, nothing. You won't owe me anything, whatever the outcome, okay?"

"Then why do it?"

"I know the pain of losing a daughter. I couldn't do anything about Kelly. It was out of my control. But with your Bella, I can try and get her back or at least find out what happened to her. Besides, I need to do something with my life. My wife passed away last year. My life's pretty empty. Apart from going to the gym every day, I've got nothing. If I don't do something useful, I'm going to lose my mind, which I've come pretty close to losing already, believe me."

Theresa said nothing but just sat there anxiously picking at her napkin until it was shredded to tiny pieces.

"And don't worry about Minchie or Venables," he added. "I'll deal with them."

"No, you can't, those guys are dangerous."

"So am I. I'm ex-SAS. Served in the first Gulf War and in Bosnia, where I hunted down Serbian war criminals. I'm good at finding people, especially people who don't want to be found. A couple of backstreet thugs don't frighten me, and I can be very persuasive, make them see sense and do the right thing." That was a polite way of saying he'd tie them to a pole and throw broken bricks at them if they didn't agree to leave her alone. "Now, do you want me to help you?"

Theresa didn't speak but just looked away while an endless stream of tears rolled down her cheeks.

"I'll take that as a yes," Savage said, smiling and gripping her hand. "It's going to be okay, Theresa. We're going to find Bella. But first, we're going to pay off Venables."

"No," said Theresa. "Absolutely not. You're not using any of your own money."

"I don't intend to."

CHAPTER 10

S AVAGE PARKED HIS VW CADDY van by the curb across the road from Hackett's office, the private investigator Theresa had hired or, more precisely, had been conned by. She'd given him the address, and Savage had no problem finding it. Sandwiched between a sex shop and a kebab house in dire need of a visit from environmental health, Hackett's front door stood out like a bad tooth.

Savage sat in his white Caddy a little over an hour, waiting for Hackett to appear. His little van made a perfect OP or "observation post" as they called it in the SAS. It was bland, average and unmemorable, the kind of van a plumber or an electrician might use. No other vehicle drew less attention. His wife had hated it. *Why can't we have a proper car?* she had moaned. Savage told her it was practical, economical and reliable, ideal for fetching and carrying things. By that, he meant the DIY paraphernalia he ferried to their flat for fixing parts of his home that really didn't need fixing. That had been selfish of him, and he knew it. Regret needled him. He should've bought her something a little classier to drive around in.

One thing was for sure: it was a hell of a lot more comfortable than the OPs he'd occupied while gathering intel on various enemies during his time in the forces. Despite what people thought of the SAS, only a tiny fraction of their activity involved the sexy stuff—sneaking around bases and setting off big explosions. Most of it was what he was doing right then: long, monotonous periods spent observing a target. *Know your enemy,* as the saying went. The only way to do that was to watch them... endlessly.

The SAS was very good at it and took it to the extreme.

He'd once hidden in a bush in an African jungle with his mate for two weeks, observing a terrorist hideout, close enough that they could smell their BO. Once hidden, moving was not an option. They had to eat in the bush, sleep in the bush and crap in the bush while bugs, worms, snakes and spiders crawled all over them, but that was how the SAS beat its enemies. They did their homework, no matter what the conditions. They got close to their adversaries and watched them day and night until they knew everything about them—when they ate, when they slept, when they scratched their backsides—until they were satisfied nothing else was left to learn. Then they'd attack them when they were at their most vulnerable.

Savage saw Hackett's front door open and got his first glimpse of the man, a slob with limited mobility, dressed in a cheap suit straining at the seams to hold him all in. Clearly a junk-food addict; it explained why he'd chosen an office above a takeaway.

Hackett shuffled over to his car, an old Audi A5, clutching an SLR camera with a powerful lens, like the paparazzi would use, although Savage doubted he'd be snapping any celebrities that day.

Unlike the private detectives portrayed on TV, their real-life counterparts rarely solved high-profile crimes. Their bread and butter was far seedier, mostly involving snooping on cheating spouses whose husbands and wives suspected they were having affairs. To do that, they needed good cameras with good lenses.

Despite that, most private investigators Savage knew were stand-up guys, reliable and professional, but a few were like Hackett, bottom feeders who made a living either by ripping off people like Theresa or catching people with their pants down.

By the time Hackett made it to his car, he was already out of breath and glossy with sweat. Savage found him painful to look at.

Breathing heavily, Hackett opened the car door as wide as it would go, turned sideways, and sort of fell backward into the driver's seat. The suspension took a massive hit, dropping by about half a foot. A second later, the engine squealed painfully to life. *Fan belt needs changing.* Then Hackett drove off, trailing oily smoke.

Savage waited for several cars to pass by then pulled out so that he wasn't following too obviously. Hackett might have been a slob, but he was probably an ex-copper, which meant he'd know every trick in the book. Savage kept his distance, never getting too close, never letting him get too far away. They were heading south, towards Dulwich, an affluent village with posh houses, good schools and a thriving café culture. Savage wondered what business Hackett would have in such an upmarket place, but the PI didn't stop in Dulwich and continued towards Crystal Palace, a more affordable area with modest homes and perpetual traffic jams.

Savage sat in a queue of cars crawling along a tarmac road that skirted the town centre. Up ahead, Hackett suddenly made a left turn, speeding off down an unclogged side street.

Savage was in danger of losing him. He waited for a gap in the oncoming traffic then darted onto the other side of the road, driving against the flow. Gunning the Caddy's engine, he accelerated hard and just made it into the side street as a truck thundered towards him, air horn blasting and lights flashing.

Savage saw no sign of Hackett on the road ahead, but what he did see was a grotesque seventies concrete block in the distance, looming over the landscape, grey and ugly. At first, he thought it was an office building until he noticed a large bright logo and an even larger one advertising a "price per night." The budget hotel was cheap, soulless and anonymous. If Hackett needed photographic evidence of someone having an affair during the daytime, that would be the most likely place.

Savage followed his hunch and pointed the Caddy in the direction of the hotel. Two minutes later, he turned into its sprawling car park, filled to the brim with the sensible hatchbacks of sales reps and middle managers.

Driving cautiously down each row, he searched for Hackett's car, starting with the outermost row then working his way in. It wasn't among any of the cars he passed, but as he turned into the last row, he caught a glimpse of it through a space between two parked cars. Hackett's Audi took up the disabled spot right near the main entrance, giving him an uninterrupted view of anyone going in or coming out of the hotel.

Savage continued driving along the row until he found a space farther down. He reversed into it so that his back doors faced the front of the building. He killed the engine and climbed over the front seats into the back. If he looked at an angle through the back-door windows, he had a clear view of the entrance and Hackett's car beyond.

Hackett had his window down and was on the phone, or maybe he was just pretending to be on the phone.

Savage slid down onto his haunches and prepared to wait. The time was quarter to two, lunchtime. Most working people took their lunch between one and two. Logically, if Hackett was indeed trying to catch a couple of adulterers doing the dirty deed during their lunch break, they would be finishing up right about then, giving themselves just enough time to get back to work, unless they'd taken the afternoon off without telling their spouses.

Five minutes later, a smart, professional couple in business suits came bounding through the sliding doors, arm in arm, giggling. Hackett put his phone down, picked up the SLR and pointed it out the window. The couple stopped outside the entrance and kissed passionately, oblivious to Hackett snapping away with his camera. They briefly canoodled like a couple of teenagers then reluctantly separated to go back to their respective cars. The man went left, the woman right.

At that moment, Hackett attempted to get out of his Audi. He swivelled his feet out onto the tarmac and rocked his hefty body backwards and forwards by grabbing hold of the edges of the door like a tobogganist at the start of a run. On the third attempt, he launched himself up and out of the car. He quickly turned, grabbed the camera and waddled after the man.

A neat red Mini zoomed past Savage's window, distracting him for a second. The driver was the woman he'd seen at the entrance, still grinning with post-coital contentment.

Savage cursed himself for losing sight of both Hackett and the man. He couldn't see either of them from the back windows, so he climbed into the front seat for a different view. He spotted Hackett first, picking his way through the grid of parked cars, but he saw no sign of the man.

Hackett stopped and leaned against a car. At first, Savage thought he was recovering from his exertions, catching his breath, but then the man emerged from the car, puzzled at the sight of a large, sweaty guy wheezing against his vehicle.

The man had a similar expression to his lover's, all dreamy and warm. That soon fell away when Hackett spoke to him.

Savage couldn't hear what they were saying. He didn't need to. The man looked horrified as Hackett revealed the camera and thumbed through the pictures on the small digital screen. Evidence of his affair, no doubt. What confused Savage was why Hackett was showing the man his adulterous behaviour. Surely, he should've taken the evidence straight to the man's poor wife, the person who had hired him.

The man's eyes darkened, and he made a grab for the camera. Hackett held it out of reach and shoved him hard against his car. Hackett might have been overweight, but he wasn't to be messed with. Defeated, the man put his head in his hands then looked all around the car park as if a solution might present itself. He was on the brink of crying. Hackett just stood there, then he leaned in and said something, pointing at the hotel.

The man's shoulders slumped down even farther. Slowly, he dragged his feet towards the building.

Savage lost sight of him, so he jumped into the back of the van to see where he was going by peering through its back windows. An ATM was embedded in the wall of the hotel, right by the entrance. The man fed his card into the slot and withdrew a thick stack of notes. As he was returning, Savage climbed back into the front seat just in time to see the man hand the money to Hackett. Hackett glanced left and right cautiously before accepting the money then quickly shoved it into his trouser pocket.

Hackett was blackmailing him. The wife had probably hired

Hackett to check on her husband, but instead he was using him as an opportunity to extort money.

The man held out his hand. Hackett shook his head.

Even though Savage was inside the van, he heard what the man said because he shouted it so loudly: "Give me the bloody card!" Presumably, he wanted the memory card with all the incriminating pictures of him and his lover.

Hackett shoved him against the car again, probably threatening him. *"Keep your mouth shut, or your wife gets these pictures."*

No way was Hackett giving up the memory card and his nice little earner. The money from the cash machine was probably just the start. He would keep milking the guy for cash for as long as he could or until the guy got a divorce.

Savage had seen all he needed to see. He had a good idea of who he was dealing with, a lowlife who scammed cheating partners. Probably one of many cons he had on the go—perfect for what Savage had in mind—someone with a ton of dirty money lying around. That was all about to end, though.

CHAPTER 11

SAVAGE DROVE BACK TO HACKETT'S office, tailing him all the way but keeping a safe distance. When he got within a few streets of the private investigator's office, he veered off and parked his van out of sight, down a bleak, residential road lined with tightly packed family houses. Savage killed the engine and sat in his car for about half an hour, the amount of time he figured Hackett would take to park his car, heave his whale-like body out of the driver's seat and wobble back to his office. He could picture him taking the stairs one step at a time, gasping all the way and maybe taking a break halfway up.

When he felt certain Hackett was comfortably behind his desk, Savage pulled on a pair of tight-fitting skin-coloured disposable gloves, got out and walked briskly down several streets until he reached Hackett's office. Neither the sex shop nor the takeaway was open yet—too early for either kind of business.

Savage turned his attention to the door between the two shops, the one leading up to Hackett's office. An ancient intercom caked with grime and cobwebs clung to the wall. Hackett's name was handwritten in faded ink behind a dirty plastic window. One screw held the outer casing together, and a stray wire snaked out of the side. It hadn't worked in years.

Savage gave the door a gentle nudge. *Unlocked.* Opening it further, he peered inside, looking and listening for any signs of Hackett. Finding none, Savage quietly climbed the dimly lit, nicotine-coloured stairs and stood in front of the only door at the top, painted over so many times that where it was chipped, he could see layers of paint like geologic strata. To complete the dilapidated look, a scratched, stick-on metallic sign read Hackett Private Investigations Ltd.

Savage gave the door a little push. It was also unlocked, releasing a pungent eggy whiff from within. He stepped inside Hackett's office.

Equally depressing, a filthy beige carpet stretched across the floor while dented, mismatched filing cabinets jostled for space on the far wall. On the opposite side sat a sofa whose springs had collapsed long ago, and jammed into every corner were stacks of battered cardboard boxes overflowing with dogeared paperwork. In the centre of the mess sat Hackett, his ample body wedged behind a desk that looked as if it had been salvaged from a dump. A large computer screen sat on one side—not the svelte, flat-screen kind but the old, bulky kind that resembled a 1950s TV.

Elbows propped up on the desk, Hackett paused mid-bite, holding the biggest triple-bacon-and-egg sandwich Savage had ever seen, dripping yellow goo and brown sauce. Savage counted the edges of at least four eggs hanging out of it and perhaps a small pig worth of bacon crammed above.

"Wow," said Savage. "You've got an appetite like the Sarlacc."

"What the bloody hell's that?" asked Hackett.

"Big hole in *Return of the Jedi*. Eats Boba Fett."

"Want do you want?" he asked, clearly annoyed that someone had interrupted his late lunch. Maybe that was his second lunch of the day, in fact. Savage noticed a large Styrofoam cup of steaming tea next to Hackett's elbow, along with his SLR camera, the most modern object in the room.

"I've come to rob you," said Savage.

"What?"

"I said I've come to rob you."

"Get lost," said Hackett. "Do you know who I am?"

"Yep," said Savage, smiling. He loved it when people tried to intimidate him. He'd seen it all before. All the big claims they made, all the threats, the showing off how tough they were. The one common denominator was that none of them worked on him. "I'm still going to rob you."

"Like I said, get lost. I used to be in the police."

"Yes, you did, until you got thrown out."

"How do you know that?"

"I Googled you. Found a little article in the local rag from a few years back. Wasn't difficult. Now, back to business. Give me all your money, as us robbers like to say."

"Is this *Britain's Dumbest Criminals* or something? I'm a private investigator. Look around. There's no money here."

"Sure there is."

"Get lost. I'm eating." Hackett rammed the sandwich in his mouth, tore off a huge chunk and chewed it without bothering to close his mouth. His teeth were the colour of the pages of an old phonebook.

Savage took a step closer. "You've just taken a wad of money off someone. I doubt you're keeping it in your wallet, and you're not going to put it in the bank, which means you've stashed it somewhere, probably in here. So get off your fat arse, and give it to me."

"That's it, I'm calling my mates on the force."

Before Hackett had a chance to whip out his phone, Savage pulled out the SIG from the back of his waistband and fired its one and only bullet into the wall, a few inches above Hackett's head. The bang filled up every space in the room, even rattling the windows. Savage was used to guns going off. Hackett wasn't.

Hackett screamed, ducking low and spitting chewed-up sandwich everywhere. He desperately clawed at the top of his head to see if he'd been shot.

"Don't worry. I just shot the wall," said Savage.

Hackett spun around to see a bullet hole with spidery cracks spreading out across the plaster. Flattening out from the impact, the bullet would've been stopped by the double-brickwork party wall separating his office from the adjoining building.

Hackett panted hard, as though he were about to have a seizure.

"That's what robbers do," said Savage. "They fire guns if you don't do what you're told."

"D-don't kill me." Hackett thrust his hands into the air.

"You're doing a pretty good job of that yourself." Savage nodded towards the messy remains of his bacon-and-egg sandwich smeared all over the desk. "Money. Now."

Hackett got out of his chair more quickly than usual, helped by the fight-or-flight adrenalin supercharging his muscles. He wasn't exactly sprightly, but even Savage was impressed by how swiftly he shuffled over to the filing cabinet on the far right. Hackett pulled at the top drawer, which wasn't a drawer at all but a hinged false front hiding a safe. His pudgy hands went to work dialling the combination back and forth until the lock clicked. The door swung open, revealing shelves stacked with rolls of cash standing on their ends. Blackmail money.

"Put them in a carrier bag." said Savage.

"I don't have a carrier bag."

"What did that bacon sandwich come in?"

"A paper bag."

"Where is it?"

"In the bin."

"Well, get it out, then."

Hackett retrieved a scrunched-up brown paper bag from the top of the bin by his desk, overflowing with empty crisp packets and chocolate wrappers. He straightened out the bag and filled it with money from the safe.

"Now take out your phone and your wallet, and drop them in as well."

Hackett obeyed, fishing out a smartphone with a cracked screen and a small, faded brown leather wallet from his grubby trousers.

"Now give me the bag."

Hackett shook as he handed it over. Savage placed the bag on the ground by his feet.

"Now give me your camera."

Hackett turned and leaned over his desk, his wide belly splaying out either side of him, almost preventing him from reaching it. He managed to hook a finger around the carry strap and dragged it across to his side of the desk.

Savage took it from him and slung it over his shoulder. "And I'll have that cup of tea, as well."

"What?"

"The tea. Give it to me."

"You want my tea?"

"Yes."

Bizarrely, out of all the items Hackett was being robbed of, the tea was the one he looked most reluctant to give up. Hackett reached across the desk. Thankfully, the tea was closer than the camera, and he didn't have to strain to retrieve it.

Spirals of steam still rose from the top of the soft Styrofoam cup as he handed it over.

Savage gave it a few blows to cool it then took a slow, deliberate sip, slurping loudly.

He nearly gagged.

"How many sugars have you put in this?" asked Savage.

"Seven," Hackett replied.

"Seven?"

"And a half."

"Of course," said Savage, "that half makes all the difference." But tea was tea, even if you could stand a garden shovel up in it. Savage waited a minute or two then took another gulp. He waited then took another, still keeping the gun on Hackett.

After the fourth sip, Hackett asked, "So what happens now?"

"Nothing. Just shut up and let me drink my tea."

Savage fixed the private investigator with a blank, unreadable stare. Every now and then, he took another gulp, letting the hot, sweet liquid swill around in his mouth before swallowing. Hackett looked at the floor. He had no option but to just stand there and let the man drink his tea in unhurried silence. Large sweat patches developed under each of Hackett's armpits. Savage had never seen anyone look more awkward. That was the intention, to make him feel how he had made Theresa feel, humiliated and helpless. He was giving Hackett time to think about his situation, to let his imagination run wild.

Hackett mopped his brow with his handkerchief. Savage knew exactly what was going through his mind. An armed robber without a mask wasn't about to leave a witness behind. Once that cup was drained, Hackett would think he was getting a bullet in the head.

Savage kept up the silent treatment for about ten minutes, stretching out his drink until the very last drop. To Hackett it would have felt like a lifetime.

Finally, Savage exhaled with delight. "Ah, good cup of tea." He crushed the cup and dropped it into the paper bag near his feet. "Now, one last thing."

Hackett shifted on his feet, as if preparing to outrun Savage's gunfire, which would've been impossible for all sorts of reasons.

"Now, what was it I needed to do?" Savage tapped the side of his head with the SIG, as if to dislodge the memory. "There was something I needed to do. Tie up a loose end."

Hackett's whole body shook. "Please, don't kill me."

"No, that's not it," said Savage. Then he pointed the empty gun at him again. "I've got it!" he said, a lot louder than necessary, making the fat man jump. "I need your suit jacket."

"What?"

"The jacket you were wearing at lunchtime—where is it?"

Hackett swallowed hard. "On the back of the door."

Savage turned his head, keeping the gun on Hackett. The jacket was hanging from a hook on the door he'd come in through.

Savage backed away from Hackett, whose face was frozen in a mask of shock. He stopped briefly to throw the jacket over the same arm that held the gun. "You stay put for the next two hours. Don't leave or talk to anyone, or I'll shoot you, understand?"

Hackett rapidly nodded.

"Do you have a landline?"

"No."

"You're lying. How do I know you're not going to call someone the second I leave?"

"No, I swear, I just use the mobile."

No office phone was in sight, although it could've been hidden under all the clutter, but Savage believed him. Hackett was probably too tight-fisted to pay for both a landline and a mobile.

Savage turned and left. Outside on the landing, he stuffed the empty SIG into the back of his waistband and pulled his sweatshirt down over it. Then he descended the stairs and walked towards the VW Caddy with Hackett's phone, wallet, camera, jacket, and bag of cash.

When he got back to his van, he took Hackett's wallet and phone and slotted them into the inside breast pocket of the jacket, which had a zip fastener. He closed the zip and laid the jacket on the passenger seat.

Next, he made a quick estimation of how much cash he'd taken from Hackett. Peering into the bag, Savage counted eight rolls of twenties, each one secured by a rubber band. He reckoned each roll contained about four to six hundred pounds. That meant he had roughly between three and five grand, easily enough for what he had in mind.

Savage peeled off three hundred pounds from one of the rolls and stuffed it into his jeans. The rest of the money he left in the bag, shoving it into the glove compartment, which he locked. The camera wouldn't fit, so he had to make do with pushing it out of sight under the seat.

Savage turned the ignition, put the Caddy in gear, and pointed it in the direction of Venables, the loan shark.

CHAPTER 12

VENABLES' PLACE WAS IN A slightly better location than Hackett's. It was another low-rent office above a parade of seedy shops with convenient parking outside. However, those shops were a little more respectable than a kebab house and porn shop. A green grocer's stood shoulder to shoulder with a betting shop, a convenience store and a discount vape shop selling cheap electronic gizmos for sucking up nicotine. Similar to Hackett's, an anonymous door on the street, sandwiched between the green grocer's and the betting shop, led up a single flight of stairs.

Savage had spent a few days watching the place, checking movements and recording habits. Venables usually stayed there all day, while his trained gorilla, Minchie, was more erratic, coming and going at unpredictable times, presumably to twist some poor bugger's arm into paying up or to slap them around as he'd done with Theresa. At the moment, both of them were up there, and that was exactly how Savage wanted it.

Savage had also observed that during the day, a steady stream of people would visit and leave, staying for only a minute or two, mostly single mums with screaming kids or older people still in their slippers. Judging by the looks on their downcast faces and hunched body language, they were coming to make payments on their extortionate loans—or more likely to beg for more time or ask for more money. Either way, they'd be deeper in crap than they were before. Bad to worse in the blink of an eye. Savage felt sorry for them. Only the truly desperate would get into debt with a man like Venables. They had nowhere else to turn, just like Theresa. That made them vulnerable. And vulnerable people were easy prey.

Well, their luck was about to change. Venables was about to go out of business or at least have a very difficult time for the next few months.

Keeping his gloves on, Savage got out of the van and crossed the road with Hackett's jacket draped over his arm, covering his right hand. The jacket had Hackett's phone and wallet zipped into the inside breast pocket. Underneath the jacket, hidden from view, Savage held the SIG, gripping it the wrong way with his fingers wrapped around the barrel.

When he reached the front door to Venables' office, he knew it would be locked because he'd seen people outside, waiting to be buzzed in. Unlike Hackett's, this door entry system looked fairly new, complete with a built-in camera, and the little plastic window even had a logo on a printed sign saying Venables Financial Services, as if it were a respectable organisation.

Savage pushed the button, making sure his head wasn't in view of the camera.

"What?" said a distorted, unfriendly voice.

"I've come to make a payment," said Savage. A second later, the door clicked open. Savage went in and climbed the stairs. Plainly decorated with white paint and tough-wearing, industrial-strength grey carpet, the place was spotless and smelt of disinfectant. Venables clearly ran a tight ship.

On the landing at the top were two doors. Straight ahead, a door ajar gave a glimpse of a bright, clean, white W.C. On the right stood the door to Venables' office, complete with a smart plastic sign and that stupid logo. Savage pushed it open.

Inside, the space was well organised. Shelves of neatly arranged box files lined the walls, and a printer-cum-photocopier blinked away in a corner. Venables had even splashed out on a water cooler and a little coffee machine that took those tiny capsules that George Clooney advertised. The overall impression was of a man trying to be respectable when he clearly wasn't.

On the far wall was another door presumably leading to

Venables' office, because in front of it, like a gatekeeper, sat Minchie, the one who'd made a habit of hitting Theresa. He sat at a desk with his face buried in *The Sun*. Up on one of the shelves behind him sat Bella's laptop, still covered in stickers.

"Name?" said Minchie without looking up.

Savage put his left hand in his pocket to hide the fact he was wearing gloves, and moved in front of the desk. "I've come to make a payment for Tucker, Theresa Tucker."

Minchie put his paper down, looked up, then sighed wearily. Savage got his first proper look at Minchie. His hair was shorn all over, nearly down to the skin, revealing little scars on his scalp – an indelible history of fights won and lost. A long nose, surprisingly not broken unless he'd had it fixed, divided two small, dull grey eyes set a little too close together.

Minchie swung his legs round and stood up, easily reaching a height of six two, maybe more. As he ambled over to the shelves, Savage sized him up: a wide back and shoulders supported by two beefy legs—an intimidating package.

"What was the name again?" Minchie asked.

"Theresa Tucker."

Minchie twisted his head to look Savage up and down. "Got herself a new squeeze, has she?" He selected a bright-red ledger then placed it flat on the desk. "I would've thought she could do a bit better than you. Likes the older guys, eh?"

"Something like that."

Minchie flipped the book open, wetted his finger and flicked through pages of columns, names and numbers. "What was the name again?"

Is this guy part goldfish or something? Maybe he'd been hit in the head one too many times. It was a wonder Venables trusted him with any paperwork with a memory like his.

"I just told you. Theresa Tucker," Savage said calmly.

"Yeah, I know. I'm winding you up, idiot." Minchie grinned, revealing a few missing teeth. "So you're paying her debts off, are you?"

"Certainly am."

"That's a pity," said Minchie, coming to a stop on a page marked with a *T*. "Another week of not paying, and we have other ways of settling up, if you know what I mean." Minchie made a hole with his left thumb and index finger then prodded his right index finger in and out. He gave a dirty laugh then turned his attention back to locating Theresa's name. While he was distracted, Savage slowly lowered his right arm, letting the suit jacket slip off and fall gently to the carpet, uncovering the gun in his hand.

Minchie kept licking his top lip as his hand slowly tracked down the list of names. Like a slow computer, he was clearly using all his available processing power on the simple task. Finally, his hand stopped on Theresa's name. At that moment, Savage raised the SIG and brought the butt of the gun smashing down on Minchie's knuckles. Over a kilogram of German-engineered stainless steel collided with his hand. The hammer blow shattered at least eight of the twenty-seven bones in that part of his body.

"That's for hitting Theresa," said Savage. Then he swung the gun in a wide arc, smashing it into the side of Minchie's head, knocking him to the floor. "And that was just for fun."

Savage came around the desk and stamped on Minchie's injured hand, adding a few more broken bones to the ones he'd already wrecked.

Minchie's high-pitched scream sounded like air escaping from a popped balloon.

The door at the back of the room flew open. A guy about the same height and build as Savage burst through it. *Venables.*

"What the hell's going on?" he yelled.

Dressed in a navy-blue pinstripe suit, Venables stank of expensive aftershave. His hair was well cut and dyed an unnatural shade of brown, probably to cover up his late-forties grey. He looked like a corporate banker, clearly trying to shake off the gold-sovereign-rings-and-sheepskin-jacket image that most London loan sharks had. It wasn't working. Cheap blueish tattoos peeked out from under his cuffs, and the permanent sneer earned from years of being dragged up on tough South London streets betrayed him. Savage shuddered. That could have been him if his life had taken a different path.

"You must be Venables." Savage switched the gun round and held it by the handgrip so the muzzle pointed at Venables. "I'd like to give you something."

Venables backed into his office, hands raised. Savage followed him.

"Whoa," said Venables, looking left and right, trying not to trip over anything as he reversed. He came to an abrupt halt, his backside shunting into his desk. "I'm sure we can sort this out."

"Sit down," said Savage. "Keep your palms flat on the desk."

Venables did as he was told. An empty espresso cup sat on his desk with a folded copy of the *Financial Times*, probably because Venables thought that's what financial people did, drinking posh coffee while checking their stocks.

"I've come to pay off a debt," said Savage.

"So why do you need the gun?"

"Good point." Savage turned the gun around and slid it across the desk to Venables.

"You're a stupid bastard." Venables snatched up the weapon and pointed it at Savage.

That didn't worry Savage. It was empty, and he'd done his research on Venables. Despite the ridiculous upper-middle-class image he was attempting to pull off, Venables had a reputation for sorting out problems with baseball bats and knuckle dusters but definitely not guns. He was no ballistics expert and wouldn't know the difference between a loaded SIG and an unloaded one, and he certainly wouldn't think to eject the mag to see if it was loaded or check the chamber to see if it had a bullet in it. If he did figure out the thing wasn't loaded, Savage knew he could drop the South London thug in a fistfight without breaking a sweat. A groan came from outside. Minchie certainly wouldn't be any help that day.

"You put Minchie on the floor," said Venables. "Not many people could do that."

"I got lucky."

"So you pistol whip my guy then hand me the gun that you did it with." He examined the weapon from all angles. "This is a nice shooter. Okay, so you've got my attention. What do you want?"

"I've come to make you a deal. Theresa Tucker borrowed three hundred quid off you, and I'm here to pay you back." Savage reached into his pocket, pulled out a wad of twenty-pound notes, and dropped them on the desk.

Venables fanned out the notes with his free hand and did a quick count. "You're short. Where's the interest?"

"Oh, here." Savage pushed his hand deep into his jeans pocket. After fishing around, he eventually pulled out a pound coin and placed it on the desk. "The interest."

Venables' face was unreadable. Then he burst out laughing, big belly laughs. Savage joined him.

Venables' laughter abruptly stopped. "That little bitch owes me over two grand in interest. And you give me a pound. Who do you think I am?"

"Here's the deal," said Savage. "You take this money as full and final payment."

Silence for a few seconds.

"What? That's it?" said Venables. "That's not a deal. That's bullshit."

"I'm afraid it's the only deal on the table."

"Or what?"

"I guess you'll have to kill me."

"You're a funny guy," said Venables. "But I need two and a half grand plus a couple of hundred more for putting Minchie out of action."

Savage shook his head. "Afraid not. Just so we're clear: there's no more money coming to you, apart from what's on the desk."

"Well, then you've got a very big problem."

"I see it differently. You have two choices: take the deal I'm offering, or kill me, because as sure as the sun rises in the morning, that's all you're getting."

Venables readjusted his aim, pointing the gun at Savage's head. "You don't make the demands, pal. I do."

"Er, I think I just did. Shall I draw it in crayon so you can understand it? There's no more money, so either we have a deal, or you have to pull the trigger."

"You don't know who you're dealing with."

"Yes, I do. A cheap backstreet lowlife who hasn't got the balls to kill me."

"I will kill you."

"Well, stop talking about it and do it. Otherwise, I'm walking out that door, and we're square, as far as Theresa Tucker's concerned."

Venables didn't move, apart from a slight twitch near his mouth. The veins on the side of his head looked ready to pop, and his skin turned scarlet with rage. Savage stared at him, waiting for a response, but none came.

"Pulling a trigger is not as easy as it looks, is it?" said Savage. "Even for a hard bastard like you. Takes a certain type of person to end a life, especially in cold blood. So take the deal, and that'll be the end of it."

Venables lowered the gun. "I'm not going to kill you. Do you think I'd be so stupid to murder someone in my own office? But I promise you one thing. You walk out that door, and you're a dead man."

"I don't think so."

"I know people, people that take care of little problems for me. Next time I see you, it'll be on the six o'clock news, being pulled out the Thames with concrete blocks round your feet."

Savage turned to leave. "You can keep the gun, but you should have taken the deal," he said, closing Venables' office door behind him.

Back in the main office, Minchie sprawled on the floor clutching his hand. Savage stood on it again as he stepped over him, giving his heel a good twist to ensure maximum pain. "That's to make sure you don't hit any more women."

Minchie squealed.

Savage reached up to the shelf and grabbed Bella's laptop. On his way out, he scooped up Hackett's jacket from the floor and hung it on a coat stand by the door. Then he left the office, walked down the stairs, and headed to the nearest phone box. They weren't as plentiful as they used to be, but he'd made sure a box was working a few streets away.

He lifted the receiver and called 999. Before the operator could answer, he spoke quickly and clearly. "I want to report an armed robbery at the office of Private Investigator Tony Hackett in Sudgen Street, South London. He was robbed by Sam Venables. Venables is in his office right now in Park Street and is still armed." Savage hung up.

Nothing jumped to the top of the list of police priorities like an armed robbery. In a service where everything was an emergency, armed robbery was the daddy of them all, second only to a full-on terrorist attack. At that moment, lit-up armed response vehicles or ARVs would be hurtling towards an unsuspecting Venables from somewhere across the city. ARVs were always on patrol in the capital. They'd find him in possession of a recently fired SIG Sauer P226 and Hackett's jacket, containing his wallet and phone, plus a bit of cash. That wasn't much, but it would be enough.

At the same time, scene-of-crime officers would be descending on Hackett's office to find a shaken-up private detective with a bullet wedged in his wall. Forensics would later analyse the bullet and confirm it came from the gun found at Venables' office. Venables would protest that he had never seen the gun before and that a complete stranger had come in off the street and threatened him. He'd probably spin them a story that Minchie had managed to get the gun off the stranger, hence his smashed-up knuckles. The police wouldn't buy it, not when they had more than enough evidence to pin an armed robbery on a well-known scumbag like Venables.

Hackett's statement would be a problem. He'd almost certainly deny Venables' involvement. That didn't matter, though. Every lowlife around had heard of Venables and steered clear of him, unless they wanted to wind up in hospital. So the police would simply think Hackett was covering for him because he was frightened. Hackett's description of Savage would match Venables', but that would just seem as though Venables had put pressure on him to get his story straight. Then Hackett would also have some difficult questions to answer. He couldn't mention the money Savage had taken because it was blackmail money. It would look highly irregular that someone like Venables would go through all the trouble of an armed robbery just to steal a phone and wallet. The police would figure something was up between those two. They'd most likely think that Hackett owed Venables money and he'd given Hackett a warning shot to pay up, literally. Because a gun was involved, the police wouldn't stop until they had answers.

Whether Venables got put away or not, life would soon be very difficult for him. His days of bullying people for money would be over, and Hackett's little blackmail racket would, too.

Savage stepped out of the phone box to the sound of police sirens heading his way, and he allowed himself a wry smile.

He'd taken out two scumbags with one bullet—not a bad day's work.

CHAPTER 13

SAVAGE UPTURNED THE CRUMPLED PAPER bag and dumped the rolls of notes onto Theresa's small, shabby kitchen table. They scattered in every direction as if trying to escape. Some rolled away, tumbling off the edge and bouncing onto the chipped kitchen floor. Savage scooped them up and placed them back on the table, butting them into a mini mountain of cash.

"What's this?" Theresa asked, her hand flying to her mouth.

Savage thrust his arm through the pile of money, dividing it in two, and shoved the larger part towards her.

"This is for you, and the rest is for me—to use to find Bella. But if there's any left over at the end, it's yours."

"But where did it come from?"

"Let's just say Hackett had a change of heart and decided to refund your money, plus a little something extra for all the stress he caused you."

"But there's thousands here."

"Listen, don't lose any sleep over a lowlife like Hackett."

Theresa bit the nail of her little finger, tearing a sliver of nail off. "And what about Venables? I need to pay him back."

"Already done it. Minchie won't be bothering you again."

"How come?"

"It's probably best you don't know."

More worry lines surfaced across her forehead. "John, this sounds dodgy. What did you do to him? What if the police get involved?"

"They already are involved. Let's just say I tipped them off, and now he's helping them with their inquiries, which means he won't be bothering you."

Savage pushed the rolls of money closer to her so that they nearly dropped in her lap. "Take the money. Put it in a safe place. Use it to pay your bills, get a new TV, get your hair done, buy some new clothes—whatever. You deserve something nice for a change. Now, I'll make us some tea, and let's get started on finding Bella."

Savage boiled the kettle. Theresa extracted biscuits from a plain packet that had Value Range written on the outside, and slid them onto a plate. They moved into the lounge, which was as cramped as the kitchen. A fake leather sofa took up most of the space. It had probably been tan once, but exposure to years of daylight had discoloured it to a jaundiced shade of yellow. On the wall opposite, a faded rectangle marked the absence of a TV screen thanks to Venables snatching it as partial payment for Theresa's debts.

Theresa slurped her tea nervously. "So what happens now?"

"First, we work the lists."

"What does that mean?"

"I'll need a list of everyone who knew Bella. Friends, family, boyfriends, girlfriends, anyone she even vaguely knew, even enemies."

Theresa shook her head. "She didn't have any enemies."

"Okay, well, anyone that she might know, regardless of how distant." Savage shifted uneasily on his seat. "I know this is painful, but can I ask when you last saw Bella?"

Theresa's hand shook, forcing her to put her tea down. "She went to work—"

"Where did she work?"

"The health club in Camberwell."

"Health club? The one called Motivation?"

Theresa nodded, picked her tea back up and took a shaky sip.

"I'm a member of that club."

"Yeah, so's half of London."

"What did she do there?" Savage took a bite of his biscuit, which was dry and tasteless.

"Cleaning. Wiped the machines down, swept up, scrubbed the toilets, that sort of thing. Not the best job in the world, but she loved it. Felt like she was part of something big and glamourous. She'd struggled to get anything before that. Unemployed for ages, almost from leaving school, but they gave her a chance—I think her looks helped. She wanted to become a personal trainer, and the manager—"

"Carl Hansen?"

"Yes, that's him. Carl promised to put her on a training course, help her get qualified."

"So you saw her go to work, and then she never came home."

Theresa got to her feet, folded her arms, and paced up and down the tiny kitchen, as though moving helped her to contain the pain. "She went off one Saturday morning to do her shift. They open at seven, and she left at about six. Then she never came home."

"What time did her shift finish?"

"Three thirty. She was meant to go out that night, so I know she was keen to get home, relax, and have a bath before getting ready."

"Did her work colleagues see her go?"

"Yes, and Carl, I mean Mr. Hansen, was kind enough to show me the CCTV tapes from the security cameras outside the club. She definitely left work. So whatever happened to her, happened..." Theresa's voice cracked and trailed off. Her head dropped into her hands, and she sobbed quietly. "I just want her to come home."

Savage stood up and took Theresa's hand. "I'll find her. I promise. Maybe we should stop for a while—"

Theresa's head snapped up, and she fixed him with a pair of sad, red-rimmed eyes. "No. We need to keep going. Please."

"Of course, of course. If you're up to it."

"I am."

"Okay, would you mind if I took a look at her room?"

"Sure."

Savage followed Theresa up a flight of narrow, bare stairs

that creaked at every step. His first impressions of Bella's room were of a girl who'd barely left her teenage years. A small pile of cuddly toys perched on the top of a neatly made bed. Posters of rappers hung on the wall. Random photos of her and her friends peppered a wardrobe mirror. She looked happy, full of life and ready to take on the world. By the window was a small dressing table. Judging by its size and tattiness, she'd probably had it since her early teens. A kaleidoscope of makeup products, hair ties and beauty tools covered its surface.

"May I look in the wardrobe?"

"Of course."

Savage opened the wardrobe door. Inside, every inch of space was taken up with clothes hanging in a line or neatly folded away.

"Was Bella always this tidy?"

"Not at all. Her room usually looks like a bomb's hit it. I cleaned up."

"Did you throw anything away?"

Theresa looked at the floor. "Yes, I'm sorry. There was just so much rubbish everywhere. I bet I've thrown away something important. I'm so stupid."

"Hey, stop that. Can't do anything about it now."

Savage closed the door to the wardrobe and quickly looked through her chest of drawers. Nothing stood out as being significant, the typical bedroom of a sociable young girl, almost a carbon copy of his own daughter's when she was that age, minus the cuddly toys, which she'd never really cared for, even when she was little.

"Okay, I've seen enough," said Savage. "There's one other thing I'd like to look at—her laptop."

"Venables has that."

"Not any more. I took it off him."

A tearful smile broke across Theresa's face. "You got it back?"

"Yes, it's in my rucksack, downstairs."

"I thought it was gone forever. It has all her photos on it. Yes, of course you can look at it."

They returned to the kitchen, cleared the money off the table, and set up the laptop, plugging it in. All the passwords had been saved by the device and the desktop screen popped up with all her social-media sites still open: Twitter, Facebook, and Instagram.

Savage carefully scrolled back through each social-media site, comparing them as he went, a complete online diary of her life up to the point when she disappeared.

In the past, before the social-media age, discovering the last movements of a missing person meant painstakingly gathering information piece by piece. Nowadays, there it was, all laid out for the world to see, every place she'd been and every thought she'd had, all digitally captured.

Savage carefully examined every photo and read every post and comment, cross-referencing them with posts on her other accounts. None of it was any help. Her posts were like those of any young girl in her twenties living at home on minimum wage: a procession of images of her in cheap bars with her friends holding up happy-hour pints of beer or glasses of wine. Those were sometimes interrupted by images of her showing off a new garment she'd bought from Top Shop or River Island with comments like, "Just blown this week's wages." Or the odd meme of a cute puppy saying something rude.

Her tweets ranged from "Yay, going clubbing tonight" to "Can't believe it's Monday." Innocuous, superficial stuff with not a clue to her disappearance, just a girl having a good time with friends.

"Do you recognise the people in all these shots?" asked Savage.

"Yes, that's Nikki and Sam, Dave who she went out with for a year, and Tim from Surrey. There's Katrina, who she went to Ibiza with..."

Savage cut short the shopping list of friends and acquaintances. "Put it another way. Is there anyone here who you don't recognise?"

"Er, no. Not so far."

"And what about her ex, Dave? Any bad feelings there?"

"None at all. Actually, I think he's gay now, so definitely not. They're really good friends."

Now and then, Bella had shared pics of celebrities at red-carpet events and exclusive parties, with comments about how she adored that dress or wanted to be famous like them, or asking why she didn't get invited to celebrity parties. Like many girls her age, she wanted to be famous, one of the "beautiful people," or at least to rub shoulders with them.

Savage painstakingly scrolled back through the previous two years of her life, and nothing stood out as significant.

"What about her photos?" asked Theresa. "She backed up all her photographs on her laptop. That's why I was so desperate to get it back."

Savage clicked on the file icon and opened the folder marked Pictures. Laid out in front of him was a neat grid of files, each marked with a year. He clicked one at random. It opened up to reveal the fresh, immature faces of Bella and her school friends. They must have been around fifteen at the time. In some shots, they were in uniform. In others, they wore jeans and hoodies and hung out at the local park, still too young to get served in pubs.

Savage went forward in time and clicked the cursor on the very last folder, the year Bella had gone missing. He started with the most recent photos and worked his way back. He recognised almost all the images. They were the same ones she'd posted on social media. A digital deja vu, except more variations of the same photograph were there—the ones she'd taken but hadn't chosen to post. Parties, rough pubs, cheap booze and the odd budget holiday. Nothing new.

Then something caught Savage's eye. In the sea of all that teenage averageness, one shot stood out. It did so firstly because he hadn't seen it before on any of her social media accounts but, more importantly, because it was far from average.

CHAPTER 14

"**I**T MIGHT BE SOMETHING, OR it might be nothing, but this image isn't like the others," Savage explained. "Have you seen it before?"

"No. Never," replied Theresa, peering closely at the screen.

"And it wasn't on any of her social-media pages," Savage added. "I would have remembered."

"Why is it different?" Theresa asked.

"At first, it looks like another shot of her out on the town. Bella's sitting at a table in a dimly lit club. No different from hundreds of shots we've already seen. But I don't recognise this place. It's a one-off. Secondly, it's a selfie. She's there alone. None of her friends are with her. I don't think I can remember any shots of her going out where she doesn't have her friends with her."

"Maybe she's waiting for them to arrive."

"But this is the one and only shot of her in this place. She'd have taken lots of others once her friends joined her."

"Maybe they got deleted."

"True, she could have gone there, had a falling out or a bad time, then deleted them all. But she's kept this one. Why would she do that? She'd either have lots of shots or none at all."

"Okay, but it's not much to go on."

"Look closely at the image. What do you see?"

Theresa's eyes narrowed. "I see Bella in a smart red dress, sitting at a table. There are some odd metal balls hanging down, with holes in them. They look like fancy lights. And there's an ice bucket on the table with a bottle of Champagne in it."

Savage pointed at the bottle of Champagne. "I haven't seen Bella drinking Champagne in any other shots. Does she like Champagne?"

"Yes."

"Then why doesn't she drink it?"

"Because it's too expensive."

"Exactly what I thought you'd say. Champagne is pricey, even if it's an average bottle of bubbly from a supermarket."

"I suppose so."

Savage enlarged the picture, closing in on the smart gold foil around the neck of the bottle. "Look a bit closer. You can just about read the name on it."

Theresa leaned in for a better look. "Yes, it says Krug."

"I'm no expert, but Krug is top-quality stuff. Only people with too much money drink it. A bottle like that costs at least five hundred pounds in a restaurant or a bar, maybe more."

"You're joking."

Savage rose to his feet. "Come with me for a second."

Without question, Theresa stood up and followed Savage up the stairs and into Bella's room. He threw open the door to her wardrobe and flicked along the hanging dresses and garments. He stopped on a red dress, the same one from the photograph, and lifted it out to lay it on the bed. It was a beautiful, well-tailored pencil dress, cut tastefully above the knee, sexy without being vulgar.

"This is the dress from the photograph," Savage said. He lifted up the label so they could both see it. "Karen Millen. What sort of label is Karen Millen?"

"A good one. Very good. It's beautiful," Theresa replied, fingering the material.

"How much does a Karen Millen dress cost?"

"I don't know. I can't afford them. Maybe a hundred and fifty, two hundred, perhaps."

"So definitely not in Bella's budget."

"No way."

"Have you seen her in this dress before?"

"No, never."

Savage slotted the dress back into the wardrobe. They both went back downstairs and sat in front of the laptop, staring at the mysterious picture.

"Something about this photo doesn't add up," said Savage. "Bella's wearing a posh frock in a place that sells ridiculously expensive Champagne, which means it's very exclusive. Way out of her league. The kind of place she dreams about being in, rubbing shoulders with the rich and famous—all she talks about in her social posts. Now, if she was in a place like this, wearing a dress like that, why hasn't she posted anything about it? She'd be desperate to share it with her friends. But she didn't. Doesn't make sense. It seems out of character."

Theresa swallowed nervously. "Why do you think she was there? To impress someone, a man, maybe?"

"Quite possibly. That's what we need to find out." Savage right-clicked on the image, and a box with a little menu appeared. He scrolled down to Properties and found the date stamp on the image. "This photo was taken about three months before she disappeared." Then he clicked the tab marked Details. "Damn it."

"What's the matter?"

"I was hoping the image was geotagged."

"What does that mean?"

"Smartphones and digital cameras have built-in GPS," Savage explained. "It records where each photo was taken. But there aren't any tags on this photograph. Some phones, you have to switch on the feature before it starts recording locations. Bella probably didn't know about it or didn't have any reason to use it."

"And that's bad?"

"It just means it's going to be a hell of a lot harder finding this place. We'll have to do it the old-fashioned way. Could you call her friends? Maybe she mentioned this place to one of them. Ask them if she talked about going to a posh club around that time."

"Yes, I can do that." Theresa went into the hall and returned with her phone.

"I'm going to contact whoever supplies Krug in this country, see if I can find out where this stuff is sold, narrow down the search."

Savage got out his mobile and made some inquiries. After a few calls, he found out he was right about Krug being sold only in exclusive establishments. The supplier told him they sold directly to about eighty prestigious venues in London. Eighty was a manageable number, and with a few weeks' legwork, he could find out which venue was in the photo. That was the good news. The bad news was that Krug could also be bought through wholesalers and sold to anyone with a liquor license. Tracking down every place that had bottles of the stuff sitting in their refrigerators would take a lifetime. London was a city full of rich people, and ironically, exclusive venues were everywhere. The supplier told him that hundreds of independent upmarket hotels, clubs, bars and restaurants that they weren't aware of probably sold Krug. He'd have to narrow that list down somehow or else visit all of them in person. Doing that would take months, maybe years, and the majority of those places wouldn't even let him through the door, let alone talk to him. Also, that was just London. If the picture had been taken outside the capital, in another town or city, it'd be like finding a needle in a haystack without knowing if he was looking in the right haystack.

Savage watched Theresa calling Bella's friends one by one. Each time, she asked the same question, and each time, she got the same answer.

Theresa hung up the last call. "It's a big zero, I'm afraid, from everyone. But they all said the same thing: Bella would have been the first to gossip about going to a place like that."

Savage scratched his chin. "Like I said, this could be nothing, but my gut is telling me otherwise. We need to get to the bottom of this before we move on. Otherwise, it's going to keep bugging me. I'd rather cross this off my list before I move on, but first we're going to need help finding where that shot was taken."

"Do you know someone who can do that?"

"No, but like I said, I'm good at finding people."

CHAPTER 15

IN THE FIFTH COMPUTER SHOP Savage had visited, he still hadn't found what he was looking for. He had been avoiding all the national chains—the big, boxy, out-of-town superstores where everyone had a name badge and tried to sell you things from the moment you walked in. Instead, he'd trawled the independent local backstreet PC-repair shops. They were dotted all over the place in odd, unexpected locations, but they all seemed to follow the same blueprint. They all had security bars on the window, and behind the bars would be an odd collection of refurbished machines of all shapes and sizes, some desktops and some laptops. An assortment of screens would also be there, some with recognisable brands, others with unfamiliar and sometimes unpronounceable names. Each store seemed like a dog's home for computer equipment. Strange mongrel machines that had once been people's pride and joy sat waiting for new owners to take them home. Day-Glo stickers were slapped on each device, scrawled with marker-pen prices and weak promises like "Two-month guarantee."

Savage opened the door to the next shop on his list of names, with Bella's laptop under his arm. Inside, the walls were lined with utilitarian metal shelving, the kind that bolted together. Towards the back of the shop sat a wooden counter piled with bits of electronic equipment, circuit boards and cables. Among all the debris was a plastic display announcing a comprehensive yet baffling price list for PC repairs.

Behind the counter, an archway led to a backroom workshop. Four young, sweaty guys with unkempt hair sat on stools, heads down, feverishly trying to fix bits of hardware. One girl sat chewing gum and playing on her phone. Clad in combat trousers and an unshapely black long-sleeve T-shirt, she had dark skin and a mass of glossy black curls shaved severely around her temples.

To the side of the room, watching over the table of workers, sat the manager, prodding away at a laptop. A thin man, he wore a collar and tie far too big in circumference for his long, scrawny neck, which poked through it like a stick through a hula hoop. His beady eyes looked over the top of his screen at the girl playing on her phone.

"Tannaz!" he shouted, his faced pinched with anger.

"What?" said the girl still engrossed in her phone.

"Have you fixed that Mac yet?"

"Yep."

"What about the Hewlett Packard?"

"Done it."

"And the new motherboard for—"

"Done that, too."

"Well, you can help Chris with his—"

"Already have, and I've done his next job and Ralph's too, so I'm just having a little break, catching up on emails." Her brash London accent had the tiniest trace of Middle Eastern.

"I don't pay you to have breaks. We're not on Arabic time here."

Without looking up from her screen, she gave him the middle finger. "I'm not an Arab, racist prick."

The manager was just about to retaliate when he noticed Savage waiting by the counter. He leapt up, tucked his shirt in, and assumed a more civil manner for his potential customer. "Sorry, I didn't see you there," he said, coming through the archway. "Bloody lazy Arabs, eh?" he said, hoping to find an ally.

Savage cleared his throat. "Like she said, she's not an Arab. And she seems far from lazy."

The girl looked up from her phone screen at Savage.

"What?" said the manager.

"Tannaz is a Persian name, I believe," said Savage. "Persians are not Arabs. They're Persians. In the same way that you are not Australian, American, or Klingon—"

"I can speak Klingon."

Everyone turned to look at the small oily lad who'd interrupted Savage.

He sat at the table, fiddling with the trackpad on a laptop. "Just saying."

Nobody spoke.

Savage returned his attention to the guy in the white shirt and continued, "So you owe her an apology."

"Well, I'm just having a laugh."

"Really? Nobody else is laughing."

"Look, can I help you with something?"

"Nope, just leaving. I've found what I'm looking for."

Savage left the shop and headed across the street to a small greasy-spoon café, where he ordered tea and waited. Several cups later, five thirty came around. The lights of the computer repair shop flicked off, and everyone left, going their separate ways. Tannaz appeared, pausing briefly outside the shop. She dug a packet of cigarettes out of her bag, selected one and fitted it between her lips. After sparking it up, she drew long and hard, breathing out a small cloud in ecstasy. She carried on puffing as she walked to an empty bus stop, took a seat and waited.

Savage tucked Bella's laptop under his arm, left the café and headed towards her.

"Hi," he said.

Tannaz didn't reply. She just eyed him suspiciously.

"I need some help of a technical nature." Savage held up the laptop.

"I've finished for the day. Come back to the shop tomorrow. We open at nine thirty."

"You're too good for that place."

"Thanks. Now, go away if you don't mind." She took another drag on the cigarette.

"So I'm asking myself, 'What is a talented person like you doing in a dump like that?'"

"Look, mate, I just want to go home. Can you go away? You're creeping me out."

Savage turned, took a step away from the young girl, then turned back. "You know, I think you do that job because it's a regular wage, pays taxes, national insurance. Nice and neat. Respectable. Someone cynical might call it a smokescreen for other stuff you do."

"Who the hell are you?" She spat the cigarette out, stood up and ground it out with her foot.

Savage backed away. "Nobody. I'm just trying to track down a girl."

"Oh, so you are a creep."

"She went missing a year ago," he said. "I have a picture of her, and I need to know where it was taken."

"Check the geotags. That'll tell you." Tannaz walked away.

"I did. There aren't any."

"Well, drag and drop it onto an image-location site. There are tons of free ones on the web."

"Tried that. They're fine for tourist photos of castles and churches, but this is a little trickier." Savage caught her up, unfolded the laptop, and brought up the image of Bella in the nightclub. Put the screen in front of her.

"She's hot," said Tannaz.

"Like her?"

"Hell, yeah."

"Good, then help me find her, and maybe you can meet her."

"I bet she's straight."

"She is, but she did have a boyfriend who's gay now."

Tannaz eyed Savage with a stare that said, *"Seriously?"*

"What about the image?" asked Savage. "Is it possible to find out where it was taken?"

Tannaz sighed. "Not without a geotag. Sorry."

"Would you at least give it a go? I'll give you three hundred quid."

Tannaz took out another cigarette, lit it and blew the smoke out. "Seven hundred."

"Three fifty."

"Six fifty."

"Four hundred."

"Five, and I get to meet the girl in the picture—if you find her."

"Done. And it's *when* I find her, not *if*."

Savage handed her the laptop and reached into his pocket. He pulled out a wad of twenties and peeled off a handful of notes. "Here's two fifty now. The other two fifty when I get the location of the picture."

Tannaz took the money and stuffed it into her pocket. "I should have something for you in a week or so."

"How about tomorrow?"

"Tomorrow! Are you insane?"

"No, but I've seen how good you are. You're quick. Quicker than all those other guys put together."

Tannaz smiled, revealing a beautiful row of perfect white teeth. She was pretty even though she was making every effort to look butch. "Yeah, I am good."

"Bella, the girl in that picture—she's been gone over a year. Every day wasted, it gets harder and harder to find her. So I need it yesterday."

"Lucky I don't sleep, then."

"Neither do I. Call me the second you have something."

CHAPTER 16

S AVAGE DECIDED TO HIT THE gym. He wanted to think, and the best way to do that was by running. Something about the monotony of rapidly putting one foot in front of the other seemed to help his brain fit things into place. He needed a lengthy jog, not exactly a marathon but at least a good hour on the treadmill.

He reached the health club in the early evening. He entered the lobby and flashed his membership card at the glamorous receptionist. Three of them were on that day, more than was really necessary to service everyone going in and out. That wasn't the point, though. The place was all about perceptions. With their unblemished skin and finely carved cheekbones, they looked like some bizarre Hollywood love triangle. Savage wondered what life would have been like if he had been that good-looking.

A voice suddenly snapped him out of his daydream.

"Mr. Savage. Mr. Savage?" Brett came trotting across the reception area, his blond quiff remaining strangely rigid as he hurried over.

Savage girded his loins, preparing for a broadside of Brett's pomposity.

"Mr. Savage, I'm glad I caught you. Mr. Hansen would like to see you."

Savage craned his neck, looking up at the giant clad in skin-tight black Lycra. The man's polished teeth were bright enough to give the sun a run for its money.

"Would he, now?" Savage replied.

"Yes, he would. This way, please."

"Maybe later. I'm just about to work out."

Brett looked at his watch. "Oh, no. Mr. Hansen can't be kept waiting. He's a very busy man."

"Well, so am I. Tell him I'll pop my head round the door when I've finished. If not, he can see me next time."

"But, Mr. Savage—"

"Ta-ta." Savage turned and headed off to the changing rooms, leaving Brett standing dumbfounded in the middle of the reception area.

Savage had never seen the gym so busy. Then again, he'd never been there at that time of day. Six thirty in the evening was prime time for people to get in their after-work exercise, which meant every machine was occupied. He had to wait for a treadmill to free up, making him irritable. He had a lot on his mind and too much nervous energy.

Waiting for a machine was a bit like picking a queue at the supermarket checkout—some were quicker than others. Suddenly, three became free at once as a trio of women who'd been talking and walking simultaneously decided they'd had enough. They were made up to the nines and kitted out with expensive gym gear. None of them bothered to wipe her machine down. Maybe they were rich and lazy, or perhaps they were used to someone like Bella coming round and cleaning the machines for them.

Savage tried to picture her in that place, her smiling face and that distinctive red hair, probably tied back in a ponytail. He could imagine her being a hard worker, eager to please, buzzing here and there and chatting with everyone. A little ray of sunshine.

Savage climbed aboard the machine and set it for hard terrain. He had a lot to think about.

The whir of the treadmill signalled the start, and Savage walked at a brisk pace to warm up, letting his thoughts slosh around his mind.

In the few hours he'd spent at Theresa's, he'd made more progress than the police had in a year. However, it was a well-known fact that the police simply didn't have the resources or manpower to properly investigate missing people. Bella's case was about more than just a missing person, though.

Her womb being found in an abandoned van was bizarre and puzzling. *Why haven't the police investigated this further?* Savage certainly didn't buy the backstreet-abortionist story. No one would go to the trouble of removing a womb to terminate a pregnancy, and a whole bagful of wombs had been found. The case was too strange for words, yet the police had shelved it. That side of it Savage couldn't make fit—not yet, anyway. He needed more information.

Savage hit the button controlling speed, shifting up to a running pace—not too fast, just a light jog.

The only part of the puzzle he did feel confident about, however, didn't give him any comfort. The scant amount of evidence he'd gathered so far from Bella's laptop made him anxious. It pointed in one very sinister direction, and he didn't need to be an investigative genius to work it out.

He had a missing girl, who like most girls that age wanted to have fun, go to parties and live the high life. However, she was stuck in a minimum-wage reality, living with her mum, with barely enough money to go out. Also, she was a rare beauty, a natural redhead. Then she shows up in a prestigious nightclub without telling anyone. That was what his assumption was all hinging on.

Being desperate for fame and fortune, she had probably decided to use her god-given assets as an escort or a high-class prostitute. A horrible assumption to make about anyone, it was the only logical reason she had for keeping the whole thing a secret. What didn't fit was the money. If she had embarked on that profession, her financial situation would have spiked. She would suddenly have a lot of disposable cash and certainly wouldn't be working as a cleaner unless she'd kept her day job to stop people from getting suspicious, as Tannaz was doing. Okay, she had bought a smart dress, but it was a one-off, and it wasn't extortionately expensive. She could've saved up over the weeks or bought it second-hand from a charity shop.

No evidence existed of a change in lifestyle, unless she'd been smart and stashed all the money away somewhere. Considering Bella's personality, that didn't seem likely. She'd have gone on a spending spree the second she'd earned it, treating her friends and partying.

The other possibility was that the picture of her in the nightclub was her first outing into that world, and she'd been unlucky. Maybe she hooked up with some rich psycho who had a thing for redheads, and he'd removed her womb to satisfy his bizarre perversion. That would mostly likely mean she was dead and a serial killer was on the loose. That didn't fit, either. The police didn't investigate missing people, but they sure as hell investigated serial killers.

Whichever explanation it was, Savage felt himself being pulled to a conclusion he didn't like.

He cranked up the speed of the treadmill a few more notches.

For the moment, Savage wasn't going to mention any of that to Theresa. However, she'd had a whole year to think about what had happened to her daughter. Her imagination must have run wild, and he was pretty sure much of that had already crossed her mind. The poor woman had been through hell in the last twelve months, not helped by Venables and Hackett bleeding her dry.

Savage made a decision to keep his opinions to himself until he had real, hard evidence to back up his theories. He saw no point in putting Theresa through any more grief unless he was absolutely sure of the truth.

"You know she's already dead, don't you?" The voice was back.

Damn it. He hadn't heard it for weeks. Its taunting tone made the sweat on Savage's forehead prickle and go cold. He scanned the gym to see if anyone else had heard it, but he knew it was all in his mind. His legs wobbled, and his head went light.

"She's dead, just like Kelly, your daughter. So why are you bothering with this charade?"

Savage pushed the speed of the treadmill nearly to maximum, hoping the hum of the motor and the pounding of his feet might drown it out.

"No point hiding from the truth. Bella is as dead as Kelly."

"Shut your mouth," Savage muttered without thinking. He became conscious he was speaking out loud and glanced left and right at the guys on treadmills next to him.

Neither of them had noticed. They were too engrossed in their workouts.

"When you do come to your senses and accept she's dead, guess what you'll have to do?" the voice said in a childish, sing-song tone. *"You're going to have to tell her mother, and we all know how that went last time."*

Savage clamped his jaw, trying to contain his rage. He had to force his breath out through gritted teeth, which made him sound possessed. The two runners on either side of him gave simultaneous sideways glances, wondering why the old guy between them was making strange guttural noises.

Savage flipped the treadmill up to full speed. To keep up with the new pace, his legs and arms flailed wildly, as if they were about to come off. The treadmill motor screamed at being pushed to its limits.

The guy on the machine next to him leaned over, concerned. "Hey, mate. You might want to rein it back a bit."

Savage didn't respond. Only one voice had his attention—the demonic tormentor inside his head.

"You remember that day, don't you? The knock at the door. The one everyone dreads. A visit from the Casualty Notification Officer—what a job that must be, going round telling people their son or daughter's been blown up in Afghanistan. Some people don't answer the door, refuse to let them in. Total denial—that's one way of dealing with it. Yours was to sidestep it. You were more worried about how your wife would react. Didn't think she could take it. Thought it would break her. How wrong you were. When she got home, you couldn't find the right words to tell her that her little girl was dead. You sounded like a gibbering idiot because you were the one having the breakdown.

"So what's it going to be like when you tell Theresa her daughter's dead? History repeating itself, I think. Going to start

bawling your eyes out like you did last time? Not very tough, is it? What's Theresa going to think of you? One thing's for sure— she'll hate you for giving her false hope. She'll know you're a fraud, so why don't you spare her the misery by killing yourself right now? Then you won't have to face it."

At that moment, Savage's right foot clipped his left. He fell forward onto his knees and collided with the spinning treadmill. Catapulted back, his whole body flew rearwards, slamming his head into the machine behind him.

CHAPTER 17

THE HARSH GLARE OF A penlight shone into Savage's eyes. Dr. Stevens moved it from one eye to the other then back again. Savage knew the drill. He'd had the concussion test dozens of times before, when he had been in the army—usually when he'd been a bit overzealous during training.

He'd been stuck in the club's clinic for an hour, sitting on a bed covered in a large swath of stiff blue paper for preserving hygiene. For most of that hour, the doctor had been fussing over him, checking and rechecking that Savage hadn't done anything serious.

"This is completely unnecessary," Savage said as the doctor held up the pen and got him to follow it with his eyes. "I feel fine."

The doctor, however, had been ignoring Savage's pleas ever since he'd sat there. "Okay, pupil response good and visual acuity good," said Dr. Stevens, flicking off his penlight and returning it to his breast pocket. "Any blurriness?"

"None."

"What about your legs and arms, any numbness?"

"None."

"Tingling?"

"None."

"Pins and needles?"

"None. Look, I just tripped over and fell off the running machine. That's all."

Savage wasn't worried about his physical health. His mental health troubled him more. The voice had come back for the first time in a long time. He hadn't mentioned it to the doctor. It had gone quiet for the time being, thank goodness. Maybe the bang on his head had silenced it for good, but he was fairly sure it would be back to taunt him, probably at the most inappropriate time. He really needed to go and see his counsellor to tell her about it, but he was too frightened they'd section him, locking him up in a soft cell, which would put an end to him finding Bella. *No time for that.*

The doctor examined the back of Savage's head for about the fifth time. "No skin broken, and a bruise is already forming."

"That's good, right?" Savage asked hopefully.

Doctor Stevens picked up a clipboard and scribbled rapidly on an accident form. "Any headaches? Nausea?"

"No. Please, I'm good to go. I just want to get back to my workout."

The doctor stopped writing. "Definitely not. In fact, lay off the exercise for a few days, and when you do return, I'd like to assign someone to supervise you, just for your next few workouts, to make sure you're okay."

"That's really not necessary."

"I insist. I can't let you back in the gym on your own until I'm sure you're safe."

"Okay, fine."

The doctor shoved the clipboard under Savage's nose and held out a pen. "Sign here, please."

Savage took the pen and signed reluctantly. He pushed himself off the bed and headed for the door.

"Oh, Mr. Savage," said the doctor. "We still need to go through the results of your health check. If you make an appointment with the receptionist on the way out..."

"Right you are," said Savage, closing the door behind him.

Out in the waiting room, the receptionist was deep in conversation on the phone, a spot of luck. Savage ignored the doctor's request, making a swift exit towards the changing rooms.

After getting showered and dressed, he was just about to leave the club when he caught sight of someone who made his shoulders sag, as if gravity had just been turned up. Leaning with one hand against the wall, almost trapping the girl he was speaking to, stood the giant figure of Brett, who was on a charm offensive, judging by the dopey grin on his face. She, on the other hand, looked uncomfortable, glancing over his massive shoulders and looking longingly at the doors.

Savage couldn't leave without passing Brett. He wondered if he could double back and find an alternative exit.

Too late.

"Mr. Savage," Brett called over. "Mr. Hansen is waiting to see you."

Don't these people ever go home? The time was nearly ten o'clock.

Brett abandoned the girl, who immediately made a bid for freedom. Brett came over and tried to herd Savage toward the offices behind the glass wall by gently pushing him in the small of his back.

"Brett, I'm really not in the mood." Savage side-stepped Brett and headed for the doors.

Brett called after him: "Mr. Hansen said it's about Bella."

Savage came to an abrupt halt and spun around. "What?"

"Mr. Hansen wants to see you about Bella Tucker. She used to work here, you know."

Savage marched back over to Brett, almost charging him but stopping short at the last moment. The smugness suddenly dropped from Brett's face, replaced with something a little more respectful.

"What does he want to see me about, specifically?" asked Savage.

Brett looked up at one of the lights in the ceiling, as if trying to recall Hansen's exact instruction.

"He said I wasn't to let you leave until I'd brought you to his office so he could give you some information about Bella. That's all I know."

"What information?"

"He didn't tell me."

"Okay, lead the way."

Savage followed Brett through the vast glass wall that separated the reception area from the office space. Once the door closed behind them, the bustle of the reception area faded, replaced by an eerie hush. The office space was definitely soundproofed. Everyone had gone home, and all the desks were empty, apart from one keen young girl in the corner, her face lit up by the glow of her PC.

"Good evening," she said politely before returning to her work.

Savage counted about thirty desks, and those were just the ones he could see. They headed down a corridor, passing doors to more and more offices and several conference rooms until eventually they were confronted by two solid-wood doors with Carl Hansen's name carved into them. "What happens if Hansen leaves?" asked Savage. "Do they get a new door carved?"

"Oh, Mr. Hansen will never leave. He's the backbone of the place. Built it up to what it is today."

Brett knocked on the door.

"Come," Hansen called from the other side of the door.

Brett pushed open both doors at once, a little too melodramatically, as if they were entering the court of a king, which, judging by the size of Hansen's office, wasn't too far from the truth. Clean, modern and unmistakably Scandinavian, the walls were covered in wide, horizontal pinewood panels. Tasteful ceiling lights hung down on long cords at regular intervals, their reflection gleaming on the highly polished wooden floor below.

Hansen rose from a high-tech office chair that probably cost more than Savage's van. He pushed his rimless glasses up onto his nose and adjusted the cuffs on his suit as he came around his desk—a thick, vast slab of laminated pine on wide, tubular chrome legs. Barely anything was on it, except for a slimline stainless-steel computer screen and keyboard and an equally svelte modern office phone. The word *impeccable* popped into Savage's mind. This guy was so precise he could have had a military background.

"Mr. Savage, thank you for taking the time to see me. Please take a seat." Hansen gestured to three smart sofas, plain and minimalist, arranged around a low glass coffee table.

Savage sat down while Brett hovered awkwardly above him.

"That will be all, thank you, Brett," said Hansen.

"Oh, right," Brett replied with a tinge of embarrassment. He left the room, closing the double doors behind him.

"Can I get you anything?" asked Hansen. "Tea, coffee, some juice, perhaps?"

"No, I'm fine, thanks."

Hansen took a seat on the sofa opposite. "Doctor Stevens informs me you took a bit of a tumble today."

"It was nothing. Just tripped, that's all."

"Please, if you'd rather we do this another time..."

"No, let's talk. Brett said you wanted to see me about Bella Tucker."

"Yes, that's correct. I heard you were investigating her disappearance."

"Who told you that?" Savage was pretty sure he hadn't mentioned it to anyone.

"I'm afraid word travels fast in this place. I heard Bella's mother hired you."

"Yeah, something like that."

"Well, I'd just like to extend my full support if I may. If you need anything, anything whatsoever, please let me know. It was a terrible tragedy when Bella disappeared. Everyone liked her— both staff and customers."

"Thank you. That would be very helpful."

Savage wondered whether Hansen was being cooperative because he wanted to help or because he was protecting corporate interests, making sure Motivation hadn't been implicated in Bella's disappearance.

"And if you need to use any rooms to interview the staff here, just let reception know and I'll arrange it."

"That's very generous of you."

"We have extensive security throughout the building, with visual and audio in most rooms, so you can record your interviews.

I want to help in any way I can. I'd also like to contribute financially if I may."

"That won't be necessary."

"Okay, but if you need us to contribute to the cost of the investigation, please let me know. I did offer to help Theresa, but she declined. That poor woman has suffered so much."

"Yes, she has."

Hansen stood up and poured himself some water from a decanter in the corner of the room. "Would you like a glass?"

"Yes, go on, then."

Hansen returned, placed the glass of water in front of Savage, then sat back down again. "Is there anything you'd like to ask me, Mr. Savage?"

Savage thought for a moment. "Did Bella ever give you the impression she had another job? Did she ever come in late or looking tired?"

"No. But there was one time when she and some of the gym staff went out drinking. She came in late the next day. Got a good telling off, I can tell you. Never did it again."

"How long ago was that?"

"I think it was just after Bella first joined us."

"Did she go out a lot with the other staff?"

"Oh yes, but after that little indiscretion, she never let it get in the way of work again."

Savage took a sip of his water. Definitely not tap water. It tasted expensive, probably from a prehistoric Scandinavian glacier.

"Any work romances?" Savage asked.

"I have no idea. Although Brett had a bit of an eye for Bella, but she wasn't interested."

"Really?"

"Yes, she said he was... Now what was the word she used? 'Cheesy,' I believe."

Savage smiled. That about summed him up.

Hansen cleared his throat. "Can I ask how the investigation is going?"

"It's early days yet. I have a small lead, which I'm following up."

"Oh, what's that?"

"I'd rather not say. Confidentiality, et cetera."

"Yes, of course, of course." Hansen took a delicate sip of water.

"Did the police ever come and question you or anyone here?" Savage asked.

"No, never."

"Even after it was revealed that someone had removed her womb? You heard about that, I take it?"

Hansen rubbed his hands together as if drying them on an invisible cloth. He took a deep breath. "It chilled me to the bone when I heard about that. Everyone here was shocked. But to answer your question, no. No, the police never came."

"Did that strike you as odd?"

"I'm afraid I'm not really an expert on these things."

"You don't need to be an expert. A missing girl is one thing. But when her womb turns up in a bag with loads of others in an abandoned van, that's a whole different ball game."

"Like I said, I'm not really an expert."

"You don't think it's odd that someone's out there, cutting wombs out of girls' stomachs, and the police aren't investigating it?"

"There could be many reasons for that."

"Tell me, what kind of reasons?"

Hansen's face darkened. A little crease appeared between his eyes. "What are you driving at, Mr. Savage?"

Savage's mobile suddenly pinged. "Excuse me." He pulled his phone from his pocket and looked at the screen. It was a short text message from Tannaz.

I have something.

"I have to go." Savage stood up and shoved his phone back into his pocket.

"Of course," said Hansen, getting to his feet and shaking Savage's hand. "Remember, anything you need, please ask me."

"I might take you up on that."

CHAPTER 18

SOMETIME AROUND MIDNIGHT, SAVAGE ARRIVED outside Theresa's house. Tannaz stood beside him on the pavement, puffing furiously on a cigarette, a rucksack slung over one shoulder. In the distance, a car alarm went off. A second later, the door opened, and Theresa ushered them inside her pocket-sized terraced house.

After an uncomfortable introduction, Tannaz unfolded Bella's laptop and placed it on the kitchen table, the cigarette still dangling from her mouth.

Theresa took an ashtray from the cupboard and placed it next to her.

Tannaz looked up through caffeine-soaked eyes. "Oh, is it okay if I smoke?"

"Only if I can have one," said Theresa.

Tannaz dug into her bag and gave her a cigarette.

Theresa sparked it up and drew hungrily on it. "I'm supposed to be giving up," she said, blowing out smoke.

"Ain't we all," said Tannaz, pulling a second laptop from the rucksack, her own. A hefty black slab of technology, her laptop made no attempt to be aesthetically pleasing. Tannaz had built it herself, handpicked all the components, then cranked them all the way up to eleven. Dual fans hummed to life when she opened it, cooling the powerful system designed for serious programming—and serious hacking.

Tannaz clicked on a program, and a grid of thumbnail pictures appeared. Savage and Theresa peered at them.

"Okay," said Tannaz. "There's good news, bad news, and more

good news." She scrolled through the hundreds of tiny images littering the screen. "This is what my program came back with as a possible match to the image on Bella's computer."

"There are thousands of them," Savage remarked.

"Thirteen thousand, to be exact."

"Thirteen thousand?" Savage rubbed his forehead. "That's going to take us weeks to go through them all."

"I know. If I had more time to finesse the program, maybe I could get that number down. But there's no point."

"Why not?"

"One, it would take too long, and two, there's just not enough detail on the image for even the best program to get an accurate match. We might as well lick our finger and stick it in the air."

"So what now?" asked Savage, pacing up and down the small patch of kitchen linoleum.

Tannaz switched to Bella's little laptop. She clicked something, and the screen suddenly filled with data.

"What's that?" asked Savage.

"*That* is lateral thinking," said Tannaz. "Okay, say you're going somewhere new. What's the first thing you do?"

Nobody said anything.

Tannaz rolled her eyes. "You Google it. You go online, check it out. See what it's like. Find out where it is. Get more info. Bella would have done that, too. She may not have told anyone where she was going, but she would have definitely Googled the place first. That's what everyone does, which means it would be in her internet history."

"I checked her internet history," said Savage. "It only went back a couple of weeks. The rest had been deleted."

Tannaz shook her head. "*Deleted* is such a redundant term. Nothing is ever truly deleted. Data gets overwritten, but it all depends on how far you're willing to go to get it back. And in this case, I didn't have to go too far. In fact, it was a walk in the park. I just downloaded some recovery software onto her machine, and it's all here."

Savage looked closer at the screen. "Are those URLs?"

"Yep," said Tannaz. "Together with dates and times and some other data."

"What are URLs?" asked Theresa.

"Sorry, it just means website addresses," Tannaz explained. "These are all the websites she visited, using her laptop."

Savage sighed. "How does that help us? There are still thousands here."

"Well, thankfully, we know the date she was in the club because it's on the original image file. That narrows our search window right down. So all we have to do is look for a URL she visited before that date, one that sounds like the name of a posh club."

"Okay, how long's that going to take?" asked Savage.

"Already done it. There's one that crops up several times." Tannaz clicked on a URL, and up popped a pure white landing page. Stark silver letters appeared: Club Zero, Mayfair. Then another line appeared beneath it: Only the Beautiful and Interesting May Enter.

"Wow, they think a lot of themselves," said Theresa.

"It's one of the most exclusive clubs in London," Tannaz explained. "Two weeks before that picture of Bella was taken, she visited this site five times. I think this is the one. Wanna have a closer look?"

"Definitely," said Savage.

Tannaz clicked on the word *Enter*, and the screen changed to a high-definition image of an empty nightclub with a lofty ceiling studded with tiny lights that looked like stars in the night sky. At the far end, placed high up on a stage resembling an altar, were the DJ's decks, flanked by two vast Greek columns. A white dance floor peppered with LED lights dominated the space, around which were two levels of sumptuous booths furnished in crushed red velvet, the upper level accessed by two wide, sweeping spiral staircases. Hovering above it all, like a giant spaceship, hung a gargantuan gold chandelier.

A temple of pleasure for the few that could afford it.

Tannaz rolled over the image with her cursor, and the image

shifted sideways to give them a full three-hundred-sixty-degree view of the club. A vast white padded-leather bar came into view with a row of stools along its length.

"I bet that's hard to keep clean," said Theresa.

The bar was stacked with chiller cabinets filled to the brim with bottles of Champagne that no average person would ever get to drink.

"Wow," says Tannaz. "It's making me feel poor just looking at it."

"We still need to be sure it's the right club," said Savage. "Were there any others in the list of URLs around about this time?"

"A few, but they were cheap places with happy hours and two-for-one shots, not in the same league as this place.

"That reminds me. Can you pull up the drinks menu?" asked Savage.

"Sure."

After a few clicks, a list of drinks appeared, ranging from extravagant cocktails to ridiculously priced bottles of Champagne.

"There," said Savage, pointing at the screen. "They stock Krug. We're on the right track."

"At six hundred pounds a pop. That's some serious jelly," said Tannaz.

"This has to be the place," Theresa said.

"It's a strong possibility," said Savage. "Are there any more images, any that look like the one in Bella's photograph, the one with the weird lights?"

"Not that I've seen. There's some stuff on social-networking sites, but they're mostly the same as this, except full of drunk rich people. I suppose we could keep looking."

"No," Savage replied. "That could take ages. We'd be back to square one. It'd be quicker to get inside, have a look round. I won't be convinced until I see the same view as the one in Bella's picture."

Savage snatched up his car keys and got ready to leave.

"Where do you think you're going?" said Tannaz.

"To get a look inside."

"Mate, there's no way you're getting in a place like that."

"Why not?"

"No offence, but you look like Jeremy Corbyn's less trendy brother. Don't you agree, Theresa?"

Theresa shifted uneasily. "Well, John... It's more of a young person's place."

"Yeah, a rich young person's place." Tannaz added. "It costs five hundred quid just to reserve a table."

"So what do you suggest?" asked Savage.

Tannaz's fingers rapidly pounded the keyboard of her laptop. She seemed to be in a trance.

"Tannaz?"

She held up one hand to silence Savage and continued typing with the other. "I'll go in. Check it out," she said without looking up.

"How will you get in?" asked Savage.

"I'm on the guest list."

"But you're not on the guest list."

"I am now." Tannaz stopped typing and swivelled around to face Savage. "Just hacked their server. Their security is crap." She folded up her laptop and shoved it back into her bag. "Let's go. You can drive."

"You can't go in there," said Savage. "These people could be dangerous."

"I'm the only one with a cat in hell's chance of getting in there. Besides, all I'm doing is having a look then leaving. No harm done. Now, come on. We're wasting time."

Tannaz shoved Savage out the door to the kitchen and into the hallway.

"Wait," said Theresa. "You can't go in there dressed like that."

"Why not?"

"You'll stand out a mile."

"She's right," said Savage, shunting Tannaz back into the kitchen. "You need to blend in, which means you need to glam up."

Tannaz folded her arms. "Oh no, I'm not wearing makeup and high heels or nothing."

"Then you're not going in."

Tannaz stared at Savage for a while, not backing down. Her shoulders finally dropped in defeat. "Fine, okay then."

"Come on," said Theresa, grabbing her by the hand and leading her upstairs, excited at the prospect of a makeover.

Savage smiled and put the kettle on to make himself a cup of tea, figuring the process could take a while.

Half an hour later, Tannaz clip-clopped into the kitchen like a new-born lamb learning to walk, followed by a proud-looking Theresa. "These bloody heels are killing me," Tannaz whined.

"What do you think?" asked Theresa.

"Tannaz, you look stunning," said Savage. "Absolutely stunning."

"Oh, shut up." Tannaz held on to the door for support. The red pencil dress Bella had worn in the photo now clung to Tannaz's curvy body. She kept pulling it down in attempt to cover her knees. Her full mouth was coloured with scarlet lipstick that set off her perfect olive skin. Just the right amount of eyeliner and smoky eyeshadow made her eyes bigger and even more beautiful than they were before.

"You'll have all the boys queuing up to talk to you," said Theresa.

"Don't like boys, and I feel like a clown with all this crap on my face." Tannaz kicked the stilettoes off her feet so they skittered across the kitchen floor. "And I'm not wearing those. Can't walk in them. I'm putting my DMs on, or I'm not going in."

"Fair enough," said Savage. "We'll compromise on the footwear."

Tannaz returned with her DMs laced up. "Oh, that is so much better. How do you walk in those things? It's torture."

Savage checked his watch. "Okay, let's go."

Theresa hugged Tannaz. "Be careful," she said. "You don't have to do this."

"It's okay. He's paying me." Tannaz held out her hand. "I'll need some spending money, Savage."

"Of course," he said, peeling off a handful of twenties. "No drinking, though. Stick to water. You're working, remember."

"You're no fun."

They got into the VW, drove onto Camberwell New Road, and headed towards Vauxhall Bridge, where they'd cross the Thames into North London, straight on through Pimlico, then skirt along the edge of Buckingham Palace and eventually into Mayfair, one of London's most notoriously expensive areas. By contrast, the tatty South London road they were currently driving along had no such reputation. It wasn't cheap by any means—nowhere was in London—but compared to Mayfair, it was an ugly mongrel of architectural styles and social experiments, designed to fit more people into an already overcrowded area. Endless rows of flats above shops stood shoulder to shoulder, punctuated here and there by pastiche modern blocks of so-called affordable housing that would still cost you an arm and a leg. The odd tower block loomed in the background, brutal and impractical.

Though it was late, Camberwell New Road still throbbed with traffic. A main route from South London into North London, the single carriageway slowed their progress. They kept getting stuck behind night buses and catching every red light, of which there seemed to be hundreds.

"Excuse me," Savage said as he reached across and opened the glove compartment. He pulled a CD out, some music to pass the time.

"What the hell is that?" asked Tannaz.

"A CD," he said innocently, slotting it into the player embedded in the dashboard.

"Yeah, I know it's a CD," Tannaz replied. "But come on, Savage. This isn't the nineties."

"What's wrong with CDs?"

"Haven't you heard? There's been a digital revolution."

"I thought retro was cool."

"That's vinyl. Vinyl is cool. CDs are, like, so not cool."

"But I'm not cool," Savage said with a smile. "I'm Jeremy Corbyn's less trendy brother, remember. CDs are perfect for me."

He hit Play. The first aggressive riffs of The Jam's "Going Underground" blasted through the speakers.

"Who's this?" asked Tannaz.

"Who's this? Who's this?" Savage made no attempt at hiding his indignation. "How can you not know who this is?"

"Why don't you stop being a dick and just tell me."

"This, my musically illiterate friend, is The Jam."

"Never heard of them," Tannaz said, nonchalantly looking out the window.

"You've never heard of The Jam? You must have heard of Paul Weller."

"Oh, yes."

"That's a start."

"He was in the Beatles."

"No! He was in The Jam. Paul McCartney was in the Beatles. This is The Jam. Bruce Foxton on bass, Rick Buckler on drums, and Paul Weller on vocals."

"He sounds very angry."

"Good. He's supposed to. He's from a time when music said something, made a statement. Not like now, when they're all sappy corporate lapdogs."

Neither spoke for a while.

"So what do you think?" asked Savage.

"It's not my kind of thing."

"And what's your kind of thing?"

"Grime."

"What the hell is grime?"

"It kinda came out of the garage and jungle scene, but it's different, harder, grittier."

"I haven't the faintest idea what you're talking about. Let's hear some, then." Savage hit the pause button, and The Jam went quiet.

Tannaz got her phone out, scrolled through a few screens, then hit Play. A deep, grungy bassline poured from the phone's speaker, followed by a fast break beat. In amongst it came rapid-fire lyrics, economical and tightly cropped to fit the beat. Just like The Jam, it was distinctly urban and hard edged but from a completely different direction.

Savage tapped the steering wheel. "I quite like this," he said. "It's real, genuine."

Tannaz grabbed her chest in a mock heart attack. "Oh my days, you get it. You get what grime's all about. There's hope for you yet."

They listened to the sounds of Skepta, Dizzy Rascal, Wiley, and Stormzy until the streets became lined with pretty mews flats and elegant Georgian terraces with white stucco walls, signalling they were in Mayfair. Tannaz shut off the music on her phone. It didn't seem to go with the highly refined neighbourhood. In this location, even a cramped one-bedroom apartment would set you back a cool ten million.

They found the club easily enough, located just off Berkeley Square in the basement of a modern office building that looked out of place among all the character properties. Savage drove past it a couple of times to get a good look. The entrance to Club Zero, in contrast to the opulent photo they had seen online, was plain and unremarkable, a single metal door. The only clue that a club hid behind it were the three doormen in hi-viz jackets standing outside.

Savage drove out of sight down a side street and killed the engine. He couldn't let Tannaz be seen getting out of a lowly VW van, not when most people probably got dropped off in Bentleys and Range Rovers.

"Ready?" Savage asked.

"Ready," Tannaz replied.

"Remember, you go in, buy a drink, look around, see if it's the right place, then come straight back out again. Okay?"

"Okay."

"Text me as soon as you get in there."

"Yes, Dad."

"I'm serious, Tannaz. This could be a dangerous place. This might be why Bella disappeared."

"All right, all right."

"And keep an eye on the security. Text me how many bouncers are in the place."

"Why?"

"Just a precaution. Forewarned is forearmed. Once you're in, I'll move the car nearer to the club so I can keep an eye on the entrance."

"Got it. Okay, here I go." Tannaz got out of the van and sashayed her way toward the club. She looked gorgeous.

There's going to be a lot of disappointed men in that club.

Tannaz paused briefly at the corner, spun around, and blew Savage a kiss.

Savage waited, phone ready.

Two minutes later, a text popped up.

I'm in.

Savage started the van and nosed it toward the club. He found a space on the street outside, sandwiched between a vast Jaguar SUV and a huge AMG Mercedes saloon. The tiny VW van had never looked more conspicuous, but at least he could see the front door to the club from his position. The three doormen hadn't noticed his humble vehicle pull up. They were too busy catering to partygoers who kept showing up. Every so often, a luxury limo or sometimes a taxi would stop, spilling loud and obnoxious rich people onto the pavement. They'd stagger up to the doormen, give their names, then disappear into the club. Savage made a mental note that two CCTV cameras were mounted high above the door on the wall.

Savage's phoned pinged.

This is one majorly cool club. Can I stay all night?

Savage texted Tannaz straight back.

No way. Find what we need then get out. What about security?

Another text came through almost immediately.

Twenty quid for an orange juice!

Savage shook his head then texted.

Don't look shocked, you'll blow your cover. What about security? Have you found the spot where the shot was taken?

Tannaz texted back.

Don't worry, Grandad, I got this. Three bouncers outside. One at the bottom of the stairs. Five inside the club that I can see. Cameras everywhere. Hold on.

Savage drummed his fingers on the steering wheel. Minutes ticked by like millennia. He'd never been nervous or impatient before, not on any of his missions. That was because he'd trained for them. That was his job, and he'd been surrounded by other highly trained soldiers who had his back, but this was different. Tannaz was a civilian, his responsibility. He'd involved her in the plan and just sent her into a potentially dangerous situation, completely unplanned. He'd rushed into it without gathering any serious intel. Big mistake.

He told himself not to worry. He'd sent her into a nightclub, not a terrorist hideout. An extremely posh nightclub at that, full of very important people, there to have fun. Nothing bad would happen. She was just having a look around. For some reason, that didn't make him feel any better. A cold hand of fear reached inside him and snatched hold of his heart. His head swam. He just hoped the voice in his head wouldn't make an appearance.

The buzz of his phone shook him out of his oncoming panic attack. A text came through from Tannaz, and Savage breathed a welcome sigh of relief. Savage opened it. A picture downloaded before his eyes: a selfie of Tannaz, showing that big, beautiful smile of hers. It was a carbon copy of Bella's picture. Same table, same angle and same weird lights dangling behind. She'd done it. That was the place, which meant the people who ran it might know something about Bella's disappearance or, even worse, might have had something to do with it.

He texted her back.

Good job, Tannaz. Leave now. I'm parked across the road.

Savage's phone pinged again.

On my way.

Finally, Savage had caught a break, a small clue. Savage had to figure out how to approach those people—not impulsively, as he'd done that night. He'd been amateurish. Instead, he would hang back and observe them to find out who owned the place, what connections they had, and who they were in bed with. He would leave no stone unturned, but he'd do it properly, taking his time.

Savage looked at his watch. Five minutes had passed since the last text from Tannaz. *Calm yourself.* Getting out of a busy club could easily take five minutes, especially if she'd gone via the loos.

Ten minutes passed.

Savage texted her.

Okay, Tannaz we really need to leave.

Two minutes later, Savage still hadn't heard anything. He texted her again.

Tannaz, you need to leave.

Savage waited, urging the phone to vibrate or ring. Neither happened. Twenty minutes had passed since her last text. He dialled her number and put the phone to his ear—straight to voice mail. He dialled again—voice mail again.

Something was very wrong.

CHAPTER 19

SAVAGE SWORE AND SLAMMED HIS hands on the steering wheel. He swore again and punched the dashboard. She wasn't coming out. That meant she was in danger.

He tried to comfort himself, imagining she'd been delayed because some posh bloke tried to chat her up, or maybe she'd met the girl of her dreams and had chosen to conveniently ignore the buzzing of her phone. None of those explanations seemed plausible. In the short time he'd known Tannaz, he'd come to realise how headstrong and single-minded she was. Nothing would get in her way unless someone was preventing her from leaving.

His stomach began to freefall like a high-speed lift in a tall building. A few minutes before, the place had been just a hunch, a loose end that needed checking out. Now, Tannaz's disappearance confirmed that something sinister was going on. Bella had gone in there and disappeared shortly afterward, and the same had happened to Tannaz. He'd royally screwed up. He should have never sent her in there. He should have waited, bided his time, and gone there during the day, pretending to be reading the meter or something. He could've found some excuse to get inside and take a look around. It wouldn't have been difficult, not for him. In his haste, though, he'd sent in someone who was completely unprepared for that kind of work. Tannaz was an IT specialist, not a field agent.

He headbutted the steering wheel.

"What's the definition of irony?" Up popped the unwelcome

voice in his head, like a turd that wouldn't flush. *"A guy who tries to find a missing girl but ends up losing another in the process."*

"Shut up," said Savage. "Tannaz is not lost. She's in that club over there."

"Doesn't matter how you dress it up. You sent her into the lion's den. What were you thinking? You are such an idiot. A fool. You can't do anything right."

"I was just following up a lead. Checking to see if we had the right place."

"Well, there's no doubt about that, is there? What are you going to say to Theresa? 'Er, I'm going to have to put the search for your daughter on hold because Tannaz has gone missing.' Well, one thing's for sure, at least Theresa will see you for the fraud you are."

"Why don't you shut up and let me think? Better still, why don't you help me?"

"Me, help you? You're the expert. Mr. I'm-good-at-finding-people. What a joke. Hey, wait. Where are you going?"

"Going to get Tannaz out of there." Savage stepped out of the van, crossed the road, and walked briskly toward the bouncers on sentry duty outside the club.

"Yes, John, yes. Fight your way in there, and get Tannaz back. There's only three of them on the door. You could take them easily. Make 'em pay. Kill them with your bare hands. Better still, get the wheel brace from the van, bust their heads open."

"I'm not killing anyone. Now, shut up."

"Come on. They're just dumb bouncers. Go on, make them pay for whatever they've done to Tannaz. You know you want to. I can feel it. Feel the hatred inside you."

"What are you, the emperor from *Star Wars*? No one is killing anyone. They probably have families. Did you think of that?"

"Never stopped you before."

"Be quiet."

Savage stepped onto the pavement and approached the three men in their thick hi-viz jackets. Their heads swivelled towards him as he got closer. Their friendly time-passing banter ceased abruptly. Savage wasn't the sort of guy who should be walking around Mayfair at three in the morning, and certainly not approaching Club Zero. He was trouble.

All three doormen closed ranks as he neared, like a battalion of Roman soldiers forming a shield wall, protecting the entrance to the club. They were easily head and shoulders above Savage— big guys, probably ex-army.

"Evening," said the doorman holding an iPad. He had a shaved head and a scar under one eye. "Help you with something?"

Savage tried his best to smile. "Yes, I've come to pick up a friend of mine."

"What's your friend's name?" asked the doorman, dabbing away at the screen.

"Tannaz."

"Is that her first or second name?"

"First."

"What's her second name?"

"Oh no, you don't know her second name, do you? Is this amateur hour or what?"

Ignoring the voice, Savage pressed on. "She's just known as Tannaz."

"What, like Sting?" asked the doorman with the iPad.

"Or Bono," said the doorman on the right.

"Adele," said the one on the left. "I quite like her stuff."

Savage got impatient and tried to look over the top of the iPad screen.

The bouncers took a defensive step away from Savage. "Whoa, back off, mate. Don't touch the iPad."

"I didn't touch it. I just wanted to have a look."

"Never touch the iPad."

Savage held his hands up in surrender. "Sorry, I'm worried about my friend. Please, could you just check? Her name's on the guest list."

The doorman swiped up and up and up then shook his head. "She's not here. You sure you've got the right place?"

"He's lying."

"Positive," said Savage. "She texted me from inside just half an hour ago."

"She may have already left," said the one on the right.

"Impossible," said Savage. "I've been sat over there watching the entrance. I'd have seen her come out."

They're a bunch of liars, John. Break their jaws. Bust their skulls open. Snap their ribs. Start with that prick holding the iPad. He doesn't respect you.

Savage rubbed his forehead. He was losing it. The voice was getting louder and stronger. He had to hold it together. "Can I have a quick look around for her?" he asked.

The doorman with the iPad smiled. "Sure, it's five hundred pounds to reserve a table."

"I just want to have a quick look inside. That's all."

"Do you know where you are, mate?" said the bouncer on the left. "This is the most exclusive club in London. You got to be rich or famous to come in here, preferably both. So if you can't afford it, I suggest you hop it."

"Don't let him talk to you like that. He's just a goon in a hi-viz jacket. You could kill him with your eyes closed and one hand tied behind your back."

Savage shook his head—not at the bouncers but at the increasingly loud voice trying to hijack his brain. He had to get Tannaz back before the voice took over permanently. "Fair enough," he said. He pushed his hand into his jeans and fished out one of the rolls of cash he'd taken from Hackett. Savage walked forward, holding out the money to the doorman. He got a firm shove back.

"Sorry," said iPad man. "You still can't come in. We have a strict door policy. Only the beautiful or the interesting can come in."

"And you're neither," said the one on the left.

"Hit him, John. Hit him so hard he never gets up again."

"Don't you think I'm beautiful?" Savage asked.

"You've got a face only your mother would love."

They all laughed.

"And those clothes. Did you get them from a supermarket?"

More laughter. Savage laughed with them.

"They're making fun of you, John. Don't let them get away with it! Show them who you are. A killer."

Savage gritted his teeth. He had to stay on their good side and keep up the friendly banter.

"You know," said Savage. "Someone said I looked like Jeremy Corbyn's less trendy brother."

Then they properly belly laughed.

"You know who said that?" Savage continued. "Tannaz, the girl in your nightclub. And if I find out something's happened to her, I'm going to break all the teeth in your mouth."

"That's more like it, John."

More laughter.

"Lucky I've got a good dentist, innit?" said iPad man.

"Look, mate," said the doorman on the right. "We get a lot of girls in here. And we never see them again. Have no idea where they go."

The guy with the iPad turned and glared at his colleague. "What he means is we can't be responsible for every girl who comes in here. So I'm very sorry, but you're going to have to leave. She's not on the list, which means she's not in the club. So you'll have to go. Or we'll call the police."

Savage nodded his head. "Okay, I get it. Thanks, guys. You have a good night, now."

"You too, Jeremy."

They all laughed.

"Going back to your care home, are you?" the same guy asked.

Savage smiled, waved a goodbye, and walked back to his car.

"What are you doing? She's in there, Savage. You can't just leave her."

"Oh, so you're worried about Tannaz now, are you?"

"Coward. Go back and break their necks. They should respect you."

"Respect, really? Ten minutes ago, you were calling me a joke and a loser."

"You're a veteran of the Gulf War. Ex-SAS. A trained killer. One of the hardest men in London. Go back and break their necks."

"And where would that get me? I'd never get in that club, and I'd never see Tannaz again."

Savage slipped back into his VW and tried calling Tannaz one more time—no reply. He sent several more texts and waited for a response. Nothing came.

A plan formed in his head. Stealth always worked better than a full-frontal assault. He started the engine, hit the accelerator, and threaded the van through the empty streets of Mayfair.

"Where are we going?"

"Shopping."

"Shopping? At this time of the morning?"

"Yep, I know a 24-hour army surplus store in East London."

"Finally, you're going to get tooled up, then go back and hurt those guys."

"Certainly am," Savage lied, but that was the answer the voice wanted to hear. It seemed to satisfy its hunger for pain and violence. As Savage drove across London, the nagging gradually ceased, ebbing away to nothing, just a blissful silence. Savage's mind calmed, and he was able to think straight again, to concentrate on getting Tannaz back.

Savage parked outside Surplus 24/7, a wide, low-slung, flat-roofed store painted in the same colour as a thousand other army surplus stores around the world, forest green.

Savage pushed open the door and nodded at the sleepy guy behind the counter, who looked up from his book with barely enough energy to nod back. The graveyard shift, always a killer. Surprisingly, Surplus 24/7 had a couple of other customers, apart from Savage. Two skinny students were pushing a shopping trolley loaded up with camping gear, probably because it cost a lot less than the stuff in the big chain stores. He doubted they were about to go hiking—probably heading to a music festival.

Savage passed racks and racks of service uniforms, boots, hats, rucksacks, and other equipment giving off that unmistakably pungent ex-army smell, damp webbing mixed with a hint of engine oil. None of that interested him. He still had plenty of that stuff at home, tucked away in a locked trunk. What did interest him lay in a corner at the back, where the store had a little side-line in work wear.

Unlike the army gear, it was all brand new, folded up in neat piles, and packaged in thin cellophane wrappers. The store had generic uniforms for cleaners, security guards, kitchen staff, builders, and what Savage needed—delivery drivers.

Savage selected a dark-brown short-sleeved shirt with matching trousers and cap. He found an empty cubicle and got changed. Piling up his old clothes, he tucked them under his arm and headed for the counter at the front to pay.

"Mind if I wear these out of the store?" Savage asked the guy behind the counter.

He didn't say anything but just put down his book and picked up a pair of scissors resting in a pot, leaned over the counter, and snipped the tags off Savage's new clothes before scanning them into the register. Savage handed over some notes and told him to keep the change.

The guy managed a quiet "Thanks" then tossed the discarded tags into a large recycling bin piled high with bits of cardboard.

Among them, Savage noticed a brown corrugated-cardboard wrapper, the kind that books and DVDs got delivered in.

"Excuse me," said Savage. "Could I have that packaging if you're not using it?"

The guy shrugged, handed it to Savage, and went back to reading his book.

Outside, Savage dumped his old clothes in his van and walked up the street a few yards, looking for a building site. In London, building sites were everywhere, pock-marking the face of the city. As the price of property went up, developers pulled more buildings down, replacing them with bigger developments to extract more profit from an ever-decreasing pool of land. He didn't have to walk too far.

Temporary bright yellow fencing encircled an area of land,

with signs announcing a new development called Woodland Park View. Savage looked around, seeing no woodland and certainly no view. *More marketing bull.* He hoisted himself up and over the fencing and lowered himself down into the building site. Work hadn't commenced yet, and the existing building had only just been demolished, rubble strewn everywhere.

Savage flicked on his mobile phone to use as a flashlight, searching through the odd-shaped shards of concrete and broken brick. He sifted through a pile on the ground until he found a roughly rectangular block of cement and aggregate about the same size and shape as a book. He tried it for size, shrouding it in the cardboard packaging—a perfect fit. If he held it by its end with his thumb underneath and his fingers on the top, the brown cardboard stayed put, concealing its heavy contents. To the casual observer, he looked like a delivery man from an online retailer, about to drop off a package. The recipients of that package, however, would not be leaving a five-star review.

CHAPTER 20

T HE TREK BACK ACROSS LONDON took a lot longer. The traffic had swelled with people eager to get into work early. Air brakes wheezed and cyclists rattled past. In the middle of it all, the little VW van threaded its way through the buses, bikes and trucks with an important delivery to make.

Savage knew Club Zero closed at six in the morning. For his plan to work, he needed to be at the club just as it finished business. Finally, he made it to Mayfair with just a few minutes to spare. As he drove past the club, a Range Rover Sport with blacked-out windows pulled out in front of him. Normally, he'd be hitting his horn at the inconsiderate driver, but the posh off-roader had vacated a space that was damn near perfect for keeping an eye on the club—not quite opposite but a few yards down on the other side of the road. From there, he had a clear, uninterrupted view of the sleek metal door to the club.

The entrance was locked up tight, but every so often, it would open to disgorge a few more revellers, who would tumble out onto the pavement, still high from their night out, their wallets considerably lighter. The doormen were nowhere to be seen. They were controlling the door from the inside, seeing the stragglers out, then closing it immediately behind. Last to leave was a girl in a sparkly silver dress cut so high that the hem hovered just below her crotch. She held up a woozy guy in a crumpled suit, his shirt untucked at the waist. He seemed to have lost all sense of direction, swaying this way and that, until she guided them both into a taxi.

Then it went quiet. The door stayed shut, but Savage never took his eyes off it.

Half an hour later, the door opened briefly to let a handful of people out. They looked tired but sober. Those were the waiters and bar staff, finishing their shifts. No taxis or limos came for them. They simply walked off in different directions, mingling with early-morning office workers, eager to catch trains and buses back home to the warm embrace of their beds.

Another half hour went by. No movement. The time was well past seven.

The door opened.

Eight large, muscular men stepped through it. He recognised two of the guys who had been on the door. They were all bouncers.

Their hi-viz jackets were gone, and they were dressed in everyday clothes: sweat shirts, jeans, tracksuit bottoms and trainers. Nevertheless, they still cut an intimidating silhouette. They fist-bumped each other before going their separate ways.

Tannaz had said she saw nine bouncers in the club. That left just one inside, iPad man.

The time had come.

Savage stepped out of the car and pulled his cap down tight. In his right hand he gripped the concrete package as he walked across the road to the club's entrance. Mindful of the two cameras above the door, he kept his head bowed as he pressed the intercom panel.

Static crackled, then a disembodied voice asked, "Yes?"

Without looking up, Savage waved the package in the air so it would be seen by the cameras above him. "Delivery."

The static went dead.

Savage stood in front of the door, took a deep breath and readied himself, holding the package up near his chest.

From inside, locks clicked and slid back. The door opened. iPad man stood there, eyes weary. They suddenly snapped wide open when he recognised who faced him.

Before the guy had time to react, Savage slammed the concrete block into the doorman's mouth, putting all his weight behind it.

Teeth splintered with an ungodly crack, and a torrent of blood followed. Savage stepped inside the door and hit him again. Same place. Twice as hard.

The doorman staggered back, hands trying to contain the masses of blood pouring from his mouth. That left the rest of his body vulnerable. Savage pulled back the block and swung it like a wrecking ball up between the guy's legs. All doormen wore groin guards to protect them against a kick to the balls. They were not, however, designed to protect them against the impact of a solid lump of concrete travelling at high velocity.

The blow sent iPad man toppling to the floor. He curled into the fetal position, attempting to minimize any more damage.

"Where is she?" Savage asked casually.

The doorman managed a gurgle of pain, the blood from his mouth pooling on the floor beside him.

Savage let the cardboard drop away from his lump of concrete—no need for the deception any more. He knelt down beside the doorman, letting him see the brutal lump of concrete that had inflicted so much damage.

"Told you I'd break all your teeth," said Savage. "It's not like I didn't warn you. However, your genitals are a different matter. I'm pretty sure they're just bruised at the moment. Your groin guard will have taken the brunt of it. But I'm guessing that it's split now and won't be much use. If I hit you in the same place again I don't need to tell you how painful that's going to be. So for the final time, where is she?"

"She's in the office... She's in the office," iPad man gasped.

"Where would I find that?"

"B-behind the bar."

"And who's with her?"

"The manager."

"Just the manager?" Savage raised the block above him, ready to smash it down.

"Just the manager, I swear. I swear."

"And who else is in the building?"

"Just me and him."

"What about the cleaners?"

"Won't be in for another hour."

"Okey dokey, then." Savage cracked him over the head with the block, not hard but just enough to keep him out of action. He stepped over him and hurried down the stairs, still clutching the block. At the bottom, he pushed open two double doors and found himself in the main part of the empty club. It looked just like the shot on the website, except a little messier. It was an impressive double-height space with a glittering dance floor surrounded by booths and, hoisted high above it all, that huge golden chandelier. The sickly odour of posh perfume and spilled Champagne hung in the air. He didn't have time to marvel at the opulent surroundings. He leapt over the white padded-leather bar lined with matching barstools and pushed through a door in the corner, leading to a corridor stacked with crates of drink on one side and more doors on the other. One was marked with a sign that read Office. Savage tried the door: locked. He stepped back and kicked it open.

He saw Tannaz immediately, gagged and tied to a chair at the far end. To the left, standing by a desk, a man gawped at him, presumably the manager. Dressed in a pair of chinos and a pink shirt with the collars turned up, he was a public-school type with rosy cheeks and floppy blond hair. He probably played polo on the weekend and summered in the South of France.

Next to his desk, a server rack and lines of security monitors showed the club from every conceivable angle. He'd obviously been watching the whole thing because he held a knife in his shaking hand.

Savage strode over to him, grabbed the knife confidently, twisting it out of his hand, then thumped him in the stomach with the concrete. The manager yelped like a dog as all the air evacuated his lungs. Savage shoved him back into his office chair.

"Stay," he said before moving over to Tannaz, pulling the gag from her mouth, and using the knife to cut her bonds. He snatched a bottle of water from the manager's desk and gave it to Tannaz, who drank deeply. He was about to ask if she was okay when she leaped up, ran over to the manager, and repeatedly punched him in the face.

"Arsehole!" she yelled.

Savage had to pull her off to stop her from beating the guy to a pulp. "Stop, Tannaz," he said, holding her by her shoulders. "There'll be plenty of time for that afterwards. But we need him to talk. Okay?"

Tannaz tried to shrug herself free from his grip, her eyes lit with anger.

"Tannaz!" Savage shouted, making her jump. "Hold it together. Are you okay? Did they hurt you?"

Tannaz shook her head.

"What happened?"

"I was about to leave when two bouncers grabbed me and put me in here with this arsehole."

"Did they tell you why?"

"Nope. Nothing."

Savage turned to face the manager. Slumped on the chair, he clutched his stomach with one hand and grasped his puffy, bruised face with the other.

"Why did you kidnap my friend?" Savage asked.

The manager looked up, surprised. "Kidnap? I didn't kidnap her. She hadn't paid. We don't know how she got in here, but she didn't pay."

"So why didn't you show her the door, tell her to leave?"

"Now, you listen to me," said the manager, shakily getting to his feet. "You broke into my club, assaulted one of my staff, assaulted me, and she somehow got into this club without paying. You're both in serious trouble. Do you know where you are? This is the most prestigious club in London. I know a lot of important people. Rock stars, film stars, and billionaires come in here. You can't imagine what I'm going to do to you. My lawyers are going to have a field day."

Savage pulled out his phone and tossed it to the manager, who just about caught it. "You'll need to report the crime then," said Savage. "Better call the police and have us arrested."

The manager looked at the phone as if it were some strange, alien object.

"Well, what are you waiting for?" shouted Savage. "Come on, call it in. Oh wait, you can't, can you. You've just held my friend against her will. That's breaking the law. It's called false imprisonment. Carries a sentence of five years."

The manager stood still, as if held by a forcefield.

"Did you know," Savage continued, "Jimmy Saville used to manage nightclubs before he was famous for being a paedophile. If someone misbehaved in his club, he'd imprison them in the basement. It's true. Used to chain them up and leave them there all night. Exactly like you've just done. So be my guest. Call the police. I'm sure they'll be very interested to hear what you've been up to."

The manager said nothing but just slowly handed Savage's phone back.

Savage took it and tapped the screen a few times then held up the picture of Bella.

"Her name's Bella Tucker. Recognise her?"

The manager shook his head.

"The picture was taken in this club."

The manager raised his weary eyes. "We get a lot of pretty girls in this club. Can't remember all of them."

"She went missing after coming here. Thing is, she's not exactly your clientele. Worked as a cleaner in a gym. So what was she doing in here?"

The manager flopped back down in his office chair and shrugged.

Savage pushed the picture of Bella in the manager's face. "Her womb was removed and found in a van along with loads of others. Ring any bells?"

The manager glanced at the image and shook his head. "I'm sorry to hear that, but it's nothing to do with Club Zero."

"Oh, I think it is," said Savage. "Mind if Tannaz checks the hard drive to your CCTV? See if we can see who she was with that night?"

"Be my guest. But we only keep footage for thirty days. It's an industry standard. Then it gets recorded over. When was she here?"

"A year ago," Tannaz replied, shoving the manager out of the way and sliding into his seat. She immediately prodded away at the keyboard of his computer.

"You won't get far without my password," said the manager, smugly.

"Don't need it. I'm already in," Tannaz replied. "Your security is crap, by the way. I hacked it and put myself on the guest list. That's how I got in here. You need to get it looked at." Tannaz searched the files, her hands dancing across the keyboard almost in a blur. After a while, she stopped and spun around to face Savage. "He's right. All video files only go back thirty days. They've been overwritten."

Savage leaned in for a closer look, not exactly sure what he was looking at. "I thought you said nothing ever gets deleted."

"It doesn't, usually. But there are exceptions. And this is one of them. It's pretty standard procedure for nightclubs."

Savage turned to face the manager. "Oh dear. Looks like we're going to have to do this the hard way."

The manager took a step back. "Hard way? What hard way? I told you I don't know the girl."

"Yeah, and I believe you. But there's something going on in this club. You're protecting someone, or you're scared of someone. Otherwise, why kidnap Tannaz? What are you afraid of? Thought she was snooping around, didn't you? Had to be sure, which was why you tied her up in here. Probably going to question her to see if she knew something. Then what were you going to do? Who were you going to call? Maybe Tannaz would have disappeared just like Bella did?"

Tannaz spun around and glared at the manager, fists clenched, ready for round two. Savage put a gentle, restraining hand on her shoulder.

The manager swallowed hard. "I'm sorry. I don't know what you're talking about."

Savage grabbed the manager roughly by the collar, dragged him out of the office, and shoved him down the corridor until they were back in the club. By the bar, he pointed toward the long line of elegant stools. "Pick one."

"What?" asked the manager.

"Pick one up, and bring it with you."

Fear and confusion wracked the man's face. "I don't understand."

Savage pushed him into the nearest stool, almost causing a domino effect. "Pick up a stool, and take it back to the office."

The manager obeyed, carrying the nearest stool with both hands, nervously bumping and knocking it against walls and corners as he went.

Back in the office, Savage snatched the stool from the manager and turned it over in his hands, examining it from every angle. It had four shiny chrome legs and soft white leather upholstery.

"These are smart, aren't they?" said Savage. "Must be a hell of a job keeping them clean, what with all that expensive Champagne flying everywhere." He turned the barstool over so the legs were pointing upwards. "I do like the fact that someone's put white rubber stoppers on the ends so they don't mark that lovely floor of yours."

The manager looked puzzled, his eyes rapidly flicking from the ends of the stool legs to Savage and back again.

With his thumbs, Savage prised one of the rubber stoppers off, revealing the end of the chrome leg, a hollow metal tube. "Now that does disappoint me," he said, examining the end of it. "This leg hasn't been finished off properly. It's all jagged and rough where it's been cut. Should've been ground down so it's nice and smooth. Anyway, it's perfect for what I need."

"What's that?" asked the manager.

"For getting answers out of you." Savage forced him down on his knees then shunted him in the chest with the stool, putting him on his back. Savage stood over him, tightly gripping the manager's head between his feet.

"What are you doing?" the manager screamed.

Savage raised the stool, positioning the exposed end of the metal leg above the manager's right eye.

"This is a game of three strikes," Savage explained calmly, as if he were the presenter of a daytime TV show. "I will ask you three times what's going on in this club. On the third time of asking, if I'm not satisfied with your answer, I will push this metal chair leg into your eye."

The manager struggled. "You're insane."

"Actually, this is wasting time," said Savage. "I'm going straight to strike three. Just tell me what's going on in this club."

"Nothing. Nothing's going on."

Savage lowered the stool so the serrated metal end of the leg was brushing against the manager's eyelashes.

"Stop! Stop! I'll tell you! I'll tell you. Please stop."

Savage lifted the leg slightly, keeping it about an inch away from the manager's eyeball. "Go on."

"They're using us," the manager gasped.

"Who's *they*?"

"I don't know. Some sort of professional gang."

Savage lowered the leg onto the manager's eyeball.

"I swear, I swear. I don't know who they are. All I have is a contact number. The gang calls up and gives us the name of a girl to put on the guest list. She gets free drinks all night, has a good time, and that's it."

"That's not enough," said Savage. "Does anyone in this gang meet the girl? Make contact with them?"

The manager screamed. "Please! I don't know. I'm sure someone is in there watching, checking the girl out. But I don't know who they are, I keep telling you."

Savage pulled the stool up slightly. "So it's a shop window?"

"What's a shop window?" asked Tannaz.

"There are two types of human trafficking for sexual purposes," Savage explained. "First one, the most common, is lure girls over here from poorer countries on false pretences, like a job offer. Take away their passports when they land and put them into prostitution. Second one is more sophisticated. A rich client will place an order for a specific girl. Take Bella, for instance. Some billionaire might have a thing for natural redheads. So he asks a trafficker to find him a redhead. The trafficker identifies a few possible girls that fit the bill, surreptitiously takes pictures of them, and sends them to the client. The client says he likes the look of Bella but wants to get a closer look before he buys, see her in the flesh. Remember, he's going to be parting with a lot of money. The trafficker sets up a shop window. Arranges a suitable date when the girl will be at a certain place so the client can take a look at the goods without her knowing. This club, for instance, although they'd probably use lots of different venues. If she's not what he's after, he can walk away, no harm done. If he does like her, then he'll pay the trafficker a deposit, who will snatch her at a later date, when it's convenient."

"Ugh, that's disgusting," said Tannaz. "And this could happen to anyone?"

"Yep," Savage replied. "You could be going about your daily business, completely oblivious that someone is targeting you to be snatched."

Tannaz looked down at the manager, still pinned to the floor. "Take this creep's eye. He's part of it."

"No, please. I had no choice," The manager said, his face a mask of fear. "They sent me pictures of my parents, my sister and her daughter. Told me I had to agree or they'd do terrible things to them. Kill my parents and"—tears streamed down his face—"turn my sister and her daughter into whores."

Savage lifted the stool away from the manager's face. "Yep, I thought you might say that. That's usually how these gangs operate." He held out a hand and hoisted him to his feet.

The manager fell into his office chair, rubbing his eye. "If you knew this already, why put me through all that?"

"You were holding my friend against her will. Had to be sure you weren't in on it. Now, back to business. All you have is a phone number for these guys?"

"Yes. We're only to call it if there's a problem."

"And have you ever called them?"

"No, never. Never seen any of them. No one has. Don't know who they are. Just that they're very dangerous. Please, you can't go after them. My family's lives are at stake. They'll know I tipped you off."

Savage shook his head. "I'm sorry. I have to. I promised Bella's mum I'd get her back. I've taken down people a lot worse than sex traffickers. Think of it this way. I can get them off your back for good. Now, you need to give me that phone number."

The manager hesitated, looking at Savage then at Tannaz. "Will you hurt me if I don't give you the number?"

"If you give me no choice, I will," Savage replied. "Look, if you don't give me the number, you'll never be free of them. You and your family will always be in danger."

"But you're just one person. What can you do?" the manager asked.

"Er, excuse me," said Tannaz.

"Sorry, two people."

Savage smiled. "That's our advantage. They won't see us coming. We're not a threat. Look what we've achieved in one night. Tannaz hacked your system, got in your club and I got past all your security guards without a scratch."

"She got caught, though."

"Yeah, and look how that turned out. You on the floor about to lose your eye."

The manager stared into space and exhaled heavily. Then he took a pen from his desk and scribbled down a number on a Post-it note and handed it to Savage. It was a landline.

"How long has this been going on?" asked Savage.

"Two years, maybe more," the manager replied.

"And how often does it happen?"

"It's erratic. Sometimes five or six girls a month. Sometimes nothing." The manager opened his desk drawer, pulled out a small bottle of whisky, and took a large slug. He offered it to Savage and Tannaz, who both declined.

"I'll need the list of names," asked Savage.

The manager glugged down more whisky. "List? What list?"

"If this gang sends girls to this club to be eyeballed, you should have a list of names."

"We're not stupid. We don't keep a list anywhere. It's all done by word of mouth."

"Don't make me use the stool again."

"Don't worry. I got this." Tannaz pushed past the manager to the stack of server units blinking away. She selected one and ripped it from its cabling then put the black slimline box under her arm. "If it's on here, I'll find it. Plus, it's got all the CCTV footage of me being held here against my will. We'll take it as a bit of insurance."

The manager took another slug. "I'm sorry. Really, I am. I was just scared."

Tannaz looked at the guy. "If Savage hadn't shown up, would I be like Bella now, getting shipped off somewhere to work as a sex slave?"

"No. Attractive as you are, they only take white girls."

"One thing's puzzling me," said Savage. "Everyone dreams of getting into this club, rubbing shoulders with the rich and famous. The girls who show up here... How do you stop them boasting about it to their friends, posting it all over social media? We only found out about this place from a blurred selfie Bella had hidden away on her laptop."

The manager leaned back in his chair. "We tell them the drinks are free as long as they come alone and they don't tell anyone. We say someone famous is going to be here that night, as extra incentive to make sure they show up. But we also tell them this A-list celebrity has forbidden anyone from taking pictures or talking about being here. No telling friends. No tweets. No posts. That's the price of getting on the guest list and getting free drinks all night. We also get them to sign some bogus form when they get here, threaten that they'll be sued for millions if they don't comply. This buys their silence. We shred it almost immediately so there's no record of them. Your girl must've snuck in a selfie when no one was looking."

"And what if no famous person shows up?" asked Tannaz.

"We get famous people in here most nights. And even if we don't, it doesn't matter. They're usually so thrilled to get in for free, they'll pretty much do anything we ask."

Savage stuffed the phone number into the trousers of his delivery uniform. "Come on, Tannaz," he said. "We've got some work to do."

She followed Savage out of the office and into the club. They were just walking across the dance floor to the exit when the manager called after them.

"There's one other thing you need to know," he said. "It's not just girls they take. It's men as well. Roughly the same number."

CHAPTER 21

THE LITTLE WHITE VW EDGED its way through the congested streets of London. Midmorning traffic had snarled up every street to almost a standstill, like driving through treacle.

Savage should've been happy. They had made a breakthrough. His suspicions had been confirmed. Bella had been trafficked for a high-profile client. She was alive, probably. Nothing was ever certain in situations like that, but it was highly likely. Nobody would have gone to such lengths to obtain her and remove her womb, probably at the client's request so she couldn't get pregnant, only to discard her. Somebody had her, and Savage was going to track them down. No matter how careful they were, traffickers of human beings relied on a chain, a chain of people. Like any chain, it was only as strong as its weakest link. The manager had proved that. Armed with the phone number, Savage could work his way along to the next link of the chain and the next and the next, putting pressure on whoever he found along the way, getting information to lead him to the next link, and so on. Eventually, he would find Bella and bring her safely back home.

That should have made him happy, but it didn't.

Something wasn't right. The situation should have been a neat case of sex trafficking, an expensive, high-level flesh trade, which would explain the van full of wombs. Horrific but logical to give the girls hysterectomies so they can't get pregnant. But the manager's confession that the traffickers also took men didn't fit the model. Sure, a sex market existed for men, but it was tiny compared to the one for females. If the traffickers had taken the odd guy now and then, he could've overlooked it, but the manager said the gender split was roughly fifty-fifty. It didn't make sense. The profit was in trafficking women for sex, not men. The only reason to take large numbers of men would be to put them into slave labour. If that were the case, though, thousands of desperate men were available to be smuggled into Europe from North Africa. They were plentiful and cheap. If the gang were snatching men to work as slaves in factories and kitchens and on farms, there would be no reason to go to the trouble of taking them from expensive nightclubs in Mayfair. It was pointless and costly, not to mention highly risky. It didn't add up.

While Savage pondered that, Tannaz pounded away furiously on her laptop. With the phone number the manager had scribbled on the Post-it stuck on the corner of her screen, she scoured the internet to find its location. Of course, it hadn't shown up on any of the reverse phone-book websites, but that was to be expected. Those guys didn't want to be found, so Tannaz employed her hacking skills, looking in places she wasn't supposed to look.

"Going to have to go deeper," she said, yawning. "These guys are good. The number's not showing up anywhere."

"Can you find it?"

"Oh, yeah, I'll get the location. It's just they really don't want to be found. They've definitely covered their arses."

"So what are you going to do?"

"Hack another hacker."

"What? Why?"

"He has software that can do this a lot better than I can, so I'm borrowing it."

"You can do that?"

"Hell, yeah. He's nicked tons of my stuff. I mean, I could write a program for it, and it would be way better than his, but that would take time. This way's quicker. Okay, I've got into his software. I'm putting the phone number in, and I'll leave it running. It'll ping when it's got something for us."

"Won't this guy notice?"

"He doesn't get up until four p.m."

"And we'll have it by then?"

"Definitely." Tannaz balled up some of Savage's clothes that he'd changed out of earlier, and she stuffed them against the door of the van, using them as a pillow. A second later, she was fast asleep.

When Savage finally pulled on the hand brake outside Theresa's, he decided against waking Tannaz up. Sleep had her well and truly in its clutches, and denying her it, after the night she'd had, seemed unfair. The laptop still rested on her legs, although the screen had gone blank to save power.

He shut off the engine and stepped out of the van, gently closing the door behind him. Tannaz stirred momentarily before dozing once more.

Before Savage had a chance to knock on Theresa's door, it flew open. Theresa stood there, eyes heavy with worry and lack of sleep.

"John. Are you okay? Where's Tannaz?"

"Asleep in the car, she was"—he was about to say *kidnapped* when he quickly changed tack—"had a busy night. The poor girl's exhausted."

"What happened? Did you find anything? Was it the right place? Why are you dressed as a delivery man?"

"It's a long story. Yes, it's definitely the place. Bella was there, and we spoke to the manager, who was very, er, helpful."

Savage told her about the club being used by high-profile traffickers, leaving out the gory details of how they came by that information.

"The good news is it's highly likely Bella is alive, and we're a step closer to finding her. Tannaz has the number of the traffickers. She's doing her hacking thing to find out where they are."

Theresa stared at Savage, unblinking. He could see every capillary in her bloodshot eyes. She wavered slightly, like a thin sapling blowing in the breeze. The next second, she collapsed onto the floor. The weight of the new information had robbed her of all her stability.

Savage immediately crouched beside her. "Theresa, are you okay?" Stupid question—of course she wasn't okay.

She sobbed with punctuated gasps for air. "Alive? Are you sure?"

"I'm fairly certain."

"But she's in danger. Horrible men have her. They'll be abusing her, torturing her."

"No, this is different. In these cases, girls like Bella are more like companions to one man." That was the most diplomatic way he could think of putting it. "It's not ideal, but she'll be well looked after, probably showered in gifts and staying in a huge mansion."

"But kept against her will, forced to have sex with some fat, ugly billionaire. You have to get her back, John."

"I will. I will." Savage helped Theresa to her feet. "I'll put the kettle on, make us some tea." He led her into the kitchen, holding her around the shoulders for support. She collapsed in a chair by the table. Savage boiled the kettle, grabbed a couple of cups, and made tea. He was just pouring the milk when a knock came at the door.

"I'll get it," he said.

He jogged to the door and pulled it open. Tannaz pushed past him, holding the laptop open.

"Got an address." She headed straight into the kitchen and placed the laptop on the table in front of Theresa. "Hey, Theresa."

"Tannaz, are you okay, love? Can I make you something?"

"No, I'm good. Maybe later. Right now, we have our first clue." Savage peered over Tannaz's shoulder. The screen showed the address of an industrial estate on the outskirts of Heathrow Airport called Finlay Business Park.

"You sure that's it?" Savage asked.

"Positive," replied Tannaz.

"What is this place?" asked Theresa. "Is that where Bella is?"

"No," said Savage. "In fact, we don't know what it is. But the people who took her may operate from here, use it as a base. Let's take a look at it. Tannaz, can you pull it up on street view?"

She put the address into Google, and up popped an image of a bland, featureless industrial estate. Using the cursor to explore the area, she clicked down along a straight road. On either side stood a continuous line of two-storey buildings, plain and boring and completely utilitarian—cheap, low-maintenance spaces for businesses that weren't bothered by aesthetics. Each one was a simple metal-clad box with a large roller door on the left, a customer door on the right, and space for parking out front. The identical buildings stretched off as far as the eye could see, as though they'd come off a factory conveyor belt. The only things that distinguished them were the signs at the top, advertising what each place did. Many were there to service the airport, like aviation specialists who dealt with hydraulics and electrical systems, but everyday firms like plumbing suppliers, window manufacturers, and printing firms were also there.

"Which one is it?" asked Savage.

"It's unit 19A," Tannaz said, spinning the picture around so that it faced the other direction. "There it is." She flicked the cursor to get a closer look. At the end of the road stood a building unlike all the others. Located in a wide concrete compound sat a squat single-storey building with no windows and no entrances, just a single roller door. Around the perimeter was a high barbed-wire fence with a cluster of CCTV cameras on each corner, facing both inside and out to the road. More CCTV cameras perched on each corner of the building. No signs indicated what the place was for or what went on within. It looked like an electrical substation or a compound for storage rather than a place where people worked. Nothing was stored outside, though, just acres of blank concrete surrounding a wide, low building, and unlike the other units, no cars were parked outside, either.

"Let's look at it from Google Earth," said Savage.

A few clicks later, they were looking at the same building from above. A rectangular building set inside a rectangular fence, positioned in the centre of a wide expanse of concrete.

"Clever," said Savage.

"Why?" asked Tannaz.

"Well, unlike the rest of the buildings, this one's purpose built. It doesn't join onto any of the others. There's space all around it, wasted space, which they've done on purpose. If you try to get close to it, you'll be seen from every angle. It's at the end of a long, straight road, too. They can see anyone approaching the building from a mile away. It's an island. No buildings around it, nothing to get in the way. CCTV has uninterrupted sight lines in every direction. Impossible to sneak up on. If I wanted to build somewhere secure, that's how I'd do it. Go back to the street view. See if you can get a close-up on the entrance gate." Tannaz did as he said, showing the closest view she could. A large black metal gate with thick vertical bars, topped with razor wire filled the screen.

"What's wrong with that picture?"

Tannaz and Theresa examined it closely. Finally, they gave up.

"What?" asked Tannaz.

"There's no entry-system panel. No intercom. No contact point. Not even a buzzer."

"What does that mean?"

"The only people that get in this place are people they're expecting. They don't like surprises. And look beyond at the roller door. That's the only way in I've seen. No other doors or windows. One door minimises trouble. Easier to control and protect. My guess is there's someone in this place, manning it at all times. Has to be. Otherwise, who opens the gate when there's a shift change?"

Tannaz said, "Maybe they have those remote-control buttons in their car. My dad had one to raise the garage door every time he came home."

"That's true," said Savage. "But if the button gets lost or stolen or misplaced, it's a security problem for this place. I don't think they'd take that risk. These guys don't take any chances. Getting in there is going to be tricky. I need to study the place, watch their movements, look for any weak spots."

"I'll come with you," said Tannaz.

"No, it's better if I do this alone. I'll be sitting in my van for a long time, which means I'll have to pee in a bottle, which I'm sure you don't want to see."

"I don't care."

"Look, I need you to stay here. Find out who owns unit 19A, then have a go at that server from the club. See if you can get some names off it. But first, get some sleep."

"I don't sleep."

"You did in the car."

"Fine, okay. But just a few hours, then I'm cracking into that server."

"Call me if you get anywhere."

"Please be careful, John," Theresa said. "Don't you want your tea first?"

"Have you got a travel mug?"

Theresa nodded.

"Stick it in there. I'll drink it along the way."

Savage changed back into his civilian clothes and bagged up his delivery-man uniform. Then he jumped into his van, tea in hand, and headed for 19A Finlay Industrial Park.

CHAPTER 22

UNIT 19A WASN'T DIFFICULT TO find, just a couple of miles from Heathrow Airport. Savage pointed his van along the straight road heading towards the compound at the end. As he neared it, he slowed to a crawl. He had to assume these guys were watching every vehicle that came close to their little citadel, and he had to be careful. He already knew they were cautious, so he couldn't get too close. When he checked a place out, he would usually just park and sit in his car, watching and waiting, as he did with Hackett and Club Zero. That wouldn't work here. They'd notice him, especially if he parked there at night after everyone else had left and the place became deserted. Short of pulling an industrial waste bin onto the side of the road and drilling two eyeholes in it so that he could hide inside, he had nowhere to conceal himself. He had to hand it to those guys—they were smart. They'd chosen their location well, a little too well for Savage's liking.

Taking another tack, he pulled onto the forecourt of a car-repair firm about three units away. He was close enough to snatch a few glimpses of the compound but far enough away not to arouse any suspicion. Savage parked and got out.

The roller door to Alpha Body Works was wide open. Through it, Savage could see men in overalls buffing body panels and removing bumpers, having a laugh and ribbing each other, typical working guys. One corner was sectioned off as a cubicle, which he assumed was the paint-spraying booth. Over the clatter and whiz of industrial power tools, he could hear a radio DJ talking the usual superficial nonsense.

A guy wandered out with a clipboard. He had a shaved head and neck tattoos but was friendly and cheerful. "Can I help you, mate?"

"Yeah," said Savage. "Got a few bumps and scrapes. Thought it was time to get them fixed. Just need a quote."

"Yep, no problem." The guy clicked a ballpoint pen that had Alpha Body Works written along the shaft and began moving around the VW. On his clipboard was a generic diagram of a car, as if it had been unfolded, showing the top, sides, back, and front all at once. Every time he came across a dent or a scuff, he noted it on the drawing. As he moved around, Savage followed him, snatching quick glances of the menacing sight of unit 19A.

"Busy?" asked Savage.

"Always," replied the guy, grinning. He had a tooth missing, a canine.

"Bet you're looking forward to driverless cars, aren't you? Won't have so many dents to deal with."

The guy laughed. "I think we'll have more work. Going to be ages until they get that right. It'll be chaos. Cars crashing everywhere."

Savage laughed with him. He gave it a few minutes, letting the guy get on with his work, then asked him, "What the hell goes on over there?" Savage nodded toward unit 19A.

"We call it Fort Knox."

"What is it?"

"Dunno. Trucks go in every now and again. And I've seen a metal-sheeting company delivering there and a foam supplier."

"Metal sheeting and foam?" asked Savage. "That's a lot of security for metal and foam."

The guy smiled, revealing the gap in his teeth. "Everyone round here thinks it's some secret James Bond base. But I bet it's something really boring like a cladding firm or something."

"There's no signage outside. Bit weird."

"Maybe they don't need to advertise," said the guy, stretching his back. "Could be just storage. Maybe all the security was left over from the previous owner."

"True." Savage didn't push it any further, as the guy

clearly didn't know what went on in there, so asking any more questions would be pointless. He'd have to find another way of gathering information.

"Okay, all done here." The guy clicked his pen top and returned it to his top overalls pocket. "Once I've done the quote, I can send it to you. Just need an address or email."

"Actually, would you mind if I waited here while you do the quote?" Savage asked.

"Sure. Could take a few hours, though."

"That's fine. I'll just sit in my van, catch up on some messages."

"Be my guest. There's a drinks machine in reception. Tastes vile, but it's better than nothing."

Savage followed him into the reception area, a grubby room with deformed plastic chairs and a tired-looking drinks machine. Savage grabbed himself a tea, holding it by the top rim. The cup was so hot he had to keep switching hands on his way back to the van. The guy was right. The tea was disgusting, leaving a metallic aftertaste. He hoped it would give his body enough stimulation to fend off a snooze. The guy disappeared into the back while Savage returned to his car.

Savage's parking spot couldn't have been more perfect. Through the windscreen, he had a clear view of the 19A compound. All the time, he pretended to be looking at his smartphone when he was really looking straight at the unit at the end of the road. He even took some footage of it, not that it would help. The footage didn't tell him anything he didn't already know from Google Street View. No discernible signs of entry, just a fence and heavy metal gates topped with barbed wire, and inside those, the windowless building. No one came in or went out—no movement, no signs of life. Nothing.

After four hours, the guy with the neck tattoos tapped on the window. He held up an envelope containing Savage's quote. Savage wound down the window and accepted it.

"I've priced up everything," said the guy. "If you want it done, there's about a two-week waiting list, so I'd book it in quick."

"Great, thanks," said Savage. "Listen, that place over there has really got my curiosity up, probably because I'm retired with too much time on my hands. But if I gave you a hundred quid now and a hundred quid later, would you mind doing me a very small favour?"

The guy's face suddenly lit up at the prospect of earning some extra cash, probably to spend down at the pub or stick on the horses. "What favour?"

"Your CCTV camera above your roller door. Could you swivel it slightly so unit 19A is in the frame?"

"I reckon I could do that."

"Just nudge it a few inches to the left. It'll still be watching your roller door, but it'll also catch anyone going in or out of that place at the end of the road."

"I think you'd be looking at four hundred quid for a service like that, seeing as you're not here to get your car fixed."

Savage smiled. The guy was smart. That was a good sign.

"Three hundred," said Savage.

"Three fifty, and I'll put all the footage on a memory stick."

"Done." They shook hands. "I'll be back in a few days." Savage went into his pockets and pulled out a couple hundred pounds and handed it to him through the window. Before he relinquished the cash, he added, "But just keep this between you and me. Nobody else knows about it. Okay?"

"Hey, this like some Jason Bourne shit?" asked the guy, stuffing the notes into his overalls.

"Exactly. Go for it, Jason."

"The name's Steve."

They shook hands again. The guy smiled and winked, excited to be part of something and even more excited to be onto a nice little earner for doing very little.

Before he left the body shop, Savage called Tannaz. "Hi, how are things? Get any sleep?"

"No, too restless. Still trying to get names off this server."

"Are you still at Theresa's?"

"Nope. At my flat. I needed my stuff to do this."

"Listen, take a break. I'm going to do the same. What about your day job?"

"Called in sick. It's fine. That place sucks. This is way cooler. What about the address? Anything?"

"Nothing, but I have someone watching the place. In the meantime, get some rest."

"Sure, boss."

"Don't call me boss." Savage hung up and called Theresa to fill her in on the details. Then he turned the VW around and drove back home, where he fell into bed with all his clothes on.

CHAPTER 23

B Y THE TIME SAVAGE WOKE up, it was seven thirty p.m. He
cursed himself for sleeping for so long, though he didn't
really sleep. More of a fidgety doze, it was somewhere
between waking and unconsciousness, the best he could hope for.

Coming out of this strange limbo made him ratty and irritable.
He shuffled around his flat, getting more and more grumpy,
not sure what to do with himself. Everything felt negative. The
investigation had hit a brick wall of sorts, which didn't help. After
the big breakthrough of getting the number and address off the
manager at Club Zero, progress had stalled.

The guys he was after were in that building. He was sure of
that. He had the urge to go barging in there right that minute
and get answers, but he knew that would be a mistake. He
couldn't sneak in, either. They'd designed the place so that would
be virtually impossible. He considered using his delivery-man
routine again, but it wouldn't work a second time. For a start,
there were no door-entry systems, and he was pretty sure those
guys were unlikely to be fooled by a random delivery man turning
up on their doorstep unexpectedly. Also, he had no idea how
many men were in there. *A handful? Ten? Twenty?* At Club Zero,
he knew what he was dealing with, but this place had too many
unknowns, and unlike the bouncers at the club, these guys would
certainly be armed.

He would have to stick with his current plan and be patient,
which had always worked in the past. He would watch and learn,
getting feedback from the CCTV footage, then decide what to do.
Vehicles had to visit it now and again, especially for changing

shifts or making deliveries. He would get some car registrations from the footage and track down who they belonged to. After finding out where they lived, he could apply pressure and work his way along the chain. That was the plan, and he needed to stick to it. If that didn't work, they still had the server full of names from the club, and he had Tannaz. With her skill, she'd surely be able to pull something useful from its files. In fact, that was probably more useful than the address of unit 19A. It was data, and data showed patterns, giving insight into movements and behaviour. The manager of Club Zero had said those guys sent girls in there at random. He probably thought that because he hadn't taken the time to analyse when they did what they did. Humans were habitual animals, and those guys would be no different. Next time they used the club as a shop window, Savage would be waiting for them.

Restlessness still troubled him, though. Sitting around waiting didn't help matters. He needed to do something, to shed some excess energy and clear his mind. *Only one thing for it.*

He threw on his gym kit, grabbed a water bottle and drove to Motivation Health Club.

Savage entered the reception area, checking for any sign of Brett so that he could avoid him. He'd didn't hate the guy, apart from the fact he was a narcissistic pervert who thought he knew it all. Savage just wasn't in the mood for interacting with anyone right then. He'd bite their heads off.

When he was sure the coast was clear, he crossed the reception and waved his membership card at the pretty girl behind the desk.

"Oh, just one moment please, sir," she said, turning to the computer screen on her desk. "I have a note here on your account: your next workout is to be monitored by a nurse, apparently."

He'd forgotten about the incident on the running machine. "That's really not necessary."

"I'm sorry, I can't allow you into the gym without a nurse being present. Doctor Stevens's orders."

Savage had been looking forward to working up a massive sweat and blowing some of the cobwebs away, but his hand was going to be held by a nurse who, no doubt, would hold him back and stop him from "overdoing it" just because he'd fallen off a stupid running machine. Right then, all he wanted to do was overdo it, wearing out his body and getting rid of some nervous energy, but he had no choice. *Might as well get it over with.* Then he could go back to exercising without constraints.

"Fine, send in the nurse."

"One moment, please." She lifted the phone and hit a button. "Hello, Gina. It's reception. Mr. Savage is here." She replaced the receiver and turned back to him. "Gina will be down in a minute. She's been expecting you."

Savage wondered how Gina could've been expecting him when he'd only just decided to go to the gym.

A minute later, Gina appeared and introduced herself. Unlike the rest of Club Motivation's staff, who barely wore any clothes at all, apart from skin-tight Lycra, Gina wore a plain white nurse uniform modestly cut below the knee. Her thick, honey-coloured hair was loosely tied back in a pony tail. She wore no makeup either—she didn't need to. Her big smiley brown eyes crinkled as she held out her hand to shake his. Savage put her at late thirties, maybe early forties. She was definitely closer to him in age than all the people around him.

"Hi, I'm Gina," she said. "Sorry about this. You look perfectly fit and healthy. This is just a precaution. Nothing to worry about." Among all the posers and fake people in the club, Gina was a breath of fresh air, genuine and straightforward.

"Er, okay," Savage replied.

After waiting for him to get changed, Gina ushered Savage into the gym, gently placing her hand in the small of his back to guide him. Savage wasn't sure why she did so. Maybe it was a nurse thing, a bit of human contact to reassure him, or maybe she was worried he might topple over at any moment.

Gina led him to an empty treadmill. "Okay, first a bit of gentle walking," she said, "just to get the heart rate up." She punched some numbers into the running machine console. "We'll do two minutes, okay?"

Savage nodded and climbed on. He noticed Gina gave a big smile after every sentence, her naturally full red lips framing perfectly white teeth. She smiled as though he was the only person in the room. Savage kept wanting to look into her eyes but didn't dare. They were like two dark magnets, pulling him in, so he kept his eyes facing front.

When the two minutes were up, Gina took Savage over to a padded bench at the edge of the gym where they sat together. "Would you mind if I take your pulse?" she asked politely.

Savage nodded, not minding at all. Gina gently took Savage's hand and pressed her fingers to his wrist. Her skin was warm and soft, and she smelled of fresh soap.

Savage never normally felt awkward or embarrassed. However, an uncomfortable prickly heat danced up his back and around his neck. He shook off the feeling. Someone as elegant and dignified as Gina would never be attracted to him. He wasn't what people would call handsome even when he'd been a younger man, just plain and unremarkable. One of Savage's mates had even gone so far as to call Savage his "cumblocker," someone he thought of to prevent himself from climaxing when he bedded his girlfriend.

Being attracted to Gina, Savage started to feel like a creep. Then again, she wasn't exactly a youngster. He tried to remember that silly formula for acceptable age difference, something like half the man's age, plus seven. At nearly fifty-eight, that meant Savage could date a thirty-six-year-old. Gina was definitely older than that, well within acceptable tolerances. He glanced down at her hand and saw no wedding ring. A fizz of excitement shot around his body.

"Okay, John, no problem there," she said, letting go of John's hand. "Your heart rate is fine. How do you feel? Any dizziness? Nausea?"

Savage wanted to say that sitting next to her made him feel light-headed. "I feel fine," he said.

"Okay, let's take it up a notch and get you on the Nordic skier." Gina led him to the waiting machines. All the while, Savage tried to keep his eyes up and away from looking at her behind. He climbed aboard while Gina set the machine for two minutes.

"Okay, same again," she said. "Nice and easy. You don't need to impress me. I can already see you look after yourself."

Savage didn't say anything. An unexpected bout of shyness held his tongue.

The machine hummed away as Savage thrust his legs and arms backwards and forwards. He was just getting into his workout, enjoying the distraction of the pleasing monotony, when Gina placed one hand on his back and the other on his stomach. More adrenalin surged through his body. Savage sped up, his legs and arms pumping more and more quickly.

"Not so fast, John," she said. "I just need to adjust your form. You're leaning over a bit too much. It puts a strain on your back." The long fingers of Gina's left hand splayed out, firmly holding the lower part of his abdominals, her other hand on the small of his back. Gradually, she changed his position, making him more upright.

Savage swallowed hard.

"Okay, hold that form for me," she said, removing her hands. "Perfect."

Savage was glad her hands hadn't lingered too long. He was worried about the effect they were having on him.

"So, John. What do you do for a living?" she asked.

"I'm retired," Savage said.

"So what do you do with your free time, apart from coming here?"

"I'm pretty boring, I'm afraid. I like DIY."

"That's not boring at all," said Gina, smiling warmly. "Do you know, I've always fancied being a plumber."

"Really?"

"Yeah. I do all my own plumbing at home. I love it."

"That's brilliant."

"I plumbed in a new dishwasher last week, saved myself a fifty-quid installation fee."

Savage felt his heart rate quicken, which wasn't from the

Nordic skier. She liked DIY. Gina just kept getting more and more attractive.

"You should give it a go," said Savage. "Get yourself on a course. You'd be great. There's not enough female tradespeople."

"I would love to, but I've only just started this job. Finished at my last place on Friday and came here on Monday. I'd feel bad about leaving so soon." Gina had integrity too. She was ticking all the boxes. "Besides, I can't do soldering yet, you know, connecting two pipes together."

"There's nothing to it," said Savage. "I could show you."

"No, that's okay. It'd be too much trouble."

"Really, it's not. It'd be my pleasure."

Gina flashed her incredible smile. "I'd love to. Are you sure you don't mind?"

"Like I said, it'd be my pleasure."

Her smile didn't fade. It just got brighter and more irresistible, like the sun coming out.

After he had climbed off the machine, Gina took his pulse again and gave him the all clear as far as his health was concerned. She scribbled down her mobile phone number on a scrap of paper and handed it to him. "Sorry," she said, "I'll get proper business cards, but they're still being printed."

Savage took the card and slipped it into his pocket. "I'll give you a call, and we'll sort out a time."

"That would be wonderful. Are you sure you don't mind?" she asked.

"Course not."

She held out her hand, and he shook it.

A firm handshake. Another box ticked.

"Well, John, it's been lovely to meet you."

"Same here," he replied.

"Bye, now."

Savage watched Gina exit the gym. Just before she reached the door, she turned back and gave him a wave. Savage waved back with a dopey grin on his face. He felt as if he were sixteen years old again.

He'd come to work out but found he couldn't concentrate on anything apart from Gina and when he'd next see her, so he returned to the changing room and had a long shower, hoping the water might douse the flames of his desire. It didn't.

He got changed back into his clothes and left the changing room, then the guilt hit him like a ton of bricks.

He didn't need the voice to shame him. The memory of his wife crept into his head and did it for him. For Savage, there had only ever been one woman, and that was his wife, Dawn. Just because she had passed away didn't change that fact. Being attracted to another woman, even one as lovely as Gina, made him feel wretched and guilty, as though he were betraying his wife's memory. Savage crumpled up Gina's number and threw it in the nearest bin.

Painful though it was, he'd accepted his wife's death, but he wished more than anything that he could have Dawn back, along with their daughter—his perfect little family together again, safe in the circle. He wanted to wind back time and just spend a few glorious moments with them again—just a simple walk in the park when his daughter was six, when all she wanted to do was ride on his shoulders and be teased. Savage recalled her little tinkling bell of a laugh. *Pure joy.* He pictured his wife holding his hand, everything right with the world.

The thought that it would never ever happen, that he would never see their faces or ask them how their day went, turned his sadness and confusion into a spear of rage.

"You know, there's one way you could fix that."

Savage's heart nearly stopped. The voice was back.

"Kill yourself, then you can all be together again. Ah, wouldn't that be nice? One big happy dead family."

CHAPTER 24

SAVAGE DARTED INTO THE NEAREST empty room, one of the exercise studios. A punch bag hung in one corner.

"Perfect."

He went in, closed the door behind himself and began hitting the bag with all his fury. He pounded the bag as if it were his worst enemy, smashing his fists and throwing in the odd elbow strike, headbutt, low kick and other dirty street-fighting moves.

"That's not going to help. I'm not going anywhere. Now, let's talk about how you're going to kill yourself. What about a simple classic? Find a bridge, nice and high. Then jump off. Nothing to it. Be like flying. Until your head slams into the concrete at about 120 miles an hour."

The supporting arm above the bag shuddered and wobbled as Savage hit it harder and harder.

"Or what about another classic? Jump in front of a train. There are loads round here. Which would you prefer, underground or overground."

Savage speeded up, punching more furiously, hoping that each whack of the bag would drown out the voice.

"Personally, I like the sound of slit wrists in the bath. Be quite comfy. Maybe you could light a few scented candles. Such a pleasant way to go."

After a flurry of rapid-fire punches, Savage staggered back from the bag, exhausted. Leaning over, hands on knees, he panted hard.

"But hold on, you're ex-SAS. That's too wussy for you. You need a manly way of dying. I know: you could do something with *a chainsaw. Rig up some kind of contraption that decapitates you. That'd be good. You could put some of your DIY skills to good use. And then the next thing you'd see would be your lovely wife and that beautiful daughter of yours waiting for you with open arms. Although maybe not your daughter—her arms blew off when that mine exploded."*

When Savage finally caught his breath, he said, "I've just realised. I don't know your name."

"My name?"

"Yeah, your name."

"Don't have one."

"Oh, that's a shame. Well, I'm going to give you one. From now on, you will be known as Jeff Perkins."

"What? Have you gone even more insane than you were before? Why Jeff Perkins?"

"Because Jeff Perkins sounds like the kind of guy who works in a boring office and orders the same thing on a Chinese menu every time he gets a takeaway. A dull but harmless little man. The kind of guy who comes back off holiday and nobody realises he's been away. That's you. Jeff Perkins."

"I'm not Jeff Perkins."

"You are now, Jeff Perkins. Sorry, what were you talking about? I drifted off a bit when I was working the bag."

"Ah, I see what you're doing. Is this some new technique your shrink has taught you? I bet she did. Give the voice in your head a name, make me seem less menacing. I bet it's got a wanky name too, like character-identity realignment. So lame."

"No, just thought of it myself, Jeff."

"Stop calling me that."

"No, sorry, Jeff. Can't do that. And just for the record, you're not menacing. You're mildly irritating, like a long supermarket queue or weak tea. Nothing to get worked up about, but it'd be better if you didn't exist. You're Jeff Perkins—mildly irritating."

Savage waited for a pithy comeback from the newly named Jeff Perkins, but none came.

"Jeff? Jeff, are you there?"

Silence.

Savage smiled at the small victory in the battle for his mental health... for the moment. He knew Jeff would be back, though, probably after going away to regroup and think of some other way to get at him.

Savage went back to his bag work, happily jabbing away, feeling a little endorphin rush from his workout or his triumph over Jeff, possibly. *Probably a combination of both.* His satisfaction was short-lived.

Brett walked in.

"Mind if I join in?" he asked, not mentioning anything about why Savage was working out in his everyday clothes.

"Yes, I do." Savage didn't stop hitting the bag or turn to acknowledge his presence.

Brett stood beside him, hands on hips. "You know, I could give you some advice, show you some pointers."

"I doubt it," Savage replied, increasing the ferocity of his strikes.

"I am a black belt in taekwondo. Second dan."

"Ah, taekwondo," said Savage. "Ancient Korean martial art, designed for kicking riders off their horses. Handy in London if you want to take out the Household Cavalry."

"I can do a hundred push-ups on my thumbs." Brett sounded like a nine-year-old trying to impress a disinterested father.

"Handy for playing tiddlywinks," Savage replied.

"Let me show you how hard I can kick that punch bag."

Savage stopped pummelling the bag, left it swinging and turned to face Brett. He wiped the sweat from his forehead with the back of his hand. His knuckles were glowing red because he really should've used gloves but hadn't seen any. Honestly, he kind of liked the stinging sensation. Made him feel alive. He faced Brett, panting like a bull about to charge.

Normally, he wouldn't engage with anyone who riled him up, but Brett's condescending tone had got under his skin. The guy had such a high opinion of himself that he was in dire need of being taken down a peg or two.

"Have you ever been in a fight?" Savage asked.

Before Brett had time to speak, Savage held up his hand to silence him. "I mean a real fight in a pub or on the street. A dirty fight with bottles and bricks, where you're fighting for your life."

Brett shook his head.

Savage wiped more sweat off his brow. "Well, it's a lot different to hitting a punch bag. Punch bags don't hit back, as Bruce Lee once said."

Brett shook his head. "No, he actually said 'Boards don't hit back.' It's from *Enter the Dragon*. I've seen it thirty-seven times. It's just before he fights Bob Hall—"

"I don't care," said Savage.

"Well, I've been in loads of competitive fights with my club," Brett said, cracking his knuckles. "I'm the current South East Taekwondo champion in the eighty-kilogram-and-over division."

"Doesn't count. That's in a ring with rules and rounds, where you get to rest and a referee steps in if things get messy. Real fights are brutal, last only a couple of seconds. Fancy kicks don't cut it. Maybe in movies they do, but not in the real world."

"Well, I disagree. Stand aside."

Savage moved out the way. He wasn't a fan of kicking in fights. It put the fighter off balance and made him or her vulnerable to leg grabs. Standing on one leg was never a good idea when your opponent wanted nothing better than to put you on the ground, so he had a rule: never kick above the waist.

Brett stepped up and danced around the bag on tiptoes, sizing it up, skipping forward and back. For such a heavy guy, he was light on his feet. Then he sprang and unleashed a powerful side kick into the middle of the bag. It bent nearly double. He followed it up with a high spinning back kick, landing it roughly where someone's head would be. It was blindingly fast. Every time his foot connected with the bag, Brett let out a bloodcurdling shout. Switching to his other foot, he attacked it with a series of wide, scything roundhouse kicks, as if the bag was a tree and his leg was the axe. A deep thud echoed around the room with every strike.

The guy definitely had skills. If one of those kicks connected with a person, it would undoubtedly send them flying across the room or, worse, knock them out cold.

While Brett carried on his assault on the bag, Savage edged out of the room, made a swift exit and closed the door quietly behind himself. He didn't want to be there when Brett stopped and started gloating about himself. Savage would have to grudgingly admit that he was a pretty good martial artist, and Brett's head was big enough already.

Savage left Club Motivation and checked his messages, finding several missed calls from Tannaz. He dialled her straight back.

"Hi, John." Tannaz sounded defeated.

"Anything from the server?"

"Nothing."

"What? Nothing at all?"

"Just loads of random names of people who have been to the club."

"Was Bella's among them?"

"No. All I have is thousands of random names. I told you their security was awful. Their IT's even worse. Their database hasn't been cleaned in years. I think the manager was telling the truth. They're not going to keep names on file of people who go missing after visiting their club."

"Damn it," said Savage, almost crushing the phone in his fist. "You're right. I just thought it was worth a try. Is there anything else you can do?"

"I could cross-reference all the names from the Club Zero database with missing persons, but there are hundreds of thousands. It's going to take days, weeks, maybe months. John, we might not get anything from this."

Savage swore and punched a nearby wall. Then his knuckles weren't just raw but bleeding as well.

CHAPTER 25

SAVAGE HAD RESIGNED HIMSELF TO the fact that the address of the compound might be their only lead. In the worst-case scenario, the database would yield nothing. Secretly, he hoped Tannaz would pull off a miracle, but he had to be realistic. He had to get into unit 19A sooner rather than later, which put him in a dilemma. The longer he waited, the more CCTV footage he'd get from Steve at the body shop. More footage meant more he could learn about the gang, possibly getting a glimpse of who they were and how many of them went in and out of the compound. He had to be patient, although doing so was killing him. At one point, he considered calling up a few of his surviving Army pals. They could put together a little assault team, storm the place, drag those scumbags out, throw them in a van, take them somewhere remote, and go to work on them until they told him where Bella was. He dismissed the idea almost immediately. Most of his pals were in no physical or mental shape to handle an operation like that, particularly when innocents could be involved. Too much could go wrong.

He was relying solely on the CCTV footage to give him answers, and that really worried him.

He gave it three days before he drove back to collect the footage from Steve. That should have been long enough to get an idea of what went on in 19A.

As he pulled onto the forecourt of Alpha Body Works, he saw Steve through the open roller door. The man looked cheerful as he buffed the body panel of a grey Toyota hatchback. Steve's face dropped as he caught sight of Savage getting out of his van. Steve switched off the power tool, placed it carefully on the ground, and held up a hand for Savage to wait there.

Five minutes later, Steve emerged from the reception area, grasping a memory stick. He still didn't look too happy, face downcast and shoulders to match.

"Everything all right, Steve?" asked Savage.

Steve ignored the question and palmed the USB stick into his hand as they shook. "It's all there, right up to the second you just pulled in."

"So why the long face?"

Steve broke eye contact, looking away as though he was about to get told off. "I've been looking at the footage. Every day before I start work. Hope you don't mind."

"Nothing wrong with that. It's your security camera. You can do what you like."

"Well, it's just there's nothing on it."

"What do you mean?"

Steve took a deep breath. "Nobody's been in 19A. Day or night."

Savage took a step closer to Steve and spoke quietly. "Nobody at all?"

"Nothing. No one's gone in or out. Will I still get paid?"

Savage took some cash from his jeans and picked out some tens and twenties until he had enough to pay off the balance. "Deal's a deal," said Savage, handing him the wad of cash.

Steve perked up. "If you need any more, just give me a shout." Then he shook Savage's hand again and returned to the workshop.

"One more thing." Savage called out. "Can you return the CCTV camera to its original position?"

Steve nodded and reached down to pick up his buffing tool.

"Can you do it now?" asked Savage. At some point, he'd need to get inside unit 19A, and he didn't want a nearby camera recording what he was doing.

With a sigh, Steve put the tool back down, fetched the step ladder, and readjusted the camera so it only pointed down at the roller door. Savage waited by his car.

"Happy?" Steve asked grudgingly when he had finished.

"Thank you," said Savage as he got back into his van. Before he started the engine, he looked at the memory stick. The thought crossed his mind that maybe the gang had got to Steve and made him doctor the footage so it showed nothing. *Unlikely.* That was too complicated and would require technical know-how to change the footage and make it look convincing, plus it would need a bit of acting on Steve's part. Savage was pretty sure the guy wasn't lying. More importantly, that wasn't the gang's style. Those guys didn't take chances. If they'd got wind of Savage using Steve to monitor the compound, then Steve would be dead and so would Savage.

He drove to Theresa's house, having arranged to meet Tannaz there. All three of them crowded around Tannaz's laptop in the kitchen as she plugged in Steve's USB. A pop-up video screen appeared, showing a daytime wide-angle shot of Alpha Body Works and a couple of other units. In the distance was an uninterrupted view of unit 19A. Cars rolled onto the forecourt of Alpha Body Works, and cars rolled off, interspersed with Steve coming out to do quotes for potential customers or to hand back their fixed-up cars. All the while, nothing went on at unit 19A.

Tannaz hit the fast-forward button, zipping the footage along at high speed. Units shut up shop. Roller doors came down. Workers went home. Day turned to evening. Evening turned to night. The footage went to black-and-white night-time mode, making everything look strangely surreal. Tannaz slowed the footage down to normal speed—nothing. She sped the film up six times. Savage glanced at the clock in the corner of the screen—eight o'clock, nothing; nine o'clock, nothing; ten o'clock, nothing. At two in the morning, a fox loped across the road, its eyes shining like two silver coins. Tannaz increased the speed to twelve times—still nothing. The image lightened, heralding the start of a new day. As the light levels increased, the image suddenly flipped back to colour daytime mode. Cars whizzed onto the screen, some pulling onto the Alpha Body Works forecourt and others into the other units nearby. Not one headed towards unit 19A. They watched another working day speeded up. Unit 19A remained eerily quiet and unchanged, a static constant in that busy little world.

Tannaz forwarded through the next day and night and the one after that, but the footage yielded nothing new.

Nobody spoke.

They had a big fat zero.

"Okay. This is a setback," said Savage, running a hand over the top of his head. "But we still know something went down in this place. I may have to step things up a little."

"In what way?" asked Tannaz.

"Not sure yet. But we still have the telephone number of this place. Could call it, see what happens. Pretend I've dialled a wrong number."

Tannaz cleared her throat. "How would that help us?"

Savage got to his feet and paced around the tiny kitchen. "Don't know. I'm trying to avoid the obvious."

"Which is?"

"Storm the place, get inside. Smash some heads. Get someone to talk."

"John, you can't," said Theresa, her face turning white. "You could get killed."

"She's right," added Tannaz. "You're no good to Bella dead."

"True," said Savage, rubbing his hand on the kitchen counter as though cleaning an imaginary spot. "But this calls for drastic measures."

"We should call the police," said Tannaz.

"They won't do anything," Theresa replied. "I've been pestering them for months to do something."

"I know," said Tannaz. "Why don't we make something up? Say drug deals are going down in this place."

Savage folded his arms and leaned against the kitchen counter. "Police powers of entry are severely limited. They'd need strong evidence that something big is going on to enter without a warrant. We have no evidence, which means, for now, they'd simply do a drive past, check it out. Trouble is, that place is as quiet as a grave from the outside. We'd lose police interest immediately. And with all those security cameras watching the outside, our bad guys could get spooked and disappear."

"But at least we'd force the bad guys to make a move," Tannaz suggested. "Get a look at them, maybe follow them."

"It's a possibility. Let's call that idea number one. Did you get anything on who owns the property? Maybe there's some leverage there."

"It's a dead end," said Tannaz, "a holding company called Vanir Properties, completely legitimate and squeaky clean." Her eyes suddenly lit up. "What about causing a scene outside? A distraction to get them out."

"Light a fire," Theresa suggested.

"That's a great idea," Tannaz said, jumping to her feet. "Setting fire to the fence would cause plenty of distraction. People always run from fire. Even scumbag gangsters. I say we do it. Make these guys feel frightened for a change."

"Hold on," said Savage, rubbing his forehead. "A fire's too risky and uncontrollable. There could be innocent people in that building—more girls like Bella being held against their will, and perhaps a few innocent men, too. Fires can rapidly get out of hand."

"But it'd only be at the fence, nowhere near the building."

Savage took a deep breath. "The difficulty with all these ideas is there's only one way in or out of there. Even if we do get them to open up, which there's no guarantee, we still have to get in through the roller door, and we have no clue about how many gang members we'll face once we're in there. This is the problem."

"What would you have done in the SAS?" asked Theresa.

"We'd observe, study the enemy, gather intel. Work out who we were dealing with. How many. What weapons they had. Put together a team according to the size of the threat. We'd know all there is to know before we went in. Thing is, we don't know anything. And even if we did, we simply haven't got the manpower or access to firearms that I'd need."

Savage felt out of his depth. He'd taken on something bigger than he was and made promises he couldn't keep. He'd made out he was some kind of one-man army, a hero who could get the job done, a real-life Rambo. That had worked, up to a point. At Club Zero, he'd succeeded, but they were just civilians. Outfoxing them had been relatively easy, but the guys holding unit 19A knew what they were doing, knew how to make the place impregnable.

What galled him the most was that he'd given Theresa false hope. He had indeed made more progress than the police and the private investigator, but that wasn't difficult. Police didn't investigate missing people, and the private investigator was a con man. He'd been a fool to think he could find Bella, and as the saying went, "There's no fool like an old fool."

A knock at the door jolted him out of his self-pity.

Theresa stood up and went to answer it.

From the kitchen, they heard the lock slide back and the door open.

Theresa screamed, "John! John! Help me!"

Savage sprang out of the kitchen, nearly knocking the table over and the laptop flying. He sprinted into the hallway to see Theresa staggering backwards, crying. He pushed past her to confront the massive form of a heavyweight thug filling the doorway.

Minchie.

CHAPTER 26

MINCHIE STOOD THERE, HIS HAND in a blue sling from where Savage had broken it during their last encounter—the perfect target. Running at full speed, Savage slammed all his weight into Minchie's broken hand. Minchie tripped over the threshold, fell onto the pavement outside, and landed on his back, banging his head against the ground. Savage landed on top of him in an instant, his knee on Minchie's bad arm, pinning him down. Savage grabbed the thug's free hand to stop him retaliating then put him in a chokehold.

Tannaz came out to see what all the commotion was about.

Savage turned to her, still keeping his grip on Minchie. "Shut the door and lock it," he said. "I've got this."

Gurgling bubbled up from Minchie's constricted throat. Syllables tried to escape from his wretched mouth.

"What do you want? Why have you come here?" Savage shouted. "I swear, if it's to hurt Theresa, I'll put you in the ground."

Minchie shook his head, as far as he could shake it with Savage holding on to him. It was more of a wobble. Savage released his grip slightly.

"P-please," Minchie gasped. "I have information."

"Information? What information?"

"Bella."

Savage looked deep into his eyes. He saw fear, ignorance, and desperation but no hint of deception.

Savage let go of him and got to his feet. Minchie remained on the pavement, panting away and holding his injured arm. After a while, Minchie extended a hand. "Can you help me up?"

"Nope."

Minchie took about a minute, with a great deal of huffing and puffing, to get to his feet.

"Tell me what you know about Bella," Savage said quietly.

"What's it worth?"

Savage grabbed Minchie by his broken arm and shoved him against the side of a car. "How about I don't kill you?"

"Okay, okay. But just listen. After you pulled that stunt with Venables, I've been out of a job. I'm skint."

Squeezing Minchie's broken hand, Savage said, "Ah, poor you. Okay, here's the deal. You tell me what you know, and I promise not to hurt you. And I'm very good at hurting people. Even creative, you might say. I can think of some wonderful ways for you to experience a whole world of pain you never even knew existed."

Minchie shook his head. "Can't do that. I need money. I know where they took Bella. It's on an industrial estate, and you'll never find it unless you—"

"It's 19A, Finlay Business Park. I already know that, genius."

Without any self-control, Minchie's mouth formed an *O* as his one and only bargaining chip fell down the drain. After a second, his brain caught up. Eyes panicking, he pretended he had no idea what Savage was talking about. "No," he said. "No. That's not the place at all. It's, er, you have it wrong. Only I know the place."

Hearing Minchie fabricate lies on the spot was like watching the world's worst actor or a chimpanzee pretending to be smart.

"Minchie, you are a terrible liar." Savage turned away and headed back to Theresa's front door.

"Wait. Wait." Minchie followed him. "I have something else. I did a job for the guys at 19A."

"Oh, so you do know them."

"Not exactly. Well, not at all, really. I never met them. But I did do a trial job for them. I kind of messed it up, though."

"Really? You surprise me." Savage exhaled. "So what good is this information to me?"

"I dunno. Thought maybe we could work together. Like partners. A crime-fighting duo."

The laugh that came from deep within Savage's lungs nearly shattered all the windows in the neighbourhood. "Me? Work with you? A crime-fighting duo? You're insane."

Minchie shifted uneasily on his feet.

"On what planet do you think you could be a force for good?" asked Savage. When the big thug tried to answer, Savage got there first. "Shut up. It was a rhetorical question."

Minchie looked confused.

Savage continued, "Think of all the misery you've caused. How many other people like Theresa have you roughed up and intimidated? Hurting innocent, vulnerable people. Fleecing them of money that they haven't got, for that bloodsucker Venables. You're crazy if you think I'd ever want to work with you. Not in a million years."

Savage turned his back on Minchie. He was just about to knock on Theresa's front door, but he stopped, hand poised and ready to rap. He turned to face Minchie. "You said you've never met these guys."

"Er, that's right," said Minchie.

"So how do you know about unit 19A?"

Minchie's eyes went blank like a shark's, nothing going on behind them. He seemed dead of thought, a creature only driven by instinct, currently trying to think of a plausible answer to the question.

"Cut the bullshit, Minchie. If you've done a job for them, you'd have met at least one of them or someone connected to them."

"Okay, that might be true."

"So who did you meet?"

"Several guys."

"Describe them. Give me names."

"Can't remember."

"This is more bullshit. How do you know about unit 19A?"

"That's where they told me to go, to discuss the job."

Minchie's story was highly unlikely. A professional gang wouldn't invite a dimwit like Minchie to their base of operations to give him a low-level try-out job. Things like that usually happened underneath flyovers among discarded shopping trolleys and dumped mattresses or in the back rooms of dodgy pubs.

Savage decided to play along with Minchie's little charade. Eventually, he'd tie himself in so many knots the truth would emerge, or Savage would force it out of him.

"What was the job?"

"I had to make a van full of body parts disappear."

"What body parts?"

"I didn't know at the time. They told me not to ask, but later I found out they were wombs."

"Are you saying that the van full of wombs found abandoned in Camberwell was you?"

"I didn't abandon it. I pulled up on a bus lane to buy some whisky, and when I came out, it had been seized. I was supposed to drive it somewhere then set it alight, destroy the evidence."

Savage shook his head and smiled. "Sounds like a cock-and-bull story to me. You could've seen that on the news. Spun it into a story so you could pretend you had some important information to sell to me."

"Okay. If I'm lying, how come I know about unit 19A?"

"I dunno. Maybe a mate down the pub told you."

"I'm not lying. I was there. It's true."

"Okay," said Savage, taking his keys from his pocket and unlocking his van. "Prove it to me."

"How?"

"We'll go there now. If they know you, they'll open up. Let you in."

"Are you crazy? They'll kill me after what I did."

"I'll kill you if you don't get in."

"No way. You don't know what these guys are like."

"What are they like? You suddenly seem to know a lot about them. Why don't you tell me on the way? Now, get in."

"No."

Savage approached Minchie, who slowly backed away. "Look, Minchie. This is your chance to redeem yourself. Do something right. You can help me find where Bella is, but I need to get inside unit 19A."

Minchie shook his head. "Forget it. These guys are serious, the real deal. I'm not going back there."

Appealing to Minchie's better side wasn't working. He didn't have a better side or care about anyone but himself, which gave Savage an idea.

"You're scared, aren't you?"

"Damn right. And I don't mind admitting it."

"Then let me get them off your back. You know I can. Look what I did to Venables and Hackett. That took me an afternoon. I'll make the problem go away for you. But you've got to get me in there. Otherwise, I can't help you. You'll be looking over your shoulder for the rest of your life. They'll track you down, eventually. I'm surprised they haven't done it already. You're not exactly in hiding, are you?"

"How you gonna do that?"

"Let me worry about it. Now, get in."

The big Londoner hunched his shoulders and nervously played with his ear. "I don't know. Sounds risky."

"Minchie. You're a marked man. You should be dead already. It's just a matter of time before they catch up with you. This way, you've got a chance of getting out."

"How will you change their minds?"

"Say you've come to apologise and have something to offer."

"What?"

"Me. I'll say I'll work for them free of charge for six months. I'm ex-SAS, a trained killer. Hitman. Hard man for hire or whatever. That makes me valuable to an operation like theirs."

"You'd do that for me?"

"Course not. Don't be daft. I can't stand you. I just want to find Bella, which is easier to do if I'm inside their operation. It's a win-win situation for both of us. I get Bella. You pay your debt off to these guys and get to sleep at night."

With more chin scratching and ear tweaking, Minchie looked as though he had a decision to make. In reality, he didn't have a choice. He knew he'd wind up dead if he didn't take Savage's offer. "Okay, fine."

Gingerly, the front door to Theresa's house opened, the security chain across it.

Tannaz's face poked through the gap. "Everything all right, John?" she asked.

"We're good, thanks. Minchie knows the guys at 19A. We're going to check it out. Go back inside."

"Be careful," she said.

"Always am."

CHAPTER 27

A S THEY DROVE TOWARDS UNIT 19A, it loomed up before them like a mini fortress, dark, intimidating and bleak. Razor wire glinted in the moonlight, and CCTV cameras pointed in every direction. The only things missing were a few machinegun towers at the corners.

Savage's VW came to a halt just in front of the gates, engine running. "What happens now?" asked Savage.

"I need to show myself, get seen on the surveillance cameras. Someone will come out." Minchie didn't move, though.

"Go for it, Minchie," said Savage. "You can do this."

Minchie still didn't move.

"You have to get out, Minchie. That's the only way to end this."

Minchie slowly unclipped his seat belt, letting it slowly slide through his fingers until it fully rewound. "I don't know if this is such a good idea. What if they kill me on sight?"

"They wouldn't do that here. Not in front of their base of operations. Want me to stand next to you?"

"Okay."

Both men got out, walked around the front of the van, and stood side by side, directly under the CCTV camera by the one and only gate. Minchie waved his hand to get their attention.

At any moment, Savage expected security lights to come on, drowning them in a blinding glow, and the roller door to rise, spitting out a group of thugs, who would open the gates and hurry them inside.

None of that happened.

Minchie and Savage waited... and waited.

"Does it usually take this long?" asked Savage.

"Never before. Gate opened straight away."

"Okay, we have two possibilities here. Either they're in there and don't want to open up, or no one's home." Savage returned to the car and took out his half-full water bottle from his last visit to the gym.

"What are you going to do with that?" asked Minchie.

"See that CCTV camera up there? It's got a heavy-duty protective housing with a wiper. If the lens gets obscured, the wiper has to be manually operated by someone inside to clear the screen. That'll tell us if anyone's home." Savage popped the small lid open on the bottle, pointed it at the ground, and squirted a little water in a patch of dirt. Using his toe, he mixed it in, creating a small puddle of gloopy mud. "How's your throwing arm?" he asked.

Minchie lifted up his damaged arm. "You broke it, remember?"

"Oh yeah, so I did. I guess I'll have to do this myself." Bending down, Savage scooped up a handful of mud from the road, took aim and threw it at the camera. The pair watched as it flew wide of its mark.

Savage tried again and missed. On his third attempt, he hit the camera square on, splattering the lens with filthy brown gunge.

They waited, looking up at the camera, as mud slid slowly down its screen.

Nothing happened.

Savage did the same thing again with a few of the other cameras, pelting them with mud, just to be sure. Same result—nothing.

"Maybe the power's off," said Minchie. "They could still be in there."

"That's true," said Savage, wiping his muddy hand on his jeans. "But up until now, these guys have been very careful. And most half-decent CCTV systems have separate backup power in case the electricity goes off. My guess is no one's in there."

"Okay, great. Well, suppose we better go back home, then."

"No way. I need to get in and take a look around, and

then you're going to tell me exactly what happened when they recruited you."

Minchie went quiet then piped up. "But how are we going to get past the gates? They're locked." He rattled them with his good hand to prove his point, and they barely moved.

Savage examined the metal obstacle in front of him. "This is an automatic gate with a magnetic lock. Very strong. But also very vulnerable."

Savage walked off, heading in the direction of Alpha Body Works.

"Where are you going?" Minchie cried.

"To find a key."

The repair shop was shut up tight. Savage looked up at the CCTV camera. It was still in its original position, pointing at the roller door, not at unit 19A.

Checking around the side of the building, he found a series of industrial bins, all overflowing with worthless junk: odd bits of car left over from insurance jobs, smashed wing mirrors, mangled plastic bumpers, torn-up tyres, and as luck would have it, a battered piece of filthy aluminium. Savage held it up. It was about the size of a tea tray with odd-shaped holes cut into the metal here and there. He had no idea which part of a car it came from, but that didn't matter. It was a lucky find that should have been locked up inside with all the good stuff they'd sell for scrap.

Savage straightened it out, flattening the thin metal with his hands, and returned to the gate.

"What's that for?" asked Minchie.

"This is our key," said Savage. "Gates like these only open from the outside with a remote control, but from the inside, it's a different matter. If a car wants to leave, it drives towards the gate, which opens automatically. I'm sure you've seen it before in car parks where there's a barrier. The barrier magically lifts when you drive towards it. Most people think this is because there's some sort of pressure pad under the concrete. But it's actually an electrical conducting loop. All we need to do is disrupt the loop, so it thinks a car wants to get out, and this piece of aluminium is going to do the disrupting."

Savage got down on his knees and positioned the flattened aluminium under the gate, then gave it a shove. The metal skimmed across the concrete, coming to a halt about five metres away.

A second later, an electric motor whirred to life, and the heavy gates moved sideways.

"Wow. Where'd you learn that?" asked Minchie. "SAS school?"

"Nope. YouTube."

Savage walked into the compound. "Well, at least we know the electricity's still on."

Minchie waited outside, timidly scratching his ear.

"Come on, Minchie. I'm pretty sure they'd be out here by now. If they were here."

Minchie reluctantly followed, attempting to make his six-foot-plus frame appear smaller, as if that would somehow save him if angry gangsters suddenly came rushing out.

They crossed the wide, flat expanse of concrete between the fence and the building, heading for the one and only means of entry, the roller door. Savage tried lifting it, but it was locked up tight.

"So how do we get through that?" asked Minchie.

"With a more traditional approach," Savage replied.

"What's that?"

"Drive my van into it very fast," said Savage.

"Bit harsh, innit?"

"How did you think we were going to get in, by osmosis?" Savage jogged back to his VW, started it up, revved the engine, and accelerated toward the roller door. Minchie leaped out of the way. The little VW punched through the door with a loud boom, making it collapse in on itself. The whole door broke free of its mountings and landed on top of the van. Savage immediately backed up, dragging the mangled door with him. He got out and started untangling it from his van.

"A little help, please." he said.

Minchie dawdled over.

"No rush. We're now guilty of breaking and entering, so it's not urgent."

"Okay, no need to be sarky."

"Well, get your arse in gear." Savage attempted to lift the door off the top of the bonnet. "This is for your benefit too."

"I don't see how," said Minchie. "They're not here."

A loud clunk from somewhere behind them punctured the air.

Looking behind himself, Savage saw the large metal gate closing, trapping them inside. Minchie saw it too. He made a run for the gate but arrived there just as it slid shut. Desperately, he pulled at it with his one good arm in an attempt to reopen it, but the gate didn't budge, so Minchie swore instead and ran back to Savage.

"They're still here," he said. "Make the gate open."

"Oh, no," said Savage, panic all over his face. "You're right. Here they come."

Minchie dived for cover behind the little VW and curled into a ball with his good hand over his head.

Savage watched the large quivering wreck on the ground, let him squirm there for a few seconds, then said, "Get up, you numpty. The gate's on a timer. It closes automatically after a minute or two."

Minchie emerged from behind the van, eyes darting left and right. "Really?"

"Yes, really. No one's here but me and a big wuss."

"Don't do that to me. It's not funny." Minchie climbed to his feet and brushed himself off.

"Real smooth, Minchie. Now, help me get this door off my van."

Together, they pulled and tugged at the mangled door, Minchie managing to be of very little assistance with only one functioning hand and stopping every second to look around in case the gang were about to leap out from somewhere.

Once the door was off, it revealed the newly deformed front end of the VW: a flattened bumper, two broken headlights and a bonnet that had been pushed back into a snarl. The car was still drivable, but Savage would be making another trip to Alpha Body Works sooner than he'd thought.

Savage opened the passenger door of the VW and took a full-size Maglite torch from the glove compartment. The heft of the black metal flashlight always felt good in his hands, reassuringly heavy and robust, especially if he was going into the unknown.

"Why do you need a torch?" asked Minchie. "I thought you said the electricity was still on."

"Just a precaution." Savage liked the fact the Maglite was big and solid enough to double as a club, should the need arise.

"Can I have a torch?" asked Minchie.

"Nope," said Savage.

As they entered the building, a metallic tang immediately hit their nostrils. Savage flicked on the torch and found a panel of light switches. He ran his hand down all of them. One by one, a series of strip lights clinked and pinged until they illuminated a large rectangular storage space.

Completely empty.

They were standing on a concrete floor zigzagged with black tyre marks where trucks had rolled in and out. The walls were stark, built from grey breeze-block. Nothing was there but dust and the smell of metalwork.

In the left-hand corner was another door, and to the back, two sliding double doors had been left ajar. Savage headed over to them, pushing them open a little wider. Minchie followed, shadowing Savage.

Inside, Savage flicked on more lights and found himself in a similar-sized space, also empty. All over the floor were equally spaced square markings where the concrete was lighter, a sign that something had once stood there, probably metalworking equipment, judging by all the offcuts scattered around the floor like breadcrumbs. Shards of metal sheeting and tiny lengths of right-angled protective edging were mixed in with metal filings and odd-shaped lumps of black foam. Savage picked one up and rolled it in his fingers. It was dense, high-quality stuff and had a give in it, but it retained its shape well, shock-proof foam for protecting something expensive. He guessed the location must have been their dummy operation, but he had no idea what that was.

Something caught Savage's eye. In the corner of the room lay a short length of discarded clear tubing, coiled up like a snake. Savage picked it up and looked it over. He'd seen that type of tubing before in army field hospitals. It was an IV tube for feeding a solution into a patient's arm from a drip. He balled it up and put it in his pocket.

In silence, the two men searched the facility, a small knot of anger forming in Savage's gut. He already knew nothing was there to help him find Bella. Like a cliché from a million movies, he'd arrived too late. The place had been abandoned long ago, cleaned out.

The two men returned to the main storage area and headed to the door in the far corner. It led to a long corridor with doors on both sides. The first room had been an office. The only evidence of that was a white board screwed to the wall and wiped clean.

The next room down the corridor was large and spotless, with one wall completely lined with cupboards and a large double sink. Savage thought it might have been the kitchen, but it didn't smell right. Kitchens usually leave behind a residue of cooking smells, old food and stale milk once they're abandoned, but that room had none of those. It smelled too clean, too clinical, so maybe it'd been a lab. Savage checked every cupboard and again found nothing.

Back out in the corridor, they came to a series of equally spaced doors. Each door had been heavily reinforced with metal plates and secured with a large sliding bolt. A spy hole had been installed three quarters of the way up.

Savage pulled back the bolt to the first door and slowly pushed it open.

Inside, the room was a perfect cube, a holding cell with a bare light set into the ceiling, protected by a metal grille—again, empty. Though it had been scrubbed clean, the room retained a faint whiff of urine. On the bare breeze-block wall, Savage noticed something bright red stuck in the pale mortar—a broken fingernail.

"Have you seen any of this before?" asked Savage.

Minchie shook his head. "I only got as far as the loading bay."

"If this is a trafficking operation, then I'm guessing this is where they kept the girls before sending them off," said Savage. "Keeping them sedated, probably. Using an IV drip." He pulled the medical tubing from his pocket.

They moved through each cell, checking each one in turn until they stood in the final one at the end. Like all the others, it was empty.

Savage had nothing—no paperwork, no forwarding addresses, no clues. The gang had left nothing behind. He still had Minchie, though.

"So tell me, from the start. What happened when you came here last?"

Minchie swallowed and looked at a point on the floor and concentrated on it. "Well, I turned up at the gate with a stolen van. Got out, showed my face. The gate opened, and I backed it through the roller door."

If Minchie was telling the truth, perhaps the gang weren't as smart or well organised as Savage had thought. They'd made one mistake—hiring Minchie. Then they'd made a second mistake— letting him inside the place. "Who was there?"

"Just a load of guys. Normal blokes."

"Were they older, younger, British, foreign, white?"

"White. Same age as me, really. You know, just blokes. But there was this one guy who seemed to be in charge. Fat guy with a beard. He had an accent."

"What sort of accent?"

"Dunno. I'm crap with accents."

"Was he Middle Eastern, South African, Asian, European...?"

"Definitely European."

"Southern Europe or Northern Europe?"

"What's the difference?"

"Northern would be German or Scandinavian, Southern would be Italian, Spanish."

"Northern. Liked his fry-ups, if you know what I mean. A right fat git."

"What was his name?"

"Dunno."

"Did you catch any names?"

"No."

"Okay, tell me what you saw."

Minchie licked his lips. "There were machines for making packing crates. You know, like the ones roadies use to put equipment in."

"What did they used them for?"

"Dunno. They were just sitting there."

As Savage had suspected, the place was just a front. Building packing boxes for air freight would be a completely believable business to hide behind should anyone come snooping around, especially being so close to Heathrow Airport. "What else?"

"There was a big blue plastic bag lying on a pallet."

"With the wombs in it?"

"Yeah, but I didn't know that at the time. I was told to shut up and listen carefully."

"Who told you this?"

"The fat guy with the beard. He said I had to burn it with fire, destroy it completely. So I opened the back of the van, and two guys lifted it in."

"What else did you see?"

"Nothing."

"So how did you hear about Bella?"

"Oh yeah, so as I'm closing the back doors of the van, I overhear this guy say—"

"Which guy?"

"The one with the beard. I heard him say something about Bella Tucker. I remembered it because Bella lives round my way."

"What did he say about her?"

"Didn't catch what he was saying. Just caught her name."

"Then you drove off across London."

"Yeah, to a building site I know, south of the river. But I left the van on a bus lane. Next thing I know, it's on the news, a bag full of human wombs left abandoned."

Savage paced up and down the small cell, churning over the information in his mind. "You're very lucky to still be alive. That was a major failure, and gangs like these don't tolerate failure. You should be dead."

"I know."

"The only reason I can think of that you're not dead is because they've shut up shop. But these people don't leave loose ends, and they're patient. They'll send someone eventually to bury you or just dump you in a vat of acid."

"You're just trying to put the frighteners on me," Minchie said, pulling at his ear again. "They'd have done it already."

"Not if they've got bigger things on their plate. Listen, it's not a question of if but when, believe me. They'll send someone back here or hire someone. Look on the bright side: you probably won't even know it's happened. Quick death."

Minchie walked to the farthest wall of the cell and gently banged his head against it. While Minchie's back was turned, Savage swiftly exited the cell, closed the door, and slid the bolt across, locking him in. A second later, Minchie was pounding on the door, shouting to be let out.

Savage said through the door, "Okay, Minchie, tell me what really happened, and I'll open the door."

CHAPTER 28

"IT'S THE TRUTH! I'VE TOLD you everything. Open the door!" Minchie's voice had been growing hoarse ever since Savage had locked him in the cell at the end of the corridor.

"I'm sure someone will find you eventually." Savage sat on his haunches, back against the wall in the corridor, waiting for the truth to emerge from Minchie's lips. "Maybe one of the gang will come back here. That'd be interesting, wouldn't it? I wonder if you'll still be alive when they get here."

"Let me out, please!" His voice was a childish scream.

"Just tell me the truth."

"I've told you everything I know."

"You've told me a bullshit story."

"Why don't you believe me?"

Savage sighed. "Because a gang as smart as this wouldn't employ an idiot like you. They wouldn't let you anywhere near this place. You expect me to believe you just happened to get a job with them? And you just happened to overhear Bella's name? It's all too convenient. So tell me what really happened."

Silence.

"I can't."

"You're not getting out of here until you tell me."

Silence followed, then more banging on the door accompanied by Minchie swearing his head off.

Savage laughed. "You can bang all you like. But you're not getting out until I hear the truth."

More silence.

Eventually, Minchie said, "I'll tell you, but you have to let me out."

"Okay, I promise."

Savage waited. From outside, he could almost hear Minchie's brain straining as he thought everything through, slotting his memory of events into the right order. He hoped it wasn't going to be another bullshit story.

Minchie spoke slowly and calmly. "They put the word out that they were looking for a redhead to snatch."

"Who did?"

"This gang. They were very specific. Natural redhead, dark eyebrows and lashes. Not dyed. Must be natural. I'd known Bella for years because she lived round my way. I always had the hots for her. Never got anywhere. Thought she was better than me. And that really got my back up."

"Maybe she just didn't fancy you," Savage replied.

"Nah. She looked down on me, she did. Like I was a lowlife."

"Yeah. She's kind of right, though."

"Listen, she was a snobby little bitch."

Savage got impatient. "Minchie, carry on talking like that, and you won't see daylight again."

"Sorry."

"Keep going."

Minchie paused then continued. "So I put the word out that I know someone who's just what they're looking for. A couple of days later, I'm walking back from the pub, and three guys shove me in an alley, say they want to know who this girl is. I tell them that I want to speak to their boss first. They say they'll be in touch and leave. Two days later, a car pulls up, and the fat guy is in the back. He tells me to get in. He asks me who the girl is and where they can find her. I ask him, 'What do I get out of it?' He hands me an envelope full of cash. I tell him I don't want it—what I want is a job. At the time, I was fed up with working for Venables. Wanted something different. Anyway, this guy laughs and says that's a first. But he likes this, asks me if I want to be part of something big and important, something that's going to make a difference, so I say hell yeah. So after he agrees to give me a job, I tell him about Bella and where he can find her."

"Then what happened?"

"They wanted to get a look at her in the flesh. If she's what they're looking for, they said they'd be in touch about making me part of their operation. Then I got out of the car."

Getting a look at her in the flesh was almost certainly when she'd received the invite to Club Zero. They wanted to check her out, to get close to her without actually spooking her, and the easiest place to do that was in a loud, crowded nightclub. "Did he mention inviting Bella to a club to get a look at her?" asked Savage.

"No, not to me. But they did say she had a very important job to do."

"Where, what job?"

Groaning sounds came through the metal plates of the door as Minchie tried to remember. "Puerto something. Puerto..."

"Come on, Minchie. This is important."

"Yeah, I know. Puerto... Puerto Vanuse. I think."

"Do you mean Puerto Banus, in Spain?"

"That's the one. Puerto Banus."

"That's where they sent her?"

"Yes."

"Are you sure?"

"Definitely."

Puerto Banus was a Spanish playground for the rich southwest of Marbella. You couldn't move for Sunseekers, designer shops, and Ferraris. It had exclusive nightclubs in the same league as Club Zero and a booming industry in hookers to service the young billionaire playboys who would roll into town on giant yachts. If Bella had been traded to work in one of its brothels, Puerto Banus would definitely fit the bill, and her distinctive Celtic looks would go down well with a certain clientele.

"And you're sure they said she had a job to do?" asked Savage.

"Yeah, course."

"They didn't say anything about her being sold to an individual, a client?"

"Don't think so. No, they definitely said she had work to do in Puerto Banus."

At last Savage had a lead, a solid lead. Most likely, Bella had been put to work in a brothel rather than sold to a fat billionaire. The former, though not as appealing, was actually better than the latter. If she'd been sold as a companion for a playboy, she'd have been put on his yacht and never seen again. At least this way, a fair chance existed that Bella was still in Puerto Banus, working in a club.

Minchie banged on the door. "Okay, Savage, let me out. I've told you the God's honest truth."

"I believe you," said Savage. "This is good intel you've given me."

"So let me out."

"Before I do that, is there anything else you want to tell me?"

"Nope, that's everything. Now open the door, Savage."

"Because if I find out you've kept something back, then it'll be better for you if you stayed in this cell."

Silence.

"Well, Minchie?"

"The packing cases, they're not a front."

"What do you mean?"

"They use the cases to get the girls out of the country... by air."

"I don't understand."

"To make it easy to get them out of the country," Minchie explained, "they drug them up, stick them in metal boxes, and send them as air freight."

With a sickening lurch in his stomach, Savage understood all too clearly.

CHAPTER 29

A COLD RAGE SWEPT ACROSS HIM like a gathering storm. That new piece of information chilled and shocked Savage, and he didn't shock easily. The gang had created a brutally efficient factory for trafficking girls, a holding pen where boxes would be custom built to fit each girl so they could be sent to nearby Heathrow and loaded aboard a cargo plane for export to the highest bidder. Vile and inhuman, it contained a sinister logic. Moving people across borders was risky. They had to be sent in large numbers to make it financially viable, and that meant the chance of detection was high, so most traffickers would throw the net wide, luring naïve girls from poor Eastern Bloc countries with the promise of high wages. This gang, however, specialised in the premium end of the market. Customers would buy to order on an individual basis, and the high cost of sending a girl in a box as air freight could be offset by the even higher price she would fetch at the other end, minus her womb. If done properly, it would raise no eyebrows. No passports were needed. The process was neat and tidy and left no trail.

Once in the box, for all intents and purposes, the girl would disappear off the face of the earth. Savage assumed she'd have to be properly sedated so she didn't become conscious halfway through the flight. Waking up trapped inside a box, she would die from the stress, and more importantly for the gang, they'd lose their investment. The dosage would be critical, which explained the presence of a lab. They'd certainly need somewhere to administer the sedative dose.

A glacial chill crept down Savage's spine. He thought he had seen some pretty despicable things in his time, but this was off the chart.

The more he thought about it, the more it made diabolical sense. Unlike passenger travel, security around air freight was far less strict, with fewer checks. To earn a place in the hold of a plane, all an item of air freight needed was a certificate of secure status. Those were issued by regulated agents who put an item of cargo through a large X-ray machine big enough to drive a van through. If they saw nothing suspicious, the cargo was cleared for the next step of its journey, the hold of a cargo plane. The gang would need someone on the inside to turn a blind eye to the living human being imprisoned inside the crate—not a problem. They'd either pay someone off or threaten them, just as they did with the manager of Club Zero.

Once in the cargo hold, the girl in the box would need to survive the flight. Cargo holds were pressurised just the same as the cabin, so that wouldn't be a problem, but the cold would. News stories abounded with horrific tales of stowaways freezing to death in the undercarriage of planes. At thirty thousand feet, the temperature could easily drop to minus forty, but the hold is a different matter. It was kept about ten degrees lower than the cabin, not exactly arctic but not comfortable, either. From all the offcuts of foam Savage had seen on the floor of unit 19A, the gang must have used the high-density foam to act as protective padding, probably cutting it to mould snugly around the occupant of each crate, ensuring they arrived in one piece. With a girl cocooned in all that foam, the cold wouldn't be a problem. After being fitted with an oxygen mask, a cylinder of air, and maybe a drip to keep the human cargo sedated, they could be sent anywhere in Europe, ready to be picked up by any scumbag brothel owner at the other end.

The wicked trade of human trafficking was horrible enough, but the gang had managed to make it even more depraved. Savage would relish taking them down once he got Bella back safely.

"Savage, are you still there?" Minchie's panicked voice interrupted Savage's thoughts.

"I'm here."

"So, you going to let me out now?"

"Nope."

"You promised!"

"Minchie, you're the reason Bella went missing. And you've been part of a ring that kidnaps young girls..."

"And men."

"And men... and puts them in boxes and sends them to work as sex slaves."

"I didn't do that bit. Well, I did the first bit..."

"Minchie, you're getting off lightly. I should put you down right now for what you've done." Savage flicked the light switch off and left Minchie in the dark, banging his fist on the door and cursing Savage's existence. He walked back down the corridor, Minchie's protests diminishing with every step he took, until eventually he couldn't hear them at all. With any luck, no one would find Minchie.

Outside, Savage found his VW where he'd left it. He fired up the engine and headed back to his flat. Along the way, he called Tannaz, knowing she'd still be up.

"John, are you okay?" Tannaz asked.

"I'm fine. Are you still at Theresa's?"

"Yeah, she's gone to bed, though. Do you want me to wake her up?"

"No, but when she does, tell her there's some good news. Minchie's given me a positive lead on Bella. I think she's in Puerto Banus."

"Where's that?"

"Spain. I'm heading to Heathrow now to catch the next flight."

"I'll come with you." Savage heard the excitement in Tannaz's voice.

"No, I need you to stay there with Theresa and get what you can from the Club Zero database."

"I'm tearing it apart as we speak."

"Good work," Savage replied, narrowly missing a red light. "And keep your phone handy. I may need some IT support."

"Yeah, of course."

Savage hung up. Twenty minutes later, he pulled up outside his flat, ran in, and grabbed his passport and a handful of euros he had stashed away—he could always change more at the airport. In less than two minutes, he was out of the flat and back in the VW again. He didn't bother to pack or bring a bag. Bags slowed him down going through security, especially at the other end. If he didn't have to wait for a bag, he could get straight off the plane and straight into a cab and into Puerto Banus to find Bella. Besides, he could get anything he needed once he landed.

Before driving off, he fiddled with his smartphone, searching for the next available flight to the airport in Malaga. Fortunately, it was midweek, the end of September. The kids were back at school, and holiday season in Britain was over. He found a seat on a British Airways flight leaving at six forty a.m. He booked it, returned his phone to his pocket, and headed straight to Heathrow, Terminal Five.

He reached the terminal at four in the morning, and it was quiet but by no means empty. Travellers booked on early flights were scattered throughout the departure lounge, trying to sleep on seats not meant to be slept on. Thankfully, a handful of bars and businesses were open twenty-four hours. He changed some money into euros, bought himself something to eat, and sat down to figure out his next move.

As Savage sipped his tea and ate his sandwich, he flicked through his phone, searching brothels in Puerto Banus. The town was quite open about its prostitution. He even found a "red map" detailing all the venues where one could pay for sex or hire an escort. Each one had its own website detailing its services, as if it were as easy as hiring a caterer or an electrician. The girls who worked the clubs were professionals. They probably even paid taxes and had accountants to make the most of all the money they made off the town's wealthy tourists. Everything was above board. That wasn't what Savage was looking for. The girls who worked those places weren't slaves. They got to go home at night. To them, what they did was a job, just like working in a supermarket or an office, except they could make ten times the amount. What Savage was looking for was the layer below that: the clubs that weren't advertised, where the girls weren't free to leave because they were bought and owned. Those places were off the radar and harder to find.

Savage felt confident, optimistic even, but one thing that still wouldn't fit, no matter how much brain power he forced into the problem, was the trafficked men. Both Minchie and the owner of Club Zero had told him that the gang took just as many men as they did women. He still couldn't figure out the economic benefit. The desires of heterosexual men fuelled sex trafficking, and while he could understand the need to satisfy people who wanted men or boys, that really didn't merit the numbers the gang was snatching. Sure, a market for it existed, but compared to the market for girls, it certainly wasn't fifty-fifty. It probably wasn't even seventy-thirty. The fact remained that the gang had taken all these fit, healthy young men, but the reason for doing it eluded Savage.

It didn't matter. All that interested him was finding Bella and getting her back. His gut told him he was getting really close.

CHAPTER 30

T HE THUD OF THE WHEELS hitting the tarmac jolted Savage awake. The flight had been uneventful, which suited him just fine. He'd slept through most of it, waking only to order tea from the trolley. Once the plane had come to a halt by the terminal, the captain welcomed everyone to Malaga Airport and informed them of the local time and temperature: 10:30 a.m. and an agreeable twenty-eight degrees Celsius.

With no bags to slow him down, Savage cleared security and customs quickly. As he stepped outside the terminal, a heady mix of fragrant Mediterranean air mixed with diesel and aviation fumes greeted him. Above him, a generous sun shone in a pristine blue Andalusian sky, and below, he could almost feel the heat from the pavement seeping through the soles of his shoes.

Savage walked past the rows and rows of taxi drivers, leaning on their bonnets, all smoking, chewing gum, and touting for business. He had rules for choosing taxis. He never chose the first one he came across or the second or the newest or the poshest, for that matter, and never the tattiest. Walking a little farther, he saw exactly what he was looking for. A small Spanish man of pensionable age leaned over an old silver Mercedes C Class, cleaning the insects off the bumper, taking pride in its appearance. It was a good fifteen years older than all the other taxis but gleamed as though it had just driven out of the showroom. The vehicle had clearly been maintained and serviced properly, and anyone who did that was all right in Savage's book.

He approached the driver, who was impeccably dressed with a crisp white short-sleeved button-down shirt, beige linen trousers and slip-on deck shoes. "How much to Puerto Banus?" asked Savage.

The man turned and smiled. His eyes were alert and brown, and he smelled of aftershave.

"Fifty euros one way."

He didn't see the point in haggling when someone offered a fair price. "Okay. Deal."

The driver smiled and opened the rear passenger door for him. Savage hopped in.

Once the taxi had driven out of the airport and its satellite industrial areas with their dusty car parks, it wove its way along the A-7, a well-kept tarmac toll road that snaked between the mountains and the sea.

Savage liked the driver because he didn't talk. He didn't play the radio, didn't make any calls along the way and kept his eyes on the road. He was in the hands of an old-school professional, which made Savage relax. He let himself gaze out at the Andalusian landscape scrolling past his window. Sleepy towns came and went. Cloud-crested mountains loomed up and then shrank into the distance. Muscular concrete bridges stretched across deep river valleys. The ever-changing landscape lulled him into a hypnotic, almost meditative state. It reminded him of his SAS days when his squad were en route to a job. Something about travelling always put him at ease, even when he was going into a war zone. Maybe because he could relinquish control to a pilot or, in this case, a taxi driver for the time being. While his mates would be jittery, tapping their feet uncontrollably, talking nonstop or fiddling with their weapons, Savage would be at his most peaceful, the calm before the storm. Then, when they got word they were a click away from the target, Savage would come back to the land of the living, focused and ready to fight, almost as though the small window of meditation had allowed him to draw on a secret reserve of energy. His buddies hated him and admired him for it, that he could muster such tranquillity just before the killing started, that he could switch between peace and aggression in a heartbeat. They saw it as an advantage. Savage had always wondered whether it made him a borderline psychopath.

A blue sign above the motorway indicated the turn off for Puerto Banus. As the driver flicked on his indicator, Savage came out of his trance and resumed business as usual.

"Where you want to go?" asked the driver.

"Somewhere I can buy clothes," Savage replied. He was still dressed in his London civvies, heavy blue jeans and a sweatshirt.

The driver dropped him off at a massive department store on the outskirts of the town. He wanted to avoid looking like a tourist, so he simply copied what the taxi driver had worn. He bought a white shirt, beige linen trousers, slip-on deck shoes and a pair of knock-off Ray-Ban Wayfarer sunglasses. He wore them out of the store, dumping his old clothes in the nearest bin.

A short walk later, he stood looking down the Avenidas de las Naciones Unidas, a grand boulevard fringed with palm trees and wide expanses of lush green grass and neatly manicured box hedges leading down to a glittering sea. A throaty rumble came from behind. A convertible Lamborghini Huracan flashed past him, quickly followed by a red Aston Martin DB11, drag racing as if they were in a video game. No one else on the street batted an eyelid—just another day in Puerto Banus.

As he walked toward the beach, more indications of the wealth of the town became apparent. The shops lining the avenue were a mixture of cosmetic surgeons, designer-label shops and posh cafés where one would easily lose ten euros just by ordering an espresso.

At the end of the Avenidas de las Naciones Unidas, a thick Doric column rose into the clear blue sky about one hundred feet, topped with a statue of some shirtless Greek god with his hands in the air. It was pretty apt because before him was a beach filled with tanned men who had the body of Adonis and bikinied women who had the looks of Aphrodite. Beautiful people were everywhere, scattered across the arc of wide yellow sand. They stretched out on sun loungers, sipped cocktails brought to them by waiters, or played in the surf with their six packs and plastic breasts on show.

To the left of the beach, the marina stood out like a box of delights. Row upon row of multi-million-pound yachts stood idle against their wooden jetties. He wondered if any of them actually made it out to sea or if they were just there as floating party venues whenever the rich felt the urge.

Savage shook his head. This was so not his world.

Standing in the sun, taking in the whole circus around him, Savage realised his shirt was already patched with sweat. He walked across the beach, past the palm trees, umbrellas and sun loungers to the water's edge. The air was marginally cooler down there. The sea lapped lazily against the shoreline. He kicked off his shoes and plunged his feet into the clear turquoise water. It certainly wasn't Peckham High Street on a wet Saturday morning. He walked a little farther and rented an umbrella and sun lounger at the end of the row. After adjusting its position so that he'd be in shade all afternoon, he checked the time: one thirty, far too early for anything to happen yet. The places he needed to go to wouldn't be open until well after the sun went down, so he leaned back, closed his eyes, and went to sleep, preparing for the long night ahead of him.

A clacking sound woke Savage from his beach slumber. He opened one eye to see the sun hanging low in the sky, dipping towards the mountains at the end of the bay, throwing splashes of red and orange onto the clouds in the west. The clacking sound continued. Glancing to his right, he realised he was the last person stretched out on a sun lounger. Two beach attendants hurried from umbrella to umbrella, closing them up with clockwork precision in a bid to get home on time.

Savage took the hint, stretched and got to his feet. He checked his phone for the time: six thirty.

Savage's stomach rumbled. He couldn't remember the last time he'd eaten. As one of the beach attendants snapped Savage's umbrella shut, he pointed at the beach bar behind them and asked if it was any good.

Without losing his stride, the guy replied, "It's okay. The one next to it is better."

"The Malibu Bar?" Savage stared at the place, a surf-themed bar decorated with flower garlands, ancient longboards screwed to its roof. Tables made of thick slices of tree trunk with straw umbrellas were scattered all over the sand. Waiters in Hawaiian shirts bustled from table to table, holding trays of drinks aloft.

"Yes," said the beach attendant. "The calamari is really good."

"Okay, thanks."

Savage made his way toward the Malibu Bar, its soft reggae tunes drifting over the sand. He needed a good meal before starting work, and a large plate of fresh calamari and fries would do just the job. As he got closer, he noticed every table was taken, full of hot, rich young things eating, drinking and laughing, still dressed in their beach shorts and bikinis. Savage took a stool at the bar and ordered his food, plus a tea to drink while he was waiting.

Savage liked the place. It had a nonthreatening, laid-back atmosphere. Boys mixed easily with girls, taking their time with their drinks and in no hurry to get drunk or laid. Maybe that was what having money did for people.

A different kind of laughter caught Savage's attention. It was the macho kind, the unmistakable sound of alpha males, beer and banter. Savage edged along the bar to get a closer look. Five men in their mid-fifties sat at a table, smoking cigars and knocking back beers with whisky chasers—English, of course. Loud, proud and badly dressed, they were away from their wives, probably to celebrate a birthday or maybe just a boys' jolly without the old ball and chain. Overexcited at being let out to do whatever they wanted, they jeered at every pretty girl that passed their way even if she was a third of their age. They spat out crude jokes about the things they wanted to do to each girl, making everyone nearby feel uncomfortable.

Savage hated them.

They were perfect.

CHAPTER 31

THE BEACH ATTENDANT WAS RIGHT. The calamari tasted heavenly, but Savage didn't have time to savour it. He had work to do. Savage settled up and asked the barman if he could direct him to the nearest tobacconist. After locating it down one of the back streets behind the beach, Savage bought himself the cheapest cigar he could find.

He returned to the bar, approaching it from the end where the group of English guys were sitting. He wandered up to them, their deep-throated guffaws filling the air.

"Excuse me, gents," Savage said, holding up his unlit cigar. "Could I trouble you for a light?"

"Why certainly," said the nearest guy, leaning over to offer Savage a lighter. The guy had his shirt off, revealing a red sunburned paunch. His hair had that seventies style to it, long over the ears and around the neck. It'd been dyed brown, presumably to cover up his grey, and it was thinning too, but he'd styled it so that it hung in a centre parting, camouflaging the receding corners of his forehead.

Savage accepted the lighter from him, a tacky heavy gold one. He clicked it a few times and sparked his cigar to life. He hated cigars normally and was careful not to keep the smoke in his mouth too long. "Thanks," he said, puffing out smoke, trying not to choke as he handed back the lighter.

At that moment, a young girl in a skimpy yellow bikini pushed past. "What I like about Puerto Banus," said Savage loudly, nodding towards the girl's behind as she shimmied between the tables, "is the wonderful view." He cringed inside as he said it, but that was the kind of crass locker-room banter those idiots loved.

"Damn right," said the guy who'd lent him the lighter. "I'm Frank. Care to join us?"

"Don't mind if I do. The name's John, John Savage." One by one, they all leaned forward and shook his hand.

"Whose round is it?" one of them asked.

"It's yours, Frank," said a guy in a baseball cap, sitting opposite.

"Are you sure?" Frank asked, getting to his feet. He was tall and skinny with rounded shoulders, giving him the appearance of a hunched-up bird. "I think the last time I saw your wallet open, a couple of pterodactyls flew out."

They all laughed.

"At least I don't have to ask my wife's permission before I open my wallet," replied the guy in the baseball cap.

A collective groan arose, as if a challenge had been laid down.

"How is your wife?" asked Frank. "Last time I saw her, she was making me breakfast."

"Sit down, Frank," said Savage. "I'll get this round."

"Now, this is my kind of guy," Frank replied.

"Yeah," said baseball cap man, "someone who pays for your round."

"Beers and whisky chasers for everyone?" asked Savage.

Everyone cheered.

Savage couldn't believe how easy it was to play those guys. With a round of drinks and a bit of crudity, he was in with them.

Savage shuffled over to the bar and ordered five San Miguels and five whisky chasers for the guys at the table, but for himself, he ordered an apple juice in a whisky glass and a non-alcoholic beer. He got the barman to pour the alcohol-free beer into an empty San Miguel bottle, so to all intents and purposes, he looked as though he was joining in with the drinking.

The barman smiled. "Smart move. Those guys have been at it since lunchtime."

"Really?" said Savage. "Please let me apologise for my countrymen's behaviour."

"Oh, it's okay. They've spent plenty of money."

Savage smiled and paid the man, telling him to keep the change.

He returned to the table with the tray of drinks. Hands dived in, making a grab for the bottles of beer and shots of whisky.

"On three," said Frank. "One, two, three."

They downed their shot glasses in a single gulp, including Savage with his apple juice. Then they switched to the beers without missing a beat, raising their bottles in the air.

"What shall we drink to?" asked one of them.

"Freedom," said Savage. "I've just got divorced."

They cheered, clinked their bottles, and took large slugs of beer.

"Good for you," said Frank. "On a divorce honeymoon?"

"Yep, it's my treat for getting away from the bitch." In his head, Savage said a little prayer, asking his wife to forgive him, telling her everything was a pantomime to get what he wanted from those guys. "And now, I'm ready to start putting the old fellow to good use again." He patted his crotch.

More cheers erupted around the table.

"Hey," said Savage, "you wouldn't happen to know any good places where I could get some action?"

"Mate, Puerto Banus is full of great sex clubs. It's the Costa Del Sex. That's why we came here, but it depends what you're into."

"Everything," said Savage. "The worse, the better."

"You're a man after my own heart," Frank replied. "See, there's plenty of brothels here, and they're okay, but if you want the good stuff, the no-holds-barred stuff, you've got to come to this one place."

"Where's that?"

"Place called Neon. You can do anything you want to the girls, and I mean anything."

"Really?" Savage opened his eyes wide with enthusiasm even though he was repulsed.

"Yep, straight up," said Frank, looking round conspiratorially. "It's a normal brothel out the front, but there's these skanks they've got in the back you can use and abuse any way you want. And believe me, I have."

Under the table, Savage's hand made a tight fist. He wanted to drive his knuckles through the prick's face and out the other side, but he had to keep his cool.

"Sounds perfect. That's where I'm going," said Savage.

"Bit tricky," said Frank. "You have to be introduced by someone if you want to go out back."

"Oh, so how do I do that?"

"I could probably get you in. They know me. Been there the last few nights."

"So how did you get in?"

"We got talking to this Spanish businessman one night in a bar by the marina. He was off his nuts. Drove us there in his Range Rover, swaying all over the road. We were all too drunk to care. He got us in. It was unbelievable the things I did to this one girl—"

Savage didn't want to hear. He was using all his self-control not to beat Frank black and blue with a beer bottle, so he cut him off. "I need to go to this place."

"What, right now?"

"Why not?"

A mischievous grin split Frank's face. "You're definitely my kind of guy, John. Hey," he said to the rest of the guys, "anyone up for an early excursion to Neon's?"

"Maybe later," said baseball cap man.

"I need food and a shower first."

"Yeah, I can smell you from here," replied another.

"Tell you what," said Frank. "Why don't I show John the delights of Neon, and we'll meet you guys there later?"

The rest of the guys agreed and carried on drinking while Savage left with Frank. They walked a short way off the beach, close to where Savage had bought his cigar, until they reached Frank's holiday apartment. He disappeared inside to quickly shower and change into some going-out clothes. Savage waited outside, leaning on a low wall. He thumbed away on his phone, trying to search the internet for Club Neon. He found no mention of it anywhere, which was a good sign. That was the kind of place Bella was most likely to be.

He thought about calling Tannaz to get her to see if she could find Neon on the dark web. Maybe they would have pictures of the girls on offer. Maybe Bella would be among them. Then he figured there was probably no point. First, he was about to go there in person and check it out for himself. Second, searching the dark web was a risky business, even for someone as talented as Tannaz. He knew what she was like. She wouldn't be content with just a quick "drive-by" search of Neon. She'd start finding out who owned it and getting dirt on them, which could get her exposed and put her in danger. Bella might not even be in the place, so Savage didn't see a point in putting Tannaz at risk.

The door opened, and Frank emerged, doused in a cloud of aftershave. He wore double denim—shirt and jeans, belted at the waist and buckled with a large brass lion's head, roaring.

"That's quite a buckle you've got there," said Savage.

"I know. Cool, huh? I bought a load of them. I'll sell you one if you want. We'd look like a couple of cool dudes, walking down the street with the same buckles."

Savage couldn't think of anything less cool than matching lion-head belt buckles. "Nah, I'm good, thanks," said Savage. "Saving my money for all the action ahead."

"Damn right, amigo."

Frank flagged down a taxi, and they both got in the back. Unlike the one that had transferred Savage to the airport, it smelled of sweat and had holes in the seats, patched over with gaffer tape.

The taxi took them away from the glamor of Puerto Banus and a little way up the motorway in the direction of the airport. Ten minutes later, they pulled off a slip road and into a modest-looking seven-storey apartment block with a gravel parking area out front.

"Is this the place?" asked Savage. "It looks a little quiet." The sun had gone down, and apart from the roar of the motorway in front of the building, the whole place seemed deserted.

"Don't be fooled. It's what's inside that counts." Frank smiled wickedly.

Savage paid the taxi driver, and the two men got out. Frank led the way across the car park and around the far side of the building to a dark alleyway. Halfway down, two lights poked out of the wall, glowing at head height. As they got closer, a small staircase came into view, leading down to a large metal maintenance door flanked by two large men leaning against the wall. They were playing on their phones, the glow of the screens lighting up their faces. Savage followed Frank down the steps.

"Buenas noches," said Frank.

The two men barely acknowledged Frank's existence, still engrossed by their phones. The one on the left pushed himself off the wall and reached over with one hand to knock on the door. Savage heard locks clicking. A second later, they were ushered into a small, darkly lit lobby, where two more doormen patted them down. Savage could hear the *thump, thump, thump* of dance music coming from behind another door on the opposite side of the lobby. When the doormen were satisfied Savage and Frank were clean, they let them into the club. As the door opened, the heavy beat of the music flooded over them.

Frank walked in, raised his arms aloft like a prophet and said, "Welcome to Club Neon."

Everything was black: black walls, black ceiling, black tables, black chairs, black sofas. However, it had all been edged with glowing pink neon, from the bar to the stage and every available corner including the edge of the stairs. It looked like the film set of a porn movie set in space. Bare-breasted girls in tiny pink hot pants crisscrossed the floor, delivering drinks to middle-aged men stretched out on high-backed sofas who each had a girl on their lap. On the stage at the back, two girls were having sex with each other. They looked like twins.

"Ain't it great?" shouted Frank over the noise of the music. "Watch this." As a waitress walked past, Frank grabbed her breasts and started fondling them. The pretty little Spanish girl with large brown eyes stopped and smiled, letting Frank carry on as if it were nothing.

Savage had to look away.

"John, you've got to have a go on these," Frank said.

Savage kept his back turned. "I'm saving myself for the main event," he said.

While Frank carried on feeling up the waitress, Savage scanned the club for Bella, but he could see no sign of her. All the girls he saw looked like working girls, not sex slaves. They certainly weren't being held against their will. They were all busy earning a living, judging by the money they were getting tipped. Every so often, one of the girls would take a customer and lead him by the hand to a corridor at the side of the club. She'd take a towel from a rack in the corner, as if the place were a health spa, and disappear with the guy into one of the rooms down the corridor, where Savage guessed they'd be paid to have sex. Savage moved closer to get a better look.

"You don't want to go down there," said Frank. He'd finished with the waitress and stuffed a ten-euro note into her microscopic shorts. He smacked her backside to send her on her way. "That's not where the good stuff is. Unless you want straight sex. We want to be over there." Frank pointed at a darkly lit door at the side of the stage, guarded by a bouncer. "That's where the all-you-can-eat buffet is, if you know what I mean." Frank laughed like a chimpanzee.

Savage forced out a smile. "Then what are we waiting for? Lead the way."

Through the mass of half-naked female bodies and seedy middle-aged men, Savage followed Frank towards the door, stopping several times so Frank could touch several different girls. Eventually they made it to the door, after Savage had to drag Frank away from a tall, blond Scandinavian girl. As they approached the door, the bouncer stepped out of the way to let Frank through, but when Savage tried to follow, he got a hand planted on his chest.

CHAPTER 32

"WHO ARE YOU?" ASKED THE bouncer.

"It's okay," said Frank. "He's with me."

"Does he know the rules?" asked the bouncer.

"What are the rules?" said Savage.

The bouncer explained, "You walk through this door, you pay one thousand euros. No negotiating. No refunds. You can do what you want to the girls, anything. No hitting in the face, and no pictures, no video. No posting on internet. Okay?"

"Okay," said Savage, his stomach churning like a cement mixer. He pulled a roll of euros from his pocket.

"Not here," said the bouncer. "Pay inside."

The two men stepped through the door and closed it behind them. Savage heard it lock. They went through another door and found themselves in a plush living room, carpeted, with elegant sofas and oil paintings on the wall. Gentle classical music filled the air, but they could still just about hear the pounding of dance music from the main club. A large mirrored coffee table sat in the middle of the room, complete with a bucket of iced beers, several bottles of spirits, and rows of shot glasses. A bowl of white powder, which Savage presumed was cocaine, had been placed on a tray together with a neat line of tiny silver spoons. At the far end of the room lay a corridor similar to the one out in the club. Four identical bedroom doors sat on each side, eight in total, plus one large metal door at the very end. At the entrance to the corridor were shelves stacked with rolls of clean white towels.

Frank spooned himself a helping of coke from the bowl and

snorted it, followed by a shot of whisky. He offered them to Savage, who declined both.

"What happens now?"

"We pay, and then we select."

The metal door at the end of the corridor opened. Through it came a tall, slender Spanish lady, elegantly dressed in a black halter-neck evening gown that reached down to the floor—the madam of the establishment, Savage presumed. Her coal-black hair was glossy and smooth, tied back into a severe bun that looked tight enough to give her a headache. A bouncer followed behind, a really big one, possibly Samoan. Dressed in a suit and tie, his neck was wider than his head, and he looked ready to burst out of his clothes at any moment. As he walked toward them, his shoulders reached nearly across the full width of the corridor.

"Good evening, gentlemen," the madam said. "Please, help yourself to as many refreshments as you want."

Frank took another hit of coke.

She continued, "Before I bring the girls out, it's our policy to take payment first. This is non-refundable, of course."

"What happens if you don't have the girl I'm looking for?" asked Savage.

"I'm afraid that's our policy Mister...?"

"Savage."

"Mr. Savage. We have some beautiful girls on offer today, and you're free to do with them as you please, but we do insist on payment up front. If this is not acceptable, please feel free to leave, and no payment will be taken from you." She smiled.

"John, honestly. These girls are amazing," said Frank. "And they're so young." He kissed his fingers in that way chefs do when something is delicious.

All that did was make Savage feel sicker.

"Okay, I'll stay." Savage reached into his pocket and counted out a thousand euros then handed the notes to the madam.

The price was worth seeing if Bella was among them. Frank handed over his money, too. The madam took the money and gave the nod to the bouncer. He pulled a key from his pocket and walked back up the corridor, one by one unlocking each bedroom door. Then he turned and waited at the end, in front of the metal door, arms by his sides. Savage noticed his suit jacket hung unevenly, sagging on the right. The fabric bulged around the jacket pocket of the same side. The Samoan was definitely carrying a firearm in that pocket, its weight making the suit jacket hang askew.

Eight young girls emerged sheepishly into the corridor. Possibly in their late teens or early twenties, they looked around like frightened mice. Once they were all out in the corridor, the bouncer gave them a gentle shove, making them head in the direction of the lounge where Savage and Frank sat. The bouncer followed them in. *A modern-day slave market.*

The eight girls took a seat on the sofa opposite. He'd never seen a group of girls so terrified. Eyes cast down at the floor, they were dressed in tatty lingerie, positioning themselves to preserve their modesty, legs closed and arms crossed over their chests. Savage scanned up and down the line.

Bella was not among them.

The youngest, at the very end, looked no older than eighteen and had a fading black eye, poorly covered up with makeup. *So much for not hitting them in the face.* She tightly held the hand of the girl next to her. They looked like sisters. Her elder sister had slicked-back hair, an attempt to make her look vampish. The bouncer cleared his throat and glared at the elder girl. She immediately let go of her younger sister's hand. The girl directly opposite Savage had scabby welts around her wrists. The one next to her had a neat line of cigarette burns on her thigh, like dots of Morse code. Another had red marks around her neck.

They were in a living hell.

"Now, girls," said the madam. "Smile for our guests."

The girls did their best to look happy, forcing out artificial grins, but their eyes betrayed them. They were rimmed with sadness, hollow and empty, as if their souls had been torn out.

"Well, I know which one I want," said Frank, getting to his

feet and smiling at the youngest girl at the end. "Come on, Inga, you're going to make me a very happy man."

The girl shook with fear. Her elder sister spoke quickly in her ear, trying to calm her or maybe warn her of the consequences of disobeying. The young girl remained on the sofa, shaking her head and mumbling something. Savage couldn't quite place the language—not Russian but something similar like Finnish or Latvian, definitely a Uralic language.

Frank stood in front of her. "Oh, come on, Inga. I'm not that bad."

The madam signalled to the bouncer, who grabbed the girl and dragged her along the corridor. When he reached the last bedroom on the left, he threw her in like a rag doll. Frank followed her into the bedroom, rubbing his hands together excitedly. Savage heard the lock click from the inside. The bouncer returned and took up position next to the girls, glaring fiercely at them as a warning not to step out of line. Each one of them looked down at her feet.

"And what about you, Mr. Savage? Which girl would you like?" asked the madam.

"I was really looking for a redhead. Do you have one here?"

"I'm sure we can get one for you. It might take a few days. In the meantime, why don't you go with Sabine? She's a very good girl."

The girl with the slicked-back hair looked up, the one he presumed was the elder sister of the girl who'd been dragged away. She looked at Savage, trying to smile, but the corners of her mouth trembled.

"Yes, Sabine is very beautiful, but I'm really looking for a redhead." Savage got to his feet. "Maybe I'll call back in a few days."

"As you wish," said the madam. "I'm afraid we can't refund your money."

"No problem," said Savage. The money didn't matter, as he was using the cash he'd taken from Hackett. "But maybe you'll give me a small discount next time."

"I'm sure we can come to some arrangement."

The madam ushered Savage back out into the club. The door closed behind him, and he found himself standing next to the bouncer, who looked slightly puzzled that Savage had returned so quickly. Savage nodded at him and walked across the club toward the exit. A girl with severe peroxide hair and silicon breasts the size of two footballs put her arms around him, telling him she could put a smile on his face. Savage must've looked downcast after what he'd just seen. He could feel bile climbing up his throat, burning its way into his mouth. He pushed past her, politely telling her he wasn't in the mood.

Girls far from home were being held captive, to be abused by horrible middle-aged men, but Bella wasn't among them. Savage resigned himself to the fact that he might have to trawl several more vile hellholes before he found her. The prospect made him nauseous, but it would have to be done.

He was just about to leave when the voice in his head piped up.

"I can't believe you're leaving."

"What do you want, Jeff Perkins?" Savage muttered under his breath. Luckily, the club was dark and noisy, and nobody noticed him talking to himself.

"Those girls—you can't just leave them there."

"I'm here to find Bella. I can't get side-tracked."

"You hypocrite."

"Oh, since when do you get all morally superior? Last time we spoke, you wanted me to kill myself."

"Still do. But that's for another day. Right now, you're alive, and you could help those girls."

"I told you I can't get side-tracked. I'm here to find Bella." Savage continued walking to the door.

"Bullshit. You could get those girls out of here before the night's over. Besides, where are you going now? You've got no leads to follow."

"I'll try some more clubs."

What clubs? These places don't exactly advertise.

"I'll go back to Puerto Banus, ask around. Find some more

dickheads like Frank. Maybe get Tannaz to do some digging, look on the dark web."

"*Hypocrite.*"

"Piss off, Jeff."

"*You know I'm right.*"

"I thought you were the voice of my post-traumatic stress, not my conscience."

"*Maybe I am. Maybe I'm both. Doesn't matter. You know I'm right.*"

"Look, I'm sorry. There's nothing I can do for them." Savage reached the exit.

"*What if it were your daughter in there?*"

Savage stopped just short of the door.

The thought of his daughter in a place like that made him shudder. Each of those girls had a mother and father at home worrying about them. He hated to admit that the voice was right for once. He could do something for those girls without affecting Bella's investigation. One night would not make a difference, but in that time, he could get them their lives back, freeing them from that terrible place and the hideous trauma they faced every night. Chances were they didn't have much longer to live. Soon, the accumulated beatings would become too much. Clients wouldn't want them anymore, and makeup could hide only so much. They'd be used up and tossed out like trash, left for dead, their bodies probably dumped in some ditch off a lonely dirt road in the mountains, to make way for another young girl to take their place and be abused.

"You're right," said Savage.

"*What's that?*"

"I said you're right."

The bouncer near the exit looked at Savage, puzzled at the guy in front of him talking to himself, although he'd probably seen people do things a lot stranger than that. Savage backed away from the door, toward the centre of the club.

"*Is the great John Savage admitting he's wrong?*"

"Okay, don't get too smug."

"Let me just savour this moment."

"Shut up now, Jeff."

"Just say it. I was right, and you were wrong."

"Jeff, shut up. I need to concentrate."

"So are you going to help those girls?"

"Yes. Now, if you don't shut up, I'm going to change my mind."

"Okay, so what's the plan?"

CHAPTER 33

T HE SAME BOUNCER STOOD GUARDING the door by the
stage, his arms folded, head slowly moving from left
to right, scanning for signs of trouble. He locked onto
Savage when he saw him approaching.

Savage smiled and said, "I'm ready for another session. Got
my thousand euros right here." He patted his trouser pocket.

The bouncer didn't smile or respond but just unlocked the
door and let Savage through. Savage went in and heard the door
lock behind him. Back in the lounge area, the girls were still
sitting on the sofa, cowering at the black shape of the madam, who
paraded in front of them, hands on her skinny hips, screaming
something at them in Spanish. The Samoan stood impassively to
one side, arms crossed over his chest. He cleared his throat when
he saw Savage, signalling to the madam that they had company.
She stopped abruptly, turned, and switched on an artificial smile,
as if nothing had happened.

"Mr. Savage, you're back again."

"Yes, I am."

"You would like a girl now, yes? It will be another thousand
euros, I'm afraid."

"Well, actually, I'd like all of them."

"You would?" asked the madam, fearing it was too good to
be true.

"Yes."

She clapped her hands together gleefully. "Well of course, Mr.
Savage. Come, come, take a seat. Have a drink, perhaps maybe
something a little stronger." She gestured to the bowl of white

powder on the mirrored table. "The price is still the same, I'm afraid, one thousand euros for each girl. No group discounts." She laughed, trying to be charming.

"Sorry, you misunderstand me," Savage said. "I would like to buy them."

"Buy them?"

"Yes, all of them."

"I thought you liked redheads," said the Samoan. His voice was deep but strangely quiet.

"I do," Savage replied. "They're not for me." He took a seat and helped himself to a beer. He took a small sip then reclined as if he was at home in front of the TV. He crossed his legs and brushed some fluff off his linen trousers. "They're for my men. I've got a hundred-and-fifty-five-foot Sunseeker parked in the marina, with a crew of nine. The men get restless away from home. As you know, men have needs, and a bit of companionship would help. Plus, whenever I have guests on board, female entertainment always goes down well." He took another swig of beer and nonchalantly checked his phone as if he had more pressing business to attend to.

"You don't look like a millionaire," said the Samoan.

The madam shot him a glare.

Before she had a chance to chastise him for speaking out of turn, Savage asked, "And what does a millionaire look like?" He didn't wait for an answer. "Five minutes ago, I just paid one thousand euros for nothing, basically to sit in this room and look at some girls. How many people do you know could afford to lose a thousand without batting an eyelid?"

The madam swallowed and said, "Apologies for my colleague's disrespect, Mr. Savage, but the girls are not for sale."

Savage put his beer down abruptly, put his phone away, and fixed the Spanish woman with a pair of cold, unblinking eyes. "Everything is for sale," he said in an icy voice. "My first offer will be one million euros. You will relay this to your boss. He will no doubt make a counter offer... which I will decline. I will make another, more sensible, offer and then we will probably meet in the middle. That is how business is done. Either way, I am leaving with these girls and their passports. Now, go and see your boss. I will wait here."

Savage knew that one million euros was well over the asking price for eight trafficked girls who had already been used and abused. Her boss would think he'd been handed the deal of the century, especially if he could hike the price up even further. Greed was a universal language that those people understood. The offer was too good not to pique his interest.

"One minute, Mr. Savage," said the madam. She disappeared through the metal door at the end of the corridor.

The Samoan didn't bother to lock it but just stood there, blocking the way to the corridor like some medieval gatekeeper, never taking his eyes off Savage.

Savage looked the Samoan up and down. He really wanted to hurt him and make him pay for the misery he'd put the girls through. They were clearly terrified of him.

"Have you ever watched *Game of Thrones*?" Savage asked him.

The guy shook his head.

"You remind me of this one character."

The Samoan looked blank, impassive. "Who's that?"

"Big guy called Hodor. You're just like him."

The Samoan didn't bite but just stood there like a dumb tree trunk. Savage's attempts to goad him into a fight weren't working, which was just as well. As much as he wanted to stamp on the guy's windpipe, that wouldn't be a good idea. First, it would scare the girls, and they could end up getting hurt. Second, the commotion would scupper his plans for getting in front of the boss and getting the girls' passports back. The boss wasn't about to have an audience with a so-called millionaire who was downstairs beating up one of his men. Savage reined in his tongue, thinking, *You'll get your comeuppance soon enough.*

Savage glanced across at the girls on the sofa, sitting motionless like seven petrified kittens—all except the one at the end. Sabine, with her slicked-back hair, kept eyeing Savage cautiously, stealing glimpses of him as though working out whether life would be better being owned by him than it was being imprisoned as a punch bag for Club Neon and its clientele of violent sex tourists.

He wanted to reach out to her, to all the girls, and tell them everything was going to be okay, that they wouldn't have to endure this miserable existence for much longer, and soon they would go back home to their families, to being young girls again. He couldn't tip them off to his intentions just yet. He had to play the arsehole millionaire for a little longer.

A muffled scream broke the silence. It came from one of the bedrooms down the corridor. Sabine jumped, reminding Savage that her sister Inga was still in there with Frank.

"How long is this going to take?" Savage asked.

The big guy just shrugged. A second later, his mobile buzzed. He answered it briefly then hung up.

"Follow me," he said to Savage.

Savage got to his feet and followed him through the metal door into a small, squarish lobby, harshly lit by bare fluorescent tubes. The Samoan locked the door behind him. To the left was a flight of metal stairs with open risers. Through the gaps, he could see an emergency fire door with a horizontal push bar. He gestured for Savage to climb the stairs.

"Hold on a second," said Savage, not going any farther. "Where are you taking me?"

"Boss's office at the top of the stairs."

"Is this one of those setups where you lure me into a room, knock me over the head, and steal all my money? Who's up there?" Savage was playing the frightened tourist to find out what he was up against.

"Relax," said the Samoan, "It's just my boss, Miss Lopez—"

"The Spanish lady?"

"Yes, and Garcia."

"Who's Garcia?"

"The boss's bodyguard."

"That's all?"

The Samoan nodded. Savage had all the intel he needed. He

faced two, possibly three men with guns, including the boss. Miss Lopez might also be armed, a concealed weapon strapped to her inner thigh. That settled it. He would need to acquire a weapon as soon as possible, and he knew just how to get one.

"Okay," said Savage, "After you."

The Samoan shook his head. "You first."

Savage knew he'd say that. As a security procedure, he'd want Savage in front of him, going up the stairs first so he could keep an eye on him, which was perfect for what Savage had in mind.

Looking at the stairs, Savage counted seventeen risers. As he climbed them, he counted each step in his head. When he got to number nine, he spun around and front kicked the Samoan, who was a couple of steps lower than Savage. The Samoan was completely unprepared. Being a couple of steps behind, the big guy was a good foot below Savage. That put his head directly in the firing line of Savage's foot, which hit him square in the nose. His head snapped back. The huge bouncer had nowhere to go except down. Gravity sent him crashing to the floor below, where he landed on his back, knocking all the wind out of him. The drop must've been at least seven feet, but Savage knew that wouldn't keep a guy that big down for long, so he leaped after him, landing square on his chest, driving his heels into the guy's rib cage. Savage felt the bones in the Samoan's chest crack and give way beneath him. But Savage still wasn't convinced he had put him out of action. To be sure, he dived for the Samoan's right-hand suit pocket, snatched the gun, and double tapped him. One bullet in the head. One in his chest.

If the fall hadn't alerted the people upstairs that something was wrong, then the gunshots would have. Savage turned to face the stairs, crouched down beside the dead Samoan, and aimed the gun toward the top step. It was a Glock 30, small, powerful and accurate. With a ten-round clip, it was the go-to concealment weapon. He brought his left hand underneath his right, cupping it for support, and aimed just above the top step.

A second later, a large bald man in a suit appeared on the landing above, gun raised, searching for the source of the gunfire.

Presumably, he was Garcia, the boss's bodyguard. By the time Garcia locked onto Savage, crouching next to the Samoan's body, Savage had fired two shots. Both of them hit Garcia in the chest, sending him reeling backwards, out of sight. Savage scrambled up the steps after him. Reaching the landing, he saw Garcia flat on his back, unmoving. Two large red stains on his chest were growing in size. Savage put another one in his head just to be sure.

Up ahead of him, the door to the boss's office was open. Nosing it open with the muzzle of the gun, Savage scanned left and right to make sure no additional bouncers were lurking there. When he was satisfied, he entered the office, gun raised. Plainly decorated with a few filing cabinets and a squat, chunky safe in a corner, the uncarpeted room was bleak and cold. A small weaselly man sat behind a desk, his body barely filling his navy-blue suit. Two small black eyes of coal stared out from his skull-like head with a mouthful of ratty teeth between two sunken cheeks. To one side of the desk stood Miss Lopez.

Their expressions weren't ones of fear, more of anger, perhaps annoyed that they'd let themselves be duped so easily.

"You're a very foolish man, Mr. Savage," said the weasel behind the desk.

"Sorry, who are you?"

"Fitch," he said. "And I have at least twenty men in this place. They'll have heard the gunshots and will be here any second."

Savage shook his head. "No one's coming, arsehole. That's the trouble with owning a nightclub where the music's too loud. No one's going to hear gunshots over that racket, especially not back here. Now, give me the girls' passports."

"Those filthy bitches belong to us," Miss Lopez hissed.

Savage shot her in the side of her left knee. She collapsed on the floor, writhing in agony, clutching her leg joint as blood spilled through her fingers.

"Give me the girls' passports." Savage pointed the gun at Fitch.

"Is that supposed to scare me?" he said. "Do you know who I am?"

Savage shot him in the forehead, right between the eyes.

He'd heard it all before, the do-you-know-who-I-am speech. In Savage's experience, it always came out of the mouths of egotistical psychopaths who had no idea of the consequences of their actions. People like Fitch didn't respond to threats, even in the face of impending death. Savage would be wasting his time. The guy would rather die than give him what he wanted, so he spared himself the trouble. Lopez, however, was a different matter.

Savage stood over her as she wriggled in agony. "Give me the girls' passports," he said, pointing the gun at her.

"They're in the safe," she managed to say.

"Then open it."

"Only Fitch had the combination."

"Don't bullshit me. A second ago, you said 'Those bitches belong to us.' *Us* is a collective pronoun. That implies you and Fitch are partners. Sorry—*were* partners. So you'd both know the combination."

"I don't have it."

Savage crouched down beside her. "Listen to me carefully, Miss Lopez. You've got the chance to come out of this with little more than a limp right now. However, I'll put another bullet through the back of your good knee. Open it up like a party popper, ligaments and tendons all over the place. Now, give me the combination."

She shook her head.

Miss Lopez cried out in agony as Savage rolled her over onto her side and jammed the muzzle of the gun into the back of her right knee.

"I won't ask again," Savage said, pushing the barrel deeper into her good leg.

"Okay, okay."

"Good." Savage hopped over her to the safe in the corner. Slowly and with great effort, Miss Lopez called out the combination. It clicked open the first time. Inside was a pile of burgundy European Union passports of the Latvian Republic and a stack of several thousand euros held together with elastic bands. He counted up eight passports and flicked the first one open. It was Inga's. Compared to the person who had been dragged into the bedroom, the girl in the passport photograph was almost unrecognisable. Her eyes were bright and lively, full of optimism, and her cheeks were plump and rosy. A beautiful, innocent girl, she'd been robbed of her youth. Snatched away by Fitch and Lopez.

Savage's anger flared. "Changed my mind," he said and put a bullet in Lopez's head. He had to. If she survived, she'd take over the business since Fitch was out of the way and carry on enslaving girls. He couldn't let that happen.

Savage stuffed the passports into his pocket, together with the stacks of euros, making both sides of his trousers bulge. He left the office, slotting the gun into the back of his waistband and hurried down the stairs, stopping briefly to retrieve a set of keys from the Samoan's trouser pocket.

After unlocking the metal security door, he went straight to the bedroom where Inga and Frank had gone. He kicked down the door. Inside was more of a torture chamber than a bedroom. A bleak cell with all sorts of contraptions screwed to the walls. In the middle, on top of a padded table, Inga was gagged and tied. Frank had his belt in one hand, holding it by the buckle. Savage didn't dare imagine what Frank was going to do with it.

CHAPTER 34

FRANK LOOKED AROUND, ANGRY AT being disturbed. "John, what the hell are you doing here?"

Savage punched him on the chin and snatched the belt out of his hand. Wrapping the end of it around his fist, Savage held it like a medieval flail and swung it at Frank's head, smashing the buckle into his temple. Frank yelped, clutched the side of his head and collapsed to the floor. Savage hit him again, on the other side of his face, slicing open his right cheek, then threw down the belt beside him. "Go back to your wife, arsehole. You're lucky to have one."

Turning to Inga, Savage gently removed her gag.

"Don't worry, Inga. I've come to get you out of here," Savage said softly.

The girl didn't respond but just lay on the padded table in shock, eyes staring into nothing, a cat's cradle of ropes holding her tightly in place. Savage searched the room. One wall had a board screwed to it, covered in hanging tools, like someone might have in a garage to keep everything within easy reach. Among them, Savage spied a Stanley knife. He unhooked it and sliced through her bonds. The rough hessian ropes fell away.

Savage lifted Inga up in his arms and carried her down the corridor into the lounge. She was light and delicate, like a little bird. Savage kept telling her everything was going to be okay. He doubted whether she heard or understood any of it.

Back in the lounge area, the girls hadn't moved from the sofa. They were huddled together, eyes wide with terror. When they saw Savage carrying Inga, they pushed their bodies closer together, scared and confused about what that meant for them, as though some cruel, new exercise were about to commence.

"I've come to get you out of this place," Savage said, "but we must hurry."

None of them spoke.

They were gripped by fear. It pinned them to the spot, preventing them from making any sort of response or rational decision in case it was the wrong one.

"Please," said Savage. "You need to trust me. We must go now."

None of the girls moved.

"Do any of you speak English?"

Still nothing. Sabine's eyes flashed with recognition, though. She seemed to be the only one who understood what he was saying. Silenced by fear, she still didn't respond.

Savage took a different tack. He'd have to be cruel to be kind.

"Get up, now!" he shouted, fire in his eyes, as if he were giving an order to a group of fresh army recruits. "Come on, move!" He kicked the end of the sofa.

Anger was the only language they understood. It was the last thing he wanted to use on those poor girls, but it was the only way to get them out of there.

Sabine spoke rapidly to the other girls in Latvian. Savage hoped she'd translated what he'd said. The girls obeyed, standing to attention.

They followed Savage, who still carried Inga in his arms, to the end of the corridor and through the metal door. Stepping over the Samoan's lifeless body, they went underneath the stairs to the fire exit, where Savage kicked the horizontal push bar. It opened onto a darkly lit car park at the back of the building. They could just make out the shapes of cars parked nose first against the building. Presumably, they belonged to everyone who worked at Neon.

"Sabine," Savage said. "In my left pocket is a set of keys. Take them out."

Sabine understood and shakily retrieved the Samoan's keys. Attached to the key fob was a remote control with an Audi symbol.

"Point and click," Savage instructed.

Sabine held up the remote control and began pressing the unlock button, pointing it in various directions. Several clicks later, a vehicle lit up, blinking its lights.

"Let's go," said Savage.

The Samoan's car was an Audi Q7, a roomy, luxury seven-seater SUV, possibly not his. More likely, it was Fitch's, and the Samoan chauffeured him around in it. Neither of them would be using it again, anyway. Savage laid Inga in the front seat and told Sabine to sit next to her. He went to the rear of the car, opened up the hatchback and ripped out the parcel shelf, tossing it on the ground, then folded out the two extra seats in the boot. He pointed at two of the girls and gestured for them to get in.

They didn't move. Maybe they didn't understand.

Sabine leaned out of the passenger door and said something rapidly in Latvian. The two girls climbed in.

The remaining four Savage told to get in the back seats. They were squashed, but the car was large enough to fit them all in.

Savage got behind the wheel, started up the engine, and reversed out. A second later, they were on the motorway.

"Where are you taking us?" asked Sabine in a quivering voice.

"The airport," said Savage. "You're all going home." He reached into his pocket and pulled out their passports.

Sabine took them and handed them out to the girls. They clutched them as if they were life preservers.

"But first," Savage added, "we're going shopping."

The time was just after nine when Savage pulled into the car park of the big department store by the motorway. That was one handy thing about being in a resort town: the shops stayed open late. Savage found a space near the entrance, parked, and killed the engine.

He turned to Sabine. "Don't move. Don't get out of the car. Don't let anyone get out of the car. If anyone approaches you, beep the horn, and keep beeping it. I won't be long."

Savage ran into the store, its cool temperature, bright lights, and soothing music a surreal contrast to the place he'd just come from. He ran up the escalators to the clothing department and searched until he found sportswear. Hunting through the racks, Savage didn't know what he was looking for, but then he came across a display full of matching sweat suits—hooded tops and bottoms dangling from hangers. It gave him an idea. He grabbed an armful of navy-blue ones, more than he needed, not bothering to look at the sizes. That would take too much time. Just buying lots and lots was better, and he would hope the law of averages would ensure some would fit. *Safety in numbers.* He dumped them at the nearest cash till, a mountain of navy-blue cotton in front of a smart young man with a bow tie and an apron.

"Put these through," said Savage. "Back in a second."

With the sound of the scanning gun beeping behind him, Savage went back to the racks and pulled eight identical navy-blue rucksacks from their hooks. He returned to the cash desk, the boy still clicking the tags of hooded tops and jogging bottoms with the gun.

"These too," said Savage, dropping the bags onto the counter. "Where are your sports shoes?" he asked.

The boy pointed, and Savage trotted over to where an unfeasibly large choice of sports shoes covered an entire wall. Hundreds of little individual shelves were there, each holding up a single right-hand shoe to try on, not what someone in a hurry wanted to see. He spun around, trying to think of an alternative, and found it. Behind him were stacks and stacks of shoe boxes filled with every colour of canvas high-top basketball shoes. Savage found a row of navy-blue ones and pulled out as many boxes as he could wedge under his arms. When he got back to the cash till, the young boy had bagged everything up in two ballooning white carrier bags. He looked horrified when Savage scattered more products on his counter to scan. All credit to the kid, he went through them like a machine, bagging them as he went. Savage slapped some of the euros he'd taken from Club Neon on the counter. He didn't wait for his change but just scooped up the massive bags and zigzagged down the escalators, running all the way.

As in all department stores, for some reason he couldn't fathom, the cosmetics department dominated the entrance, dotted with concession stands like little islands across the marble floor, for all the big brands, lorded over by beautiful women in far too much makeup. He stopped at the first one, where a stunning Spanish woman with thick, glossy black hair down to her shoulders and a red dress smiled at him.

"Buenas noches," Savage said, "Makeup wipes?"

"Of course." She reached into the cabinet in front of her and laid several different tastefully designed packets in front of him, as though they were fine pieces of jewellery. "This one has micro algae and a firming agent with—" She didn't get to finish her spiel.

"I'll take it." Savage scattered more of Club Neon's money on the counter. He snatched the wipes, stuffed them in the top of one of the bags, and headed outside.

His shopping detour had taken less than ten minutes.

Back at the car, the girls were exactly where he'd left them, still and unmoving, clutching their passports to their chests. Inga had climbed onto her sister's lap, her head resting against Sabine's chest, arms wrapped around her like a koala. They jumped when Savage opened the door.

"Okay, ladies. We have wipes if you want to get rid of your makeup. And I've bought you some clothes and shoes to change into so you don't have to walk into the airport in your underwear." Savage pushed the huge carrier bags onto the laps of the girls in the back seat.

Like giant clouds full of clothes, the bags took up all the space, obscuring the view out the back window.

"We need to get going," said Savage. "So dig in and find your right sizes. Okay?"

Nobody responded.

"Girls, you need to put them on while I drive. Please."

Sabine spoke rapidly in Latvian. Tentatively, one of the girls in the back pulled a makeup wipe and smeared it around her face, cleaning off the layers of cosmetics. She handed the packet to the girl next to her, who did the same.

Savage started the car, drove out of the car park and pointed it in the direction of the airport.

When the girls had finished cleaning their faces, they delved into the bags, trying to find the right sizes. The car was a tangle of limbs and clothes as the girls wrestled to try on tops and bottoms in the confined space. Arms and legs went everywhere. Pulling over to let them get out and change would've been easier, but Savage couldn't risk stopping. The car would certainly have a tracker, and someone would come after them very soon.

So far, the girls had been quiet, but easy chatter soon drifted around the car as the girls searched for their right sizes. Tops got swapped and bottoms exchanged. One girl even giggled a little as she put on a sweatshirt that drowned her. The simple act of trying on clothes seemed to give the girls back a small measure of dignity.

Inga, however, remained mute. Savage glanced sideways as her sister wiped her face, revealing the huge bruise under her eye. Sabine selected some clothing and pushed her sister's arms and legs into them as if dressing a toddler. All the while, Inga's eyes looked like two dark tunnels, bleak and hopeless.

"She'll be okay," Savage said.

In reality, she would probably never get over the ordeal. None of them would, but at least they were free.

"Thank you," said Sabine. "For helping us."

"Don't mention it."

The car went quiet. Only the hum of the engine was audible, along with the thrum of tyres on tarmac.

"Is this what you do?" asked Sabine. "Help girls like us?"

"Sort of," said Savage. "I came here to look for a missing girl for a friend of mine. She was taken like you."

"What's her name?" asked Sabine.

"Bella. Bella Tucker." Savage reached into his pocket and pulled out his phone. He risked taking his eyes off the road to thumb the screen until a picture of Bella appeared. "Here." He handed the phone to Sabine.

"This is her?" Sabine studied the image.

"Yes."

"I know this girl," she said.

CHAPTER 35

SAVAGE WANTED TO PULL OVER to interrogate Sabine and get answers out of her, but that was out of the question. First, he couldn't stop until they were all safe inside the airport. Second, Sabine had just had the most traumatic experience a young girl could go through. He didn't want to add to her misery by making her relive everything, but that was the best lead he'd had since getting there. He had to try, treading carefully and choosing his questions wisely.

"Was she at the club?" Savage asked gently.

"No," Sabine replied. "But sometimes I would see her at the marina."

"The marina? Where all the big boats are?" Savage feared the worst. If she'd been put on a boat, she could be anywhere, perhaps thousands of miles around the other side of the world.

Sabine handed Savage back his phone. "The men at the club would take us there sometimes. A rich man on a boat would pay money to have us for a few hours. Then they would take us back to the club."

"And did you see her on a boat?"

"No. But when we were taken on the boat, I would sometimes see her, sitting at a café by the water, drinking coffee."

"Was she with anyone? Did she look scared?"

"No. She looked rich. I wished I could be her. She was free."

"Are you sure it was her?"

"Yes. She is very different—her fiery hair."

"And how many times did you see her?"

"Five, six times."

"And when was the last time?"

"Maybe a week or two ago."

A fizz of adrenalin hit Savage's bloodstream. Bella could still be in Puerto Banus. "One more question, Sabine."

"Of course," she replied.

"What was the name of the café?"

"Sophia's."

"Sabine, that's fantastic. You may have saved Bella's life."

"Really? She did not look like she needed saving."

That new piece of information didn't fit with the facts so far. Trafficked girls looked like Sabine and her friends. They didn't hang out in cafés at the side of marinas full of multi–million-pound yachts, watching Ferraris drive past. The question was, did she want to be found? Maybe he'd read the situation wrong. Maybe she hadn't been trafficked but just wanted to start a new life someplace else. Perhaps Theresa hadn't told him the whole story. If the two of them had fallen out, there was a strong possibility that Bella had simply run off without telling her mother where because she didn't want to be found. If that was the case, she'd have a right to be left alone. After all, she was an adult. However, he owed it to Theresa to at least get some answers out of Bella and to tell her that her mum was worried sick and wanted her to come back home or at least ring her and let her know she was all right.

Turn-off signs for the airport appeared along the edge of the road. Savage pulled onto the A-7 motorway, heading down a large curving slip road. Two kilometres later, they arrived at the dropping-off zone in Malaga Airport. Savage parked the car between a minibus and a taxi. A large, lofty concrete canopy spread out above them, supported by columns that looked like abstract trees. Savage clicked the Boot Open button on the dash and told all the girls to get out and wait for him on the pavement. He took the Samoan's gun from the back of his waistband, cleaned his prints off it, and locked it in the glove compartment.

Through the windscreen, he noticed the girls standing there, head to foot in navy blue, rucksacks slung over their shoulders. He'd made a good choice with their outfits. To the casual observer, they appeared to be a sports team on their way home from a tour. The girls stared up at the vast airport structure, overwhelmed at being outside, at being free. They were back in the land of the living and were quickly adapting. Their mouths moved rapidly as they chatted excitedly. Even little Inga had some life back in her eyes, not exactly hope but maybe a lack of despair. She watched people and families as they hustled past, reminding her that normal life still existed and was waiting for her.

He looked around the inside of the car, strewn with discarded sweat tops and bottoms and empty shoe boxes, some of them still untouched, the shoes still in them. After wiping the steering wheel and instruments clean, Savage got out of the car and locked it, found the nearest storm drain, and dropped the keys down it. Then he joined the girls on the pavement.

"Okay, if anyone asks you," said Savage, "you say that you're one half of a hockey team, coming back off a tour. That will explain any bruises you have." As Sabine translated, Savage continued. "Now, let's see if we can get you a flight home."

They trouped across the road, Savage leading the girls as if he was their coach. Inside, the airy departure lounge echoed with the sounds of whiny flight announcements and busy people dragging wheeled luggage behind them. Savage quickly found the information desk and discovered a Lufthansa flight was leaving for Riga, the capital of Latvia, at midnight. They hurried over to the Lufthansa desk, where Savage used the money he'd taken from Club Neon to book the eight girls on their flight home. Next, they lined up at the check-in desk to get their boarding passes. They were on their way home.

When they'd finished checking in, Savage reached into his pocket and pulled out the remaining euros he'd taken from Fitch's safe, divided them roughly into eight equal shares, and handed them out to the girls. Each share must have been just over a thousand euros.

Dumbfounded, the girls stared at the money, probably because they'd never seen so much cash before.

"This is ours?" asked Sabine.

Savage nodded. "That's all yours." He wished he could've given them more, after what that place had put them through, but even if it had been a billion euros, that wouldn't have been enough. "Put it safe in your rucksacks," Savage said. "You'll need some for buses and taxis home after you land."

Sabine looked at him with big, innocent eyes. "Could we buy some..." She struggled to find the right word, conferred with her friends, then turned back to Savage. "Candy?"

"Well, you really need to go through security now."

All eight girls looked at him with puppy-dog eyes.

"But yes, I suppose it's okay."

A wave of smiles spread across their faces. Excitedly, they jogged across the concourse to a large airport shop that sold everything from magazines and large cartons of cigarettes to tacky souvenirs. Savage followed along behind, cautiously looking for any signs of men from the club. He saw none, and if any were there, they would be highly unlikely to try anything in an airport with armed police wandering around. However, Savage wouldn't be able to relax until the girls were safely on the other side of the security barriers. He felt he really should have insisted they go through and use the shops on the inside. However, it was too late, and they looked as though they were enjoying themselves.

Emerging from the shop with rucksacks stuffed full of tubes of Pringles, bags of M&Ms, bottles of Sprite and Coke and brightly coloured pop magazines with free gifts taped to the outside, the girls beamed contentedly. Inga had a giant bar of Toblerone nearly as big as she was. She offered Savage the bar. He snapped off a section and ate it whole, which reminded him that there was nothing quite like chocolate for making one feel human again.

"Now, ladies, we really need to get you through security."

The girls followed him, munching and drinking as they went. They were a little disappointed when Savage reminded them they wouldn't be able to take their drinks through and had to throw them away.

"You can buy more on the other side," he said. "Now, off you go."

The queue was minimal, but the girls hesitated. "You are not coming with us?" asked Sabine.

"No, I have to look for Bella. You'll be completely safe once you're through. I promise. Please, you must go."

The girls turned and joined the queue.

Sabine darted back and hugged Savage, pecking him on the cheek. Then all the girls went back to him, giving him a group hug.

"Okay," said Savage, feeling a little embarrassed. "You really need to go through security now."

One by one, they joined the end of the queue, eventually laying their rucksacks and sweets on a tray to pass through the X-ray machine. When the last girl had gone through the metal detector and retrieved her things, they turned and waved to him. He smiled and waved back then watched them disappear.

Outside, in the drop-off zone, Savage walked along the wide pavement to the other side of the airport. Past the rows and rows of waiting taxis, he found the familiar face of the driver who had first taken him into Puerto Banus, still working, still busily putting a shine on his vehicle even though it looked immaculate.

"Hello, my friend," said the driver, his leathered face creasing into a smile. "Where can I take you?"

"Do you know a café called Sophia's?" asked Savage.

"Of course. Please get in." The driver opened the rear door for him.

CHAPTER 36

THE WHINE OF A HIGH-PITCHED engine woke Savage. He'd fallen asleep in the back of the taxi and opened his eyes to find the car crawling along the road beside Puerto Banus Marina. Strewn with night-time revellers parading through the middle of the road, people surrounded the car on all sides. Expensive-looking women in designer cocktail dresses clip-clopped in stilettoes next to boyfriends in tight-fitting T-shirts that showed off how much they'd worked out. On one side of the road sat a row of brightly lit bars and restaurants, a cacophony of laughter and music spilling from their open fronts. On the other side, the sterns of ridiculously large motor yachts butted up against the quayside, dwarfing the buildings opposite. The rear decks of those floating palaces buzzed with exclusive parties. Waiters served canapes and Champagne to guests who didn't deign to look down at the peasants jostling for space on the quayside.

An engine roared from behind them. Savage looked out the back window to see a low-slung supercar tailgating the taxi, urging it to go faster.

"Where is he going to go?" said the taxi driver, throwing his hands up. "Is impossible—too many people."

"How much further is Sophia's?" asked Savage, kneading his sleepy eyes with his fists.

"Another hundred metres," replied the driver.

"I'll get out here." Savage paid the man and threaded his way through all the beautiful people, a serious face among a sea of euphoria and swaying bodies.

As he walked, waiters standing on the pavement tried to ensnare him into their establishments by shoving food and cocktail menus in his face. Savage shook them off until he finally came to Sophia's café, although at that time of night, it appeared to be more of a nightclub than a café. Its bifold doors had been tucked back to the very edges to reveal a wide-open frontage with a slightly raised wooden terrace separated from the street by a waist-high balustrade. It looked in danger of collapsing because it held so many people. Some were dancing on tables to the deafening dance track pouring out onto the street. Savage guessed a DJ was probably at the back somewhere, whipping the crowd into a frenzy. *Bella could be among them.*

A velvet rope slung across a small gap in the balustrade marked the entrance, but when Savage tried to go in a couple of bouncers barred his way.

"We are full," one of them said.

He'd already had enough of bouncers for one night.

Reaching into his pocket, Savage pulled out some notes and palmed them into one of the bouncer's hands in a handshake. They guy pocketed the money. Savage moved forward to go in but was shoved back.

"We are still full," the bouncer said.

Savage smiled at him, seeing no point in making a scene there, not when he was so close to finding Bella. He held up his hands in surrender and moved down the pavement to the very end of the café's terrace. The bouncers were still watching him. They probably thought he would vault the balustrade, which had crossed Savage's mind, but Savage changed tactics when he saw a waiter clearing a recently vacated table. A group of tipsy women eagerly waited beside him to swoop in and claim it.

Savage leaned over the rail of the balustrade to get the waiter's attention. "Excuse me," he said.

The waiter looked around, clutching an armful of dirty cocktail glasses.

"Have you seen this girl?" Savage held up his phone with the picture of Bella on it.

The waiter squinted, eyes focusing. "Oh, yes, I've seen her."

"Is she here?"

"No, she left, I think. But she's always in here. You could probably catch her tomorrow."

"What time does she come here?"

"Sometimes morning, sometimes afternoon, sometimes evening."

Before Savage could ask another question, the party of girls swarmed the table, falling into their seats, slamming their drinks down and splashing booze everywhere.

"Five margaritas, *s'il vous plait*," said a rosy-cheeked girl to the waiter, slurring her words.

The girl next to her elbowed her in the ribs. "That's French, you idiot."

The girl with the rosy cheeks cackled. "I'm a dozy cow. I meant five margaritas, *por favor*."

"With tequila chasers," added another girl.

They howled with laughter and pinched the backside of the waiter, who made a swift escape to fetch their drinks. The women turned their attention to Savage, the small balding man standing outside on the pavement.

"So, you the stripper, then?" one asked.

More cackling.

The whole group looked at Savage. "Get them off! Get them off! Get them off!" they chanted.

At that point, retreating seemed the smartest option. Savage left Sophia's and mingled with the crowd, looking out for any signs of Bella. He'd missed her. *Damn it.* Perhaps she could still be close by, wandering the streets, or maybe she'd gone to a different club or home for the night. Frustration gripped him. *So close yet so far.*

Savage trawled the length of the quayside road several more times, scanning every face, just in case he caught sight of Bella. He also tried some of the quieter side roads but came up with nothing. Staking out Sophia's tomorrow seemed his best option at that point. Glancing at the time on his phone, he realised it already was tomorrow, albeit the early hours of the morning.

Time to make a tactical retreat. He left the marina and walked until he found himself on the beach. Trudging along the shoreline, carrying his shoes, he let the cool water sift through his toes. When the noise of beach bars and seafront hotels had faded into the distance, he found a quiet section of sun loungers, lay down on one, and texted Tannaz.

Are you still at Theresa's?

Back home now. Everything okay?

Yep, Bella's been spotted here.

Amazing. I'll tell Theresa?

Nope. Hold fire. Wait until it's confirmed. No point getting her hopes up until I know for sure.

Really? She could do with some good news.

Definitely. All is not as it seems. Eyewitness says Bella sits in a cafe all day drinking coffee and looking glamourous.
Doesn't seem like a sex-trafficked slave.

WTF! Are you sure?

No, but hoping to find out. Maybe Bella wanted to start a new life.
Maybe we've got this all wrong.

But what about the gang? The nightclub? Unit 19A?
She's mixed up in something.

I know. It doesn't fit.
Will keep my distance and observe until I know more.
If I approach her she may get spooked and disappear again.

Good idea. Be careful.

Always am.

*Let me know if you need anything. Day or
night. I'm always up.*

*Good to know. I'm going to get some sleep now.
You should do the same.*
Good night.

Laters

Savage put his phone away and let the gentle sloshing of the
sea lull him into sleep.

Several hours later, a scream woke him up.

CHAPTER 37

IN THE DISTANCE, FAR DOWN the beach, Bella screamed and staggered around, blood pouring from a wound in her shoulder. He had to get to her, had to help her. When he tried to get off his sun lounger, he found he couldn't. Something was holding him back. Looking down, he saw he'd been strapped to it with leather belts, about ten of them. They were the same as the one Frank had worn, with the tacky lion's head. Savage struggled against them, but they wouldn't give. He cried out to Bella. She heard him calling and turned to look towards him. As soon as she did, a bullet hit her in the chest then another and another. Bullets slammed into her from every direction. Savage was powerless to stop it, lying helpless like someone about to be sacrificed.

Sitting upright, head pounding, breathing ragged, Savage darted his eyes left and right, trying to find Bella, but she was nowhere to be seen.

The scream came again—nothing but a seagull screeching overhead. He'd been having a nightmare.

He fell back heavily on the sun lounger and shut his eyes, trying to calm his heart, which hammered against his rib cage. The tortured image of Bella was seared onto his retinas.

After several minutes, he opened his eyes again to a faultlessly blue sky, save for two high-flying jets drawing perfect pinstripes across it. Pushing himself upright, he looked around. All was calm and peaceful. Out to sea, a lone fishing boat slid silently across the horizon, gulls giving chase. Behind him, the distance whirr of a road sweeper, doing its early-morning rounds.

The time on his phone displayed seven ten a.m. Savage got

to his feet, tucked his shirt in, and went in search of breakfast. Maybe having something in his belly would calm his night terrors.

After trekking across the sand and back to the road, he stopped at the first kiosk he came to, open early to sell the daily papers. Shuddering to think what his breath smelled like, he bought a single packet of peppermint gum. After popping two sticks into his mouth, he chewed, pushing them around every inch of his gums.

Savage headed in the direction of the marina. Every so often, a jogger ran past, taking advantage of the cool early-morning air. By seven thirty, he walked onto the quayside. Last night's crowds had gone, and the locals had returned, walking their toy-sized dogs with papers tucked under their arms or sitting in pavement cafes, sipping the first espresso of the morning. Normally, Savage was a tea man through and through, but the smell of freshly ground coffee drifting out of every café he passed was intoxicating. When Savage reached Sophia's and found it open, he took a seat on the terrace and ordered tea with an espresso chaser, as well as a plateful of scrambled eggs on toast.

Sophia's bore no resemblance to the place he'd seen the previous night. Gentle chatter filled the air, and the waiters carried pastries and shiny metal coffee pots, not garish cocktails. No bouncers were there to contend with and no deafening dance music, either—just the crinkle of newspapers being turned and the odd cry of a gull from the quay outside.

Savage sipped his tea, put on his sunglasses, and waited.

By eleven, Savage was on his third cup of tea and his second espresso, and had downed an assortment of sweet pastries, only leaving his table once to briefly nip to the bathroom.

He was just about to order a fourth cup when he saw her.

A vision in red and beautiful beyond belief, Bella Tucker strode up the street towards Sophia's, dressed as though she had just come off a catwalk in a crimson knee-length halter-neck dress. Her red hair flowed out behind her, catching the sun like a flaming meteor. Beneath oversized designer sunglasses, her cherry-red lips were ripe and full.

She was on her own, with no minder or pimp or whoever Savage had imagined had enslaved her. Instead, he saw an independent woman, a woman of means, a woman with money. Sabine had been right. Bella didn't look as though she needed saving. Quite the opposite, she looked like an A-list film star.

Stepping into Sophia's, she took a seat a few tables away from Savage at the very edge of the terrace so she could see and be seen by passers-by on the road beyond.

Savage needed all his willpower not to leap up and approach her to ask her why she'd disappeared, to say her mother was worried about her, and to ask her to come home or at least get her to call her mother.

His gut told him to stay put, though. Something wasn't right about what he saw in front of him, and he needed to learn what it was before he went steaming in, making the wrong assumption. The first rule of the SAS: observe and gather intel before engaging. He needed to find out the truth behind Bella's disappearance. Her mother deserved it.

Savage pretended to play with his phone. Surreptitiously, he snapped a few pictures of the girl. He might need them to prove to Theresa that her daughter was alive and well and happy, especially if he discovered Bella had no intention of going home, which seemed highly possible at that moment.

The waiter approached Bella, smiled and greeted her like an old friend. Bella shot him back a perfect smile. They made small talk in English. Clearly, she was a regular there. If Savage hadn't known better, he would've said that Bella lived in a villa with servants, did lunch with her friends and had a rich husband. He would hang around to see if his theory was correct. Maybe her girlfriends would show up, and they'd go off shopping for the day or back to one of their expensive houses for afternoon tea.

None of that happened.

Bella just sat there, silently staring out at the huge boats moored along the quayside, a mute siren trying her best to look perfect, which wasn't a struggle. She almost seemed to be playing a part in a movie.

After midday, Bella still hadn't moved. She'd eaten a modest green salad for lunch followed by a mint tea. Savage had eaten a cheese omelette and fries followed by another cup of tea. He would have to put his tea drinking on hold, or his bladder would explode. He chanced another trip to the bathroom, returning swiftly only to find Bella hadn't moved a muscle, even to shift position.

At three in the afternoon, everything changed. A yellow Lamborghini cornered sharply outside the café. Tyres squealing on the warm tarmac, it pulled into a parking space opposite, in front of a gargantuan motor yacht called the *Celeste*. Bella suddenly came to life. She texted rapidly on her phone then shoved it into her bag, left some money on the table, and got up to leave. Savage stayed put for the time being, not wanting to follow her too obviously. He didn't need to worry. Bella didn't go far. Outside the café, she took her phone from her bag, put it to her ear, and paraded back and forth in that way people do when they're deep in conversation. However, Savage wasn't convinced she was in conversation with anyone. Her phone hadn't rung, and she hadn't touched its screen to dial any number.

Bella was posing, acting a part in a pantomime. *But for whom?*

CHAPTER 38

BELLA STRUTTED BACK AND FORTH, heels clicking seductively on the pavement, her behind sashaying from side to side, her beautiful face spotlit by the sun itself.

Across the road, the passenger door of the yellow Lamborghini flew open. Out stepped a mountainous figure in a black polo shirt and black jeans, aviator sunglasses perched on his square head, topped with a buzz cut, grade one back and sides, grade two on top. Wide as a cathedral, he cautiously looked left and right, sizing up the street, looking for threats. Savage knew that look well. A bodyguard, ex-military probably. When he was satisfied, he went to the other side of the car and opened the driver's door while never taking his eyes off the street—textbook personal-security detail.

Out of the car stepped a well-groomed young Arabic gentleman, a phone stuck to his ear. Handsome with thick, floppy black hair, he wore a crisp open-neck white shirt tucked into a smart pair of formal grey trousers, the outfit completed by black suede slip-on shoes without any socks. The bodyguard went into close-protection procedure, never leaving the Arab's side, as if they were conjoined twins. If anything happened, he could put his body between his asset and the threat.

The Arab spoke into his phone, oblivious to the bodyguard by his side, a sign that personal protection was an everyday occurrence. By the look on his face, the call wasn't going well. Savage couldn't hear the conversation, but his tightly knit brows told him all he needed to know. The person on the other end of the line was getting a dressing down. The Arab slapped the roof of his Lambo, shouted down the phone and slapped the roof again, his face growing redder and redder. Then, as he caught sight of Bella on the other side of the road, the anger drained from him as if a switch had been flicked. His body language completely changed, shoulders relaxing.

He hung up and crossed the road without warning, not looking left or right. The bodyguard was caught unawares, allowing distance to open up between himself and his client, an unacceptable error. Being a professional, he'd berate himself later for being caught off guard. No harm was done, and he covered the two-metre gap in a second, putting himself shoulder to shoulder again, ready for any sign of danger.

Bella continued strutting outside Sophia's, almost within touching distance of where Savage was sitting. The Arab walked straight up to her with the confidence that only people with money have.

"I cannot believe it," he said, clapping his hands together in wonder and smiling with perfect white teeth. "This is a day I will remember forever."

Bella put her phone away and turned to look at the guy. "Sorry?" she said blankly, as if she hadn't been listening to him, though Savage was sure she'd heard every word.

"This is the day I have been waiting for. I knew it would come," said the Arab, hands gesticulating enthusiastically.

"What are you talking about?" Bella replied, ice cold.

"Why, the day I met the most beautiful girl in the world."

She managed a cynical half smile. "I'm sure you say that to all the girls."

"They are nothing compared to you. Truly you are a goddess, a flame-haired goddess." He got down on one knee in deference, laying the melodrama on thick.

While he knelt down, his head was conveniently level with Savage's table. Savage's phone rested on the table in front of him. All he had to do was turn it ninety degrees, and the camera had a clear line of sight of the Arab's face. Quickly thumbing the screen, Savage surreptitiously snapped off as many shots of him as he dared, then he selected the best shot of the cheesy chat-up artist and pinged them to Tannaz.

Who is this guy?

Tannaz pinged back a reply almost immediately:

Gonna take hours, got any more info?

Savage sent her the licence plate of the Lamborghini.
She replied:

Still gonna take hours.

Outside on the pavement, the clumsy flirting continued. Her admirer got to his feet, firing off all sorts of well-rehearsed lines. Bella seemed unimpressed. She removed her sunglasses, her sparkling amber eyes staring at him disdainfully.

"How is it possible?" he asked. "You keep getting more and more beautiful. I could stare at your face for eternity and be the happiest man in all of creation. Everything I have is yours. Please, I beg of you, you must join me on my yacht tonight. I am having a party. Say you will come."

"Sorry, I can't." She elegantly turned on her heel like a ballerina to walk away.

The Arab, his bodyguard by his side, went around her, blocking her path. "Please," he said. "I will simply die if you do not come."

She turned to go in the other direction. Glancing back over her shoulder, she said coolly, "I'll think about it."

Once again, the Arab stepped in front of her, bodyguard beside him. "Please, I am only here this one night. Just one evening is all I ask. I am begging."

Bella thought for a moment. She looked the Arab up and down. "Well, okay, but I can't stay for long."

"Yes! Did you hear that, Samuel?" He punched his bodyguard on the arm. "She said yes."

His bodyguard didn't react, just kept scanning the street.

The Arab continued, "I will have a car drop you home whenever you wish."

"Thank you," said Bella. "But I really can't stay long, though. Which is your boat?"

"The *Celeste*, over there," he replied.

"Pretty big boat. What's it like inside?"

"Would you like to see it, this minute?"

Bella looked reluctant. "Er, not right now. I really should go."

"A quick tour so you get your bearings for tonight," the Arab said, pleading with praying hands.

Bella shook her head.

"Five minutes is all I ask," he said. "I have some of the most wonderful art on board, and I can clearly see you have taste. And maybe a quick glass of Champagne to send you on your way, then I can have Samuel here drop you home in my Lamborghini. Have you ever taken a ride in a Lamborghini?"

Bella ignored the question, as though still undecided whether that was a good idea or not. To Savage's eyes, she was clearly pretending to play hard to get, not wanting to look too eager. Eventually, she smiled and said, "Okay, go on then, but five minutes, then I really must go."

The Arab looked to the heavens, as if to thank Allah, whom he clearly didn't believe in since he was about to ply Bella with expensive alcohol. "I swear on all that is precious to me I shall keep you no longer than five minutes."

The Arab escorted Bella across the road, shadowed by the giant bodyguard.

Savage texted Tannaz again:

He owns a motor yacht called the Celeste.

That helps. Will have something soon.

Savage would have to wait, although every cell in his brain screamed at him to run after her. However, far from being the victim, she looked more like the hunter. She'd been clearly waiting for the guy to show up and must have had her sights on him for a long time, since she'd been coming to the café for at least several weeks. Probably knew he had a yacht moored there and just had to wait it out until he showed up so she could lure him with her beauty. The situation playing out in front of him seemed pretty obvious: a young, attractive girl trying to snare a rich guy for his money.

Savage watched as Bella, the Arab and his bodyguard were greeted by two security guards at the foot of the gangplank. They ascended into the giant yacht then disappeared from sight.

Finally, a text popped up on Savage's phone:

> *His name's Saad Sharaf*
> *Son of a Saudi arms dealer*
> *Has a thing for redheads*
> *And allegedly raping them*

CHAPTER 39

SAVAGE THREW MONEY DOWN ON the table and got up. Bella was in terrible danger. He'd seriously misjudged the situation. She'd been right in front of him, and he'd let her slip through his fingers. He had to get aboard that yacht and get her out of there, but how? Two security guards stood sentry at the gangplank, the only way of getting on and off. Savage thought about using the yacht parked next to the *Celeste*, sneaking on board then leaping the narrow gap separating the two vessels. However, since that yacht was also obscenely expensive, it too had guards posted at the foot of its gangplank.

Then he heard the sound that had woken him from his beach slumber earlier that morning, the wheezy chugging of the road sweeper still doing its rounds. Savage darted around the corner, following the sound of its tired engine. Sprinting this way and that, down quiet little backstreets, he eventually came across the little sweeper, brushes spinning as it dodged in and out of parked cars, leaving a snail trail of water behind. Savage easily caught it up and flagged it down. The vehicle had no doors, so he leaned in to speak to the driver, who took up nearly all of the cramped cab, the steering wheel almost digging into his protruding tummy. A plastic Virgin Mary was tacked to the dashboard, and the cab smelled of stale sweat and rolling tobacco.

The driver glared at him, veins on the side of his neck looking ready to pop. Rapidly approaching retirement age, he was bald, save for a floppy, grey moustache hanging from his top lip. He protested in Spanish, waving frantically in his greasy grey overalls.

"Do you speak English?" asked Savage.

"Why you stop me? I have work. I am late." The driver pointed at his watch. "You understand?"

"How would you like to make a lot of money?"

The man stopped, calming down at the mention of money. "How much?"

Savage dug out everything he had in his pockets and dropped it into the man's lap. He had no idea how much there was, but it seemed enough to get the guy's attention. The big man licked his lips, shuffled all the notes together, and began counting them.

"Okay," he said, pushing the money into a pocket. "What you want?"

"I want you to drive into the back of a Lamborghini."

He shook his head, took the money from his overalls and handed it back to Savage. "Oh, no. I get in big trouble."

Savage gently pushed the roll of cash back in his direction. "Who owns this vehicle?" he asked.

"Is municipality."

"Your employer, the local government?" Savage asked.

The big guy nodded.

"They have big insurance for accidents," said Savage. "*They* pay, not you. When does your shift end?"

The driver rubbed his bristly chin. "It end hour ago. I am late, have more to do."

"But your shift ended and you're still working? That's dangerous, stressful. Too many hours without a break could cause you to have an accident. That would be their fault, not yours. You get this money here"—Savage pointed at the money he'd given him—"and you get money from the municipality. Big pay-out. They've broken the law by making you work past your shift, plus all the stress it's caused you. Maybe you can retire early. No more road sweeping. And they pay for fixing the Lamborghini."

The guy's eyes lit up, twinkling at the thought of giving up work and having money in his pocket. There was nothing like the promise of doing nothing for the rest of one's life to stimulate someone into action. The driver looked around the tatty cab of his vehicle, as if reminding himself of what he'd be giving up. Finally, he asked, "Where is Lamborghini?"

Savage squished himself into the cab and directed the driver back towards the marina. When they got close, Savage told the driver to stop just shy of the corner of a side road that led onto the quayside. They edged forward gently until the yellow Lamborghini came into view. Savage pointed at it and instructed the driver to give it a gentle nudge in the back, nothing too serious, just enough to cause a claim. When he was sure the man understood, Savage got out of the cab and crossed the road to where all the boats were moored.

Taking his time, Savage wandered along the quay's edge, gazing at the backs of the boats like a tourist lost in wonder and admiration for wealth and what it could buy. He was two yachts away from the *Celeste* when he heard the shriek of the road sweeper's engine straining at top speed. Its brushes had been retracted, and the little vehicle bumped and rocked along the road, heading straight for the Lamborghini. Savage had told the driver to give it a nudge, but judging by the sweeper's velocity, he was going for maximum damage. Maybe all the years of mounting bitterness, cleaning roads on minimum wage for millionaires to walk on, were about to be vented.

Savage quickened his pace and was only yards away when the sweeper rammed the supercar from behind. Its sleek lines crumpled like paper, bits of car flying in all directions. Every head in the marina turned in the direction of the violent thump. People evacuated nearby cafés to see what the commotion was all about. Like ants, they swarmed around the accident, phones out to record the bizarre sight of a utilitarian road sweeper and a seductive supercar, two vehicles that couldn't be further apart in the motoring spectrum, now shunted together in an ugly embrace. It had worked better than Savage had imagined.

Up ahead, two of the *Celeste*'s security guards left their post at the base of the gangplank, pushing their way through the crowds to sort out the mess. The driver of the sweeper stumbled out of his cab, scratching his head as if unsure what had happened.

Two more guards appeared on the rear deck of the *Celeste* then rushed down to join their comrades. Once they disappeared into the crowd, Savage strode up the gangplank, not looking back.

He found himself on a wide-open deck striped with narrow lengths of polished hardwood. Wide, sumptuous sofas covered in generous scatter cushions were arranged around the edge of the deck, with a large, raised padded platform in the middle, presumably for sun bathing. Beyond that, an outdoor dining table, dominated by a fountainous arrangement of fresh flowers sat next to a bar complete with a series of bolted-down stools. Towards the back of the deck, two open patio doors led to a vast indoor lounge, where more luxurious sofas faced a giant flat-screen TV.

Someone was sitting in there, a man with his back towards Savage. As he sidled closer, he could see the man was on the phone. Speaking in English, he was checking a catering order, running through a list of dishes, presumably for the party Saad had spoken of. Keeping his eyes on the man, Savage kept to the edge of the deck, aiming for the starboard side of the boat. He made it unseen to the gunnel, a narrow walkway connecting the stern of the boat with the prow. Moving quickly and silently, he came to a door halfway along its length. He knocked on it, stood to one side out of sight, and waited for a response. None came, so he tried the handle. Unlocked.

Savage slipped inside and found himself in a stairwell smelling of furniture polish and freshly laid carpet. On his right was a table against the wall with a vast bowl of fresh fruit. On the other wall hung an oil painting, abstract and expensive looking. To his left, a narrow staircase led down to the next deck. He descended it slowly, cautiously, figuring that would be where the bedrooms were. If Saad had a thing for assaulting women, that would be most the most likely place he'd taken Bella, almost definitely the master suite, to impress her. If Savage's memory served him well, naval architects usually positioned the master suite at the front of a boat to take full advantage of the width of the vessel and the view.

Savage followed the gentle curve of a left-hand corridor toward the prow, panelled with more polished wood, giving the impression of a stately home in Oxford, not a luxury yacht in Spain. At the first door he came to, he listened for sounds of movement or struggling but heard none. Gently, he knocked. No answer. Opening the door, he found an empty guest room with a made-up bed, an assortment of tasteful furniture, more fresh flowers, a bottle of wine and two glasses. He closed the door quietly and moved on to the next one. That too lay empty.

As he moved farther around the curved corridor, he noticed something up ahead on the floor. He pushed his back flat against the wall, inched his way along, chanced a quick glimpse and caught sight of a leg. As he moved closer, he realised it belonged to Saad's bodyguard. He was lying facedown on the carpet, seemingly out cold, in front of two large double doors marking the end of the corridor. Savage crept toward him, kicked the guy's foot, then backed off, just in case he suddenly leaped up and attacked him. Nothing. No movement. Savage got closer, knelt beside him and felt the guy's neck for a pulse. His carotid artery was still pumping. Still alive. Savage checked him over and discovered an empty leather holster in the back of his waistband. His weapon had been taken.

Moving quietly up to the double doors, Savage put an ear up against one of them. He heard crying.

Bella.

Savage didn't bother trying the handle. He just shouldered the door open, putting all his weight behind it, crashing into the palatial master suite.

Bella wasn't the one crying, though. It was Saad.

CHAPTER 40

THE CURTAINS WERE CLOSED, BUT just enough light crept in at the edges to illuminate the cowering shape of Saad, begging on his knees in the middle of a large Persian rug, tears streaming down his face. Bella stood over him. Her hand shook as she pointed a gun at his head, presumably the one she'd taken off the unconscious bodyguard outside.

They both swung their gazes to the surprise intruder.

"Please, help me," Saad said to Savage.

Bella pointed the gun at Savage. "You," she said. "You were in Sophia's."

"Bella, what are you doing?" Savage asked, hands up in surrender.

"You know this woman?" said Saad.

"Shut up." Bella turned her gun back on Saad. "He must die," she said. "He must die. He must die." Her voice was cold and robotic as though she was repeating a mantra, but her body language was anything but calm. Her whole body shuddered.

"No, please. Do not kill me." Saad fell facedown at her feet, weeping into the fibres of the Persian rug, which muffled his cries.

Bella took a step back, renewing her aim. "Shut up. You have to die. I have to kill you."

"Stop, Bella," Savage pleaded. "Why are you doing this?"

"I have to," she said.

"Bella, listen to me," said Savage. "Your mum sent me to find you, to bring you back home."

"Mum?" Bella spoke the word almost as if she didn't recognise it.

Savage dared to take a step closer. She immediately turned the gun on him.

He stopped and spoke softly. "Please, Bella. Your mum is worried about you. She's very upset and wants you to come home with me. Back to London."

"Mum?" she said again, trancelike.

"Yes, your mum, Theresa. She's kept your room for you. You can call her if you like." Savage held out his phone.

Her voice was distant, like that of a child with a fever. "I could call my mum, couldn't I?" She sounded as though she hadn't considered the idea before. "I haven't seen her for ages." She sounded weary.

"Yes, call her. Here, I'll dial the number for you." Savage went to his contacts list.

"Stop," she said, her voice suddenly regaining its assertiveness. "I have to kill him."

"But what would your mum say?" Savage asked. "How would you tell her that you've murdered someone?"

"It's not murder. It's justice. He's the enemy."

"What did you do to her?" Savage asked Saad.

"Nothing. I've never seen her before," Saad sobbed.

"Why is he the enemy?" asked Savage.

Bella spat the words out. "Because he sells arms to terrorists, and terrorists are the enemies of our nation."

Savage tried to calm her down. "This isn't you, Bella. You like seeing your friends and taking selfies and happy hours and two-for-one drinks at nightclubs..."

"You don't know me," she said. "You're trying to stop me. That makes you my enemy, too. Get on the floor next to him." Bella had a wild, psychopathic look in her eye.

He didn't argue and got down on his knees next to the Arab. She kept switching aim from one man to the other, unable to decide whom to kill first. Beads of sweat dotted her forehead, her breathing becoming heavy and laboured. A minute went by, and she still hadn't pulled the trigger.

"You can't do it, can you?" asked Savage, looking up at her.

"Shut up."

Savage continued, "No, you can't do it because you'd have done it already. Before I came in, how long had Saad been on his knees, waiting to die? One minute? Five minutes? Ten?"

"I'll kill you both." The gun rattled in her hand.

"I've killed people before," said Savage. "Lots of them. Did it without a second thought. But once that gun goes off, you can't take it back. Your world will change forever. You never get over it. I hear voices in my head now, telling me to kill myself. Do you want that? Because that's what it will do to you. It never leaves you. Oh, and you probably already know this, but if you're going to do it properly, it's not just one shot, either. You need to put one in our heads and two in our chests. Three shots each. Bang! Bang! Bang!" Savage shouted.

Bella flinched, blinking her eyes on each *bang*.

Saad whimpered.

"Has to be three," Savage continued. "Make sure there's no chance of us surviving. Okay, off you go, then. Execute us, but it's going to ruin this lovely rug."

Conflicted, Bella thought for a moment as if trying to figure out whether Savage was telling the truth. A moment passed. Bella stood there, a beautiful, confused statue before the two men facing death, kneeling beside each other.

Nothing happened.

Then, without warning, she turned and ran from the room through the double doors.

Savage was up on his feet, giving chase. She was quick, sprinting barefoot down the corridor, her stilettoes in one hand, the gun in the other, past Saad's bodyguard, still out cold on the floor. Savage was halfway down the corridor when he saw her disappear up the staircase. He climbed after her, only to get knocked down as a spiked heel she'd thrown caught him in the side of the head. A stinging gash made his right temple throb. Ignoring the pain, Savage strode up the stairs again and was barely halfway up when the table he'd seen earlier on the landing above came cartwheeling down towards him. Savage dashed back down the stairs, out of its way. The table came to a halt at the bottom, its legs caught up in the balustrading. Wasting valuable time, Savage tried to dislodge the obstacle, but it was wedged in tight. He abandoned that approach and climbed over it, continuing his pursuit of Bella. Her evasion tactics had worked. She now had a five-second head start on him, a long time in a foot chase.

Out on the deck, Savage saw no sign of her. He rushed to the stern, looking left and right, desperately searching for signs of the girl. The crowds were still on the quayside, surrounding the crash, but the police had turned up and were trying to quell an argument between the driver of the road sweeper and the guy Savage had seen on the phone in the *Celeste*'s lounge. Security guards stood beside him, unsure what they should be doing. As for Bella, she had disappeared.

CHAPTER 41

OUT OF THE CORNER OF his eye, Savage caught a flash of red disappearing around a corner at the end of the quayside. In the short time he'd lost sight of Bella, she'd put at least a hundred yards between them. The girl could sprint.

Savage ran down the gangplank and onto the quayside just as one of the *Celeste*'s security guards casually turned to notice him. The guy stepped into his path. Savage sprinted at him at full speed, elbowing him in the face, and the guy keeled over. Before anyone could notice, Savage was gone, dashing to the corner where Bella had made a left turn.

Rounding the corner, he glimpsed her again farther up the street, making a right turn into an underground car park. That wasn't a good sign. Most likely, she had a car parked there. He would have to get there before she drove off, or he could lose her forever.

Savage increased his pace, but the capacity of his lungs was at maximum. He simply couldn't go any faster. The early-afternoon sun drenched him in sweat, sticking his shirt to his back. Pounding the hot pavement past expensive boutiques, hair salons and estate agents, he cursed himself again for not making contact with her in the café. That had been a mistake, and he was paying for it.

Sweat dripped into his eyes by the time he made it to the car park. Darting down its concrete ramp, he was thankful to be in the blessed shade even though the air was thick, cloying his throat with stagnant petrol fumes. Since Bella had entered, no cars had emerged. A lucky break. She must still be in there unless another exit existed which he didn't know about.

Ducking under the entrance barrier, he was confronted by two rows of cars, neatly parked on each side. At least that made his job easier. He slowed his pace, jogging along, peering left and right into the windscreens of the stationary cars. All were empty, no sign of Bella. At the end, he came to another concrete ramp that curled around to reach the level below. Savage hurried down it to see a carbon copy of the layout of the car park above. On this level, though, a figure stood barefoot at the very end, in a red dress—Bella.

Savage walked slowly toward her, hoping that would be less threatening. As he got closer, he could see that she still had the gun in her hand, hanging by her side. He smiled, raising his hands.

"Bella. My name is John, John Savage." His breathless words echoed loudly off the dirty concrete walls, not the effect he was aiming for. He calmed his voice. "I'm not here to hurt you. Like I said, I'm a friend of your mum's."

"Stay where you are." She raised the gun.

Savage stopped where he was, about twenty yards away. "That's fine. We can talk from here." He took a few moments to catch his breath, wiping the sweat from his forehead. "Hot out there, isn't it? Bit different to South London."

"You must leave," she said. "Right now."

"I can't do that. I made a promise to your mum that I'd bring you home."

"I'm, I'm..." Bella's words caught in her throat as if she were struggling to push them out. "I'm not in control."

"What do you mean?"

"You have to leave. Or they'll get you."

"Who will get me?"

"You have to leave, right now." She put the gun to her head.

"No!" shouted Savage. "Stop! Bella, we can work this out. Whatever's happened to you, we can fix it, I promise."

"No, you can't." She pushed the gun into her temple. "It's like there's someone else in my head."

Savage edged closer, hands clasped together, pleading. "Please, I know what that's like. I have it too. Like a voice telling you to do things. Horrible things. But you don't have to. You can reason with it. I've even given mine a name, Jeff Perkins." He gave a little laugh to try to defuse the situation.

Bella wasn't amused. Her face switched from fear to anger. "Shut up. You don't understand," she said, taking the gun from her own head and pointing it at Savage again. "You must go, or the same will happen to you."

Just then, Savage heard the rumble of tyres above them. A vehicle had entered the car park and was accelerating quickly, the sound of its high-revving engine reverberating off the walls, funnelling down to where they were. The noise turned into a roar as a black van appeared at the bottom of the concrete ramp, its lights on full beam, blinding in the dingy car park. It headed for Savage then screeched to a halt, blocking his way, engine idling.

Savage stood in the glare of its headlights. He was trapped. Behind him was nothing but the end of the car park, a solid concrete wall... and Bella with the gun trained on him. He needed that gun if he was to stand a chance against whoever came out of that van. He was guessing they'd be armed, whoever *they* were, the mysterious gang from unit 19A.

Savage backed up, not taking his eyes off the van. In a few steps, he would be level with Bella. He would wrestle the gun off her then walk her out of there like a hostage. Whoever those people were, they wanted Bella in one piece. That was what he was banking on. If not, they were both in trouble.

None of that happened.

Savage felt a heavy blow on the back of his head.

His vision blurred, and his legs buckled. The world folded in around him, then he lost consciousness.

CHAPTER 42

"**WAKE UP, SAVAGE. YOU NEED to wake up.**"

The voice was distant, far away, like someone calling for him at the end of a very long tunnel. Savage couldn't decide whether he was awake or asleep or in that strange limbo in between, where nothing makes sense. He took a deep breath to give his brain some much-needed clarity. At that moment, he became aware of something loosely strapped around his mouth. He could feel his breath collecting in front of him, creating a cloud of warm condensation. Noisy and echoey, each breath sounded like Darth Vader's painful gasps.

"*Savage, wake up.*"

The voice was nearer and sounded genuinely concerned. That got Savage's attention. The voice was never concerned. Normally, it wanted him to suffer and die.

Every thought took Savage an age to process and everything felt in slow motion, as though he was underwater or worse, wading through treacle. Like a dinosaur trapped in a tar pit, every movement pulled him farther down into a black abyss.

Slowly and with great effort, Savage opened his eyes, but everything remained dark, not a speck of light to be seen. He blinked repeatedly, snapping his eyes open and shut in an effort to clear his vision. Nothing changed. The blackness stayed, surrounding him, enveloping him in a dark, claustrophobic shroud.

"*Savage, are you awake?*"

Savage nodded, but his head could barely move. Something soft pressed against his forehead, restricting his movements to the very minimum. He tried to move his hands. The same thing happened. They budged a little, but then a soft barrier prevented them from exploring any farther. Shifting around on the spot, he could move only an inch in any given direction before he encountered a squishy cocoon. Savage pushed harder, stretching out his legs and arms, but he stayed in an upright seated position. Completely entombed.

"Where am I?" His voice was hoarse and sore, muffled by the thing in front of his mouth.

"I have no idea."

"How long have I been here?"

"How should I know? I know as much as you do."

"What's that sound?"

"Okay, this isn't going to work. I'm in your head, remember. I have the same information as you."

Savage couldn't see, but his hearing still worked perfectly. White noise surrounded him on all sides, a quiet roar, constant and unchanging in tone and pitch. He became aware of something else. Feeling out as much as his numbed senses would allow, he detected a juddering—sometimes more, sometimes less—a quivering sensation like the top of a washing machine on full spin. His sluggish mind struggled to make sense of it. He pictured himself riding on the oversized kitchen appliance floating through space. The surreal thought made his head turn inside out. The harder he tried to think rationally, the more his mind wanted to pull him in bizarre, unreal directions. He needed to think straight, had to focus and cut through all the misinformation conjured up by his mind. So he started with something basic by asking himself a simple question: who was he?

Another trippy thought flew into his head. His mind flew off at wild tangents into deep meanings of existence. No, he wasn't being philosophical, he just wanted to know his name, plain and simple. Maybe the voice could help.

"Are you there?"

"I'm always here."

"Who am I? I mean, what's my name?"

"You're John Savage."

"Yes, of course. I'm John Savage, and you're Jeff Perkins. I was doing something before this, but I can't remember what it was."

"You were looking for a missing girl."

"That's it. Yes, I was looking for a missing girl. What was her name?"

"Bella."

"Yes, Bella. I was looking for Bella. Something terrible happened to her."

"She got taken. Snatched by a gang. But you tracked her to a place in Spain, Puerto Banus."

"Yes, I remember."

"Then you blew it."

"What?"

"You blew it, arsehole. She was right in front of you, in a café. But instead of reaching out to her, you followed her. Wanted to solve the mystery, see what she was up to."

Savage groaned. The memory of it sent a new wave of pain into his already frayed mind, as though he was waking up from a hangover and remembering something awful he'd done the night before. But this was worse, much worse. Guilt and shame stabbed at him from every angle.

Guilt and shame weren't going to help him get out of there, though, wherever "there" was.

"And now, you're in this place. Well done, Savage. You lost the girl and managed to get captured. Smooth, real smooth."

Savage remembered being in the car park, seeing Bella standing there, and feeling a blow to the back of the head. Something else happened, though.

A concept popped into Savage's sluggish mind. He tried grabbing at it as it bobbed around, drifting in front of him, just out of reach—like those weird floaty things people see when they close their eyes, tiny fragile entities with no substance.

He had to try harder. *Focus.*

Savage's head throbbed with the effort of trying to cut out all the nonsense clogging his brain.

He felt like a child clumsily trying to fit pegs into holes except the pegs weren't complete. They were just fragments, splinters that kept dropping onto the floor.

For some reason, Minchie's big, dumb face appeared in front of him. He remembered him but didn't know why. The ugly brute was saying something, his lips moving, but no sound came out, as if the volume had been turned down. Minchie kept repeating the same thing over and over again, on a loop, but Savage had no idea what it was. He watched the contortions of his mouth, hoping he could read the lips, concentrating on the form and shape of every word, but nothing became any clearer. Instead, Savage focused on the last time he'd seen Minchie. *What was that place?* He couldn't remember, but he felt a sinister wave of fear and anger come over him. Something diabolical had happened there, something to do with Bella.

"Why are you thinking of Minchie? That prick's no help."

"Shut up." Savage's voice sounded strange and unnatural. Minchie's face faded away, dissolving into the blackness. "It's gone now. I nearly had something, an important memory."

"Let's face it. You're going to die in here. Maybe they've buried you alive. What a way to go. Even I'm not that cruel. I told you to cut your wrists, jump in front of a train. But this is some evil shit. Hats off to these guys. They've put me in the shade. This is better than I could've imagined."

Something in what the voice said made sense. Judging by his current feelings—claustrophobic, trapped, oppressed—he certainly felt as if he'd been buried alive.

Think. Concentrate.

Savage's mind strained, making him cry out. He dug his fingernails into the squishy surface.

"I wonder how much air you have left. You'll die of suffocation if you're lucky, or you'll go mad. Maybe you'll go mad then die of suffocation. Double prizes."

"Shut up."

Then, with great effort, the image of Minchie returned in sharp focus, unmuted.

Minchie spoke: "They drug them up, stick them in boxes."

Then he vanished, but that little fragment of information was all Savage needed. It had been the last thing Minchie had told Savage before he left him locked in unit 19A. He remembered then.

A moment of clarity hit Savage. Reality came crashing through his consciousness like a juggernaut, out of control.

Savage knew where he was.

He gasped with horror.

He was trapped in a box.

CHAPTER 43

PANIC GRIPPED HIM. LOUD AND desperate, his breathing suddenly increased in frequency and intensity. The gang must have snatched him just after he'd confronted Bella in the car park. They'd knocked him out and shoved him into one of their packing crates.

Entombed in metal and foam, the amplified sound of his lungs pumping air in and out had a cumulative effect. The more he heard his own frantic gasps, the more he panicked. Savage shook and kicked and clawed, desperate to free himself from his tiny prison. The more he pushed against the foam, the more resistance it put up. He remembered picking up a sliver of the stuff in unit 19A—premium stuff, soft yet dense and tough, perfect for holding someone in place without damaging them. A micro padded cell.

Savage twisted left then right, as far as he could go then back again, contorting his body in the hope something would give. The thick, deep foam held him fast.

He shook in uncontrollable spasms. He was going into shock, panting rapidly.

"Keep breathing like that, and you'll use up all your air. Suffocate and die. Just saying. Death will come quicker the harder you breathe. Actually, maybe that's a good thing. As you were."

A light flicked on in Savage's brain as a clear thought landed in his fog-bound head. The voice was right. Being shut in a metal box packed with protective foam, he'd have very little space left for any air.

He had no idea how long he'd been there, but suffocation

wouldn't be far away. Even in the short time he'd been conscious, his air should have been scarce already, yet he was breathing deep, panicky breaths, taking in great lungfuls without a problem. An impossibility if he had been sealed in a box.

He must have an air supply constantly feeding him to keep him alive.

Savage knew he had something strapped around his mouth, making his voice sound odd. He squished his face against the foam and felt the shape of it digging into the bridge of his nose and around his jaw. He knew what that object was: an oxygen mask.

Air was being supplied to him. If he had a supply of air, they weren't trying to kill him. Maybe they were transporting him, as they had with Bella and all the people they'd snatched. To where and for what reason remained a mystery.

Gradually, Savage calmed his breathing and felt his heart rate lessening. The shock coursing round his body subsided—not completely, but at least it became more manageable. *This isn't the end.* Maybe that would come later. He would have to wait and see.

"I haven't been buried," he said to the voice. "They wouldn't give me oxygen if they wanted to bury me alive."

"They might do, to give you false hope. Anyway, it's not going to last forever. It'll run out soon. You're still going to die."

Savage didn't bite or get worked up. Giving oxygen to a buried man made no sense, but he couldn't think of an argument to back that up. His feeble brain was still struggling to function. Then he remembered the other thing the image of Minchie had said: "They drug them up."

That was why his brain had turned to mush and he couldn't think straight. He'd been drugged, sedated while in transit, just like Bella and all the other people the gang had snatched. They'd been knocked out so they didn't wake up and panic or go into shock, just as Savage had done, and die of fright. Keeping them drugged up and unconscious would be paramount, otherwise they would surely go insane. Yet Savage had woken up.

"They wanted to scare you. Torture you."

The voice was getting desperate. Even with Savage's reduced faculties, he could tell it was clutching at straws, running out of ideas to unsettle Savage.

"If they wanted to torture me, they could've just made me watch crappy daytime TV," suggested Savage, pleased to see some of his humour returning.

The voice had a point, though. Thinking of his predicament in terms of torture was helpful, even comforting, bizarrely. Most people would have gone into a deeper panic at the idea that torture was somehow a comforting way to regard the current predicament, but not Savage. That was familiar ground for him. He'd been trained to resist torture and endure it for hours on end, and he had done so on several occasions. He knew how to deal with that. Just another day at the office—not a nice day at the office by any means, probably the worst anyone could imagine— it was a situation he merely had to work through, an obstacle to overcome.

Savage had also been trained to resist drugs. The two went hand in hand—torture and drugs, evil twins. Both were used on prisoners to get the truth out of them. During his years in the SAS, he'd been exposed to many mock interrogations. They'd given him a variety of pharmaceuticals to see how well he could cope with their effects while being questioned. None of them had worked, and although they'd been nightmarish experiences, Savage had built up a resistance to both pain and mind-altering narcotics, probably why he'd woken up. Whatever they were giving him wasn't strong enough.

An uncomfortable thought tugged at the corner of his mind. Again, he had to strain to hold onto the thought. His befuddled mind struggled to make sense of it. He fidgeted and squirmed, as if that would help free his mind a little.

At that moment, Savage felt a small sting in his right arm. Almost imperceptible, it came from his right forearm, near his elbow—a needling, pricking sensation. He'd felt it earlier when he was shaking but had forgotten about it when he panicked.

Savage shoved his arm back and forth to get a sense of it.

A cut or graze perhaps? Moving the whole of the right side of his body as much as it would go, he became aware that small areas of skin at regular intervals up his arm felt restricted. When he moved, patches of hairs on his arms seemed trapped, held in place. He was also aware that something unnatural snaked up his arm, toward his shoulder.

Savage fidgeted again, reading the pain receptors in his arm, trying to create a mental picture. The feeling was familiar, a sensation he'd had several times before, sometimes in training, sometimes on the battlefield. His mind was a bit slow at playing catch-up, but it got there eventually.

An intravenous drip had been shoved into his forearm, the needle pushed into a vein connected to tubing extending up his limb, towards his shoulder, and secured in place with squares of tape. Somewhere above him, embedded in the foam, would be a container drip-feeding him a concoction of goodness-knows-what. Definitely a sedative to keep him in his befuddled state and most likely some electrolytes too, for keeping him hydrated.

If he wanted to clear his head, he had to get the IV out.

Using his hands was out of the question. He had minimal movement. Trapped in place by the foam, he had no way of reaching across to yank it out. He would have to use his teeth, but first he would have to remove the oxygen mask.

Savage pushed his head into the foam in front of him, turning it left and right, side to side in attempt to push it off his face. At first, the oxygen mask stayed put, merely scuffing against the foam, but as he pushed his face deeper into the foam, it began to budge, gradually sliding across his face, as if he were wiping it off. After several attempts, it eventually shifted around to his cheek, just enough to free up his mouth.

He needed to work quickly. Without the oxygen mask feeding him air, he could already feel his breathing becoming laboured, and though some air leaked out from the edges of the mask, that wouldn't be enough to sustain him.

The next challenge was to get his teeth within biting distance of the IV. From what he could tell, the nearest section of tubing was taped to the top of his shoulder. Aiming his head down and to the right, he twisted it as far as it would go but only managed an inch or two before the foam held him back. Again, he tried, pulling his head back and thrusting it down towards the top of his shoulder. He got a little closer that time, but his mouth was still nowhere near the tubing. Savage repeated the exercise again and again. Sweat gathered on his forehead, and his mind began to swim due to oxygen starvation. He realised then that he hadn't really thought his plan through. If he couldn't get his mask back on, he was in danger of blacking out, and then he definitely would die of suffocation.

Sensibly, Savage ceased his attack on the IV tube and pushed his face into the foam, turning his head in attempt to get the mask back on, but it didn't seem to want to leave his cheek. Desperate for air, Savage pushed harder, using the foam to grip and hold the mask in place while he slid his face around. Little by little, the mask returned to its original position, and Savage was able to breathe again. Gulping down huge, greedy breaths, he came back to life.

When Savage had recovered enough to make a second attempt, he tried a different approach. Keeping his mask on, he forced his head within biting distance of the IV. That way, he'd have a constant supply of oxygen while he attempted the most arduous part of the task. The tactic worked, and his head became wedged just above his collarbone at an unnatural angle, straining the muscles in his neck. He couldn't stop there but had to keep going. Next, he rubbed the mask against his collarbone to gradually nudge it out of the way, which worked better than the foam, as his collarbone was a more solid obstacle to push against. Once the mask was out of the way, he located the IV tube taped to his shoulder and bit down hard. Then in what little space he had, he pulled his head back to try to tug the IV tube out of his arm. Straight away, he realized that would never work. There simply wasn't enough space to pull the tube far enough to dislodge it from his vein. The needle in his forearm stayed firmly in place. He tried again and again, yanking his head back hard, but the foam allowed only an inch or two of movement. He hadn't even dislodged the tape holding the tubing to his arm, let alone pulled the needle out near his elbow.

Perhaps he didn't have to, though. All he needed to do was prevent the flow of the drip. He had another way to achieve that. With what little oxygen Savage had left, he used his tongue to push the length of tubing into his mouth to the back of his jaws. His molars ground away at the plastic tubing, pulverising it. It was tough and put up plenty of resistance, but it was no match for the hundred and seventy-one pounds of pressure a human jaw could exert. The tubing soon shredded, and Savage felt the bittersweet taste of the IV fluids flooding his mouth. He spat both tubing and solution out. Without pausing, he shifted his head back into its original position and set about getting the mask back on. An easier task the second time around, although Savage still gasped for air by the time it was back in place.

All Savage could do then was sit and wait. *How long will it take for the drugs to wear off?* He had no idea. Fluid from the severed IV tube dribbled down his arm and soaked into the foam around him, but that was the least of his worries. He had to sober up before the box reached its final destination, or all his efforts would be for nothing. He didn't know where he was going or what was in store for him, but he knew he had to be ready for whoever was waiting to open the box. Sluggish and slow-witted, he was in no shape to face whoever would be on the other side of his metal-and-foam prison.

CHAPTER 44

S AVAGE'S HEAD POUNDED AS IF it had been filled with wet
cement and rusty barbed wire, and some bastard was
stirring it all with a rotten lump of wood. Sickness swirled
around in his stomach. He went to puke, but nothing came out.
Just acid making him gag and gasp.

That was a good sign that the drugs were wearing off, and
though he would've killed for a couple of paracetamol, at least he
could think straight—sort of—although it hurt like hell.

He had no idea how long he'd been in the box—an hour,
two hours, or eight hours. Being denied any outside stimulus
played havoc with his internal body clock. However, his cognitive
reasoning had returned to full strength, so he could at least
gather and analyse some evidence about his surroundings. He
had very little to go on, restricted by what he could hear through
the dense padding around him, but that was enough to form some
rudimentary deductions.

The white noise and rattling he'd heard earlier wasn't part of
his drug-induced hallucination. It was real. He could still hear it
all around him, a constant rumble. While he'd been a soldier, he'd
sat in the back of enough transport planes to know he was in the
hold of one right then. The noise of the engines was unmistakable,
definitely jets. That led him to believe he was in the hold of an
airliner—it needed to be something big enough to fit that box in
its hold. That ruled out budget short-haul bucket flights, as their
bulkhead doors were only wide enough for baggage, not large
items of freight. Then he remembered the Boeing 777, a pretty
common choice among the major airlines because it could handle

short and long haul and had a large rear door big enough to take both freight and baggage. Or maybe he was in the back of a freight plane. Those came in all shapes and sizes. Thus, he was none the wiser about where he currently resided or where he was heading, still in Europe or flying farther afield, to another continent.

Maybe the gang had its own plane. That seemed highly unlikely. Running a plane was costly, an unnecessary expense. It involved ground crew, pilots, and a whole support infrastructure on the ground, not to mention independent safety inspections, which would create plenty of opportunity for people to pry into their operation and get found out. The other alternative was they had leased a plane or chartered one, but that was also risky, with too much paperwork and legislation arousing suspicion. He came to the conclusion that they were using a public airline to move him.

That posed Savage with a dilemma. Once the plane landed, the airport ground crew would begin unloading the freight. That would be his chance. He could kick up a fuss, shout and scream and make a commotion, and get them to discover him and let him out—as long as the foam padding didn't muffle his cries for help. A problem existed with this. Yes, he'd be free, but once he escaped from the box, the trail would go cold. The gang would get spooked, and no one would come to retrieve it from the airport. They would disappear just as they had back at unit 19A, and he'd lose them again. That meant he'd jeopardize his only link to Bella's whereabouts. *Back to square one.*

Savage made a decision. Though doing so went against all his natural instincts, he would stay put, riding the journey out as far as it would go, right until the box opened and he got his first proper glimpse of his captors. Therefore, he would stay passive for the time being. He would let the gang come and collect the box, thinking he was unconscious inside.

That presented him with another decision. He had to work out what to do once they opened the box. Outnumbered and unarmed, he would be their helpless captive. He still had no idea what they wanted with him or why they had kept him alive.

Savage's best guess was they wanted information out of him. Not a watertight theory, by any means. If they wanted to pump him for information, they could have taken him somewhere remote in Spain and beaten it out of him. Why go to all the hassle of putting him in a box aboard a plane and smuggling him out of the country, if, indeed, that's what they were doing. It didn't add up.

That was the only workable theory he had, though. Savage figured he was being kept alive because they wanted to find out who else he had told about the gang and their operation—in other words, Tannaz and Theresa. They'd want to know so they could tie up loose ends and conveniently make them disappear to safeguard their anonymity, which raised another problem with his theory—Minchie was a loose end, but they hadn't bothered to silence him. Perhaps they were waiting to find out what names Savage gave up so they could eliminate them all at once, Minchie included, a package deal of assassinations.

One thing was sure: he would never give them the names of Theresa and Tannaz despite whatever elaborate torture scenarios they had in store for him. They could beat him, electrocute him, starve him, waterboard him—they'd get no names, well, apart from Minchie's, of course.

He remembered being tortured during the first Gulf War. The Iraqis had gone through a whole menu of pain: beating him with sticks; starving him of food, water and sleep; humiliating him and making him stand naked in the same position for hours on end, which was by far the worst. His Iraqi captors had been wasting their time. Savage told them nothing.

This would be harder, though. Back then, he only had himself to worry about. He didn't care about dying because it was his job. This was different. He had Bella to worry about. He had to find her and stay alive long enough so that he could get her home safely, but he'd have a better chance of doing that if he kept his enemies close, putting his head in the lion's mouth, as it were. That was a chance he was willing to take. Besides, he had no other plan. He had to follow this through, or he'd lose her again. He wouldn't make the same mistake twice.

One element was on his side—surprise. When they opened the box, they'd expect to find a heavily sedated middle-aged man—at best, someone confused and disoriented who wouldn't put up a fight. They'd be relaxed. That's when he would strike. He wouldn't have long. The moment the side of the box came off and the foam was removed, they would see he'd bitten through his IV and know something was up. He would have to be lightning fast.

That led to a problem. He'd been sitting in the same position for several hours. His joints and muscles would be cramped, next to useless for fighting. His opponents would probably be armed, too. The odds of success weren't great. He'd have to get a weapon off one of them. That was his first priority.

In the meantime, he needed to ready himself. In what little space he had, Savage pushed his arms and legs, stretching them out as far as the foam would allow, trying to loosen them up. He shrugged his shoulders, raised his calf muscles and flexed his hands. Any movement he could make was better than nothing.

Suddenly, the plane's engines changed pitch. Their tone lowered, and Savage felt his stomach drop. They were making their descent.

CHAPTER 45

THE WHINE OF HYDRAULICS SIGNALLED the undercarriage easing itself down, followed by a loud clunk as it locked into place.

Butterflies hammered in Savage's stomach as he got the first hit of adrenalin in his bloodstream, which was a little premature. A long time might pass before he got out of the box and had to face down the people who had put him there. Savage tried to remember that famous Churchill saying, something about the end of the beginning or the beginning of the end. He couldn't remember. What he did know was the next stage of the journey would be the last.

An almighty thud made the box shudder violently as the plane's undercarriage hit the runway. Engines screamed as they were thrown into reverse, helping the plane tame its monstrous momentum. Over seventy tons of metal, people and cargo was coming in at around one hundred and seventy miles an hour—not easy.

The box juddered and shook as though it would come apart. Forward inertia pushed his whole body into the dense foam, crushing the oxygen mask against his face. Just when it felt as though the plane would never slow, the engine noise subsided as the plane's speed fell away and gradually settled into a more sedate pace, rumbling along the tarmac. Once it reached taxi speed, Savage felt the whole plane make a hard left turn, and he pictured it in his mind, exiting the runway towards the terminal. It trundled along for a while then came to a halt, the engines shutting off. Savage wondered about all the passengers above him, if indeed he was in a passenger plane and not a freighter, unclicking their seat belts even though the captain hadn't turned off the Fasten Your Seat Belt sign and gathering their things from overhead lockers even though they were supposed to stay in their seats. Every one of them would be oblivious to the fact that a man was shut inside a box in amongst their bags of holiday clothes. Maybe one or two of them knew. Perhaps the gang had sent a couple of men to ride in the plane, just to keep an eye on proceedings in case Savage broke out and went all *Die Hard* on them.

Outside the box and to his left, Savage heard a clatter followed by one loud bang and several smaller ones. Then came men's voices and bodies clambering around inside the hold—ground crew, most likely, hooking the ramp up to the plane so that the bags could be offloaded. He strained to hear what language they were speaking, to give him some idea of where he'd landed, but the foam in the box muffled their words.

Every second or two came the thud of what he presumed was another bag being thrown onto the loading-ramp conveyor belt. They'd probably empty the bags first so that the passengers could be on their way, leaving the cargo—i.e. him and whatever else was being transported—until last.

Then everything went quiet.

The box suddenly shifted, and Savage's whole world moved surprisingly quickly and smoothly. He was being shoved backwards and then changed direction, going sideways briefly, until he stopped abruptly. A second later, Savage felt the box descending ever so slowly. He guessed he must be outside the plane on a hydraulic lifting device lowering him down to the ground. A moment later, the downward movement ceased, and he felt himself moving forward again, the motion slow and constant. Every so often, the box bumped and wobbled slightly. Savage pictured it in a convoy of other boxes, like a miniature train being hauled across the tarmac by one of those odd little tractor vehicles only seen at airports. About five minutes later, the box became stationary again.

Waiting, waiting, and more agonising waiting.

Savage felt his sanity slipping away and regretted not having the drip in his arm to numb his brain and shield him from that claustrophobic nightmare when the box rose into the air at a slight tilt. *Picked up by a forklift, maybe?* The box travelled a short distance before being dumped down with a jolt. Gentle thuds and bangs went on all around him until they were cut short by the distinctive rattle of a diesel engine and the grind of gears. *A truck?*

Savage was on the move again, judging by the stifled sounds of dense traffic around him, the odd car horn and impatient revving of a car engine, the usual stop-start congestion around an airport. Soon, the truck's speed increased and continued on its journey without holdup, and Savage guessed he must be on some sort of motorway.

As the truck sped along, Savage began singing The Jam's back catalogue in his head to pass the time. He knew every song, chorus and key change intimately, right down to the running times of each album. He started with their debut album *In the City*, released at the height of punk in 1977, running time precisely thirty-two minutes and two seconds. Once he finished that album, he moved on to their second, *This Is the Modern World*, released in the same year, running time thirty-one minutes and nineteen seconds.

At the end of that album, he calculated he'd been traveling on a motorway in the back of the truck for exactly sixty-three minutes and nineteen seconds, just over an hour away from whatever airport he'd landed in. If anyone had had the misfortune of travelling in the box with him, they might've thought Savage was doing that to get a fix on his location, a secret SAS technique for triangulating one's position on the earth by using time and the average speed of a laden truck to calculate distance travelled.

The truth was nothing of the sort, though. Since the drugs had worn off, he was acutely aware that his bladder had swelled to the size of a melon. Singing The Jam's back catalogue took his mind off the fact that he desperately needed to go.

He wasn't averse to peeing in his pants and had done so on many occasion while concealed in hedges, staking out an enemy encampment for days on end, but in the confines of the box, he would rather that be his last resort.

He was just in the middle of *Sound Affects*, released in 1980, their fifth studio album, when the truck turned sharply, ending its so-far smooth journey along whatever mysterious highway it'd been travelling. In contrast, the lorry bumped and shuddered its way along what Savage guessed was a dirt road, throwing the box left and right as it turned abruptly.

Savage totted up his albums and worked out that he'd been in the truck for approximately two and a half hours.

The jolting gradually subsided, and the going became smoother. He felt the truck swing round in a wide arc then stop abruptly. With a monotonous *beep, beep, beep*, the vehicle went into reverse, slowly edging back until it came to another stop. The engine shut off, and a door slammed. Once again, he felt the box lift slightly at an angle, just like it had back at the airport. A forklift was removing it from the back of the truck. Savage felt the box travel a short distance backwards before finally being lowered to the ground.

This is it. Showtime.

Savage got in some last-minute shrugs of his shoulders and flexed his arms and his legs, doing as much as he could manage to limber up. Then he got mentally prepared, which wasn't easy, considering he had no information about where he was or whom he was up against. Savage quickly banished those negative thoughts from his mind, as they were of no use. Without any plan, apart from getting a weapon as soon as possible, he'd have to rely on improvising, and for that to work, he'd need a cool head. Breathing deeply and slowly, he reduced his heartbeat and put his emotions to one side, replacing them with controlled aggression—calm but alert. Whoever faced him on the other side of the box he wouldn't see as people or even enemies, just obstacles that needed to be removed.

The screech of an electric screwdriver came from the top left corner of the box. They were opening the side directly in front of him. The noise of the screwdriver shifted to the top left, then the bottom left, and finally the bottom right. One by one, all the screws holding the front side of the box in place were removed.

Savage clenched his fists and switched on the part of his brain marked Violent Behaviour.

CHAPTER 46

A FTER A MOMENT OF JIGGLING, Savage felt the front of the box lifting off. The foam encasing him stayed put, but a sliver of light crept in all around the edge of the box, forming the perfect outline of a square, the first light he'd seen for hours. He opened his eyes wide, trying to take in as much of the minimal light as possible so they could adjust to not being shrouded in absolute darkness, but as soon as he'd opened them, the block of foam in front of him suddenly came away from his body, and he had to shut them tight again. Brightness flooded the box. Even though his eyes were closed, the glare was painful—like a sun exploding—not surprising since he'd been shut up like a calf in a veal crate for several hours.

The back of him was still wedged in a block of foam, keeping him in a seated position, but his front half was now exposed, free from the suffocating packaging. Air circulated around him, caressing the skin of his hands and arms, an intoxicating sensation. He wanted to leap up, rip the oxygen mask from his face, and indulge in the freedom of being released from the cramped metal cell. Keeping still took all his willpower, body rigid, to keep the deception going. The only thing that would give him away was the chewed-up IV tube dangling beside his shoulder. He had to hope they wouldn't notice it, not until he was ready to make his move.

Relying on only his ears to gather information, he heard the squeaking of wheels coming towards him. Expecting to be lifted out of the foam at any moment and placed on a stretcher like a hospital patient, Savage risked stealing a glance. He fluttered his eyes just once to snatch the briefest of glimpses. Anyone looking might have thought it was an unconscious reaction, like a nervous tic. A good tactic, apart from the fact that it nearly burned out his retinas. His eyes still weren't used to all that brightness pouring in through his pupils. The world around him appeared as a blur of white, a bleached-out photograph. Savage shut them again, gave them a few moments to recover, and tried again. That time, he was more successful. In the millisecond he opened his eyelids, he saw two men in the distance, resting the side of the box against the far wall. Also, a man was walking toward him, carrying a clipboard. Lucky for Savage, the man looked down at the clipboard, not at him. He also noticed that it wasn't a stretcher they'd wheeled in front of him but a low stool like hairdressers use when they're cutting a customer's hair.

Savage clamped his eyes shut just as the man with the clipboard sat down in front of him on the stool. A waft of freshly laundered clothes drifted off him. The guy was so close Savage could hear him breathing through his nose, making a slight whistle.

With both hands, the man gently pulled Savage's head forward, popping it out of the protective foam hollow it had been resting in. Something prodded him in the ear. It stayed there for a few seconds then disappeared. Savage risked a quick look. The man held a small plastic device in his hands with a digital readout on the front, an ear thermometer. Savage closed his eyes again. He guessed the guy must be some sort of doctor, checking the vital signs of all the new arrivals to see what state they were in after being drugged and shut in a box for hours on end.

Next, he took Savage's hand and held it with two fingers pressed against his wrist to take his pulse. That meant he'd be looking at his watch, not Savage.

Savage momentarily flicked his eyes open to test his theory. He was right. The doctor was looking at a gold wristwatch and yawning. Savage shut his eyes again and prayed the man hadn't yet noticed the detached IV tube. He would soon though, and once that happened, the element of surprise would be lost.

Savage stole another glance. Looking over the doctor's right shoulder, he saw that the other two guys, who had lifted the side off his box, were opening more boxes with a large electric screwdriver that screeched loudly every time they undid another screw.

He could see them, but they couldn't really see him. The doctor sat with his back to them, blocking their view. That didn't matter—they looked engrossed in what they were doing, as if opening large metal boxes with unconscious human beings inside was just another part of their daily duties.

From what little he could make out, Savage was in a loading bay not dissimilar to the one in unit 19A, only far larger. More metal boxes had been stacked against the far wall, big silver cubes with reinforcing on the sides and corners. Savage wondered what poor wretches were inside them, more people taken against their will.

Savage watched the doctor, whose eyes were still focused on the watch on his wrist, concentrating on the ticking of the second hand as it made its way around the face back up to the twelve. He was using the full minute to calculate Savage's pulse, and with what few seconds he had left, Savage would go on the offensive.

He waited until the next whine of the electric screwdriver then headbutted the doctor square in the face, using the noise to mask the thwack of his skull against the doctor's. It was the perfect strike for the situation, requiring minimal movement on Savage's part but having a devastating effect. Savage swiftly followed it up with a second, just to be sure the doctor was out cold.

Before the doctor could topple off his stool, Savage grabbed him by the neck to hold him up, keeping him in place and shielding himself from view of the two other men working on the other side of the loading bay.

Savage pulled the doctor closer, improving the cover he was providing, so if the two men did happen to look over in his direction, all they would see was the doctor sitting in front of Savage, and they would assume he was still checking him over. Savage took the opportunity to carefully remove his oxygen mask with his other hand, letting it dangle beside him.

Looking just past the doctor's head, Savage spied on the two men to get a better look at them, sizing up his enemy. Both guys were dressed in tight white T-shirts, jeans and Doc Marten boots, their heads shaved almost down to the skin—the default uniform of a skinhead. Each had a handgun stuffed in the back of his waistband.

They were busy removing the front half of packing foam from another box they'd been working on, revealing another victim. From that angle, Savage could just see the slender, lifeless legs of a woman, another drugged and trafficked victim of the gang.

Still holding onto the doctor with one hand, with his other, he attempted to pat him down, desperately searching for a weapon while keeping a cautious eye on the two men. By contrast, the doctor wore a plain navy-blue sweater with a white shirt underneath and beige chinos. His hair was thick and messy, swept back like Tarzan's. After a quick search, Savage found he was unarmed, apart from a stethoscope in his pocket.

"Magnus," one of the skinheads called over to the doctor. "Hey, Magnus." He had an English accent, Midlands, maybe.

Am I back in the UK? Savage froze and closed his eyes, playing the unconscious victim again.

"Hey, Magnus!" the other skinhead shouted. "We haven't got all day." His accent was definitely German.

When Magnus didn't respond, Savage heard one set of footsteps approaching. He didn't dare look up and kept his eyes firmly shut while still holding onto the doctor by the neck.

"Magnus," the guy repeated.

As he drew closer, Savage released his grip on the doctor, letting him slump off the stool and onto the floor. Savage opened his eyes just in time to see the skinhead, who was less than a foot away, jump in surprise as the doctor collapsed in a heap. That bought Savage a second's worth of distraction. Plenty of time to get to his feet, snatch up the wheeled metal stool and smack the guy in the face. Swung in a huge arc, it made a godawful crack as it collided with the unsuspecting skinhead, hitting him in the temple. Savage would have followed it up with another, but his legs were too stiff to respond. The guy staggered back, eyelids drooping as he fought to hold on to consciousness.

The other skinhead ran towards Savage, drawing his gun from the back of his waistband, but his buddy got in the way, stumbling around semiconscious, trying to keep his balance. The two skinheads nearly collided. The one with the gun couldn't get a clear shot and had to dodge out of the way. As he did so, Savage flung the heavy metal stool at him, knocking the gun from his hand.

Savage ran at him but only got a few strides in before his legs gave way. That didn't matter. Savage turned the stumble to his advantage, adapting it into a rugby tackle as he charged into the guy's midriff, knocking him onto his back and smacking his head against the concrete floor. Before he could recover, Savage punched him in the throat, crushing his larynx. Climbing off him, Savage retrieved the gun he'd knocked out of his hand and pointed it at the skinhead writhing on the floor and struggling for breath.

"Where am I?" Savage asked.

The man could barely get enough air down his throat to stay alive, though, let alone speak. After several painful gasps, his eyelids slowly came down as he blacked out.

The other skinhead was also out cold.

Just at that moment, Savage heard the clatter of feet approaching, lots of them.

He had to work fast. Savage stuffed the gun into his waistband, searched the pockets of the skinhead nearest him, found his smartphone and went straight to Google Maps. A blue dot appeared, showing his precise location. He was in the centre of Norway, towards the south. He had no time to examine his location or take in any names or details. Savage hit the share button at the bottom of the screen and sent the map link straight to Tannaz's phone, together with a hurried text message. He dropped the phone on the floor, smashed it with his heel, then put it back in the pocket of the unconscious skinhead so it looked as though it had been broken in the fight. Next, he pulled the gun from his waistband and pointed it in the direction of the rapidly approaching footsteps.

CHAPTER 47

T HROUGH TWO DOUBLE DOORS AT the far end of the loading bay poured about twenty skinheads, mostly men, but a few women were there, too. Dressed the same as the men Savage had knocked out, they were armed with Kalashnikov AK-47 automatic rifles, the terrorist's go-to weapon of choice, and with good reason—they were light, easy to maintain and fiendishly simple to use.

Fanning out around Savage, they cocked their weapons and aimed them at him, looking for any excuse to pull the trigger. Savage slowly lowered his gun to the floor and put his hands in the air. He saw no point putting up resistance, not unless he wanted to be peppered with bullet holes, which would not help Bella in the slightest.

None of them moved or spoke. They all had hateful looks in their eyes.

"Aren't you going to introduce yourselves?" Savage asked the armed ensemble in front of him. "Although I'll probably forget your names. All you skinheads look alike to me." Savage smiled.

None of his captors saw the funny side of it. They just did their best to look mean, guns poised to spray him with bullets.

A large man with oily receding hair and a neatly trimmed beard marched in behind them and pushed his way through the skinheads, not caring that he shouldered a few of them aside. Overweight, his large belly hung over a military-style webbing belt with a holstered firearm at the side of his waist. His olive-green trousers had been tucked into a pair of black combat boots, and he wore a navy-blue sweater the same as the doctor's, straining at the midriff to contain his massive girth.

The man paraded up and down, stroking his beard while examining the scene in front of him: three unconscious men lying on the floor. After making several thoughtful sighs, he smiled and clapped his hands in applause.

"Bravo! Bravo!" he guffawed. His voice was heavily accented, definitely Norwegian, with a grittiness in the back of the throat, probably from too much brandy and cigars—he looked like the type.

In contrast, the men behind him looked on, confused.

"You see this," he said to them. "This is the work of a skilled warrior. This man has been shut in one of our transport crates for how long?"

"Seven hours," said a ginger-haired skinhead standing closest to Savage, the end of his weapon almost touching him.

If fewer of them had been there, Savage would've attempted to snatch the weapon from him.

The big man slapped his forehead. "Seven hours! Seven hours! Drugged and unarmed, and he takes out three of our men like they were nothing. This is what I'm talking about. This is the kind of soldier we need to be. Resilient, resourceful, unmerciful. Better than our enemies. So that one of us is worth five, no, ten of theirs. That's how we will win this war." He suddenly swung round to face Savage. "But where are my manners? My name is Kurt Thorsgard, and this, my friends, is the legendary Captain John Savage."

Thorsgard applauded, and his men quickly joined in, shouldering their weapons so that they could clap for him.

Savage had no idea what was going on. Not exactly the sex-trafficking HQ he had been expecting. It felt more like a self-help retreat run by skinheads with automatic weapons and violence instead of yoga and incense. And he still had no idea why he'd been taken there, but he remembered Minchie saying something about the head of the gang at unit 19A having a beard and an accent. This Kurt fellow certainly seemed to be the same guy.

When the clapping subsided, Thorsgard looked toward the ginger skinhead. "Patrick," he said, "organise some men to take care of our fallen comrades."

Patrick pointed at several men, who then set about lifting the unconscious bodies of the doctor and the two skinheads Savage had knocked out. They carried them out one between two, holding them by their legs and shoulders.

When they'd left the loading bay, Patrick turned to Thorsgard and asked, "What about the other people in the boxes?"

Savage noticed Patrick's voice had a soft French lilt.

"They're fine for the moment. This is more important." Thorsgard paced up and down with his hands clasped behind his back, contemplating his next words. He stopped, pointed at Savage, and said, "Let me tell you. This man is the real deal. A deadly individual, as we have seen. British Army and SAS. Served in the first Gulf War, where he probably killed more Muslims than all of us put together. Please stop me if I get any of this wrong. After that, he hunted down Bosnian war criminals, although we won't hold that against him. He was just following orders."

Some skinheads sniggered, but Savage noticed others did not. Clearly, they thought hunting down a war criminal who killed innocent Muslim men, women and children in the most unspeakable ways was the wrong thing to do.

"This man is a master at murder, a black belt at killing—no, an artist! A true warrior of the modern age."

Not the reception Savage was expecting. The last thing he would've anticipated was getting smoke blown up his arse for taking out three of their guys, then being told his war exploits were to be regarded as some sort of artistic expression, like painting or synchronised swimming.

Not one for the limelight at the best of times, Savage thought that was quite possibly the most bizarre situation he'd ever found himself in, and he'd been in some of the worst, most messed-up places imaginable. Being surrounded by gun-toting skinheads and their demented leader, who came across like an amateur Shakespearian actor, having praise heaped on him for being good at killing, after being kept in a metal box and flown across Europe—it was the stuff of flu-induced hallucinations.

All he wanted to do was find Bella and get the hell out of that crazy place.

Kurt Thorsgard suddenly stood to attention, snapping his heels together and saluting in Savage's direction. Collectively, the skinheads did the same, popping smart salutes to their foreheads, all except for the ginger-haired one, Patrick, who wouldn't take his eyes or gun off Savage. *Smart boy.*

Savage stood there, looking at the gathering of his new admirers. They looked back at him expectantly, as if anticipating Savage might give some grand speech or give thanks for the wonderful introduction.

Savage shifted uneasily on his feet, looked around him and said, "I really need a piss."

CHAPTER 48

"WHERE'S BELLA?" SAVAGE ASKED AS they led him along a windowless corridor, occasionally prodding him in the back with the barrel of an AK-47 to hurry him up. Four of them were trained on him at all times. Patrick held one, and three other skinheads held the others—two British guys and a Swede, from what Savage could tell. One of the Brits was called Stu and had a rich west-country accent. He had thick wrists, a thick neck and a swastika tattooed on his muscular left arm. The guy looked as though he could bench press a cow without breaking a sweat. The other guy was called Rich, equally sturdy but carrying a bit more weight, giving him a chubby, doughy appearance. Savage found his accent harder to place. It was neutral, possibly south of England or home counties. The Swede was called Jörgen, a big bear of a man, bigger than Stu or Rich. He had an expressionless face, absent eyebrows, pinprick blue eyes and very little to say.

They'd taken the extra precaution of securing Savage's hands behind his back with a set of quick cuffs, as they were called—two thick interlocking zip ties, one for each hand, linked in the middle. Quick cuffs were only a temporary measure, and they would really need to be replaced by some proper metal ones. Otherwise, Savage would have them off at the first chance he got and would relieve one of them of their automatic rifles then go on a killing spree until he found Bella. He just had to bide his time, get hold of something sharp and wait for the right moment when they weren't looking so he could saw through them, break free and snatch a Kalashnikov.

Just at that moment, another skinhead came bounding up to them, breathlessly enthusiastic and eager to please. He was young, not much older than eighteen. A gopher on a mission, he held out a pair of metal cuffs to Patrick. Patrick wasted no time in clamping them on Savage's wrists, not bothering to remove the quick cuffs. Two sets of cuffs were better than one. Patrick was clearly a belts-and-braces man who didn't like to take chances with dangerous prisoners. If it were the other way around, Savage would have done the same, but that meant his chances of getting his hands free were about as good as getting a decent cup of tea, which he was gasping for, apart from the fact that his bladder was the size of a zeppelin and he had nowhere to put any more liquid.

The young skinhead disappeared back the way he came, and the small party and their prisoner continued until they came to a door marked as a men's toilet.

At last, thought Savage, his eyes watering.

Patrick shoved Savage through the door and followed him in with the other three skinheads in tow. "You need to piss, so piss," said Patrick.

Savage found himself in a large, square, no-frills utilitarian bathroom. The place was spotless and smelled of strong industrial disinfectant.

"Well," said Patrick, "relieve yourself."

Savage was standing a good two metres from the nearest urinal. "What, from here? That's a little Tony Hancock joke for you."

Patrick looked unimpressed, and Jörgen's blank expression didn't change.

However, Stu, the British skinhead with the swastika, suddenly became interested. "That's not Tony Hancock," he said. "That's Ronnie Barker in *Porridge*. Classic. First episode, where Fletcher has a medical, and the doctor asks him for a urine sample."

"You know, you're right," said Savage. "That was *Porridge*, wasn't it?"

"You're getting it mixed up with *Hancock's Half Hour*," said Rich, the chubby British skinhead.

"Oh yeah," Savage replied, "The old memory's not so good."

Patrick interrupted. "I thought you were desperate to pee."
Everyone ignored him.

"*Hancock's Half Hour*," said Stu, reminiscing. "That was my old man's favourite TV show. There's that one where the doctor asks him to donate a pint of blood and Hancock says, 'That's nearly an armful.'"

Savage and the two Brits laughed, but Patrick, clearly not a fan of early British TV sitcoms, didn't.

"Shut up!" he screamed. "All of you!" He grabbed Savage by the collar and dragged him over to the nearest urinal, banging his head against the wall. "Now, take a piss."

"Er, a little help here," Savage said, nodding down toward his privates. "You need to uncuff my hands so I can go."

"Nice try," said Patrick. "I'm not taking the cuffs off. I'm not stupid. I'll get your junk out. Now, stand still, old man."

"Be gentle with me," said Savage.

Patrick unzipped Savage's fly, reached into his trousers, and rummaged around a bit until he got hold of his privates.

"Hey, aren't you supposed to buy me dinner first?" asked Savage.

Patrick didn't see the funny side of that and squeezed Savage's manhood hard, making him yelp.

"Not so tough now—"

Before Patrick could finish his sentence, Savage let out a stream of warm urine into Patrick's hand. Patrick leaped back, shaking the wet pee off his hand and swearing. He kicked Savage in the leg then rushed over to the basins and washed it off with copious amounts of liquid soap from a dispenser. "You're going to regret doing that, arsehole."

"Sorry about that," said Savage. "Couldn't hold it in, what with you squeezing and everything." He straightened up and managed to aim the rest of his bladder's contents into the urinal. "Ahh, that's better."

Savage glanced over his shoulder and noticed the other skinheads were sniggering at Patrick, a good sign. Laughing at a superior meant a lack of respect, and a lack of respect meant weakness, and weakness could be leveraged.

After washing his hands, Patrick marched over to Savage, who had just finished his business. Patrick shoved Savage's head hard against the white tiled wall above the urinal. "You're a funny man, aren't you?" he said.

"Yeah," said Savage. "Uncuff me, and I'll show you how funny I am."

Savage's head got cracked against the wall once more.

"You haven't got a clue, have you, Savage?"

"Don't get too close, or I might piss on you again, or maybe you like that sort of thing."

Savage's head hit the wall once more.

"I thought you were supposed to be smart." Patrick pushed his face close to Savage's and grabbed him by what little hair he had, yanking his head back. "Kurt thinks you're some super soldier who needs to be respected. But you're nothing but a clown. You have no idea where you are or what we do here. You're not smart. In fact, you're a disappointment."

"You're from the South of France, aren't you?" Savage said out of the blue.

"What?"

"What part of the South of France are you from?"

"How did you know that?" Patrick released his grip on Savage, a curious but cautious look on his face. He took a step back and raised his weapon. "I said, how did you know that?"

"Don't worry. It's nothing. Your accent gave you away. The way you roll your r's. It's very subtle. But it gave me a clue. It's a bit of a party trick of mine. See, I like guessing accents. It's a sad hobby. So whereabouts in the South of France are you from?"

Patrick thought for a moment, as if telling him his hometown would give Savage some sort of advantage. When he couldn't figure out how that would help Savage in his current predicament, he said, "Nice."

"Nice?" asked Savage. "Wasn't that where that terrorist drove a lorry into all those people? Was that what made you join this organisation, to get revenge?"

"Maybe."

"Interesting."

"Interesting?" Patrick's tone changed from one of cautious curiosity to anger. "Interesting! That Muslim maniac killed eighty-six people, and you think it's interesting!"

"No, I think it's terrible, I really do. What I find interesting is that the attack wasn't long ago. So you must be fairly new to this organisation. A year at the most. Yet you seem to be Kurt's right-hand man. Must have risen through the ranks quickly, leapfrogging all these other guys who've been here longer."

"So what?"

"Kurt must really like you. Taken a shine to you. If you know what I mean." Savage winked then got a hard shove in the small of his back so that his crotch collided with the porcelain urinal.

"Shut your mouth," said Patrick.

"Listen, I think people should be who they want to be. You shouldn't have to hide who you are."

Patrick violently yanked Savage back by his collar, kicking his legs from under him so that he dropped in a heap on the floor, jarring his spine. "Toilet break over. Get him up and out of here," he said to the others.

"What about his cock? It's still hanging out," asked Stu.

"Leave it," said Patrick. "Let everyone see his prick, because that's what he is, a prick."

"Fine by me," said Savage. "I'm sure your beloved boss will be happy to see me flashing my old fella. Maybe I'll see if I can rustle up a stiffie for him. I bet he'd like that, wouldn't he, Patrick." Savage winked again.

Patrick rolled his eyes and kicked Savage in the side, winding him, then turned and pointed at Stu. "You, put his cock back in his trousers."

"Why do I have to do it?" said Stu. "I ain't touching another man's cock."

"That's an order," said Patrick.

"No way," said Stu. "Get Rich to do it."

"Why me?" said Rich, his doughy cheeks suddenly flushing red. "Get Jörgen to do it."

"Because I told you to. Otherwise, I'll tell Kurt."

Patrick was weak—that much was sure. Not strong enough to stand up to Stu, he had to resort to threats to get Rich to do what he asked. His leadership hadn't been earned. It had been handed to him. Whether he was Kurt's boyfriend or not didn't matter. The men didn't respect him.

Rich sighed and ambled over to where Savage lay. Looking the other way, he quickly stuffed Savage's manhood back into his trousers.

"Thank you, darling," said Savage.

"Get him on his feet," said Patrick.

Rich and Stu helped Savage up.

Patrick leaned in so he and Savage were face to face. "You're going to regret getting on the wrong side of me, SAS man."

"I thought we were getting on like a house on fire."

Patrick head butted Savage on the nose. Blood leaked from Savage's nose all down his white linen shirt. *Pity.* He really liked that shirt.

"Things are about to get a lot worse for you," said Patrick. "A lot worse."

CHAPTER 49

THE TEA WASN'T STRONG ENOUGH for Savage's liking. Some idiot had obviously committed the unforgivable sin of putting the milk in first, but it was warm and wet, as they say. *Good enough*. He drank it down quickly then attacked the egg sandwich on the plate in front of him, gulping it down in huge mouthfuls.

"How's that sandwich?" asked Thorsgard, looking out the window. Hands clasped behind his back, his large frame almost blocked out the light.

"It's good," replied Savage. "Very good. Tea could do with being a bit stronger, though."

"I'll remember for next time," replied Thorsgard. "Those eggs were laid today, right here on our farm."

"You should sell them at the local farmers' market," said Savage. "You could call your stall Egg White Supremacy."

No one responded to the joke. Maybe they didn't get it.

They were in Thorsgard's office, a handsome high-ceilinged room lined with overflowing book shelves and smelling of wood smoke from an open fire. It would have been beautiful had it not been for a massive picture of Adolf Hitler staring down from the wall above Thorsgard's grand desk, which was piled high with papers and several computer monitors.

Savage sat on the other side of the desk. He'd changed out of his bloodied clothes and into bulky dark-blue overalls they'd given him, a one-size-fits-all number that did nothing for his figure, rolled up at the cuffs and hems.

The plastic quick cuffs had been removed, but the metal cuffs were still securing him. They'd cuffed one of his hands to the chair he was sitting on. The other they'd released so he could eat and drink.

Patrick, Stu, Rich, and Jörgen, his ever-present guards, stood at the back of the room, guns poised to fire.

Thorsgard turned away from the window to face Savage, who was finishing the last mouthful of his sandwich.

"I hear you've been a bit uncooperative, John," said Thorsgard. "That's unfortunate. Although I have the highest respect for you, my generosity isn't limitless."

"Fine," said Savage. "Let me get Bella, and I'll get out of your greasy hair."

"See what I mean?" Patrick interjected.

"Patience, Patrick." Thorsgard parked his ample behind on the window sill and folded his arms. "John, what do you think it is we do here?"

"You're a sex-trafficking gang."

Everyone in the room laughed except Savage.

"Sex trafficking? Is that what you think we do?" said Thorsgard. "Never. Never in a million years. That kind of thing is abhorrent to us."

"Then how do you explain all those boxes in your loading bay with people inside them, people you've taken against their will?"

"That's recruitment, not sex trafficking."

"Recruitment? Is that what you call it? It's kidnapping, plain and simple. Just like you took Bella. I want to see her right now."

"All in good time. Maybe we should start at the beginning. I think that will help you understand our cause better. Come and join me by the window."

Patrick shouldered his weapon, moved over to where Savage sat, released the cuff from the chair and resecured Savage's hands behind his back.

Savage got to his feet and joined Thorsgard by the generous floor-to-ceiling window with its thick wooden mullions. Through the glass, he got his first real glimpse of the location. They were in an elevated position high above a green valley flanked by mountains and patched with dense forest. In the distance, dividing the two sides of the valley, lay a wide sleeve of flat, lush farmland, a river curling its way through the middle. In the foreground, sheep and cows lazily munched away on grass.

"Beautiful, isn't it?" said Thorsgard. "This is Norway, near Lillehammer in a region called Gudbrandsdalen. Come winter, this will all be covered in snow. A magical sight. But that's not why we chose to base ourselves here. We knew this was the right place for us because of the name, Gudbrandsdalen. Know what it means?"

Savage shook his head.

Thorsgard continued, "In old Norse, Gudbrandsdalen means God's sword. A perfect description of who we are—God's sword against the Islamists."

Savage sighed heavily. "Don't tell me—you think God is on your side. I hate to shock you, but so do Muslim extremists and every other religious nutter on this planet. You're the same, just on opposite sides of the spectrum."

Thorsgard's face went red with rage. "Don't ever compare us to Islamists!" he shouted. "We are the only thing standing between them and their quest for world domination. ISIS, Al-Qaeda, Taliban—whatever name they go by, they all have the same intention, the Islamification of this planet. Do not be fooled. They won't stop until they have achieved their mission, and when one group fails, another springs up in its place. They are vermin. And vermin must be killed. That is the only solution. While governments pussyfoot around, we are the ones who have chosen this crusade. Pushing them back into the sewers and wiping them out. Wherever they are, we will be there too, fighting them, as a sword of God." Thorsgard took a handkerchief from his pocket and wiped the spittle from around his mouth.

Savage took a deep breath. "Okay," he said. "That's your thing. But what's this got to do with Bella? I mean, I'm pretty sure she's not into right-wing politics, so why's she here?"

"Ah, good question. And I'm coming to that." Thorsgard's tongue returned to civility remarkably quickly, one of the signs of a psychopath, being able to switch moods in an instant. Savage really didn't need convincing. Obviously, anyone who snatched people and put them in boxes was in dire need of being locked away from society forever.

Thorsgard continued his speech, pacing across the carpet, hands behind his back.

"There is one thing I do admire about Islamic extremists, and that is their commitment. They think big. Look at 9/11 and specifically the idea of an Islamic State, a terrifying but interesting concept, so I thought, 'Why aren't we doing that? Why aren't we creating our own white utopia, free from the infection of ethnicity? A place where pure white folk can live in safety, knowing that no murderous Muslims can hurt them.' That was the day I conceived our organisation, the Aryan Nation."

Patrick clapped.

Thorsgard raised his hands as if giving a benediction. "On the one hand, we are an attacking force, but on the other, we are a safe haven for decent white folk. After a modest beginning, the Aryan Nation is growing. This is just the beginning. People are flocking to our cause every day, and every day we grow bigger and stronger, expanding our borders. I have big ambitions, but I am under no illusions. To achieve our goals, we need more people, racially pure people who are convinced that the Muslim threat is real and that the only solution is to build an Aryan Nation. We are already planning to take root in other countries like Britain, Germany, France and Sweden. Their governments can't protect them, but we can—"

Savage would've raised his hand at that point, like a schoolboy in class, but he couldn't because of the handcuffs, so he flapped his hands around, trying to catch Thorsgard's attention midspeech. "Excuse me one second. I still don't see what this has got to do with Bella."

Patrick suddenly hit Savage in the stomach with the butt of his AK-47, winding him. "Never interrupt Kurt when he's talking," he snarled.

"Patrick, it's okay. I'm just coming to that." Thorsgard cleared his throat. "Okay, so I have a hard core of roughly one hundred men and women who have joined me since the Aryan Nation began. These are my elite troops, like Patrick, Jörgen, Stu and Rich here. Totally committed, they're always armed and wear the uniform of the skinhead. They chose it themselves: strong, intimidating—"

"And gay," Savage added. "Just need moustaches to go with those big boots and tight jeans, and they'll look fabulous," Savage said camply. Patrick hit him the stomach again with the butt of his rifle. Breathlessly, Savage continued, "It's good you're LGBT friendly. Inclusivity is so overlooked by the far right."

Patrick went to hit him again, but Thorsgard stopped him. "I can see what you're trying to do, Captain Savage. Belittle our organisation with your humour. Very British, but I think by the end of the day, your humour will evaporate. I guarantee that."

Patrick threw Savage a sadistic smile.

Thorsgard continued, "Now, to answer your question, we need more men and women to bolster our numbers so we can achieve our plans. Numbers are growing, but not fast enough, so we also have what we call 'acquired recruits.'"

"Acquired recruits?" asked Savage. "What are they?"

"We seek out racially pure individuals from all over Europe. Strong white people who have specific skills we need to build our nation. Now, they may not have heard of us or have an opinion on the Islamist threat, but they soon do when we've educated them. Bella was one such person."

"So you mean you press-gang them into joining the Aryan Nation, but how do you get them to stay? What do you do if they don't agree with your *education,* brainwash them?"

"Yes, except we call it belief reassignment."

"What? That's insane."

"Not insane, just practical. Some people have been conditioned by liberal Western thinking, deceived into believing Muslims are benign. They need to be purged of this and given a new set of values, the truth about the current crisis we face. We have a very powerful and effective method for doing this. Once completed, ninety-nine percent of recruits are utterly committed to our cause and would even die for it. Come, let me show you."

CHAPTER 50

THEY LED SAVAGE THROUGH A network of corridors to what he presumed was the rear of the building. The high-ceilinged corridors and Scandinavian period features gave way to a plainer extension that appeared to be more recent, judging by the pungent paint smells and utilitarian rubber flooring.

Along the way, skinheads both male and female rushed here and there, Kalashnikovs slung over their shoulders or sidearms in holsters at their waists. Civilians were there too, dressed in everyday clothes, blankly moving through the building, their eyes glazed over—presumably the acquired recruits. Wherever they went, Savage noticed one or more skinheads were always escorting them.

Eventually, they came to a heavy grey door with a round porthole window inset with wired safety glass. Patrick rapped on the outside. The face of a skinhead appeared in the window briefly. From the other side, they heard bolts shoved back, then the door opened with a deep sucking sound. Rubber trim ran all around the edge of it, an acoustic seal for soundproofing the interior.

Inside, the room appeared to be a basic recording-studio setup. Two skinheads sat behind a large sound desk with a control panel peppered with all manner of knobs and switches, plus an array of computer monitors. The screens formed a grid of live black-and-white images, eight in total. Each image showed a person tied to a chair with headphones strapped to his or her head by a sort of belt arrangement. Some struggled and shook their heads violently as if trying to shake the headphones off.

Others slumped forward, presumably passed out. A large glass wall separated the desk from the main recording space, but instead of microphones and musical instruments, there stood a line of small cube-like booths, numbered one to eight. Each had a little door made of blacked-out glass.

"How are our new recruits doing?" asked Thorsgard.

The skinhead sitting nearest replied, "Good. Just another day, I think, and they'll be ready for stages two and three, then boot camp."

"Boot camp? What, are you grooming them to enter *X Factor*?" asked Savage.

Thorsgard ignored him and continued speaking to the skinhead at the desk. "Can you show us a close-up on cubicle two?"

"Sure." The skinhead tapped a few buttons on a keypad, and the image on the screen inside cubicle two enlarged dramatically.

Out of all the people on the computer monitors, that man seemed to be convulsing the most, rocking backwards and forwards as far as his bindings would allow. He twisted from side to side, his face grimacing.

"What's wrong with him?" asked Savage.

"He's listening to our greatest hits," said the skinhead at the desk. Everyone laughed. "Want to hear it?"

Savage nodded.

The skinhead hit a button. From large speakers mounted in the corners of the room came the deafening cries of a baby. Its screams cut through the air like a blunt hacksaw, painful and impossible to ignore, designed that way by nature so the baby got attention and was fed by its mother—a primal survival response. This was a recording, though, relentlessly played over and over on a loop. The poor guy couldn't escape it.

"How long's he been listening?" asked Thorsgard.

The skinhead at the desk said, "Nearly forty-eight hours."

"That's inhuman," said Savage. "He'll lose his mind."

"That's the idea," said Thorsgard. "We keep them in here for about a week, deprived of outside stimulus. Sometimes, we turn off the crying for an hour or two. Sometimes, it's only a minute or two. The silence in between is actually worse because they never know when it's coming back. Shut it off, let's have a look at him."

He hit the pause button, and the two skinheads at the desk rose and went through an exit at the side of the room, leading to the booths. They unlocked the door to number two and untied the man, removing his headphones and dragging him out into the light, his legs trailing uselessly along the floor.

The poor guy was in shock, eyes blinking wide open even though the light must've been blinding. After hauling him over to a sofa at the far end of the line of booths, they sat him upright. A water bottle was pressed to his lips.

After a minute, Thorsgard pushed a button on the intercom. "Okay, put him back in."

Savage watched the poor man as they dragged him, crying, back to the nightmare, his spirit utterly broken.

"Who knew a baby's cries could be so effective?" said Thorsgard. "I thought of it myself on a flight back from London. A baby cried the whole way. By the end, all I wanted to do was strangle it. And that was just a couple of hours. This guy's had it for forty-eight. What do you think, Captain Savage?"

Savage said nothing but just looked straight ahead as they held the guy's head and strapped on the headphones. He knew how torture felt. The outside world ceased to exist, and all that remained was pain. At least he had been prepared for it, trained for it, but that sorry wretch was probably someone off the street who worked in an office, played squash in the evening, and went out with his friends at the weekend.

"What, no jokes or puns?" asked Thorsgard. "I told you we'd make that sense of humour disappear."

"Is this what you put Bella through?" asked Savage.

"Oh, yes. All our acquired recruits go through this process. This is only stage one—disorientation. Stage two is desensitisation, my personal favourite, then boot camp, where we educate and train them, completing their belief reassignment."

"But why did you remove her womb?"

"Each of our new recruits has a part to play in the Aryan

Nation. This fellow here, I believe, was handpicked for his IT expertise. He'll help us attack the Islamists online."

The two skinheads closed the door to booth two and locked it. They returned through the door at the side and sat themselves back down behind the control desk.

"Ready to continue, sir," said one of the skinheads.

Thorsgard nodded. Savage watched as the skinhead pushed a sliding knob, presumably raising the volume in the headphones, inflicting the baby's cries once more, slowly vapourising the guy's mind until his personality would be completely malleable, like wet clay. Then the Aryan Nation could impose their beliefs on him and redirect his energies towards the destruction of Muslims.

If I ever manage to get Bella out of this place, how much of her will be left to return to her mother?

"Very good," Thorsgard said to the men at the sound desk. "Keep up the good work." Then he turned back to Savage. "Where was I?"

"Bella's womb," Savage said.

"We need some people for their practical skills like building, plumbing, farming or cooking. But we also have very specialised roles that need filling. Like Bella, for instance—she was picked to be one of our field agents. Unfortunately, our female agents from time to time have to use their sexuality to get close to targets. I'd prefer it if they didn't, but sometimes it's the only way. We can't afford for them to get pregnant. They're too valuable, so we remove their wombs. It just makes it less complicated. No contraception to remember, etc. In Bella's case, her job was to get close to a Saudi target. And we definitely wouldn't want her getting pregnant with some filthy half-breed Arab brat."

"Saad Sharaf?" asked Savage.

"Yes. He and his father supply arms to Islamic terrorists. We knew Saad had a thing for natural redheads, especially ones with dark eyebrows and lashes. It's a very rare combination, and we couldn't run the risk of simply dyeing the hair of one of our current operatives. Saad might notice if he's a redhead connoisseur. So we needed to find the real thing."

"That was where Minchie came in," said Savage. "He found Bella for you."

"Yes and no. By the time Minchie approached us with information about Bella, we already knew about her from another source of ours, plus we had a couple of other suitable candidates we needed to vet."

"And you did that at Club Zero?" Savage asked.

"Correct. Once I'd observed all three in the flesh, there was no doubt. Bella stood out from the other two girls. It had to be her. We made preparations to snatch her, got a box ready, and smuggled her out of the country."

Savage felt his guts twist. Bella and the others were just a commodity to be taken by The Aryan Nation whenever the need arose, no better than cattle.

"We trained her for months for that mission: self-defence, infiltration, assassination. Her job was to get close to Saad, get onboard his boat, and kill him."

Savage looked puzzled. "Seems an extravagant way to kill one person. Why didn't you just hire a hit man? Get a sniper to take him out."

"Because we wanted to send a message," said Thorsgard. "Make these people feel vulnerable. Paranoid. To fear us. So they know we are an organisation of means. We inserted Bella in Puerto Banus and kept watch over her. She went to a café every day, opposite where Saad's yacht was moored. Sooner or later, Saad would show up, see Bella and want to bed her. The idiot has no self-control when it comes to women. We knew he'd try to get her on board and seduce her, then she'd take him out and anyone who got in her way."

"Then I came along and ruined all your plans." Savage smiled.

"Oh no," said Thorsgard calmly. "We knew you were coming. We engineered it."

CHAPTER 51

THORSGARD'S WORDS REVERBERATED IN HIS ears. Savage was rarely caught off guard and felt a powerful dropping sensation in his gut, like a lift descending too quickly. His mind, which had so far followed a logic that had always served him well, hit reverse, backtracking to see where he had gone wrong.

"No, that's impossible," said Savage.

"John," said Thorsgard, resting his hand on Savage's shoulder, "We've been watching you the whole time, ever since Club Zero. The manager kindly informed us of your interest in our operation—you really should have killed him, you know. We saw you clumsily follow the trail of breadcrumbs until Minchie had to step in and give you a hand."

Then the penny dropped. Everything became clear. They hadn't failed to tie up a loose end by letting Minchie live. They'd left him alive on purpose so that he could lead Savage right to them.

Thorsgard stroked his beard, clearly enjoying the sadistic pleasure of catching Savage out. "Didn't you think it was strange that Minchie was still alive after the complete farce he pulled with the van? Anyone else would've executed him for such a diabolical mistake. But I always like leaving people in my debt. You never know when they'll come in useful. Minchie played his part very well. Turned up just when you were out of leads. Patrick here was convinced you'd sense a trap. Thought it was too obvious. But you'd didn't suspect a thing."

Patrick sniggered. "Told you you're not as smart as you think."

Savage felt the blood drain from his face. He'd been played, set up from the start, and he hadn't even realised it. Maybe Patrick was right. Perhaps he wasn't as clever as he thought he was.

He shook these feelings off. Couldn't give in to negativity. None of that could be helped, and the situation hadn't really changed. His intention all along had been to get inside this organisation and get Bella back, and he'd achieved the first part. Plus, he still had his advantage. He just had to be patient.

The self-satisfaction dripped off Patrick like a sweet, sickly goo. "We got Minchie to feed you enough information to get you to leave London. Make you head for Spain, where it was a lot easier to snatch you."

"How so?" asked Savage.

"We'd wound up our operation at unit 19A, as you'd seen," replied Thorsgard. "Never good to stay too long in one place, but we still had an active transport hub in Spain at Puerto Banus, so we could prepare a box for you there and all the necessary sedation. You don't realise how precise an art that is. We knew you'd come once you knew Bella was here. Plus, you were on your own. Didn't have that Iranian bitch to watch your back. What's her name? Tannaz. But you did take a detour along the way. Risking your life to save those whores. Very noble of you. We nearly stepped in at that point, thought you were going to get yourself killed in there. Very impressive, though, taking out the head of a criminal gang on your own. Next thing we knew, you were in the café with Bella. How did you know she'd be there?"

"Got lucky," said Savage. "One of the girls I rescued had seen Bella on the quayside a few times."

"Blind luck, eh?" said Thorsgard. "You disappoint me."

"Like I said, not as smart as you think you are," added Patrick. The guy was beginning to irritate Savage.

"You found us a little quicker than we expected," said Thorsgard. "Your timing wasn't great. You showed up when Saad finally arrived, after we'd been waiting weeks for him to appear. Not ideal. But one thing we are good at is having backup plans and adapting. After Bella failed to pull the trigger and you caused all that commotion on the quayside, another one of our field operatives slipped aboard dressed as a deckhand and planted a bomb. So we killed Saad and got you. Two birds with one stone."

"Why didn't you just snatch me the second I touched down in Spain?" asked Savage. "Would've been much easier."

"Yes, but far less fun. Besides, we want to see how good you were. Like an initiation test. Wanted to know how you coped with problems."

"And why would you need to know that?"

"You're a valuable asset to an organisation like ours. Someone with all your SAS experience... We could learn a lot." Thorsgard cleared his throat. "You will train my elite troops. Impart your SAS knowledge to them, so we can use it against the threat of Islam. Make us an unstoppable fighting force. Men and women the Islamists will be terrified of."

"I don't think Islamic extremists are terrified of anything," replied Savage.

"Perhaps not. But you *will* train my elite troops."

"If I refuse, are you going to try and brainwash me? Because I can tell you now, that shit will not work on me—I've had far worse."

"I believe you, but first I'd like to show you the second stage, desensitisation. Come, follow me."

Just as they left the sound studio, Stu and Rich sidled up to Savage.

Stu spoke quietly in Savage's ear. "That business rescuing those young girls from that whorehouse... We really respect that."

Savage didn't know how to take that, coming from a couple of guys who worked for an organisation that did basically the same thing but under a different banner. *Ridiculous double standards.* Everyone here was deluded, especially the ones who hadn't been brainwashed. In fact, they were worse. They had one weakness, though—a weakness he could exploit and use to bring about their downfall.

CHAPTER 52

A T THE END OF THE corridor stood two skinheads guarding a wide double door. As Thorsgard and his little entourage approached, the two men saluted and snapped to attention. Thorsgard saluted back. One of the skinheads pulled out a bunch of keys on a retractable cord and unlocked the door, holding it open for the group to pass through.

Stepping out into the open air for the first time since arriving, Savage got his first proper look at the HQ of the Aryan Nation. Surrounded by patchy woodland, it nestled on a gently sloping hill, facing south. Savage had no idea of the time, but the sun had passed its zenith and was making its descent towards the horizon, so he guessed late afternoon or early evening.

As he suspected, the building he'd just exited was a bland concrete extension. Wide, unpainted and windowless, a bleak bunker with no aesthetic quality whatsoever, existing purely to contain rooms and spaces. By contrast, the building it butted up against was a traditional Norwegian farmhouse. Clad in thick burgundy-stained timber, it had a wide, gently pitched roof and tall, finger-like chimneys. It looked more like a fairy-tale farmer and his wife should live there rather than a bunch of dangerous neo-Nazis.

Turning back to the view in front of him was like looking at a hastily constructed college campus. Mismatched buildings were haphazardly scattered all over the gently rolling hillside. At least three buildings were in various stages of construction, and to the far left, a bright-yellow Caterpillar digger hacked away at the earth, preparing deep foundations.

"That's going to be our new meeting hall," said Thorsgard, pointing at the digger. "At the moment, we use the mess hall located in the extension. Not ideal."

To the far left stood a two-storey grey concrete structure with rows and rows of tiny round windows, barely bigger than dinner plates. More guards were posted outside.

"What's in there?" asked Savage.

"That's the accommodation block for all our acquired recruits, where you'll also be staying."

It figures. The place looked more like a prison, just in case their brainwashing wasn't as effective as they thought it was and someone had the smart idea of making a run for the treeline.

They intended to imprison Savage there for the foreseeable future, forever, in fact. The very fact that Thorsgard was happily showing off his entire operation, leaving nothing out, meant they had no intention of letting him leave, ever. When he outlasted his usefulness, he would probably be shot in the head and dumped in one of the foundation trenches and smothered in wet concrete.

"So where do your elite troops live?" asked Savage.

"In the extension behind us," replied Thorsgard. "It was the first building we constructed, but even that is now too small." He pointed out other buildings from the hodgepodge of constructions in front of them. "That's the armoury. Those are the stores. Garages over there, library including classrooms, and in the distance is our farm. We grow most of our food on site. We're very proud of its organic credentials, and we're almost self-sufficient."

Savage wanted to laugh at the irony of it all, the warped self-righteousness of environmentally friendly Nazis. Maybe they were following in Hitler's hypocritical footsteps. He had been a vegetarian and couldn't abide cruelty to animals but had no problem exterminating millions of innocent people. Then again, logic and fascism never really saw eye to eye.

Thorsgard continued, "We have over seventy hectares of land, plenty of room for expansion, and our nearest neighbour is ten kilometres away, far from prying eyes. Nobody comes up here, and we're left to get on with things, growing stronger every day."

"What's that round building?" Savage pointed at a drum-like structure in the centre of everything. Like all the other new buildings there, it was made from a depressing grey concrete.

"That's our next destination, the Desensitising Zone. Follow me."

It sounded like a spa where they would offer you bathrobes and play soothing music and give you rubdowns while you sipped complimentary coconut water. Thorsgard certainly liked branding things with poncey names when, in reality, all his activities involved some sort of torture, and Savage had a strong feeling that place would be no different.

Roughly double height, it looked like a small version of the old cylindrical gas holders that Savage used to see in and around London when he was a lad. As they walked around the circumference to the entrance, Savage noticed a large, low square block joined onto the back of the building. As they passed it, several dog barks came from inside.

"Is that a kennel?" asked Savage.

"Yes, we also breed dogs here," said Thorsgard, who then glanced at his watch. "And we're right on time for today's performance. Come on."

Savage followed Thorsgard in through a modest-sized door guarded by a couple of skinhead sentries, followed by Patrick, Jörgen, Rich and Stu. Inside, the space was like a miniature coliseum. Sunken into the ground was a circular area with a drain in the middle, surrounded by a concrete retaining wall about five feet high. Set into the retaining wall was a single metal grille door on strong hinges with a dark cement tunnel behind it. Above the retaining wall, bolted into the top of the concrete, was a metal rail and barrier, and behind those were arranged three tiers of simple stepped concrete seating. Apart from the guards, the place was empty.

Thorsgard, Savage and the rest of them shuffled along the topmost tier and sat down.

"What happens here?" asked Savage.

Thorsgard smiled proudly. "This is the second stage of

Belief Reassignment. After new recruits have completed a week in the sound studio, listening to our greatest hits"—he made air quotes—"they come here until desensitisation is complete. Sometimes, it can take only a couple of sessions. With others, they need to keep coming back until the treatment works. We've just got a few minutes to wait until their daily session begins."

"What happens in a session?" asked Savage.

"Ah, that would spoil the surprise."

"Could I ask you something else?"

"Of course. What's on your mind?"

"The business with the wombs being found in the van when Minchie messed up... How come the police didn't pursue it? The investigation just stopped. Did you have anything to do with that?"

"A good question. We have a key figure in the UK police force, who is extremely supportive of our cause. In fact, high-ranking officers in many forces across Europe are sympathetic to what we're trying to achieve. Of course, they can't admit it. They have to be seen to favour equality and all that nonsense. However, behind the scenes, they help us whenever they can—make things go away, like the van and its contents. I know you still see us as well-meaning amateurs, Captain Savage, but we are the real deal, as our Aryan brothers in the States call us. We have powerful patrons and supporters everywhere, big corporations that back us financially. They see us as an investment, safeguarding Western capitalism. You need to start taking us seriously."

"I've always taken you seriously. It's just now I'm taking you even more seriously."

"I'm glad to hear it. Ah, here they come."

Escorted by a couple of skinhead guards came a handful of new recruits. They looked confused, glancing around the space they were in, presumably for the first time. They were led to the lowest tier of seating, just above the arena. Another group of recruits entered after them, but those had troubled expressions on their faces, and some were crying. One girl tried to make a run for it, back out the door she'd come in from. A skinhead caught her round the waist and dragged her back.

"No, no, no!" she screamed as he shoved her into the second tier and forced her to sit down with the others.

He pulled some quick cuffs from his back pocket and secured her legs at the ankles so she couldn't run away. Finally, a third group entered, whose faces appeared ghostlike, totally devoid of emotion. Like a procession of automatons, they calmly sat on the third tier alongside Thorsgard, Savage and the others.

"They're all at different stages of the treatment," noted Thorsgard. "First tier is new to this and don't know what to expect. Second tier have already had several sessions and are still emotional, but that won't last long. Soon, they'll be like the people in the third tier, desensitized and ready to move on to boot camp for their education and training."

When everyone was seated, the metal grille door in the sunken arena automatically flew open. Seconds later, from the tunnel came the clip-clop of small hooves on cement. Into the arena bounced a pretty lamb, not a new-born by any means, but not fully grown either. Maybe a few months old, it skipped happily around the arena, taking in its environment. Savage had heard that lambs were far more intelligent than most people give them credit for, and the little creature seemed to be proving the point as it curiously looked up at all the human faces surrounding it, almost as if questioning what they were doing there. Trotting and bleating happily as it went, the lamb made several circuits of the arena, stopping now and then to snuffle on the floor or to get a closer look at the people by reaching up against the retaining wall on its hind legs.

Everyone seated in front of Savage in the second tier began crying at the lamb's appearance. One woman covered her eyes and ears.

A skinhead standing at the side pushed his way along the row to where she sat and knocked her hands away with the butt of his Kalashnikov. "Watch and listen!" he shouted mercilessly. When he was convinced everyone's undivided attention was on the lamb, the skinhead took a whistle from his pocket and blew a shrill blast.

Painful groans rose from people in the second tier and from some in the first tier, who sensed something sinister was about to happen.

Guttural growls echoed from somewhere down the cement tunnel. Five emaciated pit bull terriers suddenly charged into the arena, their coats grey and dull like the concrete around them. The lamb instinctively ran to the far end of the arena, as far away as it could get. It turned and faced the dogs, watching them as they slowly closed in around it, their jaws hanging open in salivating grins, revealing rows of sharp spiked teeth.

The whistle blew a second time.

All five pit bulls dived for the lamb. The poor creature made no sound as the dogs tore it apart.

Everyone seated in the rows in front of Savage sobbed. Some looked away but got a swift crack on the head from one of the nearby skinheads until they returned their gaze to the horrific sight.

The people in the third row alongside Savage remained impassive, though, sitting calmly as if nothing had happened. Desensitisation was obviously complete for them.

The skinhead blew the whistle a third time. Automatically, the dogs left their prey and returned through the cement tunnel, blood dripping from their mouths.

Thorsgard looked at Savage expectantly, hoping he'd be shocked and appalled.

"Like I said," Savage remarked. "That shit's not going to work on me."

"And like I said," replied Thorsgard, "I don't expect it to. But what I've got lined up next will."

CHAPTER 53

THORSGARD AND HIS MEN LED Savage over to the library, perhaps the only new building that had any aesthetic quality. Modern and boxy, with large expanses of green-tinted glass, it was clad in wood that had been charred, giving it the look of a burnt matchbox—all very Scandi.

"An architect designed this for us," remarked Thorsgard.

"What happened to him?"

"Sadly, the belief reassignment didn't go so well, and we had to put him down. But not to worry. When the time's right, we'll simply snatch another one."

That was how Thorsgard saw the world: one large sweet shop where he could take what he needed as long as the main ingredient was pure and white, like refined sugar.

Inside, the library was a surreal experience. Just like a regular library, it had a couple of librarians behind a desk, a skinhead man and woman processing a pile of books, presumably not *Fifty Shades of Grey* or *The Very Hungry Caterpillar*, but instead books about why white people were so much better than everyone else.

As they passed through the lobby, Savage spotted a noticeboard with a mess of flyers and posters pinned to it, but rather than advertising events like cake sales and coffee mornings, they were emblazoned with slogans for talks and meetings such as Why Islam Is Not a Religion, What to Do if You Suspect a Comrade Is Homosexual and Why White People and Ethnics Should Not Co-exist.

"We call this a library, but it's much more than that,"

Thorsgard said proudly, his hands aloft, ever the showman. "Upstairs, there are classrooms and meeting rooms where new recruits start boot camp and their re-education, or *true education* as we like to call it."

"What's downstairs?"

"Let's go upstairs first—I like to leave the best until last."

Savage followed Thorsgard up a flight of sculptural wooden stairs with open risers supported by steel stringers and flanked with a steel-cable balustrade. The architect who had designed it clearly had talent, a talent cut short by a mindless narcissist with greasy hair and fledgling type 2 diabetes—hardly what you'd call the master race.

Patrick, Jörgen, Stu and Rich joined Thorsgard and Savage on the first-floor landing, a wide, rectangular space with a generous atrium that threw light down the stairwell. *Another nice touch.*

Off the landing were five doors, each with a vertical window allowing Savage to glimpse into each room.

"Take a look," said Thorsgard. "Have a listen."

Savage edged closer to the nearest one. Through the door he saw a brightly lit, neat and pristine classroom full of rows of American-style school desks, the kind that a person slides into from one side with a desktop fixed on the other side. Each desk was occupied by an adult. The teacher at the front flicked through a PowerPoint presentation.

The slide projected at the moment was titled Islam: The Rise of Evil. It showed a world map dated AD 632, the death of Muhammed. The entire map was white apart from a small black splodge covering some of the Arabian Peninsula. She clicked to the next slide, one hundred years later, and that small black splodge had grown to include North Africa, Spain, Portugal and the whole of the Middle East, just stopping short of India. As she clicked forward to the present day, Islam receded from Spain and Portugal but spread to engulf a third of Africa, pretty much all of the Middle East and Central Asia and around a third of South-east Asia. Europe and America were also peppered with black dots.

An annotation on the slide read Islam—World's Second Largest Religion, World's Fastest Growing Religion.

The teacher clicked to the next slide, and the class gave a collective gasp. On screen was a map of the world titled 2100—The Islamification of the Planet. The black of Islam dominated the entire map apart from some spots of white scattered around Europe, Australia and, of course, America.

"This is what will happen in the future unless we do something!" cried the teacher, slapping her hand on the nearest desk. "Islam intends to rape this planet, drive out decent white folk and the society we have created and worked so hard for. They hate the progress we have achieved and want to return this earth to the Middle Ages. The only people who can do something about it are you and you and you and you." She pointed at everyone in the classroom. "Remember where we are and why this place was chosen. Gudbrandsdalen. Remember what it means—God's sword. That is what we are. Every one of us is God's sword and will cut down the Muslim, hack them back to the worthless desert hellholes they came from while growing the borders of our own Aryan Nation. A paradise free from their filthy practices and backward ways."

Savage turned back to face Thorsgard and the others. "Quite a speech," he said. "Are you sure that last map was accurate?"

"It's a calculated projection we found on the internet," said Patrick.

"Really?" said Savage. "Oh, well it must be true if it was on the internet."

Thorsgard jutted his chin out defiantly. "Something must be done about the Muslim threat. You must realise that."

"By Muslims, you mean extremists. Because I've met plenty of Muslims who just want to live in peace with everyone else."

"No, I mean all of them. They're all jihadis at heart, John. There's a war coming, and you're lucky to be on the right side."

"Firstly, they're not all jihadis. Secondly, what do you know about war? Have you ever been in one?"

"I did my national service."

Savage laughed. "Not the same, not by a long shot. Think of the worst hell you can imagine, and it won't even come close to a real war. There are no winners, just the side left with the least number of casualties. There's a saying: 'War is a series of disasters that ends in victory.' It's a complete bloody mess, sucking in lives like a fire sucks in oxygen, and if you'd experienced it, you'd be trying to find another way around. I saw the atrocities committed in Bosnia, what they did to young Muslim families. They machinegunned their husbands in front of them then raped the wives while they cut their children's throats. Girls as young as eleven and twelve were raped. Is that part of your glorious vision?"

Patrick went to say something, his mouth opening in an angry O shape, but Thorsgard held up a hand to silence him.

"We could get into an argument here, but we'd just go back and forth without getting anywhere, you entrenched in your beliefs and us entrenched in ours."

"They're not beliefs," said Savage. "They're facts. I was there."

"Of course, of course. But this is all beside the point."

"And what is the point?"

"That you will start training our elite troops. We have done okay up to now. I have passed on some of my limited military knowledge to my men, and we have a few ex-soldiers here and some self-defence instructors, plus information about bomb making that we can get off the internet, but what you can teach us is far superior, possibly the best in the world. Your firsthand experience will take us from being good soldiers to great ones. You will start tomorrow. We'll give you everything you need and—"

Savage held up his hand for silence. "Yeah, I've had a think about that, and I'm afraid it's going to be a no on that front."

Rather than being angry, Thorsgard smiled and stroked his beard. "I thought you might say that. Please follow me."

Patrick gave Savage a hard shove in the back towards the stairs. *So,* thought Savage as he descended the steps, *this is where my torture begins.*

"Oh, Savage, what have you done?"

Jeff Perkins. Savage hadn't heard a peep out of him since he'd been trapped in the box. *Nice of you to join me.*

"Stop mucking about. This is serious. You're going to get tortured again. Remember what happened last time? What it did to your head. All the beating you got in the Gulf War was pretty much where I came from."

True, but it was also because I killed a lot of people and couldn't handle it. Listen, why do you always appear at the worst times?

"Because I'm your fear, anger and guilt all rolled into one. That's why. You need to get ready. You're far too casual about this. Things are going to get really bad from now on. Don't you realise that? Just give in, do what they ask and avoid all the pain. You're older now. You won't be able to take it."

To be honest, I don't give a shit. I'm not helping these pricks so they can hurt innocent people, so I'll take the consequences. If that means being tortured, then so be it.

Down in the lobby, they took the next set of stairs into the basement, where the interior changed dramatically. Gone were the wood and tinted glass, replaced by bleak concrete blocks and rough cement flooring. A few bare bulbs dangled from the ceiling, and at one end of the small rectangular landing sat a heavy steel door guarded by two more skinheads, as if it were a bank vault. They jumped to attention when they saw Thorsgard, saluting quickly, desperate to impress.

"Open the door please, gentlemen."

One of the men twisted a key in the lock and pushed it open.

Thorsgard turned to Savage. "This is where we store our files and documents, but now we've found a whole new use for it."

The space was dark as they entered the room. Patrick reached his hand around the corner and flicked the lights on, revealing a large, low-ceilinged room lined with rows and rows of identical filing cabinets.

In the centre of the room, a large, square wooden post had been set into the concrete. Shackled to it was Bella.

CHAPTER 54

"Bella!" cried Savage.

Dressed in the same baggy overalls as Savage, she raised her head as though it took all her effort. Her eyes were weary yet terrified.

Savage tried to run to her, but Stu grabbed him by the handcuffs and yanked him back like a dog on a lead.

"Patrick, give her some water," said Thorsgard.

The Frenchman obeyed and removed a small bottle from a pack of six on a table to the left of them. Savage noticed a cattle prod lying next to it.

Patrick approached Bella, unscrewed the cap of the bottle and up-ended its contents into her mouth. The water filled up her mouth far too quickly for her to swallow, spilling everywhere. Bella coughed and spluttered.

"Let her drink it properly!" yelled Savage.

Patrick ignored him, threw the empty bottle on the floor, and walked back to the table, where he picked up the cattle prod and flicked it on. He held it in the air and tested it a few times. The long, thin rod fizzed at the end, streaks of electricity leaping between the two contact prongs. Then he calmly walked back towards Bella, the cattle prod by his side.

"No, no, no!" shouted Savage. Struggling against Stu's grip, he nearly broke free until Rich came and helped restrain him. Savage writhed and twisted and swore at Patrick, screaming for him to leave her alone.

"Don't," said Rich, quietly in Savage's ear. "You'll only make it worse for her."

When Bella caught sight of the cattle prod in Patrick's hand, she too struggled and screamed.

"Stop!" pleaded Savage. "Stop!"

"That cattle prod carries a thousand volts of electricity." Thorsgard casually remarked. "Would you like Patrick to try it out on Bella?"

"No," Savage shouted. "I'll train your troops. Just don't hurt Bella."

"What was that?" asked Thorsgard, stringing it out.

"I'll do it. Just stop him hurting Bella." Savage spat out the words.

"Very good," said Thorsgard. "Okay, Patrick, Captain Savage has seen sense, stop now."

But Patrick continued walking towards her, the menacing cattle prod hissing by his side.

"That's enough, Patrick," Thorsgard shouted.

"Leave her alone!" Savage cried, still struggling against Stu and Rich's grasp.

Without being asked, Jörgen strode over to Patrick, grabbed him by the arm and pulled him away before he had a chance to use the cattle prod on Bella.

Eyes ablaze, Patrick wheeled around and pointed the prod at Jörgen's chest. "Don't ever do that again," he said, venom in every word. "I outrank you in this organisation. Do you hear me?"

"You ignored an order from Kurt," Jörgen said in a thick, blunt Swedish accent. "Kurt outranks you."

"Everyone, calm down," said Thorsgard.

"We're too soft," Patrick said, throwing the cattle prod on the floor.

Savage turned to Thorsgard. "I'll train your troops, but I have conditions."

"You're in no position to make demands," said Patrick, now standing beside Thorsgard.

"Patrick, be quiet," said Thorsgard. "Go on."

Savage continued. "You move Bella from this place and put her somewhere comfortable with a bed."

"She'll still be under lock and key, but fine," replied Thorsgard.

"I see her every morning and every evening to check she's okay."

"Fine, too."

"And lastly, you keep your pissy little French-poodle lapdog away from her."

Patrick went for Savage, but Thorsgard blocked his way. "Get a hold of yourself, Patrick. Let him have his little victory. We are getting what we want, remember? Why don't you get yourself a coffee from the mess, and calm down, okay?"

Patrick looked at Thorsgard then back at Savage, hatred still pulsing through his veins. A second later, he turned tail, but before he climbed the stairs, he shouted, "We're too soft!"

Savage made a mental note of Patrick's little outburst, which might be useful, then he asked, "May I speak with Bella?"

"Quickly," Thorsgard replied.

Stu and Rich relinquished their grip on Savage, who strode over to the girl, hanging limply from the post.

"Bella? Bella?" he said quietly. "It's me, John, a friend of your mum's."

She managed to raise her head, though that took all her effort. Through tearful eyes, she looked at Savage. "I want to go home." Her voice, little more than a whisper, sounded brittle, small and raspy.

"You're so brave, Bella. Not long now," he said. "Just hang on a bit longer. And it will all be over."

"Really?"

"I promise."

"Okay, that's enough," said Thorsgard. "You need to get some sleep, Captain Savage. You've got a big day tomorrow."

Yep, tomorrow is the beginning of the end for the Aryan Nation.

CHAPTER 55

SAVAGE WAS ALREADY AWAKE WHEN they came for him. He'd hadn't slept but just did his usual dozing-but-awake thing. Too much was on his mind, and he'd been running through various scenarios in his head, making sure what he did next would create the best outcome without raising too many eyebrows. It would be tricky, but people with strong beliefs were always a lot easier to manipulate than people who weren't bothered about anything. It didn't have to be perfect, either—just effective.

He'd been placed in the accommodation block for new recruits, the one that looked like a prison. A modest locked room with no windows and not much of anything else, apart from a shiny metal built-in toilet and a thin mattress slung on the floor, it felt like the Hilton after what Savage had been through. Also, they'd taken his handcuffs off for the night. Things were looking up. All he needed was a decent cup of tea or two.

As soon as the skinheads unlocked the door, the cuffs were back on Savage. Patrick, Stu and Rich had pointed their weapons at him from out in the corridor, while Jörgen, the biggest of the four—and therefore the safest bet to take on Savage should he try something—went into his room and clamped the metal cuffs behind his back.

Savage complied like a good little captive, following them out into the corridor and past several doors until they came to the last room at the end, where they let him look through a spy hole. Peering into the fish-eye lens, he got a distorted view of the room inside. Bella was asleep on the mattress, a thin blanket twisted around her. He made them wait until she'd turned over so he knew she was still alive. From what he could see, she looked comfortable. He didn't know what state her mind was in, but he could do nothing about that right then.

Then they led him to breakfast in the mess hall.

"Really looking forward to your training," remarked Patrick. "See if you're worth all this hassle."

"Like the advert says, I'm worth it," Savage replied.

Patrick looked at him as if trying to figure out whether he was being straight or sarcastic and whether he could do with being butted in the head with a gun.

When they got into the mess hall, an intoxicating cloud of breakfast cooking smells hung in the air, instantly making Savage's mouth water. Along one wall, several trestle tables had been placed, and a handful of cooks were carrying out large stainless-steel serving dishes, the kind with lift-up metal lids to keep the food warm. Reminding Savage of an all-inclusive holiday buffet in Spain, the so-called elite troops had formed an orderly queue, trays tucked under their arms and their ever-present automatic rifles slung over their backs, eagerly waiting to gorge themselves.

"Bacon and eggs for breakfast?" asked Savage.

"That's just the start," replied Rich, enthusiastically. "Breakfasts here are legendary. There's scrambled eggs, fried eggs, poached eggs, Scotch eggs, omelettes, three types of sausage, smoked salmon, fried bread, cheese, ham and some weird pickled fish the Scandis like."

"Herring," Jörgen added.

"Don't forget the pastries," said Stu. "There's donuts, pain au chocolats, Danish pastries, something Norwegian called krumkaker..."

"Oh, man," Rich added, licking his lips. "Krumkaker is the best, sort of a rolled-up pancake."

Just at that moment, Thorsgard arrived. Everyone in the mess stood to attention and saluted except Savage, of course, whose cuffs prevented him, but he wouldn't have saluted anyway.

A hearty grin spread across Thorsgard's face. "Morning,

Captain Savage. Glad you could join us for breakfast. Remove his cuffs, gentlemen."

Patrick immediately protested. "Do you think that's wise, Kurt?"

"He's in a room with over one hundred armed members of our elite troop. I doubt he's going to try anything."

Patrick rolled his eyes, believing it was a mistake, but he still fished the keys from his pocket and took the cuffs off Savage.

"That's better," said Thorsgard. "Now, how did you sleep, Captain Savage?"

Savage ignored the pleasantries and got straight down to it. *Time to put things in motion.* "What the hell is all this?" he asked, a disapproving sneer across his face.

They frowned at Savage's insolence.

"I'm not sure what you mean, Captain Savage," said Thorsgard.

Savage moved closer to Thorsgard so that he could speak more intimately. "Are these all your elite troops?"

"Yes, apart from the ones on guard duty."

"What are you doing, fattening them up for Christmas? I know you have a farm, but I didn't realise you were breeding man-pigs as well."

Thorsgard looked along the line of skinheads as they shuffled along the line of trestle tables, piling their plates with rich, greasy breakfast food. A few of the men were in good shape, but the majority spilled out of their tight jeans and T-shirts. One was so large he had broken into a sweat just from the exertion of standing upright in a queue.

"Look, I've agreed to train your troops," said Savage, "but I can only do that if you're going to take this seriously. You need to make some drastic changes. They look far from elite. In fact, they only thing they could defeat right now is a three-course meal."

"Okay," said Thorsgard. "Do what you must." He cleared his throat and addressed the troops. "Listen, everyone." In an instant, the room was quiet. "There are going to be some changes, and I have instructed Captain Savage here to carry them out. Obey him as you would me." Thorsgard turned to Savage. "They're all yours."

Savage stepped forward, flanked by Rich and Stu on one side with Patrick and Jörgen on the other. "All of you, stop," said Savage. "Put the food down. No one is eating any more of that crap. You are elite troops. You need to start acting like it."

A collective groan rose up from around the room, including a few grumbles from Stu and Rich.

"From now on," continued Savage, "it's porridge for breakfast. You need good-quality carbs for hard training. And hard training starts today."

More grumbles.

"Silence!" shouted Thorsgard. The room went quiet.

A single hand rose in the air. It belonged to a skinhead in the queue with a red face, who kept scratching himself nervously. "I don't like porridge. Can I have toast?" he asked.

Savage sighed. "Toast is fine."

Another hand raised belonging to a tall skinhead with glasses.

"What?" Savage snapped.

"In Norway, it's traditional to have scrambled eggs and smoked salmon for breakfast."

A lot of murmuring of assent broke out along the queue from a big Norwegian contingent.

"That is true," said Thorsgard.

"Okay," replied Savage. "You can have scrambled eggs and smoked salmon. But no milk or butter in the scrambled eggs. Fatty food is only good for slowing you down. The same goes for lunch and dinner, which will now be restricted to grilled fish and chicken with steamed vegetables."

Protest broke out among the ranks. A wave of whining spread throughout the hall, a surreal sight coming from a horde of tough-looking skinheads. They were nothing but a bunch of fussy eaters with shaved heads. None of his changes were going down well. *Perfect.*

"What will the vegetables be?" asked someone at the front of the queue. "Because I can't eat green beans."

"I'll have your green beans," said the guy next to him. "I like green beans."

"I love green beans," said someone else. "But no asparagus. Makes my piss stale." Mumbles of agreement broke out around the hall.

"Shut up!" Savage shouted. "Shut up! Stop talking about green beans and asparagus and stale piss. This is not a holiday camp. You are not children. You'll get what you're given, healthy food to keep you fighting fit. Now, put your trays down and await instructions."

A reluctant clatter of trays piling up echoed around the hall as over one hundred skinheads were denied their favourite food perks.

A good start. Take their food away under the guise of healthy eating. Difficult to argue against. Difficult not to justify, especially by white supremacists calling themselves elite troops. Right now, they'll all be bitching about their new diet and about their new short-arsed British instructor with an attitude.

They had no idea things were about to get a whole lot worse. Savage turned to the four men standing next to him. "Anyone here know a good five-k run we could do, preferably in a loop across country?"

"I do," said Patrick.

"Great," said Savage. He then turned back to address the hall. "Okay, look sharp, everyone. We're going on a five-k run."

"But we haven't had breakfast yet," said the green-bean guy.

Savage marched over to him. Rich, Stu, Jörgen and Patrick went with him. Savage got all up in the guy's face. "You think you get a buffet laid out for you when you're in a warzone, sweetheart? You think your Islamic counterparts are chowing down on all-you-can-eat breakfasts? Course not. They're living in mud huts, eating whatever they can scratch out from the dustbowls they live in. I've seen them survive on nothing but mouldy flatbread and dirty water for weeks." Taking a step back, Savage addressed the rest of the men. "No wonder they think you're soft. They're certainly not frightened of you. A bunch of lazy, overweight, overprivileged babies. You think a skinhead haircut, some tattoos and a Kalashnikov make you tough. This is where we start finding out who's tough, and let me tell you, anyone who can't cut it leaves the elite troops. And to answer your first concern, you get breakfast when you've finished the run."

Savage looked over at Thorsgard, who nodded his head in agreement.

Savage continued, "To be an elite trooper, you have to earn it. Anyone who isn't up to it and can't handle the training and the discipline joins the rest of the civilians, doing chores around the place. Is that clear?"

No one spoke.

"Is that clear?" Savage repeated.

Some heads nodded, but the one nodding the most was Patrick's. He was loving all the hardcore stuff. That was what he wanted—tough, uncompromising ideals—and Savage was serving it up to him by the shedload.

"Right, anyone want to leave now?" asked Savage.

They glanced at one another, shuffling uneasily on their feet. Nervously, about eight or nine hands rose in the air, including green-bean guy and the massively overweight one who couldn't stop sweating.

"Okay, guys," said Savage. "Take your weapons to the armoury."

"They need to keep their guns," said Thorsgard.

"No. No way," said Savage. "It makes a mockery of the guys who are training. What incentive does it give them? If every Tom, Dick and Harry can have a gun, there's no point having elite troops. It doesn't mean anything."

"He's right," said Patrick. "We can't just hand out guns to any slob who feels like having one. We have to have standards. Levels that must be met."

"Yeah," said Stu, smiling. "It's survival of the fittest, not survival of the fattest." He laughed at his own joke. No one joined in.

"Okay," said Thorsgard. "Hand in your weapons at the armoury. We'll find alternative activities for you."

Ten men left the mess hall, heads down, shoulders slumped.

"The rest of you!" Patrick cried out. "Know this: no one's position in the elite troops is safe. You must earn your place. Anyone who falls short will be out. Is that clear?"

A collective "Yessir" came from the remaining skinheads.

Savage's plan was going better than he had hoped. Patrick had not just taken the bait, he'd swallowed it whole and was trying to jump into the fishing boat as well.

CHAPTER 56

T HE FIVE-K RUN TOOK THEM around the edge of Aryan
Nation land. Patches of dense woodlands flanking its
borders gave way to open countryside, fields and gently
sloping hillsides. If he hadn't been in such a precarious situation,
Savage would have enjoyed running through an idyllic fairy-tale
landscape of lush meadows and mountain backdrops, leaping
over clear streams that twinkled in the early-morning sunshine.
Instead, his mind analysed the terrain, noting places to hide and
vantage points from which to mount an attack. The landscape
was good for those purposes, with lots of variety and plenty of
opportunity for concealment.

He just had to wait.

Savage had been cuffed for the duration of the run, although
they had done him the courtesy of securing his hands around the
front to make running a little easier. However, Stu and Jörgen
had tied ropes around Savage's waist and were holding him like a
dog with two leashes.

Patrick led the way, maintaining a fast pace. They were in a
group of about fifteen men at the front. All the men still carried
their Kalashnikovs, a little harder to run with although a lot more
realistic. In the SAS, they'd have run like this with a weapon and a
spine-crushing backpack full of kit weighing twenty-seven kilos.

As they entered the final leg of the journey, coming back
round on the loop, they skirted alongside the open farmland
owned by the Aryan Nation. Savage glanced to his rear and saw
a stream of skinheads trailing behind him. Some were clustered
in groups, and others ran alone. They all looked in pain. He did

a quick estimate of numbers. He reckoned about seventy men were behind him. With ten men already having dropped out that morning, that left around twenty men who were nowhere in sight, twenty men who weren't going to cut it and would most likely be kicked out of the elite troops. Not a bad start to the day.

Back at the mess hall, Patrick finished first. Savage, Stu and Jörgen came in a little later, around joint tenth. They released him from his ropes and recuffed his hands behind his back.

After that, several more men staggered in and collapsed on the floor. A couple threw up. That went on for the next half hour, men returning in dribs and drabs with bright-red faces and weary limbs.

The cooks had cleared away the earlier breakfast and replaced it with a healthier one—porridge, toast and low-fat scrambled eggs—but no one wanted it. All that running causing their stomachs to bob up and down had robbed them of their appetite. The only thing they craved was water, and the cooks handed it out by the jugful. A few took a gulp then poured the rest over their hot, sweaty heads.

Savage watched the last stragglers come in, those who had completed the run in an acceptable time. Then came a large gap, possibly another half an hour during which no one came in at all. Half an hour turned into forty minutes and then an hour. Finally, a sorry group of about twenty skinheads dragged themselves into the mess hall. Heads red as berries drooping against their chests and barely able to breathe, none of them had a weapon.

Savage looked over at Patrick, who sat draining a large cup of water. He stood bolt upright and marched over to them.

"Where are your weapons?" he demanded.

The men had thrown themselves on the floor and were coughing and gasping for air.

"I said, where are your weapons?"

One of them looked up, his eyes bloodshot, an unhealthy sheen of sweat on his pale forehead. "We had to leave them," he said breathlessly. "Too heavy."

At a little over three kilos, the Kalashnikov was hardly heavy.

"You left your automatic weapons lying around the countryside?" Patrick yelled.

"Y-yes," replied the skinhead on the floor.

By then, everyone in the hall had swivelled around to see how this was going to pan out.

"We'll go back and get them, won't we, guys? Just need a bit of recovery time." A few of them with enough energy managed to nod in agreement.

"Get out," said Patrick in a quiet voice.

"But we've just got back. We haven't had breakfast yet."

"Get out, go back, and retrieve your weapons. Then hand them into the armoury."

"We'll just get breakfast first and—"

Patrick kicked him in the head before he could finish his sentence. The guy went over onto his side. Patrick kicked him again, knocking him out.

"Someone clean this shit up," said Patrick. "You men on the floor, go back and get your weapons, then return them to the armoury. You're out of the elite troops. There'll be no food for you today." Patrick turned to address the rest of the hall. "No food for these men. Anyone found giving them anything to eat will also be out."

Savage kept a straight poker face, but inside he grinned from ear to ear. He'd planted a nice little seed in Patrick, and it was growing far better than expected.

As the men on the floor pulled themselves to their feet and exited the mess hall, Patrick came over to Savage, looking somewhat pleased with himself. *Why wouldn't he?* He was asserting his authority, getting rid of the dead weight, the chaff. His elite troops were losing their soft underbelly, on the way to getting a rock-hard, bulletproof six-pack. At least, that's what Patrick thought.

"What's next?" asked Patrick enthusiastically.

"Milling," replied Savage.

"What the hell's milling?" Patrick asked. "Is it painful?"

"Very. But I'll need these cuffs off."

Patrick shook his head.

"Okay, well, could you at least cuff me round the front again?" asked Savage.

Patrick thought for a moment then did as Savage asked. "If you try anything, I'll shoot you, and I'll enjoy it. Just give me an excuse," he said, smiling wickedly. Then he turned and made an announcement. "Everyone, fifteen minutes, then we continue training. If you need to eat, I suggest you do it now."

After their time was up, Savage stood in the middle of the mess hall. The cooks were clearing away the last of the food, most of it untouched. The men still had no appetite, and what was coming next probably wouldn't change that.

"I want everyone standing in a circle around me," Savage said. "We're going to do something called milling, which is a tradition in the British Army."

"Sounds like a dance for queers," said a stocky skinhead with broad shoulders and a mean face. He looked like he'd been in a few fights in his time and won all of them.

"Okay, handsome, you can go first," said Savage. "Give your weapon to a mate and step into the middle with me."

The stocky skinhead sniggered as though he was about to play a party game. He handed his weapon to the guy next to him and came and stood with Savage.

"Okay, pick a partner," said Savage.

The skinhead looked around, and his eyes alighted on a young guy who Savage recognised. He was the one that had brought Patrick the handcuffs when Savage first arrived.

"Him," said the stocky skinhead.

The kid smiled, relinquished his weapon, and made his way into the centre. Without asking, everyone moved in closer, eyes filled with curiosity. What new world of pain had this Englishman invented for them now?

"Okay," said Savage. "Rules of milling are simple. Anyone seen the film *Mad Max Beyond Thunderdome*?"

Only a couple of hands went up.

Savage rolled his eyes. "Is that all?"

They were all too young to remember the post-apocalyptic movie from the eighties.

"I've seen the Tom Hardy one," someone said.

"Not a patch on the original," said Savage. "Okay, rules of Thunderdome are...?"

One of the guys who'd put his hand up answered, "Two men enter. One man leaves."

"Perfectly correct," said Savage. "Milling is just like Thunderdome except without chainsaws and hammers. You fight until you can't fight anymore. Two men enter. One man leaves."

Savage caught a glimpse of Patrick, who almost couldn't contain his sadistic joy at the thought of some kind of gladiatorial fistfight.

"You stand toe to toe," Savage continued, "and you hit each other. And that's it, really. No dancing around, no fancy moves. No dodging out of the way. You just gotta stand there and take a beating until you've got nothing left. And when you've got nothing left, I still want to see you go for it. No backing down. No quitting."

Savage turned to the stocky skinhead and the young lad who were first to fight. "If your opponent goes down, you stop. Let him get back on his feet and face you, then I'll start the fight again. Got it?"

They nodded.

Savage brought them together. The two men shook hands then got into fighting stances, fists raised, feet nearly touching. Savage held his cuffed hands between them, separating the pair.

Then he pulled them out of the way and shouted, "Fight!"

The mess hall nearly exploded with men cheering. The simple act of a fistfight brought out their most primal, testosterone-fuelled instincts.

A volley of punches hit the young kid in the face. He barely had time to react and was on his backside in the first couple of seconds. Drunkenly, he shook his head, trying to regain his faculties. Savage stepped in, giving him time to get back up again and face his opponent. When he was ready, Savage restarted the fight. That time, the kid managed to get a few half-hearted hits to his opponent's face. They barely made an impact. Fast, powerful jabs flew back at him. The stocky guy even got a hooking punch in, slamming into the young guy's jaw. The lad went down again. Again, he got up, faced his adversary, and continued. And got knocked down again. The pattern continued over and over. The boy got hit. The boy went down. The boy got back up again. Blood flowed out of both nostrils, and he had a cut above his left eye, but still he kept getting to his feet, ready for another beating. After several more rounds, he couldn't see or stand up straight. Savage stopped the fight.

Hands aloft, jumping up and down, the stocky guy celebrated his victory. There wasn't a mark on him. Men flocked around to congratulate him.

Meanwhile, Savage pulled the young lad up to his feet and made sure he was okay.

"I can go again," the boy said, blood spilling out of a split lip.

"That's the spirit," said Savage, "but I think we'll call it a day."

Savage called for calm, which descended quickly over the hall. He brought both fighters together so they were standing on either side of him. "Well done, to both of you," he said.

More cheers.

"The winner of our first bout is…" Savage paused for dramatic effect. Then he raised the hand of the young lad.

The whole room gasped in disbelief.

"What?" said the stocky guy. "I'm the winner. I won." He raised his hands in the air again and paraded around the circle like a peacock.

"Nope," said Savage. "I mean, you did well. Good boxing, by the way, but this isn't a boxing match. This is milling, and the lad won."

He wheeled around on Savage. "This is bullshit. I'm the best here."

Savage faced the stocky skinhead and prodded him in the chest. "You weren't listening. I said fight until you can't fight anymore. And when you've got nothing left, I still want to see you go for it. Milling is a test of determination. Of heart. You knocked that kid down. He got straight back up again. He's got balls. He never quit, even when he was getting beaten to a pulp. You lost. You're out of here."

Patrick didn't like that at all. He grabbed Savage by the arm and pulled him aside. "You can't dismiss Seth. He's one of our best men. A fierce fighter."

"The best men are the ones with unbreakable determination," said Savage, "the ones who never give up even if the odds are stacked against them. Not bullies like Seth. Notice how he picked on the smallest guy here."

Patrick thought for a moment. "Okay, I see your point, but we can't just get rid of Seth. The men respect him too much. He misunderstood the aim of the fight. We give him another go. Make it a more even match."

"Fair enough." Savage turned and walked up to Seth, who looked ready to go volcanic. "Seth, how would you feel about fighting again?"

"Hell, yeah. I'll flatten anyone here," he replied.

Savage addressed the rest of the men. "Would anyone like to fight Seth?"

The over-excited skinheads suddenly lost their enthusiasm. Heads bowed or turned away, looking anywhere but in Savage's direction.

"No one?" Savage stared at Stu, Rich and Jörgen, the biggest men in the room, but even they looked intimidated.

As Patrick had said, this Seth guy must have thought he was something special, but Savage knew a bully when he saw one.

Savage held his cuffed hands out toward Patrick. "Okay, I'll fight him."

CHAPTER 57

RELUCTANTLY, PATRICK FREED SAVAGE FROM his cuffs. He didn't have any choice. No one in the room wanted to stand up to Seth, not even Patrick. Savage was the only one prepared to go toe to toe with him.

When the cuffs were off, Savage approached Seth and asked, "Do you need to take a minute or two, get your breath back?"

"No, I'm ready to go right now, old man." Seth was bouncing up and down on his toes, limbering up, throwing a few combinations of punches.

The rest of the men gathered around once more, forming a circle, eager to see how the fight would go. Even the young lad joined them. He held paper towels to his face to stem the bleeding. One of the cooks had given him a bag of ice to press against the side of his face.

Shouts of encouragement filled the air, none of them for Savage.

"Go on, Seth!" they roared. "Kill him, Seth!"

That didn't bother Savage. He just focused on the task ahead. Clearly, the guy had skills as a boxer, good skills. He'd definitely been in a ring before, but this wasn't a boxing match—no three-minute rounds, no bell to save him, no Queensbury rules and no boxing gloves. Every punch would hurt him, especially ones to the head. Seth had an easy ride with the last guy. Still in that awkward, gangly stage, there was barely anything of him, like fighting a tall blade of grass. Savage was a different case altogether. He knew how to take a beating and could grin and bear it for as long as it took.

They squared off in the middle of the hall, and Patrick stepped in as referee. Around them, the gang of skinheads bayed for Savage's blood.

Savage raised his fists and looked at his opponent, still wearing a cocky expression. As far as the skinhead was concerned, the fight was already won.

"Ready, guys?" asked Patrick.

The two men nodded.

Patrick shouted, "Fight!" and stepped out of the way.

Savage didn't bother punching but just went straight for a cover-up, dipping his head, fists and arms protecting his face. Seth rained blow after vicious blow down on Savage, a nonstop barrage of bombs exploding on the top of Savage's skull.

They hurt, but they'd be hurting Seth more. The top of the skull was the hardest part of the body, and on unprotected knuckles, that would be like thumping concrete.

An unexpected punch made it through Savage's guard, hitting him square on the nose. Dazed, Savage staggered back, his vision suddenly doubling. Seth kept up his relentless attack, taking advantage of Savage's sudden weakness. He landed another on Savage's chin, a couple more on the side of his head.

Savage felt himself fall, then his backside thudded on the floor.

Patrick stood over him, temporarily blocking Seth's assault. "Ready to go again?" he asked Savage.

"Never better," replied Savage, shakily getting to his feet, facing his enemy once more.

Patrick stood between them then restarted the fight, stepping briskly out of the way.

Savage went back to covering up. Seth resumed his role as the aggressor, firing blows thick and fast. Savage got hit in the ear, which made the inside of his brain ring.

The blows kept coming, but they were becoming softer and slower. Seth was tiring.

Savage was tempted to mount a counterattack, but the longer he waited, the easier and more devastating it would be.

Seth's punches were little more than slaps.

Savage risked opening his guard slightly and saw Seth's arms were punching lazily, as though he couldn't be bothered. They were low blows, swinging wildly from his waist, leaving his top half completely exposed.

Savage leapt forward and drove the heel of his hand up underneath Seth's chin, like a ramrod. Seth's head snapped back. With his other hand, Savage hammered his knuckles into Seth's solar plexus with as much force as he could muster. The strike caused the cluster of nerves massed underneath the centre of Seth's breastbone to overload, temporarily shutting down Seth's body as though he'd been hit by a power outage.

Seth's body went limp and collapsed to the floor.

Patrick stepped in to stop Savage doing more damage.

When Seth came back to the land of the living, his swagger had gone. Arrogance was replaced by fear and a new respect for Savage. One thing was clear: the guy had never been knocked on his arse before.

"Get up," said Savage.

Slowly, Seth dragged his frame into the upright position, taking his time to give himself a few extra seconds of recovery. His body might have rallied, but his confidence hadn't.

The Seth that stood in front of Savage was more timid, more worried about getting hurt. He raised his fists, but his heart wasn't in it.

Patrick yelled, "Fight!" and Savage went for him, throwing everything he had. All finesse and technique went out the window. Savage pummelled the guy like a lump of tough meat that needed tenderising, his frenzied punches knocking Seth across the mess hall. Combinations of body blows and headshots hit Seth from every angle.

Seconds later, Seth was back on the floor, face streaming with blood.

"Get up," said Savage.

Seth didn't move, couldn't move. He looked like a frightened child waking from a nightmare.

"I said get up!"

Seth shook his head.

Savage turned to Patrick. "Told you. He's a bully. Used to winning. He's got no heart. He's a quitter. First sign of trouble, he'll turn tail and run."

Patrick stood in front of Seth. "Get up. Relinquish your weapon at the armoury. Go see the farmers and ask if they have any work for you."

Seth found his weapon, slung it over his shoulder and left the mess.

No one cheered or gave him a second look.

"Right," said Patrick. "Does anyone else want to quit? Because we need everyone to have the heart of a lion. People who don't back down. If you can't make it through milling, you're no use to us."

About ten more men followed Seth out of the mess hall.

CHAPTER 58

SAVAGE WAS BACK IN THORSGARD'S office, hands cuffed behind his back. Stu, Patrick, Jörgen and Rich were guarding him as usual. Savage had been held captive by the Aryan Nation for two days.

The fire wasn't lit that morning, and the atmosphere was icy, but not just from the lack of heat. Thorsgard was furious. Sitting behind his desk, he wouldn't look at Patrick or anyone. His gaze was far away, focused on the hills through his window.

"You mean to tell me our elite troops are now down to just thirty men?"

"Thirty determined men," Patrick corrected. "The running, the milling, the food—it's sifted out the wheat from the chaff. The men have been tested, and we now have the ones we know won't back down in a fight."

"You had quantity. Now, you have quality," added Savage. "These are men I can train, that I can turn into elite troops. Before, you just had wannabees. Thugs."

Thorsgard got to his feet and walked around his desk, hands clasped behind his back. "Thirty men," he muttered. "That worries me. That worries me greatly."

"Look," said Savage. "This is not my army. You don't have to do anything I say. Bring them back if you want. Put guns back in their hands. I don't really care. It's your choice. Do what you want. You asked me to train them—"

"That's right," said Thorsgard. "I asked you to train them, not reduce them down to a handful of men."

"You can't train men who haven't got the heart for it," Savage replied. "It's not going to happen. If you want more men, more good men, you need to be pickier. You are with your acquired recruits, so why not your elite troops? After all, they've got a harder job to do. They're your first line of defence, your boots on the ground. Or you could brainwash them, see if they grow a backbone that way."

Thorsgard rounded on Savage, eyes blazing. Savage could see he wanted to shout, scream, bang his hand on the desk, but he couldn't because he knew Savage was right, and he would never inflict brainwashing on men who'd joined him of their own free will. That went against his perverted sense of right and wrong.

Thorsgard looked away, back out the window. Eventually, he spoke again. "Very well. But from now on, I want to see proper training, no more weeding out. I want you to impart SAS knowledge to my men. You need to impress the hell out of me. Otherwise, Bella will have another date with the cattle prod, and this time I'll let Patrick have his way."

"Okay," said Savage. "Let's get on with it, then."

They made their way to the mess hall, led by Thorsgard, keen to see what Savage had planned for his depleted troops. When they arrived, the men had already finished breakfast and were eager to get started. Gone were the casual, paunchy groups of men, busily chatting about nothing in particular, waiting to stuff themselves on calorific fried food. In contrast, these men were quietly warming up, running on the spot and stretching. They looked serious, determined.

Savage looked at Thorsgard to gauge his reaction. He hid it well, but Savage knew he was happy, mostly because he didn't say anything or make any critical remarks.

When the men caught sight of Thorsgard, they stopped what they were doing, stood up straight, and saluted.

"Get to it, Savage," said Thorsgard. "Remember, I want to be impressed."

Savage moved into the centre of the hall. "Gather round," he said.

The men formed a perfect semicircle around him.

"Anyone know what the motto of the SAS is?"

Hands shot into the air. Savage picked one.

"Who Dares Wins," said the young lad, his face still busted up from the previous day's milling.

"Correct. Now, most people think this is a pompous way of saying be brave or courageous. Personally, I believe it's about a lot more than being brave. I think it's about believing you can win without any shred of doubt creeping in. Because when doubt creeps in, you've already lost. It's a mindset, an unshakeable way of thinking. Let me give you an example. At the height of his boxing career, they used to say that Mike Tyson won his fights before he'd even got in the ring. His opponents were terrified of him. He used to say, 'I don't try to intimidate anybody before a fight. I intimidate people by hitting them.' That's the same mindset as the SAS. We don't try to win. We know we can win.

"For instance, in the SAS, we have a technique we adopt when we're outnumbered. When a superior force is attacking us, we do the opposite of what they expect us to do. We attack them, start advancing on their position even if we're outnumbered. We turn the fear on them. More often than not, they start to retreat, thinking that we're the superior force. But you can't pull off something like that unless you have rock-solid confidence that you can win. Okay, I'd like to show you something." Savage looked at Patrick and said, "I need my cuffs removed, and I need someone to point a gun at my head."

Patrick laughed. "Finally, my wish has come true."

Everyone laughed except Savage.

"I'm serious," said Savage.

"So am I," Patrick replied.

He approached Savage and freed him from the cuffs, stuffing them into his back pocket. Then he took his sidearm out of its holster and pointed it at Savage's head, right where he stood. "This okay?" he asked.

Thorsgard interrupted. "Remove the magazine first. I don't want Savage getting injured. I know how much you love him."

Patrick slipped the magazine out of the weapon and tossed it to Stu.

"And the one in the chamber," added Thorsgard.

Patrick huffed, pulled the slide back on the weapon, removed the chambered round, and stuffed it in the front pocket of his jeans. He returned the gun to its original position, right up against Savage's head.

"Let's make it more interesting," said Savage. "How about I get down on my knees? Hands on my head." Savage knelt on the floor, hands clasped behind his head, the default position for a captured enemy.

Patrick stood in front of him, the muzzle of his gun touching the hairline above Savage's forehead.

Savage continued, "A no-win situation, right? He's got me. I'm on the floor with a gun pointed at my head. There's no way I can get out of this."

The next moment seemed like a magic act, too fast for anyone's eyes to follow.

Savage was suddenly up on his feet and had snatched the gun from Patrick's hand and had it pointed at him.

A collective gasp rose from everyone gathered.

Patrick swore then asked, "How the hell did you do that?"

"Simple body mechanics and psychology," said Savage. He handed Patrick back the gun. "Let's do it again, but I'll slow it down."

They resumed their positions—Savage kneeling, hands behind head, and Patrick pointing the gun at him.

"First thing I did was grab the gun with two hands and redirect the line of fire away from my head." With one hand, Savage gripped the muzzle and pushed it away from his face. At the same time, he brought his other hand around the back of the gun, cupping it around the hammer. "Now, I have a good grip on the gun. Patrick's natural reaction is to pull the gun away, try to get it out of my hands. Now, this is the clever bit. By trying to snatch his gun back, watch what happens."

Patrick pulled on the gun, and Savage magically rose to his feet.

"He's actually helping to pull me to my feet. And while he's thinking, 'Oh shit, my prisoner is on his feet,' I'm busy using my superior two-handed grip to twist the weapon out of his hands. He has to let go. Otherwise, I'll break his wrist." Once more, the gun was in Savage's hands, pointing at Patrick. "Bang, bang, bang!" shouted Savage. "And Patrick's brains are all over this nice wooden floor. No offence."

"None taken," said Patrick.

Thorsgard clapped. The rest of the men joined in. Patrick didn't, although he did manage a half smile.

Savage took a theatrical bow and tossed Patrick's gun back to him. When they'd quieted down, he said, "Right, get into pairs and have a go. Slow it right down to begin with. When you've got it mastered, start speeding it up. And remember what I said earlier. Who Dares Wins. The important thing is you must believe you can do it. Otherwise, you'll get a bullet in your head. Practice builds confidence. By the end of today, I want you to do this so fast it's like a blur. But before you start practicing, empty your guns first. No magazines and no rounds in the chamber."

As the men paired up, Thorsgard came over and patted Savage on the back. "Bravo," he said. "Bravo. This is what I'm talking about. Please tell me there's more of this."

"Oh, yes, I've got loads of it saved in my brain. There's plenty more I can teach your men."

"Yes, yes." Thorsgard clapped his hands.

Savage had never seen him so happy.

Savage was also happy, not because Thorsgard was pleased but because the technique he'd just taught the men, along with others he would be teaching them in the days ahead, had been devised by a brilliant Hungarian called Imi Lichtenfeld. Long before Bruce Lee or cage fighting, Lichtenfeld took moves from a range of martial arts such as aikido, judo, karate and boxing, but only the ones that would work in a real situation. He blended them together, adding his some of his own practical techniques, and called it krav maga, meaning "contact combat." Imi Lichtenfeld was Jewish, and his self-defence system was later adopted by the Israeli Army.

Savage was teaching Jewish martial arts to neo-Nazis.

The delicious irony of it all caused a huge grin to crack across Savage's face. He would tell them eventually, just to see the looks on their faces. He figured the longer he left it, the more insulted they'd be. All those hours of dedication spent mastering techniques invented by a Hebrew... They were not going to be happy. But for the time being, that would be his private little joke to sustain himself while he waited.

CHAPTER 59

I T HAPPENED ON THE FIFTH night of Savage's imprisonment by the Aryan Nation. He'd finished another day of teaching krav maga to the troops. They were lapping up the magical fighting techniques, but in reality, most of the stuff could be found on YouTube. It seemed to satisfy them for the time being, and he was never going to reveal anything about SAS tactics and strategy that they could use against innocent people. Besides, Savage had signed the official Secrets Act.

After the final training session had ended, he'd been led to Bella's room to check she was okay. They even let him speak to her. She was tearful and didn't want him to leave. He told her everything would be okay and she replied by saying she wanted to go home. Their conversation ended prematurely when, without warning, Patrick shoved her back into her room and locked the door. Savage couldn't wait to kill that guy, but he had to be patient.

Then, as with every night, they marched Savage up the corridor and locked him in his room. At least they took his handcuffs off before locking him in.

The boredom was killing him. Usually, he was in his room by seven in the evening. He had no TV, no radio, and no books to read, just a blank wall to stare at. Savage had had worse. At least the room was comfortable, sort of. He would sit on his thin mattress, back against the wall, legs stretched out in front of him, as he waited for lights out. That happened every night around ten thirty, although that was just a guess as he had no watch.

Tonight was no different.

The lights in his room clicked off automatically, and he

could see a thin horizontal rod of light at the bottom of the door, coming from outside in the corridor. The lights out there always remained on.

Every night, guards were posted outside his room, three of them. He didn't know the first shift. They must've been elite troops that had escaped his culling, because he didn't recognise their names or their voices. Savage had never seen them in the flesh, because his door was always locked tight when they arrived. Then, in the early hours of the morning, the shift would change, and another set of guards would take over. Finally, possibly around five or six in the morning, he would hear the familiar voices of Stu, Jörgen and Rich. They were always grumpy at that time of the day until they had their first cup of coffee. He could smell the fresh brew wafting under the door. It always made his stomach gurgle.

This morning was different, though. About half an hour after Stu, Jörgen and Rich had taken over, the lights in the hallway went off without warning. Savage heard their confused exchanges outside. Jörgen, laid back, told them it was nothing, while Rich got in a flap, cocking his gun.

"What's going on?" Savage shouted through the door.

"Nothing to worry about," Stu replied. "Just a power cut."

"Has that happened before?"

"Er, don't think so," said Stu.

A place that remote would be off the grid and must have had its own power.

"Sounds like your generators have broken down," said Savage.

"They never break down," Rich replied nervously.

Rapid footsteps came drumming along the corridor. Savage heard a hurried, whispered conversation outside, then whoever had delivered the message took off again.

"That's a worry," said Savage. "Wonder what's caused that. Whole place must be in the dark. I suppose if the generator goes out, the whole place goes out."

"The place is too big for one generator," Rich said, a tinge of panic in his voice, bringing out his West Country accent. "We've got three generators in different places. One for the main house, one for the farm, and one for all the outbuildings."

"And they've all gone out at once?"

"Yeah, so we've just been told."

"Are they connected at all?"

"Don't think so."

Savage didn't say any more. He'd probably said too much already and didn't want to jeopardise things by tipping them off, but they'd told him what he wanted to know already. Three unconnected generators all going off at the same time—music to Savage's ears. Something was going down, something he had planned since he'd got here. One thing was sure: Thorsgard and his men were about to encounter the pant-shitting experience of real war. Playtime was over.

They were being raided.

Outside in the corridor, more footsteps approached, followed by more frantic conversations.

Patrick had arrived.

Keys jangled, and the next second, Savage's door swung open. A light shone in his face. The dark figure of Patrick stood in the doorway, his Kalashnikov pointing in. He had gaffer-taped a Maglite to the end—in a rush, judging by the ragged taping. Savage made out the silhouettes of Stu, Jörgen and Rich behind him.

"What's going on?" Patrick asked Savage.

"Why are you asking me?" Savage got to his feet.

"Because I think you've got something to do with this."

Savage laughed. "Me? You think I caused the power to go out? Patrick, you have eyes and ears on me every second of the day. And when you don't, I'm locked in here. How the hell could I have caused a power cut?"

Patrick's phone buzzed. He answered it immediately. "Yeah, I'm here with him now. He hasn't moved. What shall I do with him? Okay, understood." He hung up.

"Who was that?" asked Savage.

"Thorsgard," Patrick replied. "And this is more than just a power cut. Several guards aren't at their posts."

"What?" said Rich.

"You heard me," Patrick replied, renewing his aim on Savage. "And I think this arsehole has something to do with it."

"Wait," said Rich. "So what the hell's going on?"

"You're going to tell us, Savage," Patrick said. "Otherwise, Thorsgard has ordered me to kill Bella."

Savage raised his hands, playing the innocent victim. "I had nothing to do with this," he said. "I've been here all the time, and when I'm not, I'm with you, handcuffed."

"That's not what I mean," said Patrick. "You may not be doing this, but you know what's going on. Are we being attacked?"

"I have no idea—"

Patrick stepped forward and jabbed Savage in the stomach with the muzzle of his gun, making the gaffer-taped torch go askew. He straightened it out, but it still drooped. "You know how these things go down," Patrick said. "You're going to tell me so we can take evasive action. Tell us the best defence."

"Like I said, I have no idea."

Patrick relaxed his shoulders and lowered his gun then turned to leave. "Okay, you're going to go down this road. Fine, I'll give Bella a visit and put a bullet in her head."

CHAPTER 60

SAVAGE WAS OUT OF OPTIONS. Patrick had the upper hand. While they held Bella, Savage would always be at a disadvantage, but maybe he had a way to turn the situation to his favour.

"Okay, I'll tell you," he said. "But on one condition: you let Bella go."

"Fine," said Patrick. "I promise I'll let her go."

"Not good enough," said Savage. "You open her door right now and tell her to walk to the tree line with her hands raised."

Patrick thought for a moment. "Done." He turned to Jörgen. "Unlock Miss Tucker's room and escort her out of the building. Tell her to walk to the tree line with her hands raised."

Jörgen nodded and disappeared down the corridor. They heard the door unlocking and Bella's sleepy voice. Jörgen repeated what Savage had said word for word. After a moment of confused exchanges, Savage was finally relieved to hear footsteps descending the stairwell. Bella was free.

After five minutes, Jörgen hadn't reappeared.

"Jörgen, get back here!" shouted Patrick down the darkened corridor.

No response.

"Jörgen! Jörgen! Rich, see if he's down there."

Rich went to look and came back empty-handed. "He's gone."

"He's been killed, hasn't he?" Stu said, his big, hulking frame quivering in the dark.

"Shut up, and hold it together," Patrick replied.

"He hasn't been killed," said Savage. "He's been smart. You

really should've specified emergency lighting when you built these places. Building regulations are there for a reason—stops cowards like Jörgen slipping off in the dark."

"Shut up," said Patrick. "Now, you're going to tell me what's happening, or I'll kill you too."

Savage had thought about spinning him some bullshit yarn and playing dumb, but Jörgen's disappearance had given him an idea. He'd do the opposite of what they were expecting. He'd tell them everything, a blow-by-blow account of what they could expect. That would fill them with fear, weaken their resolve, destroy their hope and make them turn tail and run, just as Jörgen had done. Stu was already halfway there, so Savage just had to work on Rich and Patrick.

"You are under attack by Norwegian Special Forces," said Savage.

"That's impossible," Patrick replied. "No one knows we're here."

"That's not entirely accurate," said Savage. "First thing I did when I got out of that box you put me in was to grab a mobile off one of your comrades after I knocked him out. I sent a text to my friend Tannaz. Nothing much. The Google Maps location of this place and three numbers: the telephone number of my old regiment then my army serial number and a special code."

"What code?" asked Stu.

"An old one, but still works. Roughly, it means 'terrorist cell located.'"

The last three words hung in the air like icicles.

"You're bullshitting me," said Patrick. "Trying to frighten us."

"I'm just telling you what I did. The rest you can make up your own minds about. Once Tannaz made the call, my old regiment would have got in touch with Norwegian Special Forces to pass on the intel, which wasn't much to go on but would have been enough to pique their curiosity. They'd have sent a satellite over or maybe a couple of guys up here to check out the lead, set up a concealed observation post to watch everything you do."

"We never saw anything," said Rich.

"That's because it's concealed, idiot," said Stu.

"He's right," Savage continued. "They're not going to rock up and knock on your front door. These guys are the real thing. Not just a bunch of blokes carrying guns who think they're hard. Day and night, they'll have been watching this place, passing all the information back to HQ, who'd be putting together a plan to take you down with minimum fuss and maximum damage. They probably knew enough about you after five days to make an assault. Personally, I would have left it longer, maybe a week or two. But there you go."

"So we're being attacked?" asked Rich nervously. His automatic rifle rattled in his hands.

"But we haven't heard any firing," Stu added.

Savage sighed. "This is a stealth raid. You picked this place because of its name, Gudbrandsdalen, but it's probably the worst place you could have chosen for defensive purposes. It's surrounded by elevated positions with trees and rocks, lots of places to hide. Heaven for a sniper. There'll be dozens of them covering the teams who are currently infiltrating your base, going from building to building. There's been no sniper fire yet because the teams haven't been challenged. They'll be using night vision with silenced weapons or knives, getting up close and slotting anyone who gets in their way."

"Slotting?" asked Patrick.

"Killing," Savage answered. "My guess is there are four teams of five or six men, a coordinated attack starting with simultaneously taking out your three generators to knock out the lighting. If you can't see, you can't fight. Then they'll have secured the armoury. Next, they'll converge on the main house, where your men live. Combining their forces, they'll work their way through the house in the darkness, room by room."

"Shit," said Patrick, pulling out his mobile phone. "Got to warn Thorsgard and the others. Goddammit, there's no signal. Rich, Stu, try your phones."

In the darkness, the small screens of their phones lit up their anxious faces.

"Can't get through," said Rich.

"Me neither," said Stu.

"Ah, they'll have engaged the jammer, then," said Savage.

"What! They're jamming our signal?"

"Yes, they'll have positioned a StingRay nearby. Clever device that mimics a cell tower, you must have heard of them. Small enough to fit in a van, it intercepts all nearby calls. They'll have heard every conversation you've had, even the last one you had with Thorsgard. Now the raid's underway, they've started jamming your calls so you can't communicate and raise the alarm or coordinate a counter-attack."

"Hold on a minute," said Patrick. "You've just sent Bella out into the open. She'll get shot."

"They know who's a civilian and who's a threat by now, and she doesn't have a gun. Plus, you've made it easy for them by wearing that ridiculous uniform—skinhead haircut, jeans and black boots. And remember that cross-country run I told you to go on? Nice way of getting a good look at you all. Gave them an idea of who they were up against and the numbers involved."

"Shit," said Stu.

"Our elite troops will fight back," said Rich. "We're always armed."

"Most of them are asleep, and the ones who are on guard duty are... Well, you can already guess the answer to that. You had over a hundred before. That's a small army. But now you're down to thirty, not much of a threat."

"Wait," said Patrick. "Are you saying you've been reducing our numbers because you knew this attack was coming?"

"Yes. At first, I thought it was obvious, you know, thought you'd see through it. But I guess you're not as smart as you think you are. You loved all that weeding-out-the-weak stuff I was spinning you. It was just a smokescreen to make it a bit easier on the guys who are now raiding your base. I mean, a fat guy with a gun is still a threat. Don't need to be an athlete to pull a trigger."

Patrick was losing his temper, and though Savage couldn't

really see him behind the glare of the Maglite, the anger in his voice was clear. "I don't believe this!"

A sudden crack from outside split the air in two, then another and another.

"Uh-oh, looks like it's not a stealth attack anymore," said Savage. "That's the sound of sniper fire. Big, powerful, American-made Barrett MRADs—that's what the Norwegian Army uses. Brutal weapon. Very cool. Very effective. Love to get my hands on one of them. Fitted with night sights. The Norwegian Army produce excellent snipers. They'll be picking off panicking skinheads left, right and centre. It'll be like a video game down there. Anyone with a gun in their hand will have their head popped open by a red-hot sniper round. Going to be one hell of a mess."

Outside the building, a series of explosions went off. "That'll be the room-clearance teams," Savage said, enjoying himself. "Going door to door with their flashbangs. G60 stun grenades, most likely. Just like *Call of Duty*, except the real thing will blind and deafen you and make you lose your balance. Hundred and sixty decibels, like having your head in a jet engine while staring at the sun. Toss in the grenade, disorientate the enemy, then..."

"Then what?" asked Stu.

"Look," said Savage. "I've been laying it on a bit thick. They're not going to shoot people sleeping in their beds. They're not monsters. The aim of the exercise is to avoid a massacre and take prisoners—shooting is a last resort. However, if anyone puts up resistance, they're fair game. Bit like that film *Predator*: if you have a weapon in your hands, you're a target. Best thing to do is surrender, lay your guns down, walk to the tree line, hands up, and you'll be fine."

"Don't listen to him," said Patrick. "Can't you see what he's doing? Trying to psych you out."

"Yeah, and its working," said Stu.

"Face it, Patrick," said Rich. "This has gone tits up."

Patrick swung his gun around on the two men, throwing a

cone of torchlight that illuminated their terrified faces. "You will stand and fight for the Aryan Nation."

"Bollocks to that," said Stu. "I want to live, even if it's in a prison cell. I've heard they let you play Xbox inside."

"That's right," Rich added.

"You cowards. This is serious!" Patrick yelled.

"We know," said Rich.

They threw their automatic rifles down on the floor along with their sidearms, walked out into the corridor, and disappeared into the darkness.

"Come back here," called Patrick after them. "That's an order. I'll shoot, I swear."

A second later, he was back in Savage's room, pointing the gun at him.

"Couldn't kill them, eh?" asked Savage.

"No," he said. "I thought they were my friends, my comrades, loyal to the cause. I was wrong. But I won't have any problem killing *you*."

CHAPTER 61

PATRICK MOVED CLOSER, AIMING HIS gun at Savage's belly. "I should have done this a long time ago," he said.

Savage raised his hands, edging to the back of his tiny room, the Maglite covering his face in brightness. Soon, he'd run out of space, and his back would be against the wall. As he moved back, Savage stepped over his mattress on the floor and gave it a gentle shove with his foot, pushing it into Patrick's path.

As his foot caught on the edge of the mattress, Patrick faltered slightly, dipping the gun. At that moment, Savage snatched the barrel of the gun with his left hand, redirecting it away from his body, just as he'd taught the men in the mess hall.

Patrick pulled the trigger, spraying bullets harmlessly into the wall behind him. The barrel of the gun instantly became hot, burning Savage's fingers. Thankfully, Patrick stopped firing, trying to conserve rounds until he had a proper shot on target. Thinking that Savage was trying to flip the weapon out of his hands, Patrick slammed his body forward into Savage's while keeping a firm grip on the weapon, but that wasn't Savage's intention. Twisting an automatic rifle out of someone's hands was far harder than a pistol and a lot riskier. Savage was going for the easy win—the Maglite badly taped beneath the gun's barrel. He got his fingers round it and wrenched it away first time. Holding it like a club, he brought it down on Patrick's skull. Patrick still wouldn't relinquish his hold on the weapon, which at least kept his hands occupied. That meant Savage could keep beating him with the Maglite, unimpeded.

Smash, smash, smash. Savage repeatedly hit Patrick, throwing shafts of light around the room. Struggling with the weapon, Patrick twisted it this way and that, trying to get a clean shot on Savage, but after being cracked on the head several times, he was losing consciousness. In desperation, Patrick squeezed the trigger. Bullets flew everywhere, but none of them struck Savage. The hot barrel burned the skin off Savage's fingers, but he wouldn't let go. He held on tight with one hand while pummelling Patrick with the Maglite in the other.

The sustained attack to Patrick's skull became too much. He fell to his knees, the grip on his gun weakening. Savage snatched it away, flipped it around, and shot him in the head.

Savage had no time to recover, because from the darkness of the corridor came a gentle thud followed by a metallic rolling sound, as if a large ball bearing was coming his way. He knew that sound.

Throwing the gun down, he slammed the door to his room shut, rolled into a ball, and covered his ears.

A deafening boom came from outside, accompanied by a flash of blinding light that lit the room up even though the door was shut and he had his eyes closed.

A stun grenade.

The pungent stink of magnesium and ammonium nitrate wafted through the thin gap at the bottom of the door.

When the noise and light had subsided, Savage got into a kneeling position away from the door, his hands on his head. A second later, the door was kicked in, and three Norwegian Special Forces soldiers burst in, screaming at him, guns pointed at his head.

Savage didn't dare move but just shouted out his name, rank, and army serial number, over and over.

The men gradually ceased their barrage of shouting. Savage stole a look at the men standing over him. One by one, they flipped up the night-vision goggles attached to their helmets and switched on the lights at the end of their weapons. Savage instantly recognised the Heckler & Koch 416 assault rifles pointed at him—unlike Patrick's hastily improvised taped-on torch, their lights were an integral part of the weapon's design.

One of them approached him, pulled his gas mask down, and placed a conciliatory gloved hand on Savage's shoulder. He looked up and saw that he was a she.

"Captain Savage," she said in nearly perfect English, save for a very slight Norwegian tone. "We've been looking for you. I'm Lieutenant Hanna Olsen."

Savage had heard Norway had females in their special forces and had a whole unit completely made up of women, known as the Hunter Troop. The Scandis could always be trusted to be forward thinking.

"Thanks for responding to my invitation," Savage said, getting to his feet.

"Not a problem. Would have got here earlier but needed to assess the situation. Sorry about the stun grenade," she said. "We heard shots fired and wanted to neutralise any hostiles in the building, but I see you got there before us." She shone her light on Patrick's lifeless body. "Who was he?" she asked, her piercing blue eyes glimmering in the torchlight.

"His name was Patrick," Savage replied, "the number two around here. Kurt Thorsgard's the one you need. He's the boss man. Big, bearded guy, thinning on top. Probably saw him strutting around."

"Ah, yes," said Lieutenant Olsen. "The one everyone kept saluting. Our observation team highlighted him as the probable head of this organisation."

"That's the one," replied Savage.

"Any idea where he might be?"

"Farmhouse, most likely," Savage replied.

"We've swept that clean. No sign of him."

"Then I'm afraid I don't know."

"Don't worry, we'll get him. Now, let's get you to safety." She tried to usher Savage into the hallway.

Savage stayed put. "Before we do that, I sent an innocent out to the tree line to surrender, a girl named Bella. She's the reason I'm here. I promised her mother I'd bring her home. I just need to know if she's safe. She's got red hair, very distinctive. Would've been the only civilian you encountered. The rest of them are locked up tight in this building."

Lieutenant Olsen turned away and used her tactical helmet, which had built-in headphones and microphone so she could communicate with the rest of her team. She rapidly exchanged words in Norwegian then turned back to Savage. "I'm sorry, Captain Savage. None of my teams have reported securing an individual of that description."

"Are they sure?"

"Positive."

"I need to find her," Savage said, leaving the room and walking into the dark corridor. "I'm coming with you."

Olsen and her men followed him out. "I'm sorry, Captain Savage, but I can't sanction that."

Savage turned to her. "Do you know what goes on here? They kidnap people and brainwash them into becoming racist automatons. I'm sure you noticed, when you were observing this place, all the civilians being escorted around like cattle. You won't believe what they do to get them in that state. Well, Bella is one of them. And I made a promise to her mother to bring her back. So I'm coming with you. Plus, I know this place better than you."

Savage fished around in the dim light until he found the weapons Rich and Stu had discarded. He picked up a sidearm and stuffed it into the side pocket of his overalls then found an AK-47 and cocked it so it made a deliciously clean click.

"Very well," said Lieutenant Olsen. "But stay behind us. We need to clear and secure this building."

"No point," said Savage. "As I said, this is the accommodation block for all the civilians. They're locked up tight in their rooms, nice and safe. Better to leave them here, keep them contained until the nasty stuff's out of the way."

Olsen thought for a moment, and Savage knew he would get an idea of what type of leader she was. Leaving the civilians there was the right thing to do. Trying to extract hundreds of innocent people during a raid was a headache she could do without, but some officers didn't like their judgement being challenged even if something else was the logical thing to do.

"A good idea," she said. "I'll position a couple of snipers on the roof and more inside to stop anyone coming in or out."

"Even better." Savage smiled.

Olsen was all right.

She touched her headset and radioed the order, calm and assertive, but then her tone changed. "*Gjenta*," she said.

Savage didn't know much Norwegian, but he knew that word. It meant "repeat." Olsen bowed her head, concentrating hard on the repeated message. She then spoke a rapid reply, never taking her eyes off Savage. She listened again, responded briefly, then clicked off.

"My men have located Thorsgard in the basement of a wooden building on the east side of the compound."

"That's the library," said Savage. "Let's go."

Olsen held him back. "He has taken someone hostage, a young woman with red hair. I think it could be this Bella you are looking for."

CHAPTER 62

L IEUTENANT OLSEN ORDERED THE TWO men she was with to guard the entrance of the accommodation block. Two more men were on their way to join them, plus a couple of snipers. They were just a precaution. Most of the Aryan Nation's skinheads seemed to have deserted the cause, laid down their weapons and surrendered. But it took only one of Thorsgard's so-called elite troops to go all trigger happy and work his way through the accommodation block, kicking down doors and spraying everyone inside. With Olsen's security measures in place, he wouldn't get within spitting distance of the place.

As they left the accommodation block, a smudge of inky blue light on the horizon announced the end of the night, just enough to make out buildings and pathways.

Savage led the way to the library, taking point while Olsen assumed the role of tail gunner, covering the rear. Weapons raised, the pair of them moved quickly and silently, instinctively knowing what the other was thinking, as though they had been training together for years.

Avoiding open areas and hugging the cover of buildings, they kept low as they moved so that they didn't silhouette themselves against buildings, presenting a target for the enemy. Savage took them on a wide arc around the bloody arena where the lamb had been ripped apart. The dogs in the kennels barked manically at all the commotion, sensing something wasn't right.

Gunfire to their left.

It came from the entrance to the arena, long bursts of automatic weapons fire. *Definitely not Olsen's men.* A trained soldier would fire in short bursts, no more than three or four rounds at once. Any more than that, an automatic weapon becomes uncontrollable, aim going all over the place. *Must be one of Thorsgard's men.*

Savage edged nearer to the circular building, Olsen following closely behind, until he got a glimpse of who was firing. He recognised the shooter instantly. It was the young lad who had taken a beating when they were milling. He seemed to be firing at nothing, sending bullets from his AK-47 into the damp morning air. As soon as the mag emptied, he discarded it, fitted another one and resumed firing.

He was scared.

Savage waited until he had to change another mag and called out, "Hey, kid."

The boy wheeled around, pointing the gun at Savage and Olsen, total fear on his young face. Tears streaked down both of his cheeks.

"It's okay. It's me, Savage."

The boy froze.

"Put the gun down," said Savage. "Those hills are full of snipers."

"Don't come any closer," the boy said, voice trembling.

"Not going to. Just saying, I'd put down the gun. Otherwise, one of those crack shots will take you out." Savage turned to Olsen. "Tell them to hold fire. This kid's not a threat."

Olsen spoke into her headset microphone and called them off.

"I am a threat," the boy said.

"Course you are," said Savage. "You've got spirit. I've seen it. Don't waste it on this place."

"This was my life. Something I believed in."

"And now what do you believe?"

"I don't know. It's all turned to shit."

"Yes, it has, but that doesn't mean you have to go down with it. Come on. Put the weapon down—"

Before Savage had a chance to finish his sentence, a shot rang out. A split second later, the lad was on the floor. Savage ran over to him to assess the damage. The back of his head was missing.

Olsen got on her comms device, reprimanding whoever took the shot.

"Damn it," said Savage. "I thought you told your men to cease fire. He was just a boy."

"I'm sorry, Captain Savage," said Olsen. "I did order them to stand down, but mistakes happen."

Olsen was right. Savage knew that only too well from experience, but he'd thought his days of seeing young kids die for pointless causes were over. *Another wasted life to add to all the others.*

"Come on," said Olsen. "There's nothing you can do for him now."

Savage reluctantly left the lad on the ground, his dead eyes staring up into the new morning sky. "This way," he said.

Savage and Olsen made it to the library without further incident. One of Olsen's men met them in the lobby and led them down the darkened staircase into the basement, where Bella had been tortured with the cattle prod.

As they entered through the open metal door, Savage saw the backs of two Norwegian Special Forces men with their automatic rifles raised, their torch attachments throwing a surreal yellow light into the basement room. They were both aiming at Thorsgard. He held Bella by the throat with one hand and had a gun pointed at her head with the other.

Thorsgard grinned wickedly, although his eyes were saggy and tired.

Bella looked like a mannequin, her eyes staring lifelessly straight ahead, as if her brain had shut down to preserve whatever tiny measure of mental well-being she had left, if she had any left at all.

"Good morning, Captain Savage," said Thorsgard. "And who is this young lady?"

"I'm Lieutenant Hanna Olsen, Norwegian Special Forces. Release your hostage, and surrender."

Thorsgard shook his head. "I think we all know I can't do that."

"Kurt," said Savage. "What exactly do you think is going to happen?"

"You're going to let me go. Otherwise, I kill Bella. It's quite simple. Would you like me to draw a picture?"

"So what is it?" asked Savage. "Helicopter and secure transport to South America? Briefcase with a million dollars?"

Thorsgard nodded. "Something like that. Let's make it five million."

"How many of those scenarios do you think have actually worked?" asked Savage. "Because I can't think of any."

Thorsgard gave a rattly chuckle. "You'll make it work because you care for Bella. You made a promise, didn't you? To bring her back to her mother alive. Well, I'll make a promise to you. Once I'm safely in South America, I'll release Bella."

Savage chanced moving a couple of steps closer, and Thorsgard closed his fingers around Bella's windpipe, making her gasp.

"Forgive me if I don't trust what you say," said Savage. "Seeing how you abandoned everyone who believed in you just to save your own skin. I mean, were you serious about any of this, or was it just to bloat your already inflated ego?"

A flash of red crossed Thorsgard's face. "They betrayed me! Stinking cowards. First sign of trouble, and they ran."

"Your boyfriend Patrick didn't until I shot him in the head."

Thorsgard pushed the gun harder into Bella's temple. "Don't push me, Savage."

Bella's eyes were dead already. She'd given up, gone beyond fear.

"You won't shoot Bella," said Savage calmly. "She's your ticket out of here. Kill her, and we kill you. Game over. And one thing I do know about you is that you're a survivor."

Thorsgard removed his hand from Bella's throat and grabbed a fistful of her hair, yanking her head back. She didn't scream or wince but just kept that same blank expression fixed on her face. Savage tried to guess what was going on behind her stony eyes. It certainly wasn't fear. The brainwashing had rendered her catatonic, emotionless.

"Who says I won't kill her?" Thorsgard snarled. "Then what will you tell her precious mother? *I found your darling daughter, but I wasn't able to save her.* I'm your only hope, Savage. If I don't get what I want, then Bella will never see home again. Never see her mother. Never feel the warmth of her embrace. Do you hear that, Bella?" Thorsgard leaned in, speaking quietly in her ear. "You'll never see your mother again."

He slowly licked her cheek.

Life came back to Bella's eyes. Darting left, they stole a look at the gun that had been against her head. Thorsgard had moved it away from her left temple, resting it on her shoulder so he could lick her cheek a second time, a long, laborious swipe of the tongue.

As his tongue was at its full extension, Bella suddenly twisted her body and swung the heel of her right hand up and under his chin. Such was the force of the blow, it clamped his teeth together, snapping his jaws shut and cleanly severing the tip of his tongue.

The howl Thorsgard made didn't seem human. As he grabbed at his mouth to stop the flow of blood, he dropped his gun on the floor. It landed next to his lopped-off tongue.

Savage, Olsen and her men readied themselves to shoot at Thorsgard, but Bella got in the way. She hadn't finished with him yet.

While Thorsgard held his hands around his mouth, Bella dropped low and punched him twice in the crotch, making him double over and cry out, sending torrents of blood over himself and her. She straightened up, grabbed him by the ears and pulled his head down. Her knee came up to meet it, slamming squarely into his nose, producing a sickening crack as bone collided with soft nasal cartilage. Thorsgard's head jerked back, revealing a wide-open target, his throat. Bella landed a punch right in the middle of his windpipe.

Thorsgard staggered back, groaning drunkenly, hands clamped around his mess of a face, blood spurting through his fat fingers.

Thorsgard had grossly underestimated Bella. He'd wrongly

assumed she would play the victim and be his passive hostage, but she was nothing of the sort. His brainwashing had seen to that. He'd conditioned her to be a cold-blooded assassin and taught her how to fight, take lives and survive against anyone who threatened her. He was reaping what he'd sown.

Bella snatched the gun up off the floor. Thorsgard, struggling for breath, garbled a few desperate words of surrender from his bloody mouth.

Bella aimed the pistol at him. "You're the enemy," she said coldly. "You have to die."

Collapsing to his knees, Thorsgard held up his hands.

"You have to die," Bella said again. Unlike the time when she'd tried to assassinate Saad, her hands weren't shaking. They were calm and steady. She would go through with this.

Savage didn't really care what happened to Thorsgard. The racist, scumbag terrorist could die right then and there for all he cared. He did, however, care about what effect that would have on Bella. She wasn't a killer—that was an artificial personality they'd programmed into her. But if she pulled the trigger, that's what she would become. She'd already had enough disturbing experiences to give her mental-health issues for the rest of her life. He didn't want to add "killer" to her list of traumas.

Savage shouldered his weapon and slowly made his way towards her. Trying to placate her was clearly not going to work. Her mind had flipped into attack mode, so she wanted Thorsgard dead and wouldn't be satisfied until that happened. He'd have to find another way to get her to put the gun down.

"Stay back," she said to Savage.

"Bella," said Savage. "I just want to ask you a question."

Bella said nothing, so Savage continued.

"Do you want this man to suffer?"

"Yes," she said.

"So do I. Pulling the trigger is too good for him. His suffering will be over in a second. What if we made him suffer for the rest of his life?"

Her head turned slowly to look at Savage. She didn't say anything, so Savage continued.

"Let him live, and the whole world will know what he's done here. He'll be brought to trial, humiliated in front of the world. People will despise his name. He'll be locked away for the rest of his life to think about what he's done, every waking hour."

Bella thought for a moment, her expression softening. She lowered the gun and looked at the floor. Savage edged closer, one hand outstretched to take the gun away.

Tears streamed from her eyes. "He did terrible things to me," she said.

"I know," said Savage. "But I promise it will get better."

"I saw horrible things," she said. "I can't get them out of my head."

Savage was a few feet away. Just a bit farther, he would have her gun, and this would all be over. "We can help you with that. It will take a bit of time, that's all."

Bella looked at him, her face childlike. "I just want to go home."

"Yes," said Savage. "That's where we're going, right after you give me the gun."

Bella sobbed. "I can't forgive him for what he's done."

"No, he doesn't deserve your forgiveness."

"And that's why I have to kill him."

"No!" said Savage, but he was too late.

Bella fired one shot.

It hit Thorsgard perfectly in the crease between his eyes. A red full stop, killing him instantly.

CHAPTER 63

O LSEN HAD KICKED UP A fuss. She wanted things to be done by the book, which meant keeping Bella in Norway until she had been processed appropriately. The Aryan Nation had been a Norwegian problem on Norwegian soil and had to be dealt with according to Norwegian law. Innocent civilians needed to be held for questioning. Statements needed to be gathered, although Savage didn't know how successful that would be after all the brainwashing they'd experienced. Their mental health would have to be assessed, and they would need counselling before any questioning could begin. The process could take weeks, maybe months. One thing was certain: Olsen didn't want anyone leaving the country until the authorities had dotted every *i* and crossed every *t*.

Savage had a problem with that. He wanted to take Bella home immediately. They didn't need her. They had hundreds of kidnap victims of the Aryan Nation to question. One more wouldn't make a difference. However, she had killed Kurt Thorsgard, which created a big dilemma, but he had been holding a gun to her head. She had acted in self-defence... after kicking the crap out of him. If Savage took Bella home, Olsen would have to cover that up and explain why Thorsgard had been beaten before being shot by his own weapon—tricky but not insurmountable. Governments had covered up a lot worse.

Besides, Olsen owed him. Without his tip-off, they would've known nothing about the Aryan Nation and its despicable activities. If not for Savage, Olsen wouldn't have this victory to put on her CV. Not only had he flagged up the problem, he'd also made it easier for her by whittling down the numbers of the elite troops from the inside. Consequently, her team had fewer armed men to face and fewer casualties. Not one of them had been killed or injured during the raid.

Savage didn't want any praise or recognition for that. As far as he was concerned, Captain John Savage hadn't been here. That would put the success of the mission squarely at Olsen's feet. Bottom line, she'd be getting a medal for it. Olsen had countered by saying she didn't care about medals. Savage liked her for that. Medal or not, she knew he was right, though. She owed him big time.

After half an hour of debate, Olsen agreed to let Bella return home to Britain with Savage. Savage had pushed his luck by asking if they could hitch a ride on a Norwegian Army transport plane, as neither Savage nor Bella had a passport. They had no idea where they were—locked up in some secret Aryan Nation bunker, probably. The last thing Savage wanted to do was go on the hunt for them. He wanted to get Bella out of there as quickly as possible and back to her mum.

Olsen pulled some strings and arranged for a Norwegian Hercules to take a detour to RAF Brize Norton, the largest station of the Royal Air Force, located sixty-five miles northwest of London.

Five hours after the raid ended, Bella and Savage touched down on Brize Norton's main runway.

A miniature city, the base was home to strategic and tactical air transport, including over ten different RAF squadrons, air-to-air refuelling, military parachuting and numerous other units. The base also had an extensive medical wing with a psychiatric team, which Savage was keen to avoid. If they took one look at Bella, they'd detain her under the mental health act. Thankfully, Brize Norton was also the base for all major airborne operations in the UK, including those of the SAS. Savage knew the station commander well, who turned a blind eye for an old colleague landing without any paperwork. He arranged onward transport for them both.

An unmarked RAF saloon and driver waited by the runway to meet them. They exited the Hercules and got straight into the back of the car and drove towards the security gate, where they were waved through by the guards.

A dull and unremarkable twilight descended as they approached the outskirts of London, cloaking the city in grey. They came in via the M4, passing close by Stamford Bridge, Fulham's football ground, then turning onto the Chelsea Embankment, where they followed the Thames until they crossed it at Vauxhall Bridge, heading into South London towards Camberwell.

The journey from Brize Norton had taken them a little under two hours. Throughout, Bella hadn't uttered a single word. She hadn't said anything on the plane either, just sitting, staring forward, looking into space, eyes glazed over as if she were a robot awaiting instructions. She was still in there, he hoped, but to what extent he didn't know. Part of Savage thought Olsen was right. Maybe he should have let Bella get some counselling or therapy before returning home. With hindsight, that seemed the smart thing to have done, but at the time, he'd just wanted to get her away from all the misery she'd experienced.

As they pulled up outside Theresa's house, Savage asked the driver if he wouldn't mind parking a little farther down the road, out of the line of sight of Theresa's front door.

If Theresa opened the door and saw Bella sitting in the car, she'd be right out to welcome her home. Savage didn't want that. He wanted to talk to Theresa first, to prepare her for Bella's mental state. Her little girl was back, but she had been changed. He had to at least give Theresa prior warning, to prepare her for a Bella who'd been altered.

"You stay here, Bella," he said. "Let me just talk to your mum first. I'll be back in a minute."

"Okay," she said without looking at him, her hands resting on her knees.

Savage got out, jogged the short distance to Theresa's door, and knocked.

"Who is it?" Theresa said from within.

"It's me, Savage," he replied.

The door flew open immediately. "John, where have you been? I've been worried sick. I thought you'd been killed."

Savage stepped into the hallway and closed the door behind him. "I'm so sorry. I've been tied up."

"Why didn't you call? I kept asking Tannaz what had happened to you, but she didn't know either. Said you were in Norway. What have you been doing? Are you okay? You look tired." Theresa's words came thick and fast, running into to one another. All her worry was coming out in a barrage of questions.

Savage took Theresa by the hands. "I have news about Bella." Theresa fell silent.

"What news?" she asked quietly, her face contorted in pain.

"Good news. Bella is alive. I found her."

For a moment, Theresa seemed as though she'd stopped breathing. Her mouth flickered as if she were about to say something, but no words were uttered. Maybe she'd been thinking about this day, hoping but never dreaming it would actually happen.

"My Bella is alive?" she whispered.

"Yes, but I have to warn you, she's been through a lot. She may not be the same girl you knew."

Theresa's eyes opened wide, scared at what was coming next.

"Physically, she's fine, but mentally, she's going to need therapy, probably for the rest of her life."

"What's wrong with her?"

"I'm not an expert, but I'm guessing she's got something similar to what I have, post-traumatic stress. A more intense version. You'll have to get her help as soon as possible. She'll need sedatives and all sorts of medication, I'm guessing. I can give you the name of my therapist."

"Where is she? How soon can I see her?"

"You can see her right now. She's outside."

Theresa pushed past Savage, nearly knocking him to the floor. She made it out onto the pavement, desperately looking left and right. "Bella!" she shouted. "Bella!"

Savage followed her out.

A few yards down the road, Bella emerged from the back of the RAF saloon. "Mum," she said, her voice croaky and uncertain. The sight of her mum seemed to kickstart Bella's brain. The lost, empty gaze disappeared, and her eyes instantly brightened. Her whole posture changed. She shouted, loudly and passionately, "Mum!"

Theresa spun around, saw her daughter and ran to her. The pair embraced on the pavement. Thick tears dropped from the pair of them like rain.

"Oh, my Bella," Theresa cried, bear-hugging her daughter. "My Bella."

"Mum, you're crushing me."

Theresa relinquished her grip but only a little. "Sorry, but I'm never letting go of you again."

Savage smiled.

Being reunited with her mum had seemed to make the old Bella re-emerge, which was a good sign. She was still in there. Good enough, for the time being. Savage was happy for them both, but he was under no illusions and knew some dark times were ahead for Bella and her mother.

After things settled down and Theresa stopped thanking Savage for about the thousandth time, they drank tea together. Savage tried steering the conversation away from what had actually happened in Norway. They would need to deal with that with a professional in the room, not someone who was also facing his own demons.

Theresa couldn't stop laughing then crying alternately. Bella kept joining her. After half an hour, Theresa's lounge was littered with damp, screwed-up tissues.

Savage made his excuses to leave, but before he did, he asked if he could use Theresa's phone.

Out in the hallway, he called Tannaz.

She picked up after the first ring.

"Tannaz," he said. "What have you got for me?"

CHAPTER 64

LATE IN THE EVENING A couple of days after he'd arrived back home with Bella, Savage waited patiently on a sofa in the lobby of Club Motivation, a gym bag by his side. To pass the time, he played on his new phone, the one Tannaz had picked out for him. She'd got him a good deal, making mincemeat out of the salesperson. The guy didn't know what had hit him. That was always the case when the person buying knew more than the person selling. After a while, the guy had just given up and rolled over, probably just to get her out of the shop.

Savage wasn't used to the interface yet. Actually, he preferred his old phone, but that had disappeared when he was taken by the Aryan Nation. Tannaz had assured him this one was better and faster and could stream footage in milliseconds without the dreaded wheel of death appearing.

Through the window in the lobby, Savage watched the swarm of glamourous people trying to work up a sweat, but not so much that it would ruin their makeup. Savage had no intention of joining them. He was sitting by the door separating the lobby from the office area. People were still working behind the large glass wall even though the time was well after seven p.m. Presumably, no one wanted to be the first to leave, as they thought it would be unprofessional and the others would look down on them for going early or, more likely, tell on them to the boss. Competitiveness and job insecurity in places like these had turned work colleagues into modern-day Gestapo informants.

At that moment, Savage thought of Jeff Perkins, the voice in his head. He realised he hadn't heard his shaming accuser for quite some time, not since the Aryan Nation. After returning Bella home, Savage noticed the voice had clammed up altogether. Did Bella's rescue have something to do with it? Had her safe return and the destruction of the Aryan Nation somehow atoned for his past sins, alleviating his guilt? He hoped so, but it wasn't over yet. Maybe the voice was just regrouping, gaining strength for its next assault. Or perhaps Savage would have to keep atoning for his sins to keep the voice quiet and satisfy its need for penance, like an ancient deity that could only be appeased with regular sacrifices.

Finally, a young woman logged off her computer, threw her bag over her shoulder, and waved goodbye to her workmates. Everyone smiled and waved back, followed by a few raised eyebrows and disapproving sideways glances. Savage watched as she made her way past the rows of desks, towards the door. Pulling it open, she hurried out, not giving a backward glance. The door began to close, the hydraulic piston at the top ensuring it returned to its locked position. Before it did, Savage slipped through and briskly made his way towards Hansen's office. No one challenged him. They were all engrossed in their late-night work, probably desperate to finish whatever spreadsheet needed completing.

Savage didn't bother knocking when he reached the double doors of Hansen's office. He just marched straight in.

Hansen sat behind his desk analysing a document, his frameless glasses perched on the end of his nose. They nearly fell off when Savage appeared.

"Mr. Savage," Hansen said, filing the printout in his desk drawer. "I'm afraid this is a private office. You can't be in here."

"Oh, I think I can, especially when you hear what I have to say."

Hansen stood up, straightened his suit and pushed his glasses back up his nose. "You'll have to make an appointment. I'm afraid I'll have to ask you to leave."

Savage ignored him. "Do you know a guy called Kurt Thorsgard?"

Hansen paused for a second, thrown by the question. "No.

No, I don't think so. Mr. Savage, these are my private offices. You have to leave—"

Savage unzipped his gym bag, pulled out a wad of printouts and threw them on the desk.

"Well, he seems to know you."

Hansen snatched them up and examined them, sheet after sheet of email messages, back-and-forth communications between Hansen and Thorsgard.

Hansen shook his head. "I've never seen these before. I don't know this man."

"Are you sure?"

"Positive." Hansen butted the sheets neatly together, placed them squarely on the desk in front of himself, then pushed them across the desk in Savage's direction. "Who is he? What's it got to do with me?"

Savage pulled up a seat and sat down in front of Hansen's desk. "Thorsgard is a despicable Norwegian neo-Nazi who, up to a few days ago, was head of a terrorist organisation known as the Aryan Nation, who basically kidnapped people and forced them to work for their cause. They're the ones who took Bella."

Hansen sat back down. "That's terrible. What happened to her? Is she all right?"

"She's back with her mum now but will probably be in therapy for the rest of her life."

Hansen poured himself a glass of water and drank it down in one go.

"You okay?" asked Savage.

"Yes, just shocked, that's all."

"I found out something else too," said Savage. "Actually, that's not true. Can't take the credit for this. My friend Tannaz found all this stuff out while I was away."

Hansen frowned. His hands shook as he poured more water into the glass.

Savage continued, "You used to be a member of a fascist group in Bergen when you were a teenager."

Shock turned Hansen's face pale. "H-how did your friend find that out?"

"Her IT skills would make your eyes water."

Hansen got to his feet and wiped his brow, which was beginning to sweat. "I know how this looks," he said. "But I swear I don't know any Kurt Thorsgard, and that *thing* I did when I was younger was a mistake, a stupid, foolish mistake. People do idiotic things when they're young, things they regret for the rest of their lives, and that was mine. I'm ashamed of it. Truly I am."

"Okay," said Savage. "I think I believe you."

"You do?"

Savage picked up the emails. "All this," he said. "It's too neat. A nice email trail laid out, waiting for someone to find. It's not that difficult to do either, apparently. Hacking someone's email and sending messages back and forward is simple as long as they cover their tracks, which they did very well. And then there's you being a Norwegian, same as Thorsgard and having a short flirtation with neo-Nazis. It fits too well."

"I don't understand," Hansen said, sitting back down.

"I think you're a patsy. Here to take the fall for someone else. A bit of distraction to take the heat off the person who's really pulling the strings, should anything go wrong, which it has. You're a scapegoat for the operation they've got going on in this club. And now the Aryan Nation has fallen, it won't be long until the trail leads to you. Luckily, I got here first."

"I still don't understand. What operation?"

Savage poured himself some water and took a few sips. Hansen's expression changed from abject panic to worried curiosity.

"Do you know how many people go missing in the UK each year?" asked Savage.

Hansen shook his head.

"Two hundred and seventy-five thousand."

Hansen's eyes widened, his brows rising in surprise. "That's shocking. What happens to them all?"

"No one knows. Police haven't got the resources to deal with them all. Just haven't got the manpower, so they stay missing, disappear off the radar forever."

"Why are you telling me this?"

"Well, turns out that point zero four percent of the people who went missing last year were members of your clubs."

Hansen scowled then laughed. "Don't be ridiculous. Lots of people are members of gyms. That's like saying five percent of people who went missing owned mobile phones or drove cars or drank coffee. There's no connection. Surely, you're not suggesting we had anything to do with this."

"That's the brilliant thing about it. No one would make that connection, and if they did, they would have the same reaction as you. It's too tenuous to be taken seriously. No copper would give it the time of day. They haven't got the resources, and on the rare occasions they do investigate disappearances, it's done on an individual basis, not large groups of people disappearing. No one would think to connect the dots on a theory that's so thin. Not exactly a breakthrough, is it, discovering that out of the thousands of people who go missing, some had a gym membership? But that's the sinister genius of it. Someone's playing the system, knowing the odds are stacked heavily in their favour."

"How so?" asked Hansen.

Savage continued, "Point zero four percent sounds tiny, and it is, compared to the overwhelming number of people who disappear. But that figure works out to about a hundred people a year, all of them members of your clubs. All of them missing."

Hansen's mouth fell open. Eventually, he said, "But surely someone would notice?"

"Not if it's done carefully. How many clubs do you have in the UK? Five hundred is it?"

Hansen nodded.

"If someone wanted to snatch a lot of fit, healthy, skilled white people without raising any eyebrows, they'd have a pot of five hundred clubs to choose from. But they don't get greedy. They only take the people they need, a hundred a year at the most, spread out across all five hundred clubs. If you do the arithmetic, they could take someone from one of your clubs then move onto the next club, always making sure they're miles apart, geographically. They wouldn't have to go back to that first club to snatch someone else for another five years. Anyone going to notice that? People stop going to gyms all the time. They lose enthusiasm. Willpower goes. Nothing out of the ordinary there. How long does someone stay a member of your gym for?"

"On average, most people stop after twenty-four weeks," Hansen replied.

"There you go. Twenty-four weeks. No one would bat an eyelid if someone stopped going, certainly not the staff. How long do they stay for?"

"Staff turnover is every two years," Hansen said quietly.

"So a person goes missing. Police can't investigate. Maybe family and friends ask around, stick up posters. Last place they'd think of looking is the gym. And if they did, how would they connect one disappearance with others from your gyms around the country? It would never cross their minds. Someone in, say, Southampton isn't going to start asking about a missing person in Birmingham or Liverpool or Cardiff."

Hansen looked horrified. "And you think it was this Aryan Nation that was snatching people?"

"Yep," said Savage. "And not just here but from all your clubs across Europe."

"But why us? Why our members?"

"Simple. Their DNA."

CHAPTER 65

H IS EYES SHARP, HANSEN LEANED forward in his chair, desperate to get to the bottom of the situation, desperate to know if this was all some bizarre mistake made up by an old fool who'd seen too much action, or if his beloved chain of prestigious health clubs were indeed spiriting young people away right under his nose.

"This guy, Thorsgard," said Savage, "he was quite open with me. A real show-off, bragging about his plans for eradicating Muslims. Said he needed people to build his Aryan Nation, people with the right skills. No one in their right mind is going to join a bunch of fascists living in the hills outside Lillehammer. So Thorsgard had the idea of taking the people he needed, press-ganging and brainwashing them, but only people he knew were racially pure."

"That's disgusting." Hansen winced.

"So Thorsgard needed to know who was whiter than white before he ordered them to be snatched—who's fit and healthy to build his master race. Your club is unique. It has health screening for every member, the full works, including taking blood samples, from which DNA can be extracted. Armed with this, Thorsgard's doctors could find out a person's racial heritage before deciding to take them. Plus, because of the health screening, he knew exactly how fit and strong they were, only picking the ones without any health issues, just like ordering off a menu."

Hansen put his head in his hands. "This is appalling. But how did he get access to our club's records?"

"Simple. Someone on the inside. Thorsgard's partner in all

this, the man who came up with the idea for health screening in the first place."

Hansen shook his head manically. "No, no, not Doctor Stevens. I simply refuse to believe it. He's a good man. Trustworthy, reliable."

"Course he is. That's his cover. He'd never get away with it if he wasn't. I bet he presented the health screening as a marketing idea, didn't he?"

"Yes. Yes, he did."

"And did it work?"

"Our clubs are nearly full to the brim."

"And would they be full to the brim if you didn't offer health screening?"

Hansen looked doubtful. "I don't know."

Savage continued, "The real reason he introduced it was so he could harvest DNA. Create a vast database of racially pure, fit and healthy people he could snatch and send to the Aryan Nation."

Hansen collapsed back in his seat, removed his glasses and rubbed the bridge of his nose. "This is all so overwhelming. And you think he set me up in case anything went wrong, so it'd look like I was the one behind all this?"

"Who worked here first, you or him?"

"He did."

"Who interviewed you for the job?"

"He did, along with the board."

"So he could've swung it in your favour?"

"I suppose."

"I think he made sure you got hired," said Savage, "checked your background and probably saw an opportunity to build himself a nice little safety net if it all went wrong. If the connection between the Aryan Nation and Motivation Clubs was ever made, the finger would be pointed at you, not him."

At that moment, the double doors of the office flew open, and like a pantomime villain, Brett bumbled his way in with blond hair, perfect as ever, and muscles big enough to burst. Following Brett, walking calmly and confidently, white coat billowing out behind him, chestnut hair impossibly thick and lustrous, came Doctor Stevens.

"Mr. Savage," he said. "What a nice surprise."

Jeff Perkins had been right about one thing. Savage should've stabbed the smug doctor in the throat when he'd had the chance.

A gasp came from Hansen as he saw his colleague through new eyes. He reached for the phone on his desk.

"Who are you calling, Carl?" asked Doctor Stevens.

"The police," replied Hansen. "I've heard all about your little operation."

"Brett, would you take the phone off Mr. Hansen and remove his mobile."

Brett looked confused and worried. "But Mr. Hansen is the managing director," he said. "I can't do that."

Stevens looked determinedly at Brett. "Yes, but he and Mr. Savage are part of a terrorist organisation, like I told you."

Brett didn't know where to look. Stevens prodded Brett in the chest. "This is deadly serious. Now take the phone off him."

Brett spoke quietly. "Yes, Doctor Stevens. But shouldn't we call the police if they're terrorists?"

"That's right," said Savage. "You should call the police."

"No!" said Stevens. "We have to deal with this ourselves, quickly and efficiently, to save the credibility of the club. If the police get involved, it will ruin our reputation."

"That's all right," said Savage. "We'll go quietly, won't we, Mr. Hansen?"

Hansen nodded.

"We'll drive straight to the police station right now, turn ourselves in."

"Don't listen to them, Brett," said Stevens. "They'll escape the first chance they get."

Savage turned to Stevens. "The real reason you don't want the police involved is because you haven't got a blue-uniformed buddy protecting you anymore. Kurt Thorsgard told me all about the high-ranking officer in the Met who covered up your little slave trade and that nasty business with the wombs in the van.

I'm guessing he doesn't want to get involved anymore, now the Aryan Nation has been discovered. Abandoned you, has he?"

Stevens snatched up the pile of printed emails on Hansen's desk and shoved them under Brett's nose. "Hansen's a terrorist," he said. "Look. Here are the emails to prove it. He's been communicating with this Nazi, Thorsgard. They're both Norwegian, for crying out loud."

Savage rolled his eyes. "Brett, this is a setup. It's so obvious. Stevens concocted those emails to frame Hansen."

Brett got out his phone and started thumbing away.

"Wait," said Stevens. "What are you doing?"

"Just Googling this guy Thorsgard," said Brett. He read from the screen. "Kurt Thorsgard, the neo-Nazi leader of the Aryan Nation, was killed outside Lillehammer by Norwegian Special Forces."

Brett put his phone back in his pocket and looked at Hansen.

Hansen said, "Just because I'm Norwegian doesn't mean I had anything to do with this."

"He's right," said Savage. "That's what Stevens wants you to think. Those emails are fake. It's pretty easy to do."

Stevens stood in front of Brett. "Don't listen to them, Brett. These two are dangerous criminals. You need to take their phones away. Stop them from calling for help."

Brett stood there, not knowing what to do, looking from Savage and Hansen to Doctor Stevens. His brain was deadlocked.

"Call the police, Brett," said Savage.

"No," said Stevens. "Think of the club. We can't have police swarming all over it. We wouldn't survive a scandal like that. The club would suffer, and you'd be out of a job."

The last remark caught Brett's attention. Savage knew Brett liked his job. It made him feel important. Plus, he liked looking at all the girls in their skin-tight Lycra. No way would he jeopardise that.

Stevens carried on. "Take their phones away, Brett. Then we could say you single-handedly apprehended two dangerous terrorists. You'd be famous, a hero."

Brett's eyes lit up at the word "famous" and the promise of him being a hero. "I would, wouldn't I?" he said, trying not to smile.

"Oh good grief," said Savage. "What is it with young people and being famous?"

Brett unconsciously licked his lips, almost salivating at the prospect. He put his phone away, walked over to Hansen, and unplugged his desk phone.

"Don't do this, Brett," said Hansen.

Brett ignored him, wrapping the cord around the phone several times and shoving it in a filing cabinet.

"I'm sorry, Mr. Hansen," Brett replied, "but I'll need your mobile too."

Hansen reluctantly reached into his pocket and handed it over. Brett gave it to Stevens, who put it in the front pocket of his white coat. Brett then turned to Savage. "I'll need your phone, Mr. Savage."

"That's going to be a no from me, I'm afraid." Savage stepped away from Hansen's desk into the middle of the room.

Brett followed him then swiftly overtook him, blocking his way because he thought Savage was making for the exit. Towering above Savage, he held out his hand. "Phone, please."

Savage shook his head. "I've just got a new one, and I really need it."

Brett frowned. "I really don't want to hurt you—"

"Brett, don't implicate yourself in this," said Savage. "You don't want to get involved with Stevens. He's behind that whole thing in Norway. He kidnapped Bella plus hundreds of other innocent people. I know you've got nothing to do with it. But if you continue down this road, the police will see it differently. They'll think you're his accomplice."

Stevens laughed. "Ridiculous. Take his phone off him, Brett. Actually, you better knock him out. He's a danger to the public."

Brett looked unsure. "Please, Mr. Savage. Just give me the phone. I really don't want to hurt you."

"I believe you," said Savage. "But you're not getting my phone."

"You need to use force, Brett," Stevens urged. "That's the only language terrorists understand. Hit him, Brett."

Brett and Savage stood facing each other, neither backing down.

"Brett, may I remind you that Mr. Savage is a member of this club," Hansen remarked. "Striking a member is a sackable offence."

"Shut up, Hansen," Stevens snapped. "Brett, what are you waiting for? Hit him. Hey, I'll record you doing it. You can stick it on YouTube, go viral—hot blond guy beats up terrorist. Think of all the hits you'll get."

Brett looked like a child who had just been told he had the week off from school to go to Disneyland, and not just the Paris one but the proper one in America.

Savage doubted very much whether Stevens would film anything. He would never want to create footage of what was happening. That was just a ruse to get Brett to do his bidding.

Brett started limbering up, shrugging his shoulders and shaking out his limbs. "Okay," he said to Stevens. "I'm going to be performing some very fast, powerful kicks. Make sure you catch them."

"Well, this is a first," said Savage, moving away from Brett's warm-up routine. "I don't think I've ever been in a fight where my opponent's been giving out film directions. Is there anything you want me to do, Brett?"

Brett didn't reply. He just kept dancing around in the middle of the room, throwing the odd punch or kick. Savage stood out of his way, leaning his backside on one of the tubular metal chairs around the conference table, a classic Alvar Aalto replica, straight out of the sixties.

"Let me know when you've finished, Brett," said Savage.

"Okay, Brett," said Stevens. "That's enough now. You need to take Savage out and get his phone."

Brett nodded and headed toward Savage, bouncing on his toes and holding his fists up, ready to fight. Savage remained where he was, backside still perched on the conference chair's backrest.

"I've got an idea, Brett," said Savage. "If this is going on

YouTube, you should show off that hot body of yours. Fight me with your shirt off."

Brett stopped jiggling. The thought of showing off the results of all those hours in the gym on the internet intoxicated him—catnip for a narcissist.

"Brett!" shouted Stevens. "Stop being so vain and hit him."

Brett ignored him. The idea of fighting with his shirt off for thousands of followers to see had ensnared him. Brett reached down to the hem of his tight Lycra top and began peeling it up and over a set of tanned abdominals that looked like waves about to break on a Hawaiian beach. As he got the top higher, he pulled it over his neck and head, temporarily covering his eyes. That was when Savage reached back, grabbed the metal chair he'd been resting on, and swung it hard into Brett's perfect midriff. The blow bent the big man over double, knocking the wind out of him. He fell back, his top still obscuring his face.

Savage brought the chair down again, that time hitting Brett's Lycra-covered head. Brett collapsed on the floor but managed to flip over onto all fours, trying to push himself up. Savage hit him again, square on the back, the metal tubes of the chair thrumming like an off-key tubular bell. Brett finally collapsed spread eagle, groaning. Discarding the chair, Savage reached down and pulled the top back off Brett's face so that he could breathe.

"Sorry, Brett," Savage said. "But I did warn you I fight dirty."

Hansen and Savage looked at Stevens, who put his phone back in his pocket.

"Okay," said Savage. "So you've lost your muscle. Why don't you just come clean now, and we can put this all behind us. Otherwise, you might end up like poor Brett, here."

Stevens' face remained cold and calm. He reached behind himself and pulled a small handgun from the waistband of his trousers, a Russian-made Makarov 9mm, by the look of it, with a short, stubby silencer already screwed into the barrel.

Stevens cocked the hammer and shot Brett in the back.

CHAPTER 66

"I WAS REALLY HOPING IT DIDN'T have to come to this," Stevens said. "But you've left me no choice."

Hansen panted hard as if he were having a panic attack. Savage knelt down beside Brett and felt his neck. "You've killed him, you arsehole."

"Oh, come on," said Stevens. "He was an annoying prick."

Savage got to his feet. "Brett didn't deserve to die. He had nothing to do with this."

"You're right," said Stevens. "He had a black girlfriend, or we would've recruited him. Shame I had to kill him, but you're partly responsible. If you hadn't got involved, we wouldn't be standing here and Brett wouldn't be lying on the floor."

"You know it's over, don't you? Your little Aryan Nation dream. It's finished."

"It is, but I'm not. I'll come out of this unscathed."

"How do you work that out?"

Stevens smiled, keeping the gun pointed at Savage. "Simple. I shoot you and Hansen. Then I put the gun in your dead hand and raise the alarm. Looks like an ex-SAS soldier with post-traumatic stress syndrome—and yes, I did know about that." Stevens tutted. "You didn't put that on your form, did you? Very naughty. Anyway, where was I? Oh yes. It looks like an old soldier with issues has gone crazy and shot these two dear employees before turning the gun on himself."

"Okay, so why are you hesitating? Why not just shoot us now and get it over with?"

"I need to know something before I kill you," Stevens replied.

"How did you find out? How did you connect this health club to the Aryan Nation? I thought I'd been careful."

Savage picked up the chair he'd hit Brett with, turned it the right way up, and sat down on it. "You were careful. Very careful. Apart from one tiny thing you did, which made me suspicious."

"Which was?"

"Gina, the pretty nurse. That was clumsy and desperate. You planted her, didn't you? She was supposed to gain my trust and find out how close I was getting so you could monitor my progress."

Stevens nodded, disappointed. "Something like that. But how did you know?"

"Firstly," said Savage, "have you seen me? I mean, what would an attractive woman like Gina want with an ugly spud like me? Secondly, she was a bit too good to be true. I mean, congratulations on doing your homework. She was just my type, especially the plumbing bit. Some men like breasts, some like legs, but I love a woman who can handle a wrench. Usually, if something's too good to be true, it probably is. But that wasn't what gave her away. She made a mistake."

"No. No way. Impossible," said Stevens. "Gina is one of our best agents."

"I'm a details person," said Savage. "Never forget anything. I've been trained to retain information whether I like it or not, and I remember one of the first things Mr. Hansen told me about this club when I joined."

Hansen, who'd gone into shock, his face pale and paralysed, suddenly turned to look at Savage.

"What was it you told me about staff inductions?" Savage asked Hansen.

"I can't remember," he said, his words barely audible.

"I can," Savage replied. "All staff have to do a three-week induction before they're let loose in the club. However, Gina told me that she'd left her old job on Friday and started here on Monday—no mention of an induction. So I knew she'd been placed here in a hurry. Something wasn't right about her. Trouble is, I had nothing else, no evidence. So I put it on the back burner. But I did have the database from Club Zero, the place you used for eyeballing potential victims."

"Acquired recruits, we like to call them," Stevens said proudly. "And that's not the only place we use. We have different venues around the country."

"Had," Savage corrected. "You *had* different venues. This thing is over, remember?"

Stevens ignored him.

Savage continued, "What I don't understand is why you sent Bella to Club Zero. If she already worked here and Minchie had told you about her, you must have already known whether she was right for the job."

Stevens pulled up a chair and sat opposite Savage, flipping the tails of his white coat up so he didn't sit on them. "Even though I knew she was perfect, Kurt always had final say on who we recruited. But there was no way I wanted him wandering around the place, staring at her. He'd have stuck out like a sore thumb. We couldn't risk having him connected to the health club. So he flew over here to vet her and a couple of other possible candidates. Kurt always liked having a choice. So we arranged a shop window at Club Zero. A little over the top, I think, but Kurt liked going to those places. Liked to feel important, rubbing shoulders with VIPs."

"I bet he did."

Stevens cupped the gun with his left hand to steady his aim. "Go on."

Savage cleared his throat. "So before I'm taken captive by the Aryan Nation, my friend Tannaz tells me she's going to take the database from Club Zero apart until she finds something. She's going to rip it to shreds. Get to the bottom of it. And do you know what she found?"

"What?"

"Nothing. Absolutely nothing. Not a dickie bird. Nothing to connect that nightclub with anyone who's gone missing."

Stevens grinned. "I thought as much. We told the manager at

Club Zero not to record or leave any of the names we gave him anywhere. Or we'd kill his family."

"Yep, and he kept his word. She hacked his computer too. Found nothing."

"Told you," said Stevens. "We're smart, we cover our arses. We knew she had nothing."

"Well, you underestimated her, didn't you? She's a gay, Iranian woman, someone you think is a second-class human. How much of a threat could she be?"

"That's putting it mildly," said Stevens. "I can think of worse ways to describe her and her people."

Savage paused. "Big mistake. She was the real threat, not me. Two things I've learned about Tannaz. She's like a dog with a bone when it comes to solving problems. Tannaz the tenacious I should call her. And secondly, she's a brilliant lateral thinker."

Stevens jutted out his chin, clearly not liking the praise Savage was piling on an ethnic minority.

"When Tannaz couldn't find anything on the database, she hacked their office printer."

Stevens laughed. "Their office printer. What good was that?"

"Well, I didn't even know a printer could be hacked, but there you go. You see, they're all on Wi-Fi these days, and most people forget that a printer has a memory. Every time you hit print, your document is sent to the printer's memory. Someone hacking it can see everything that's come off that printer, and in the case of Club Zero, it was full of boring documents: invoices, letters and correspondence. Nothing of any interest. But in amongst all the dull stuff were some invitations.

"Now, a posh place like Club Zero gets all its literature done professionally by a high-quality outside printing contractor. So why would they create their own invites in house? The quality was okay. Office printers aren't too bad if you shove some glossy paper in the tray. But it still doesn't make sense unless they were done at short notice, say, because a criminal gang has given them the name of a person who needed to be in that club so they could be eyeballed for snatching. They can't phone or email them. It looks a bit unconvincing, and it leaves a trail. So they send out a printed invite on short notice, created quickly on a PC without being saved, so there's no electronic record of it anywhere. The person receives it in the post, can't pass up the opportunity to go to the most expensive nightclub in the country, but they have to bring it along to get in.

"The invite is collected at the door and is then destroyed—no record of it ever existing or being connected to anyone who's ever gone missing. Drinks are complimentary all night too. Must have cost the club a bomb, but they don't want anyone using their credit card. They can't risk having a financial record of them ever being there. You guys eyeball them, see if they're right for your little Third Reich, but you don't snatch them straight away. You wait at least a month so the club's security footage is taped over, then there's no record of them being in the club. All nice and neat. However, you and the club forgot the invites stored in the office printer's memory." Savage gestured to his gym bag on Hansen's desk. "May I?" he asked Stevens.

Stevens nodded. "Slowly," he said.

Savage gently upended his gym bag onto Hansen's desk. Gradually, sheets of printed red paper slid out onto the desktop. Each one had Club Zero's logo on the top and a smart, modern typeface inviting the recipient to join them for a complimentary evening.

"Tannaz cross-referenced all these names on these invites with the missing-persons database. Turns out ninety-two percent of people who received an invite later went missing. Always at least a month or more after the date on the invite. I'm guessing the other eight percent were people who didn't show up or didn't make the cut. Maybe you didn't like the look of them when they were eyeballed in person."

Stevens clenched his jaw, making the muscles pop out the sides of his face.

"But the people who don't show up," Hansen interjected, "they'd still have an invite. Wasn't that a risk, leaving behind proof?"

"Proof of what?" asked Savage. "Those people never went to the club, so they never got snatched. Nothing sinister happened to them. Didn't matter that they left an invite lying around. Probably got thrown away eventually."

"Okay," said Stevens. "So the Persian bitch finds out these people are missing, but how does she connect them to this health club?"

"Like I said, sheer tenacity," said Savage. "She starts analysing all these missing people, finding out who they were, what they did—seeing what connected them. She cross-references them with other databases. She hacks bank records, phone bills, shopping habits, anything she can think of that might reveal a pattern or clue or connection. Hacks into loads of systems. Girl is up day and night, sifting through data, much of it a waste of time, like more of them drink Starbucks than Costa. More shop at Waitrose than Marks and Spencer. Pretty useless stuff, but she perseveres. Starts looking at their leisure time, what films they downloaded, bars they hang out in, and of course, gym memberships. She hits the mother lode. All the people who disappeared were members of a Motivation Health Club, except for Bella, who worked at one."

"Very impressive," said Stevens.

"So Tannaz knows something's going on in here. Starts hacking Motivation Health Clubs left, right and centre. Still doesn't find anything incriminating. She looks into everyone's emails—still nothing. But then she finds a hidden email account."

"The one you set up to frame me," says Hansen, his pale face suddenly flushing red with anger. "How could you do that, Stevens?"

"How did you know they were a setup?" Stevens asked.

"Tannaz told me they were hidden but not hidden well enough. Like whoever set up the account wanted it to be found, a little insurance policy you took out just in case things went pear-shaped."

"Guilty." Stevens smiled, holding a hand up. "But that didn't point the finger at me."

"True," said Savage. "The finger was supposed to point at

Mr. Hansen. But, like I said, it was too neat and tidy. Plus, I had my doubts about Gina, who, after all, is a nurse, which means you'd be responsible for hiring her. So I asked Tannaz to dig up everything about you. And there it was, hiding in plain sight, something very difficult to cover up, even for you, or maybe you didn't want to cover it up. Was it your ego that stopped you?"

Stevens looked confused. "I've got no idea what you're talking about."

"You were an anaesthetist before you came here, a brilliant anaesthetist. I remember seeing the awards on your wall. One of them was for innovation in anaesthetics. Tannaz found out you've won quite a lot of international awards for your work. So what's a cutting-edge doctor in your chosen field of medicine doing in a health club? Unless it's to use your expertise to smuggle innocent people out of the country in boxes."

Stevens grinned. "Okay, you got me. I really didn't think anyone would notice. Most people don't even know anaesthetists are real doctors. It's not exactly the sexy side of medicine, not like being a neurosurgeon or a heart specialist." Stevens took a deep breath. "Well, I'm glad you told me all that. Otherwise, it would have bugged me for the rest of my life. Now, I'm afraid I need to shoot you both."

"You know what I've always liked about this place?" Savage remarked, looking up at the ceiling. "The security system. High definition. Lots of cameras everywhere, and with audio. I mean, you've got three in this room alone, covering all the angles. Nothing gets missed."

"Nice try," said Stevens. "How dumb do you think I am? I cut the feeds to this room before I came in here. None of this has been recorded."

"Really?" said Savage. "Can I show you my new phone?" Savage didn't wait for permission as he pulled it out of his trouser pocket.

"Put that down," Stevens said, standing up, renewing his aim on Savage.

Again, Savage ignored him. "I'm still getting to grips with it.

Tannaz picked it out for me especially for this moment. Now, let me see if I can remember what to do—"

"Put the phone down. I mean it," said Stevens.

Savage stopped what he was doing and placed the phone flat on Hansen's desk.

"Now, slide it over to me," Stevens ordered.

Savage did as he was told, sending the phone skimming across the surface of the desk straight into Stevens's hand. He picked it up and gazed at the screen.

"It's okay," said Savage. "I wasn't going to call anyone, just wanted you to see some footage. Press the play button."

Stevens eyed Savage suspiciously, knowing he should smash the phone, but curiosity got the better of him, and he pressed Play.

Savage and Hansen couldn't see what Stevens could, but they heard the audio playback coming from the phone's speaker. Clear as a bell, the little speech Stevens had just made about putting a bullet in each of their heads filled the air.

"It's really good quality, isn't it?" said Savage. "Pin sharp, as they say. It's the feed from the security cameras up there in the ceiling. Tannaz also hacked the surveillance system, made sure all the feeds you turned off were back on again. It's being sent straight to the phone, oh, and someone else too. Now, who was it?"

"Who?" asked Stevens, worry lines popping up all over his forehead.

Savage prevaricated a little longer. "Sorry, it'll come to me in a minute. Oh yes, the Metropolitan Police Force. They've been watching it since you came in here. I guess they ignored the first part. Just looks like three middle-aged men having a squabble. Could be a hoax. But when you shot poor Brett in the back, that would really have got their attention. And you know nothing gets the attention of the police like a suspected terrorist waving a gun around. They'll be here soon. Now, what was the response time for the London Bridge attack?"

"Eight minutes," said Hansen.

"Eight minutes," Savage repeated. "Phenomenal response

time, that was. Hold on, it was about eight minutes ago that you shot Brett in the back. That means..." Savage cupped his hand to his ear, listening hard. "No, can't hear anything yet."

Stevens backed away from the desk, still holding Savage's phone in one hand and the gun in the other. "You're bluffing," he said. "I'll shoot you both and breeze out of here."

"Oh yeah," said Savage. "The footage is also being sent to everyone with a PC in this building. I'd imagine the place is being evacuated and locked down. Health and safety and all that."

A spike of panic shot across Stevens's face. He rushed over to the window, pried the blinds open, and stole a quick glance while keeping his gun on Savage and Hansen. "Damn it!"

"What's happening, Doctor, is everyone okay?" asked Savage with mock concern.

"Shut up," said Stevens.

"Hold on..." Savage cupped his hand to his ear once more. "Yes, I'm definitely getting something this time. Can you hear anything, Mr. Hansen?"

"Sirens," Hansen replied, relief in his voice. "Police are on their way, Stevens."

"Not just any old police either," Savage added as the whine of sirens grew louder. "They'll have sent ARVs, armed response vehicles, sexy BMW X5s. I've always fancied driving around in one of those. Much nicer than the military vehicles we had to put up with. But I'm digressing. ARVs never stop patrolling the city. They're always on the move. That's how they can respond so quickly. You're never far away from an ARV in London. Bit like rats except they carry three highly trained police officers armed with a ton of automatic weapons and a shoot-to-kill policy for pricks like you. They want you out of action sooner rather than later. And don't think you can go all *Die Hard* and enforce a siege with us as hostages. There are only us three left in the building. No offence, Mr. Hansen, but two middle-aged men like us are an acceptable loss. They'll storm in with a full-on assault. And they won't stop firing until they've put several rounds in your chest, Stevens. They go for chest rather than head as it's a bigger target."

Stevens raked his perfect hair with the edge of the gun, pacing up and down the room as his options became scarcer and scarcer and his breathing became heavier and heavier.

He flicked the blinds open once more. The flash of emergency lights popping on and off lit up his desperate face. The drone of police radios came loud and clear from outside.

Keep looking out that window, arsehole. Savage hoped a police marksman outside would get a positive ID on Stevens and stick a bullet through his head. No sooner had Savage thought it than Stevens moved away from the window.

He hurried to the centre of the room and did that quick-pacing thing as if it would help him think better. He stopped abruptly, smiled at Savage, and said, "What am I worrying about? I'll cut a deal. I have valuable information about the Aryan Nation and its plans."

Savage's face split into a smile. "Your beloved Aryan Nation is gone. Haven't you heard?"

"Idiot," said Stevens. "You think Norway was our only operation? We have fledgling bases in other countries all over Europe, including this one. I can tell them everything."

"Oh dear," said Savage. "I'm afraid that position's already been taken. Eighty percent of your men surrendered to the Norwegian Special Forces. What do you think they're all doing right now? They're making deals, spilling their guts. Police don't need your information. They've got information coming out of their arses."

"They might not know everything," Stevens said weakly.

"True," said Savage. "But here's the kicker. Do you think that the high-ranking police officer who's been covering your back up until now is going to let you walk out of here? Is he going to allow you to sit in a cosy interview room while you point the finger at him? You're a fool, Stevens, a deluded fool. I bet he's instructed those armed officers out there to put as many nine-millimetre rounds in you as they can, whether you surrender or not. Face it, Stevens, you're in a lose-lose situation."

Stevens looked away, as if trying to ignore the truth. He

paced more, rubbing the gun against his head, but this time with a frantic rapidity, as if he had OCD.

He looked over briefly at Savage then at Hansen.

Stevens put the gun under his chin.

Neither Hansen nor Savage tried to stop him.

Closing his eyes, Stevens pulled the trigger.

CHAPTER 67

THE SKY WAS THREATENING TO drizzle when Savage met Tannaz on a park bench in Camberwell Green. The taste of moisture hung in the air. That was the ever-present risk of planning anything outside in the UK. Rain had more than a tendency to show its miserable face whenever a date was stuck in the diary. Like true Brits, they weren't going to let a little drizzle put them off. Savage had suggested they go to a café, but Tannaz wanted to smoke without having to nip outside like a leper every time she wanted to spark up.

They found a free bench just before lunchtime and plonked themselves down on the damp wood. Tannaz couldn't stop yawning despite her rapid sips of takeaway coffee. The triple-shot flat white didn't seem to be having any effect on her early-morning start. Tannaz considered any hour before two p.m. to be early, though.

Savage smiled as he gulped his tea and handed her a brown bag full of money.

"It's all there plus a bit more on top," he said. "Actually, a lot more on top. You went over and above what I asked you to do."

"Ah, you shouldn't have." Tannaz accepted the bag and peered inside. "Holy crap, Savage, there's thousands in here."

"Well, you earned it. You saved my life. I don't think I'd have got out of the Aryan Nation without your help."

"I'm sure you would've found a way, but this is too much."

"Okay, I'll have some of it back then." Savage reached for the bag.

Tannaz held it out of the way. "I didn't say that. I'm already spending it in my head." She scrunched up the bag and pushed it deep into the pocket of her oversize green parka. From another pocket, she retrieved a packet of cigarettes, lit one and blew smoke out into the dank air.

"That reminds me," said Savage. "I've got something else for you." He handed her a small box covered in gold wrapping paper.

"What's this?"

"A present. Open it."

Tannaz wedged the cigarette in the corner of her mouth and tore the paper open with both hands. Inside was a vape kit containing a rechargeable electronic cigarette and a selection of flavoured vape liquids to use with it. "Thank you," she said, pecking Savage on the cheek. "That's very kind of you, but you really shouldn't have."

"Thought it might be a bit healthier."

"That's very thoughtful of you, but I already have one. Sorry, Savage, I still prefer the real thing." She held her cigarette up. "But that's so sweet of you."

"That's okay. I've still got the receipt."

Tannaz took another drag then asked, "How's Bella doing? I still want to meet her, you know. That was part of our deal."

Savage sighed. "Well, she's still not in any fit state to talk to anyone new. Even someone who clearly fancies her."

"Shut up." She slapped Savage on the arm. "Seriously, though, is she getting any better?"

"A little each day. Theresa said the therapy is going well, but she keeps having times where she just shuts off, like she's not there. I don't think she'll ever fully recover. But she's gradually learning to keep the horrors at bay."

The pair were quiet for a while. Savage drained his tea then asked, "So I guess you're not working at the PC repair shop anymore?"

"No way." Tannaz sneered. "Gave that up as soon as I started helping you find Bella. Way cooler than fixing broken laptops."

"So what are you going to do for a job?"

"Dunno. Thought I could help you catch bad guys."

Savage laughed. "Tannaz, I don't do this sort of thing every day. I'm retired. This was just a one-off."

Tannaz looked crestfallen. "Oh. But I mean... If you did. If something else came up... You'd call me, right?"

"Course. I'd be a fool not to. You're the smartest person I know."

Tannaz smiled, thought for a moment and said, "There was something else I wanted to ask you. Do you do lessons?"

"Lessons. In what?"

"Being a badass?"

Savage looked at Tannaz. "Are you serious?"

"Yeah, why not?" Tannaz replied. "I want to look after myself if things go pear-shaped."

"I think you already can. I saw the way you punched the manager of Club Zero."

"Yeah, that's just brawling. I want to learn that flippy stuff you do." Tannaz made awkward jerky movements with her hands.

"Flippy stuff?"

"You know. You told me about flipping guns out of people's hands. That krav maga shit."

Savage cleared his throat and got serious. "Listen, that krav maga shit is dangerous, only to be used when your life is threatened."

"My life was threatened, sort of," said Tannaz. "Back at Club Zero when I got kidnapped."

Savage looked away. "That was my fault. I shouldn't have sent you in there."

"Well, then, you owe me one. Teach me krav maga, and I'll teach you how to spy on people with your phone."

Savage swivelled around to look at Tannaz. "You can do that?"

"Hell, yeah. I spy on you all the time."

"What?"

"Course I don't. I'd never spy on you, as long as you agree to teach me some krav maga."

"Okay, okay. Jeez, you're a dangerous person to know."

"I'll be even more dangerous once you start teaching me

some moves." Tannaz took one last drag and flicked her cigarette butt away.

"When do you want to start?" asked Savage.

"Right here. Right now."

Savage looked around. "In the park?"

"Why not? There's lots of space."

Savage shrugged. "Okay, then. First thing you must learn... and this is very important."

"I'm listening."

"You must never do any krav maga, under any circumstances, without first having a decent cup of tea."

"You just had a cup of tea."

"There's always room for more tea," Savage said, tossing his empty cup into a nearby bin. "The SAS was built on tea, and you're paying, by the way, seeing as you're flush."

Tannaz elbowed him in the ribs.

"That's not a bad elbow strike. I think you'll make a good student."

Rain started falling, the proper stuff—not that misty drizzle but big fat raindrops pelting them from above.

"You still want to train here?" asked Savage.

"Forget that," said Tannaz. "Let's go to yours."

JOHN SAVAGE WILL RETURN SOON.

If you've enjoyed this novel, why not download *Savage*, the FREE short-story prequel available at Instafreebie.

Thank you for reading *Savage Lies*. I'd love it if you could leave a review on Amazon and recommend it to your friends. Your opinion makes a huge difference helping readers discover my books for the first time.

You can also drop by for a chat on my Facebook page. I'd love to hear from you.

OTHER BOOKS BY PETER BOLAND INCLUDE:

The Girl by the Thames – a gritty urban novel
The Spiral Arm – a teen sci-fi series

ACKNOWLEDGEMENTS

I think most people realise how hard it is to write a book, but what they don't tell you about is the sheer weight of doubt that creeps up on you during the process. From the insignificant: *Was that really the best word I could've used? Surely there's a better one.* To the overwhelming and destructive: *This is a complete load of rubbish. No one's going to read it. What was I thinking? I am a fraud.* So biggest thanks must to go to my wife Shalini who supported me through several large wobbles and one humongous crisis of confidence, encouraging me when I was ready to quit. She also guided me through the marketing process, which is probably just as important as writing the book itself. Massive, massive thanks, I definitely could not have done this without you. Next, I have to thank Kelly Reed who edited the book for me and got me up a very steep learning curve, and Lynn McNamee from Red Adept. Big thanks to David Gilchrist at the UK Crime Book Club and Helen Boyce at The Book Club, and Deanna Finn, Amara Gillo, Terry Harden, Kath Middleton and Kim Husband for being brilliant beta readers. I also have to thank Neil Nagarkar whose professional knowledge of the aviation industry ensured I got the air freight bits right. Lastly my cover designer Simon Tucker who always creates something wonderful, and Glendon Haddix at Streetlight Graphics for formatting and turning my ebook into a lovely print book. Thanks everyone, hope you're all up for Savage's next outing.

Hear about all the latest free and bargain e-books by signing up at: www.ebooksoda.com